THE SPEARHEAD OF
CREATION
A SEAN LIVINGSTONE ADVENTURE: BOOK THREE

The Sean Livingstone Series

Crown of the Pharaohs
A Sean Livingstone Adventure (Book One)

Ark of the Gods
A Sean Livingstone Adventure (Book Two)

The Spearhead of Creation
A Sean Livingstone Adventure (Book Three)

Also available:

Crown of the Pharaohs (Special Edition)
Includes the prequel novella:
Monsters, Myths, and Microchips
A Sean Livingstone Adventure (Book Zero)

andrewdconnell.com

THE SPEARHEAD OF
CREATION

A SEAN LIVINGSTONE ADVENTURE: BOOK THREE

ANDREW D. CONNELL

EREBUS BOOKS

The Spearhead of Creation
Copyright © Andrew D. Connell 2020
1st Print Edition, December 2020
Published by Erebus Books

Find out more about the author and upcoming books online at andrewdconnell.com

ISBN 0-9953543-2-4

ISBN 978-0-9953543-2-6

For Sharon and Grace, two bright stars
in the centre of my universe.

CONTENTS

Message In The Fire

Henry galloped down the side of the half-finished pyramid, hooves slipping on the smooth red granite. His dual hearts pounded like drums. He kept sight of the Isharkute hunter-craft approaching from the west. They swooped across the jungle canopy, camouflaged within the blood-orange sunset. Their covert approach meant one thing – they were about to unleash hell.

The construction gantry came up faster than Henry expected. He dug his front hooves in and leapt. His flank slammed into the metal railing, winding his horse lungs. He untangled his legs and peered over the side, relieved to avoid the eighty-metre slope into the dense treetops. The impenetrable wall of green blanketed the nameless landscape.

In modern times, he knew this country as Bolivia.

Henry bolted along the gantry. His friends on the opposite side of the pyramid were oblivious to the threat. In less than a month, they were nearing completion on the biggest pyramid ever constructed on Earth. It served one purpose; to equip Sean and Nocao with the means to fight Senetep in the distant future.

Henry rounded the corner onto the eastern side.

Further along the gantry, a line of tribespeople laid casing stones with Isharkute anti-gravity technology. The floating forklifts allowed them to assemble hundreds of blocks a day. Nesuk stood behind the group, helping guide the blocks into position. His gangly frame, pale-blue skin, and white beard were a stark contrast to the olive skin and dark hair of his human companions.

'Nesuk!' Henry screamed.

Nesuk peered over the workers. 'What is it?'

'Isharkute vessels approaching from the west.'

'Leave your work. Get inside the pyramid. Now!'

Henry skidded to a stop beside Yeesha. She left her forklift hovering in place and helped corral her people inside the pyramid. Henry kept watch on the sky, confident she had the situation under control.

Yeesha had become a respected tribal leader. After the bitter yearlong winter created by the supervolcano, she led her tribe from the caves, united the scattered survivors, and built the first sustainable villages, creating the foundation for human civilisation. All this, and she was only seventeen.

The two hunter-craft swooped in and hovered over the gantry. Armed Isharkute warriors rappelled down ropes and blocked both directions.

A hybrid transport landed on the pyramid's flat, unfinished apex. Two Isharkute emerged, their appearances silhouetted in the dying light.

Henry recognised the physically mismatched pair. They were Senetep's First Commanders: Nefaro, with his skinny, skeletal frame, and Vogran, a muscular, towering brute of an alien.

Yeesha followed her people into the passage and turned to Nesuk. 'What do we do now?'

'Head to the control room. Lock down the pyramid.'

Nesuk withdrew a palm-sized cube covered in glyphs. He pressed them in a specific sequence and the cube unfolded into a flat cross. He held it against the passage wall. The cross created an outline of luminous energy and a thick stone block closed the exit.

Henry followed everyone down the long dark passages, deep into the pyramid's core. They entered the control room, a vast circular chamber with a domed ceiling. Four granite pedestals arose from the middle of the floor. Each emitted a holographic control panel that managed the pyramid's functions.

Rootuk joined them from another passage. 'I've sealed the lower hangar.'

Nesuk checked the holograms. 'Good. Now there's no way inside.'

'And no way out,' Yeesha added in a grim tone.

An uneasy silence followed.

Henry couldn't think of anything positive to add. Yeesha was right. They were trapped. Had it been a week later, the pyramid armoury would be stocked full of weapons salvaged from the Isharkute evacuation. They could have fought back. Instead, all they had were anti-grav forklifts and construction machinery.

'We must destroy the pyramid,' Nesuk said.

Gasps of disbelief echoed through the chamber. Yeesha shared a pale-faced look of shock with her tribe. Henry sympathised with them; after all the work they had put into constructing the pyramid, it seemed ludicrous to destroy it.

'What about Sean and Nocao?' Yeesha said. 'We built this pyramid for them.'

'We will start again at a new location.'

Yeesha rounded on Henry, eyes wide in desperation. 'Do you agree?'

Henry stared at her, consumed by his failure. This endeavour was his responsibility. He thought he'd chosen a safe location, where the pyramid would remain hidden for 10,000 years. He was wrong. Pre-empting the future and erecting a structure that fit into the history he knew was more difficult than he imagined.

One mistake, and the repercussions would change the course of human civilisation. Sean and Nocao might awake in a world they didn't recognise.

'Nesuk's right,' Henry said. 'I chose this location for a reason. The surrounding valley doesn't exist in my time. This pyramid was designed to be forgotten, buried beneath 10,000 years of soil and sediment. Sean and Nocao are meant to find it intact, with the clues we're leaving them. We didn't count on Senetep's forces finding us. Our work is undone. We have to start again in a new location.'

Yeesha gave a solemn nod.

BOOM! A thunderous explosion shuddered through the walls.

The hologram displaying the pyramid's layout lit up with flashing red dots swarming down the passage to the control chamber. Henry watched the fast-moving dot leading the pack. His stomach turned.

'Only hybrids move that quick!'

'They've broken through the gantry level entry,' Rootuk said. 'Everyone down to the hangar. Now!'

Yeesha directed her people into the descending passageway.

Nesuk manipulated the hologram control and sealed every passage in the upper half of the pyramid. 'This will hold them back.'

'Not for long,' Henry said. He unslung his polearm, his weapon of choice since the Great Arena. The shaft had been modified with an Isharkute stave, making it twice as powerful. 'I'll stay here – give you time to escape before I close the remaining doors. Whatever's coming, I'll make sure it doesn't get past this chamber.'

'When you're ready, deactivate these pedestals. It will close every door from here down.'

Henry aimed his polearm at the shadowy passage. 'Got it.'

'Move quick or you'll be trapped in the passages between here and the hangar.'

'Okay. Just make sure you figure out how to flatten this pyramid before we leave.'

'I have an idea.'

Henry grinned. 'Thought you might. See you soon.'

Nesuk disappeared. A series of explosions rumbled through the pyramid. The intruders were making quick work of the sealed passages.

Henry swallowed the nervous lump in his throat and scraped his rear left hoof across the floor. Human and horse in perfect sync. He was so accustomed to his hybrid physiology, it was hard to remember his body before. His former life felt like a half-forgotten dream, though one feeling remained as strong as ever: his love for Sean. Over the last few months, he had been recording holographic messages for Sean to find on his quest for the Ark. But even now, there was still so much he wanted to say.

Henry steeled himself, ready to face whatever monstrous creation screamed out of the passage. The red dots infested the holograms.

Soon the control chamber would be overrun.

A shrill scraping noise echoed down the passage, worse than fingernails on a chalkboard.

Henry recognised the sound of talons on stone. He backed up, hand poised over the hologram to seal the doors. Two piercing eyes glinted at him from deep within the passage. They blinked, then disappeared. A gust of air blew into the chamber.

That's enough! Henry thought. He punched the button and retreated.

Granite blocks lowered from the ceiling, sealing the four entrances into the chamber. The metre-thick stone moved too slow.

Come on, hurry up!

Henry edged for the exit, ready to run. He had to hold the chamber for as long as possible.

A blur of grey wings and yellow fur swooped into the chamber. The hybrid had the body of a lion, the talons and wings of a giant eagle, and the head of a woman with long brown hair. A sphinx! Her haunted expression reflected her tortured mind; another innocent soul living in a hybrid hell. She circled the chamber with a bloodcurdling screech, glossy black eyes glaring at him through matted, greasy hair.

Henry lunged after her, wielding his polearm. She dodged his attack, scraping her talons along the walls, then rounded on him, flicking the debris at his face.

'Whoa!' Henry shielded his eyes.

The sphinx used the distraction to attack, talons spread for maximum carnage. Henry raised his polearm. CRACK! She cleaved the polearm in two and flew around for another pass, screeching excitedly.

Henry tossed the useless end of his polearm aside and activated the stave section. The forks snapped open and crackled with deadly energy. The sphinx circled him in a blur. Her momentum created a vortex of wind that whipped the dust off the floor.

The Isharkute warriors raced down the passage, staves drawn.

Henry eyed the granite blocks. They were over a third closed. If he delayed his escape any longer, he wouldn't fit under the block – a disadvantage of his ten-foot-tall centaur body. Crawling on horse legs wasn't an option.

He fired a volley of blasts into the whirlwind and retreated, scraping the underside of the closing block. He reared up, spun about, and bolted down the passage. Trailing energy blasts ricocheted off the walls.

Henry galloped hard. His two hearts and four lungs heaved in unison. A gust of air cooled his back – the sphinx was flying right above him! One devastating swipe from her talons would slice him like a tomato. The exit to the hangar was coming up.

Fifty metres... thirty... twenty...

He would not make it at full height, even if he bent his human torso forward.

Ten metres... five...

The inhuman screech filled his ears. Her wings brushed his back, her talons next.

Henry dropped to his front knees and slid for his life, grazing the thin skin off his equine knees. He cleared the block just in time and slid into the hangar. His friends fired into the gap behind him, forcing the sphinx back. The block closed with a thud, silencing her screeches.

'Thank God that thing didn't get in here or we'd never stop it,' Henry said.

Nesuk helped him to his hooves. 'I've set the power crystals in our quarrying vessels to overload. The blast will trigger a chain reaction through the pyramid.'

Henry nodded. It was unfortunate they had to destroy the utility vessels. They couldn't afford to lose more resources.

Rootuk rubbed a rejuvenating salve over Henry's red-raw knees. 'We have three minutes before the power core shuts down and the crystal disintegrates.'

Henry had developed a deep respect for Rootuk. At eighty years of age, he was young for an Isharkute, but displayed a maturity and compassion beyond his years. Rootuk reminded him of Nocao.

It was easy to see why Nesuk chose him to remain on Earth to aid humanity. Like Nocao, he represented the next generation of Isharkute, an initiate of the Sciences Guild, and more open-minded to a human-Isharkute future than most elders.

The block sealing the passage rumbled. Cracks appeared in the stone.

'That's a two-metre–thick stone door,' Henry said. 'They're breaking through!'

Rootuk waved everyone away. 'Please...everyone to the transports.'

They split into two groups. Rootuk took half the tribe in one transport, Nesuk the other. Henry and Yeesha joined Nesuk in the cockpit. Sunlight bathed the windscreen as the pyramid's hangar door rumbled open: a single stone megalith the length of a football field. Beyond, the verdant jungle awaited.

The sealed passage exploded open. The sphinx swooped into the hangar and dive-bombed their windscreen, scraping deep talon marks into the surface.

'One more pass like that and it might get through,' Henry said, peering through the scratches. A squad of warriors raced out of the passage and opened fire. 'Okay, the hangar door has opened wide enough. Let's go!'

Nesuk hesitated, hand paused over the accelerator. Energy blasts bounced off the hull.

'Waiting for something?'

'Watching our utility vessels, making sure the warriors don't cancel the self-destruct. I'm drawing as many inside as we can before we leave.'

'That looks like enough,' Yeesha said.

Henry nodded. 'I agree.'

'Thirty seconds until detonation,' Rootuk announced over the communications. 'I'll lead the way.' His transporter shot through the opening and over the jungle.

Nesuk held a second longer, then accelerated out of the hangar. He activated the clear-hull technology and the rear section of their vessel became a window to the destruction. An explosion shattered the lower third of the pyramid. Flames erupted from the hangar like a dragon spewing fire. Ravaged granite blocks spiralled through the landscape, stripping trees of their foliage.

Atop the disintegrating structure, Nefaro and Vogran raced to their vessel and took off as the pyramid collapsed in on itself. The mushroom cloud remained visible for tens of kilometres.

Nesuk confirmed they weren't being tracked and set a course for their camp in the mountains. Nobody spoke during the journey.

Henry reflected on his failure, realising he had seen the unique interlocking blocks from their pyramid in the future. They were the mysterious megaliths scattered over Puma Punku, an archaeological site in Bolivia. He'd visited the location. Touched the blocks with his own hands. If he'd remembered sooner, he would have realised they were destined to fail.

That night, Yeesha and her tribe prepared a meal of fresh fish and vegetables with the Peruvian tribe they had been living with for the last few months. They ate, overlooking the tiered crops cut into the steep mountainside.

Henry stood by the fire, sipping on his latest attempt at a coffee. After weeks of experimentation with the local coffee beans, he was inching closer to success. He swallowed with a grimace – still a little bitter for his liking.

Nesuk and Rootuk joined him.

'We need to narrow down our choices for the next location,' Nesuk said.

'It's my fault.' Henry sighed. 'I should've realised the last site wasn't going to work.'

'The blame cannot fall upon you alone,' Rootuk said. 'Every decision is complicated and affects the future in ways we are yet to discover.'

'I appreciate your candour, but it's still my fault.'

'Do you have any ideas for a new site?'

'I've been thinking about it since we returned. We can't build another pyramid on a forty-five-degree angle. They're too high and easily discovered. But we still need a pyramid with the capacity to store the vessels and weaponry we've collected. It has to be built upon by later generations – something so large that when it disappears beneath the jungle, people will think it's a mountain.'

'Are there any sites like this in your time?'

'There's only one site on Earth with the scope to accomplish this... the La Danta pyramid in El Mirador, Guatemala.'

'I'll compare Earth's current topography against the geographical data we copied off Sean's laptop,' Rootuk said, sounding more confident.

'Rest tonight. We'll survey the area tomorrow,' Nesuk said.

Henry remained by the fire as Nesuk and Rootuk returned to their vessels to work. They didn't need much sleep and would remain up most of the night. Henry sipped his coffee and gazed into the fire. His eyelids weighed heavily. Now that he slept like a horse, he was content to fall asleep where he stood.

Embers stirred deep in the fire. They swirled skyward, chased by the twisting yellow flames. The flickering light lulled Henry into a sleepy state. Feelings of failure and disappointment took him to a dark place. More than failing his son, he had failed humanity. A spectral face shimmered amongst the flames. Was he dreaming? Obscured within the yellow glow, the youthful features felt strangely familiar. It was Sean, gazing back at him through the flames! Henry relaxed, content for his son to carry him off to sleep. His eyelids became too heavy to fight. As they closed...

'Dad!' Sean cried, loud and clear, as if he stood right there.

Henry jolted back, dropping his coffee.

He bumped into Yeesha. She stood beside him, staring at the fire. 'That was Sean!'

'You saw him?'

Yeesha nodded, trembling.

Henry trembled as well. It was like they had seen a ghost. Henry looked around, unsure what to make of it. Had they just shared a vision? It felt as though Sean reached across time and space, and for that fleeting moment, his consciousness manifested before them.

There was a distinct urgency in his son's voice.

It sounded like a warning.

— CHAPTER 1 —

World Meeting

The East China Sea had become a parking lot, chocked full of warships. Vessels stretched as far as Sean could see, and more arrived by the hour. With the Yonaguni beacon activated and Emperor Neberun's fleet now orbiting Earth, Senetep had fled into deep space after the *Spearhead of Creation*, a mythical vessel believed capable of creating and destroying all life in the universe.

Sean watched the warships from the Yonaguni platform, a football-field–sized rock megalith jutting several stories above the water. The beacon towered over him like an Ancient lighthouse. Instead of warding ships away, it was drawing them in. It felt like the world was closing in, pressuring him into the next dangerous endeavour.

Nocao joined him. 'Ramin says we need to leave in a few minutes. Time to say your goodbyes.'

Sean didn't respond. This was all happening so fast. He wasn't ready to commit to another mission straight away. He needed some downtime. Nocao didn't mean to be pushy, but time was against them.

'Is something wrong?' Nocao said bluntly.

'Are you serious?'

Nocao shot him a perplexed look. 'Why wouldn't I be?'

'We just slept for 10,000 years and woke up to a future under attack. After racing across the world for an ancient relic; solving mysteries; and escaping death, torture, and a labyrinth full of hybrids, my DNA turns out to be the Ark of the Covenant. Then I had to convince the United Nations to help us. And to top it off, when I finally activate this beacon, it shoots my consciousness across the universe, waking Neberun's fleet from cryogenic sleep.' Sean took an exasperated breath. 'Did I forget anything?'

'Technically, your consciousness never left your body–'

'You know what I mean,' Sean snapped. 'We just finished one crazy adventure and another one's already begun. I haven't even had time to sit down yet–'

Nocao went to open his mouth but Sean cut him off.

'–and don't tell me to sit down!'

Nocao acknowledged his frustration with a nod. 'For a human, you've experienced more than your species is accustomed to. I understand. It's a lot to comprehend.'

'That's an understatement,' Sean said, rubbing his eyes. His head throbbed. He'd barely slept and eaten for days. Exhaustion had caught up with him.

Nearby, Ramin and Nesuk were in deep conversation about human and Isharkute politics. The Bonaforte family squeezed as many hugs as they could into the precious time they had left. Tears flowed as Bella said goodbye to her brother Arturo, parents Marco and Francesca, and her aunt Carla.

'I'll tell Bella we're about to leave,' Nocao said.

Sean grabbed Nocao's arm. 'Wait. They don't have much time together. Give them a little longer.'

It was the least they could do. Sean felt guilty for making Bella leave her family so soon, but their mission to save the last female Isharkute was a crucial step towards a united future. He recalled the kiss they shared earlier that day, moments before he plunged into the sea at Yonaguni. It filled him with hope. Together, they would get through this. Bella's fearless nature and unflinching determination was just the support he needed. Of every human being, he couldn't imagine facing the unknown with anyone else.

The voices behind him became louder.

'No, don't approach the beacon,' Commander Hazim Al-Amin yelled into the bulky satellite phone. 'Hold your position and coordinate with the fleet commanders.'

Hazim and Colonel Powell had been busy since the first US warship arrived, instructing the approaching vessels to hold their positions and not to engage the Isharkute forces. It wasn't straightforward. Skirmishes were erupting all over the world, even though Emperor Neberun had decreed a ceasefire. There was a palpable tension in the air. One wrong move could trigger an all-out intergalactic battle.

Ramin strode between everyone and clapped his hands. 'Sean. Bella. It's time to leave.'

Sean joined Bella and said his goodbyes to her family. Arturo gave him a firm hug. 'Look after my sister. If something happens to her, I know where to find you.'

Sean laughed.

Arturo glared at him. 'I'm serious!'

'I know; so am I.'

Arturo smiled and roughed his hair.

Carla approached, arms open, teary eyes brimming with pride. They held each other for a few seconds. 'I'm so proud of you Sean... Your dad would be too.' She pulled back and looked him in the eyes. 'He always saw the strengths in people, even when they didn't see it themselves. That's why he made such an outstanding leader. You're just the same. Always believe in yourself.' She kissed him on the cheek.

Sean blushed. 'Thanks.'

Carla stepped aside and Sean caught Bella's gaze across the throng of people. Her deep-brown eyes glistened with excitement and a hint of terror. His thoughts exactly.

Powell pushed through a group of soldiers. 'Sean, you can't leave yet.'

'Why not?'

'We've got a world full of anxious nations. Many are preparing to attack the Isharkute. The UN has done the best they can to spread the word, but with communications and the internet down, news is slow to spread. Truth is, seven billion people don't feel comfortable with city-sized saucers hanging over their capitals. Ninety-nine per cent of the world's population have no idea what we achieved here today, but worse, they're unaware of the growing threat. If Senetep finds the *Spearhead,* the entire universe is in danger. You need to reassure them before you leave.'

Sean never considered what all this looked like to an outside observer. He had always been at the centre of events, aware of everything going on. Only a handful of people knew the full story. The thought of speaking to that many people filled him with dread. He needed an excuse. Fast.

'I can't do a worldwide press conference. I just convinced the UN. I'm so tired I can't even think straight.'

Hazim put down the satellite phone and joined them. 'Sean, the world associates the Isharkute with Senetep, a genocidal maniac intent on wiping out humanity. We need to change that perception. Instil trust.'

'How do we do that?'

'You must reassure your species with a friendly face,' Ramin interjected.

'Got any ideas?' Sean said, relieved to see his former master willing to take the spotlight.

Ramin puffed out his chest and raised his chin. 'You need a handsome yet trustworthy face. One that intuitively appeals to any species, regardless of origin.'

Sean opened his mouth in mock surprise. 'Oh, I know! What about you?'

Ramin smiled. 'I thought my appointment to such an esteemed position needed no confirmation...but you've chosen wisely.'

'If your diplomatic skills are as well-honed as your ego, we're in excellent hands,' Powell remarked.

Ramin raised an eyebrow with a haughty sniff.

*   *   *

Four hours later, Sean, Bella, Ramin, Nocao, Hazim and Powell were standing on the steps of the Lincoln Memorial in Washington,

DC, flanked by a contingent of US military. Five high-ranking Isharkute Commanders stood beside Ramin, gleaming in their gold-plated armour. Their long white beards hung heavy with multicoloured beads of rank. The intricate tattoos decorating their elongated craniums gave them an austere, mysterious presence. Each Commander had been selected by Emperor Neberun to coordinate the Isharkute arrival with Powell and Hazim. An audience of half-a-million people lined the Memorial Reflecting Pool, stretching all the way back to the Washington Monument, an Egyptian inspired obelisk that soared over 550 feet high. Neberun's massive disc-shaped mothership hovered overhead. The obelisk, pool and mothership represented the past, present and future coalescing.

Sean stared in awe, butterflies racing through his stomach. They stood where Martin Luther King Jr gave his famous, 'I Have a Dream' speech. Countless US presidents and politicians had addressed the nation from this very spot.

Sean leant close to Bella. 'There's so many people.'

'I know,' she remarked. 'It doesn't look real.'

For security reasons, the US president remained in hiding. He appeared via a satellite linkup projected onto cinema-sized screens around the pool. Every soul on Earth had tuned in to the event, either by television broadcast or the enormous holographic projections provided by the Isharkute. The president wrapped up his address, a twenty-minute speech that detailed the events from the Giza Plateau to Yonaguni.

Sean was a little disappointed. The president sounded like he was reading from a list of bullet points, with no real insight into the pain and sacrifices made by those involved.

The president requested Ramin to step forward.

Ramin grasped the lapels of his gold-laced gown and took to the podium like a seasoned politician. 'People of Earth, I am Ramin, Royal Consult to Emperor Neberun.' His voice boomed across the city. 'I speak on the Emperor's behalf for all matters. Firstly, I want to assure you that Senetep's reign of terror is over. He is a fugitive of the Isharkute Empire and wanted for treason. Senetep has fled this planet, but we vow to hunt him down and return the traitor to Earth. Senetep will answer for his crimes on your soil. I will join this mission, but leave in my stead five of our most respected Commanders. They will assimilate with your governments going forward. Also, as an opening gesture of goodwill, we offer humanity a cure for many types of cancer.'

There was subdued applause from the cautious-looking audience.

'Did you know about that?' Bella whispered.

Sean shook his head. 'I had no idea.'

'That's so cool.'

Sean gave an enthusiastic nod. Finally, there was something to be excited about. The Isharkute possessed a universal wealth of knowledge worth sharing; this was merely the first step towards a brighter future.

'The Isharkute have lived for millennia and travelled the universe. Over this time, we have encountered and studied millions of viruses, diseases, and genetic mutations. We want to share that knowledge with you. In return, we ask humanity for your help. Ironically, even with all our accumulated knowledge, our species is dying. We suffer from a collapsing genome, a sickness that endangers our existence. Isharkute reproduce through sequential hermaphroditism, which means males transform into females to give birth. These life-bearers, as we call them, only give birth once. But our male populations have failed to make the transformation, and our younger generations are showing signs of the affliction. The only cure for this heinous sickness is found within the human genome, a combination of male and female DNA. The situation has become so dire we must return to our homeworld of Akanae at once and find a cure for our last six life-bearers. They are stuck mid-transformation and are our last hope to create offspring. Emperor Neberun has already chosen two human ambassadors to represent your species. They stand behind me now: Sean Livingstone and Bella Bonaforte.'

Ramin motioned them forward.

Sean and Bella held hands and approached the top of the steps. Thousands of camera flashes went off.

'They have shown incredible bravery in the last twenty-four hours. Without their efforts, Senetep would dominate this planet and Emperor Neberun's sabotaged fleet would still be locked in cryogenic sleep, thousands of light-years away.'

The camera flashes didn't stop. The crowd became livelier. A cheer sounded from one corner. Then another.

'Are we supposed to say something?' Bella asked.

'I don't think so,' Sean said.

'Should we wave or something?'

'I suppose so.'

Sean and Bella waved their hands and the crowd erupted. The applause of half-a-million people crashed into them like a wave.

'But they weren't alone,' Ramin announced heartily over the cheers. 'They wouldn't have succeeded without the help of Nocao, Colonel Brett Powell and Commander Al-Amin Hazim.'

The three of them joined Bella and Sean. It was surreal. Sean never expected to be acknowledged by the entire world, nor did he want to. As the applause subsided, Powell and Hazim addressed the crowd. They explained how every nation on Earth was coming together to work with the Isharkute and integrate them with humanity.

After the speeches, the military escorted Sean and their entourage towards the Lincoln Memorial's rear carpark. Several Isharkute vessels were parked alongside two Black Hawk helicopters and a larger CH-47 Chinook heavy transport helicopter.

A smaller contingent of media eagerly assembled behind a barricade guarded by armed soldiers. The select group of international reporters represented a dozen or more foreign countries.

Powell directed them towards the flashing cameras and waiting microphones. 'Sean, we just need to do a quick interview before you and Bella leave.'

'What am I supposed to say?'

'Don't worry – Hazim and I will do the talking. Just give them your best smile.'

The reporters jostled for the front position, shoving their cameras and microphones over the barricade. It leaned precariously under their weight. The soldiers forced them back and demanded order.

'Your information collectors are like rabid hounds waiting to be fed,' Ramin mused.

'They're called "reporters",' Sean said.

Bella smiled. '*Si*, but I like Ramin's description better.'

'We should skip this unnecessary repeat of information and leave,' Nocao said.

Sean noticed the frustration in his friend's voice. Nocao's patience was shorter than usual, in no doubt because of the affliction ravaging his body. His left hand displayed a continuous shake and the bruising had progressed up to his elbow. Sean tried not to stare, but he was sure more bruises were developing on Nocao's neck. The genetic degradation was attacking him at an accelerated rate. No wonder he sounded stressed. He shared his friend's urgency to leave. This interview was a waste of time.

Powell and Hazim fielded the questions. They worked well as a team, keeping their answers short and sharp.

'What about you, Sean. When do you leave for the Isharkute planet?' asked one reporter. All eyes stared at Sean.

'Straight away.'

'Why did the Isharkute choose you and Bella?'

'How did you and Bella meet?' asked another reporter. 'Are you boyfriend and girlfriend?'

Bella laughed out loud. Her cheeks flushed pink.

Sean felt the same. That was a weird question to ask, and a little too personal for the world to know. 'My dad was engaged to Bella's aunt, Carla Bonaforte.'

'Your dad is Henry Livingstone, the archaeologist. Isn't that right?' asked another reporter.

Sean gave an apprehensive nod.

The reporter continued. 'Sean, the first reports that came out of Egypt and Paris after the Isharkute invasion said your father was responsible, that he found something buried under the Sphinx... some kind of ancient alien device that started all this. What do you have to say about that?'

'My dad wasn't the first to find evidence of their civilisations. The Isharkute have always been here.'

'Where is he now?'

'Why hasn't he come forward?' interrupted another reporter. 'He obviously knew about the Isharkute. Why didn't he warn us?'

'He didn't have time,' Sean shot back. He was taking the reporter's bait, but couldn't help himself – he had to stick up for his dad. 'Others already knew...but they kept it a secret.'

'Like who?' the reporter demanded.

The reporters fell silent. Every camera focused on Sean. The microphones hovered in front of his face. Sean wanted to smack them away. Instead, he bit his lip and glanced at Powell. The colonel gave him a subtle head shake. Now wasn't the time to reveal the US government's dirty secrets, even though they had known about the Isharkute since the alien crash at Roswell in 1947, and probably even earlier than that. General Maddock had admitted these things to Sean during his interrogation at Giza, stating the US government had already reverse-engineered the crystalline-based technology from the crashed Isharkute vessel. Other governments were also *in the know*, but self-made billionaire Azar Hawati was the most informed. He had collected more Isharkute artefacts and technology than every government combined, including one of the pharaoh's crowns. But none of that mattered anymore. Azar was most likely dead. The world required peace and unity. Dredging up old government secrets only undermined the way forward.

Hazim stepped in front of the cameras. 'These questions will be answered in time. Until something is confirmed by us, consider it a rumour. And there's one thing I will confirm...Sean and his father are considered heroes in my home country of Egypt.'

Hazim's words gave Sean a huge sense of relief. Cairo was in ruins and the Egyptian people had suffered more than any other nation.

They left the frenzy of insatiable reporters behind and prepared to board Neberun's royal transport. Sean approached Hazim. 'Thanks for saying that back there. It means a lot.'

'I meant it,' Hazim said, placing his hand on Sean's shoulder. He acknowledged Bella and Nocao. 'Earth's future is in good hands. You're all heroes.'

'Good luck with everything here.'

'I wish I was coming with you. I'm envious of the things you're about to see and learn. I had a taste of it when I touched the crown in the Hall of Records. Whatever that power was, it opened my mind to the universe – made me realise we're all connected to something greater. I have no idea what that is, but I think you're about to find out.'

Sean took a sharp breath, trembling momentarily. 'I'll let you know when I get back.'

'Look after yourself, kid,' Powell said, throwing his arms around Sean in a crushing hug. 'I'm gonna miss having you around to save the day.'

'I'll miss you too,' Sean wheezed.

*   *   *

Minutes later they were flying over the Lincoln Memorial, leaving Powell and Hazim with the Isharkute Commanders. Sean had been on a royal transport once before, when he was escorted from Ramin's capital to the Great Arena. This new vessel was spacious and sparsely detailed. They sat in the centre of a vast oval-shaped room on soft, lounge-style seating.

Bella stared at the beautiful crystal structure hanging over their heads. The latticework of crystals pulsed with different colours, like a chandelier.

The central floor turned opaque, showing their ascent high above Washington, DC. Sean picked out the White House and its green lawn. Within seconds it was a distant speck obscured by clouds. Light shimmered over the hull as they passed through Earth's upper atmosphere. The ride was smooth, without a hint of turbulence or acceleration.

Two Isharkute dressed in elegant robes entered with gold trays, offering a selection of luminous liquids in slender glasses and exotic-looking fruit.

'So, this is what it's like to travel Isharkute first class!' Bella said.

Ramin laughed. 'This is a taste of things to come. Consider it an introduction to a finer, more civilised way of Isharkute living.' He took a drink and offered it to Bella. 'Don't be shy. You must try everything.'

Bella accepted the glass and took a tentative sip. Her eyes lit up. 'Mmm.. I could get used to this.'

Ramin chuckled. 'I feel we shall get on extraordinarily well.'

Bella clinked her glass against Ramin's. 'Cheers!'

Ramin eyed his glass with a look of surprise, then clinked hers back. 'Cheers! Come, let me show you everything we have on offer.' He escorted Bella over to the bar to experience the full spread of delights.

Nocao leant closer to Sean. 'There's something important about our mission. It will change your mind about involving Bella.'

Sean shifted in his seat, certain he wasn't going to like the news. 'What's that?'

'Akanae is twenty light-years from Earth. For us, travelling at the speed of light, the journey will take several hours, but here on Earth, several days will have passed. The phenomenon is called "time dilation". Time moves slower for us because we're travelling at light speed.'

'I get it. When we return, everyone will have aged more than us.'

'Correct. More time has passed for them.'

'Yeah, but a few days difference isn't so bad. Is it?'

'Bella can safely make the journey to Akanae, help with the cure, and return to Earth within a few months. But she can't stay with us beyond that. When we track Senetep and the *Spearhead*, we'll be travelling thousands of light-years. That means we won't return for hundreds, maybe thousands of years. Bella's family will have been dead for generations. Everyone she cares about will be gone.'

Sean's mouth dropped open. The thought of continuing without her hit him like a gut punch. 'How will everyone on Earth know if we stop Senetep or not?'

'They won't, but future generations will.'

Sean looked over to Bella, deep in thought. Prior to this moment, he had never considered the side effects of space travel. He needed to tell Bella. It was her decision. Join him or return home after they finished the Isharkute cure. What if she said no? Nocao was his best friend, but he was Isharkute. The unfathomable reaches of space were too empty for one human. He wanted Bella to stay with him more than ever. 'There has to be another solution. I travelled through time...when I came back and met you in ancient Egypt. Why can't we create a wormhole like that and come back to Earth whenever we want?'

Nocao paused and rubbed his head. 'Theoretically it's possible... but unlikely-'

'But there's a chance.'

'A very remote chance-'

'Also, didn't Ramin say once the Emperor made up his mind, the decision is final? He said Bella had to come with us.'

'Only as far as Akanae. But don't use that as an excuse to avoid telling Bella the truth. You can wait until we've completed the cure, but you need to tell her before we leave for the *Spearhead*. That's her last chance to come home.'

Sean gave a confident nod to hide his uneasiness. He needed a foolproof solution: one that would keep Bella by his side.

— CHAPTER 2 —

Leaving Earth

Sean had never seen anything like it. He stared in awe, mouth agape. The silver hull of Emperor Neberun's gargantuan mothership stretched out like the surface of a smooth metal planet, not a spaceship. The distant edges reflected the Sun, forming a gleaming horizon against the blackness of space. As they flew around the far side, the monolith eclipsed their view of Earth. Sean thought he had seen everything. Until now. Were there even enough Isharkute alive to pilot and maintain these incredible vessels?

'Wow! It's as big as the Death Star,' Sean remarked.

'What's a Death Star?' Nocao asked.

'It's a moon-sized space station from *Star Wars*. If we ever get through all this, I'll show you the film.'

'Are you talking about *Star Wars*?' Bella said, rejoining them on the couches. 'I love those films.'

'Me too!' Sean blurted out. His overenthusiasm had gotten the better of him. Most of the girls he knew from school were into horror films and comedies. It thrilled him to learn she loved his favourite film series.

They descended upon the dark side of the hull, zipped through an opening and followed a long octagonal tunnel filled with a myriad of guiding lights and adjoining shafts. Isharkute vessels of all shapes and sizes flew by, keeping in lanes like a floating highway. After several twists and turns, they entered a cavernous mechanical void, the core of the mothership. In the middle loomed a metallic pyramid, five times bigger than the Great Pyramid.

Sean jumped to his feet. 'Whoa!'

It was a capital city within a mothership. The immense sloping faces glinted with the lights of countless windows. Vessels darted to and from the structure. They circled around the apex and ascended to the bright docking bay near the top.

'The pyramid is designed to disengage from the mothership and land on the surface of a planet,' Nocao said. 'It's useful for terraforming new worlds.'

'It's a luxury only Isharkute royalty and the elite few can afford,' Ramin grumbled.

Sean noticed a lash of bitterness in his comment. 'You sound jealous.'

'I have become accustomed to the finer things, but even when I was an Overseer, luxuries such as this were pure fantasy. Motherships not owned by the Empire are controlled by elite members of society. They have an unlimited wealth and power that stretches back millennia to the first emperors.'

'Why did Emperor Neberun bring us here?' Bella asked. 'Aren't we meant to be going straight to Akanae?'

'He requested an audience with us before we leave.'

Neberun's seven-foot-tall royal guards greeted them upon landing. They were elaborately dressed in gold-plated armour with long, decorated beards. Each bore multiple nose piercings with gold rings. Gold chains hung between their nostrils and pierced earlobes. They brandished double-ended staves powered by huge crystals. Sean had never seen such powerful weapons before.

'You wouldn't want to mess with these guys,' Bella whispered.

Sean chuckled.

The guards glared at him with their cold, no-nonsense eyes.

Sean gulped and gave them an innocent smile. The guards marched them into a nearby lift and filed in, forming an impenetrable wall of blue muscle. Even Ramin remained tight-lipped, wary of invoking the ire of Neberun's finest guards.

The lift doors opened to a dimly lit area resembling a high-tech laboratory, not a royal quarters. A row of enclosures spotlighted a curious collection of alien species. Enormous tanks brimmed with exotic, luminous fish. Camouflaged birds chirped and whistled from gold-barred cages. One of the glass-walled tanks encompassed trees with striking yellow and purple foliage. Lizards with multicoloured scales hung from the branches, phasing in and out of view like chameleons. A sturdier-walled tank concealed its inhabitants within clouds of dense, swirling vapours. Pairs of glowing yellow eyes tracked them as they passed. Sean glimpsed their dark leathery skin and spiny backs through the mist.

The collection made Sean nervous, reminding him of how close he'd come to being stung by one of Senetep's lethal slitherquills.

The guards led them down a flight of stairs to a lower mezzanine level where the surrounding walls featured floor-to-ceiling windows overlooking the core of the mothership. Emperor Neberun sat with his back to them in a mechanical chair atop a rise of steps. A hologram of a gigantic sphere hovered in front of him, its hollow interior surrounded by concentric layers of rings within rings, all rotating inside each other. The elegant design reminded Sean of a Russian wedding ring. It didn't resemble any Isharkute device he had seen.

The hologram dematerialised.

Sean noticed an open-lid chamber built into the floor behind the throne. The interior glowed with an intense white light. Icy vapours rose from within and unfurled down the side like ghostly fingers. The design resembled an ancient Egyptian sarcophagus, like something a pharaoh from the future might use.

'You should ask Neberun if you can use his cold therapy chamber,' Sean whispered.

Nocao observed the sarcophagus. 'He must be suffering the affliction.'

Neberun rose from his throne, stiff and crooked like an old man. His skeletal limbs creaked and cracked. In the dim light, his light-blue skin presented dead and leathery.

'Cold therapy might extend your life, but judging by our esteemed Emperor, it doesn't do much for your complexion,' Ramin whispered.

The royal guards assembled around the steps to the throne.

Neberun descended the steps. He spoke in a creaky voice. 'In light of our new interspecies relations, Sean and Bella, you may speak freely.'

'Thank you,' Sean replied, nodding appreciatively.

Bella copied his show of respect and nodded.

'Thank you Emperor Neberun,' Ramin said humbly. 'As always, a wise and intuitive decision.'

'My Royal Consult.' Neberun huffed with an air of amusement. 'Is there no end to your self-serving platitudes?'

Ramin bowed and wisely kept his mouth shut.

Neberun approached Nocao and took hold of his forearm, turning it over with his spindly fingers to display Nocao's bruising. He let go and faced everyone. 'There is a truth, one deliberately concealed from the Isharkute population for generations. I believe the time has come for that truth to be revealed.'

Nocao and Ramin shared a surprised look.

Neberun waved his hand, activating a holographic projection of the Moon and Earth.

'When our ancestors first arrived on designation 4793, now commonly known as Earth, they found evidence that the Moon had been artificially created and intentionally positioned in orbit to incubate life. This wasn't the first time our ancestors had discovered this phenomenon. We only find these artificial moons in solar systems where the host planet sits in a habitable zone from its sun, where water survives in liquid form and the building blocks of life can evolve.'

'On Earth, our scientists call it the "Goldilocks Zone",' Sean said.

'The Goldilocks Zone?'

'Yeah. It's based on a children's fairy tale called *Goldilocks and the Three Bears*. A little girl called Goldilocks stumbles into a house where three meals are sitting on the table. She tries all three of them, ignoring the one that's too hot, and the other that's too cold. She chooses the meal in the middle, the one with just the right temperature.'

'Interesting...but simplistic metaphor.'

'They also call it the CHZ, short for circumstellar habitable zone.'

'Our Isharkute ancestors in the Guild of Theology forced the Guild of Sciences to keep the revelation a secret, arguing Isharkute society wasn't ready to learn they were not the first civilisation to travel the galaxy. They surmised it would unravel society and disrupt belief in the First Light theory. To conceal the truth from future generations, they erased all scientific data. The truth was only passed down verbally from one emperor to the next. Echoes of this long-forgotten technology and knowledge have survived only as myth and legend: what you call the *Spearhead of Creation*.'

'But Senetep didn't discover the *Spearhead* through these manufactured moons,' Nocao said. 'He figured it out with his own scientists, tracking planets with life through the universe. He discovered a pattern, the trajectory of the vessel seeding life.'

'Indeed, the *Spearhead* travels through galaxies in a spiral configuration. It has been seeding life for billions of years. Now that Senetep has unlocked this knowledge, more of our scientists will uncover the truth. That's why the secret ends today.'

'How many of these moons have been found?'

'Over 30,000. But that was generations ago. By now there's estimated to be hundreds of thousands, if not millions more.'

'Are there any close to Akanae?'

Neberun rounded them and stooped over Nocao, his mummified-looking face fixed with a menacing glare. His skin appeared fragile, like it could crack and fall apart. 'Nek-Karani.'

Nocao's eyes widened. His breath caught in his throat and he shared a horrified look with Ramin.

'What's Nek-Karani?' Sean asked.

'Akanae's moon,' Nocao said. His vacant stared peered straight through Sean. After a moment of deep contemplation, he continued in a sombre voice. 'That means...we were all created by the *Spearhead*. Isharkute...humans...probably every living organism we've ever encountered.'

'That's ridiculous!' Ramin bellowed.

Neberun didn't respond, but the upper corner of his lip twitched oddly. Sean could tell the Emperor wasn't comfortable revealing such secrets. He seemed to resent the burden.

Nocao and Ramin remained silent, stunned. Their reaction was no surprise. The history of their race, everything they were taught to believe, was unravelling before them. Sean understood how that felt. Not that long ago, the same happened to him.

Bella leant close to Sean and whispered, 'Looks like our governments weren't the only ones keeping secrets.'

Nocao broke the silence. 'Who were they?'

'The emperors who came before me referred to these creators as the Ancients.'

'But Earth's Moon is billions of years old. How do you know it's artificial? Where's the evidence that a race of Ancients built it?'

Neberun peered up to his throne as the hologram reactivated over their heads. A perfect projection of the Moon rotated, glowing brightly as if it hovered in the chamber. The outer crust disappeared, revealing a hollow spherical structure of gigantic rings – the same hologram Neberun had been observing when they entered his quarters.

'Unbelievable!' Bella gasped.

Sean had heard of the Hollow Moon or Spaceship Moon theories before, but never really believed something the size of the Moon could be manufactured. It was a common and fairly well-known conspiracy theory that wasn't even that new. The famous science fiction author H.G. Wells wrote about a hollow Moon in his book *The First Men in the Moon* way back in 1901. Decades later, to fuel the conspiracy fire, NASA reported that the Moon rang like a bell for over an hour when the Apollo 12 mission deliberately crashed a section of its lunar module on the surface. Seismometers installed on the Moon from other Apollo missions had also recorded strange moonquakes, with NASA scientists consistently describing the Moon as 'ringing like a bell'.

'I know the Moon has something to do with tides, but I don't get it,' Bella said. 'Why's the Moon so crucial for life on Earth? I always thought it was just a big hunk of rock that somehow ended up rotating around the Earth.'

'You're right, there is a gravitational pull between the Earth, Moon and Sun that causes tides,' Nocao said. 'But more than that, the reason your Earth has four seasons is because the Moon keeps the planet tilted at 22.5 degrees relative to the equator of the Sun. It makes sure most of Earth stays warm and habitable throughout the year. That also keeps the majority of water in a liquid state – one of the essential building blocks for life to evolve. If Earth wasn't on this tilt, then the equator would get too hot and the world's weather patterns would change dramatically.'

'Now the distances between the Sun, Moon and Earth make sense,' Sean cut in. 'They were planned and calculated all along.'

'What do you mean it was planned?' Bella asked.

'I studied heaps of astronomy for my astro-archaeology. There was one thing about our solar system I couldn't believe was a fluke–'

'What?'

'A perfect solar eclipse.'

'What's so unbelievable about that? The Moon just blocks the Sun. Doesn't it?'

'Yeah, but did you ever wonder why the Sun and Moon are exactly the same size in the sky? Even though the Moon is way smaller than the Sun.'

'Not really.'

'It's true, the Moon is 400 times smaller than the Sun, but because it's closer to Earth, exactly 1/400th the distance between the Earth and the Sun, it makes them look the same size in the sky.'

'That's just a weird coincidence.'

'It's not. The Moon mimics the Sun across the sky. When the Sun's at its weakest in winter, the Moon's at its highest and brightest.'

'Sean's right,' Nocao said. 'To be more precise, the Moon orbits the Earth in 27.3 days, almost the same number when you compare the size of the Moon to the Earth, it's 27.3 per cent. Then if you compare that with how many times the Earth rotates on its axis as it orbits the Sun, which is 366.2 times, that's nearly a perfect size comparison match between the Earth to the Moon, which is 366.1 per cent larger.'

'Thanks for clearing that up,' Sean said with a smirk.

'*Si, Si*, I get it!' Bella said. 'That's too many numbers for me to think about. It's hurting my brain. I just want to know what it all means.'

'It means these Ancients, whoever they were, positioned the Moon with these deliberate mathematical relationships. The sizes and distances are so obvious and neat, it's like they wanted us to question its existence. As if it was all organised with a purpose.'

'Those relationships are like Akanae and our moon, Nek-Karani,' Nocao said.

'So, what are they saying to us?' Bella asked. 'What's in it for the Ancients? Why would they go to all the trouble of seeding a planet with life and just leave behind a cryptic message?'

'It's a message for the life forms that evolve on those planets,' Neberun said. 'When the indigenous species reach the appropriate level of intelligence and evolution, they will recognise the unique patterns within their solar system. The Ancients have a grand plan for the universe - one that we're yet to comprehend.'

'Maybe it's not that hard to understand,' Sean said. 'Sounds like the *Spearhead* has one simple job...to spread life through the universe.'

'It may be a life form itself,' Nocao said. 'The vessel acts like any other form of life. It evolves, survives, and propagates.'

'Why would it seed a solar system and move on?' Ramin said. 'It doesn't make sense.'

'Because what's a universe without life?'

'Empty,' Bella said.

Sean glanced at her and smiled, comforted to have her by his side. He wasn't going to be alone in this unexplored universe, or worse - empty.

Neberun trudged up the stairs and slumped into the throne with a sigh. His short jaunt had consumed his dwindling energy. He caught his breath and addressed them.

'It's imperative we finish the cure and begin the hunt for Senetep. If he gains control of the *Spearhead*, he wields the ultimate power of creation. And destruction. His corruption threatens all life, future and present. But before you leave for Akanae, there's something we must investigate inside the Moon.'

'Inside the Moon?' Bella exclaimed.

'My scientists have discovered a signal emanating from within its core.'

'Is it from the Ancients?' Sean asked.

'We believe so. Senetep has a head start, but this signal could be a vital clue he has overlooked. It might be crucial to understanding this ancient race and their universe-seeding vessel, the *Spearhead of Creation*.'

— CHAPTER 3 —

Alternate Course

Senetep steeled his muscles against the blast of freezing air. Glistening ice crystals blanketed his skin. It felt like he was on fire. The miniature freeze raced through his muscles, bones, and organs like a blizzard, snap-freezing every cell. His mind blanked and his body went rigid. His consciousness hovered in a frozen void. Neither dead nor alive. An alarm pierced the silence and the cold therapy chamber slid open.

Senetep collapsed to the floor.

His frozen knees took the brunt of the fall. If they were any colder, he'd be picking up the shattered pieces of icy flesh. He had pushed his body to its limits. The affliction had advanced tenfold since leaving Earth. His DNA was in a rapid state of decay. It had reached a point where he couldn't give orders because his jaw locked in spasms.

His regular body heat returned in waves. Electrical signals from his brain exploded through his nervous system, twitching and flexing his muscles.

Senetep fought his trembling legs and stood. He was alone inside his personal quarters, suffering in isolation. None of the crew knew about his affliction. It had been a well-kept secret, even from his former Commanders, Nefaro and Vogran. Just thinking about their failure ignited his body with rage. He needed a replacement Commander, one with experience who could take over while he managed his affliction.

Senetep wiped the condensation off his skin. He smacked his

biceps and thighs to settle the twitching. Satisfied his body would support him for the next few hours, he returned to the bridge.

The bridge was noisy and chaotic. The escape from Earth had taken a severe toll on their annihilator and the crew were dealing with multiple system failures. Fighting through Neberun's fleet had depleted their shields and destabilised the main energy crystals, leaving them limping through space, barely able to hold light speed.

Senetep watched the pandemonium with dismay.

It would be impossible to find the *Spearhead* in this condition. They needed a new vessel, capable of travelling into deep space. But first, he needed to appoint a First Commander. The best of his crew stood around him. There were several older Isharkute, all second and third ranked Commanders. Many had served him since Ranatar's tenure. They were loyal, but stale and unambitious.

Then there was Erund Griss, a young, enthusiastic Fifth Commander. Erund's swift and decisive actions helped them escape from Earth. His willingness to serve without question made him the perfect candidate.

Senetep straightened, conjuring his loudest voice. 'Fifth Commander Erund Griss!'

Erund looked up from his control panel and nodded. He instructed a technician to take over his work and marched proudly across the bridge. His confident step, muscular physique, and gold armour reminded Senetep of himself at a similar age. Erund's commanding presence drew sideways glances from those around him. His pure white beard was decorated with the platinum and azure beads unique to the Guild of Arms. Tattoos of rank inked half his forehead, an impressive achievement for such a lowly ranked Commander.

Erund stood before him and straightened his shoulders, chin high in the air. 'Overseer Senetep, how can I serve you?'

'Erund Griss, you have been a loyal citizen of my capital since your birth.'

'Yes. My father and generations before him have prospered under your leadership.'

'Where does your father serve me now?'

'He died of the affliction.'

Senetep's lip twitched. He rubbed his beard to mask the spasm and marched behind Erund, deliberately concealing any further tics and tremors. 'You're an initiate to the Guild of Arms, like your father.'

'That's right. I trained under First Commander Ranatar, whom I considered your best Commander.'

Senetep laughed. Erund's compliance sounded deliberate and rehearsed. Regardless of his willingness to please, the young Isharkute was skilled and disciplined. 'With Nefaro and Vogran dead, I'm looking for a First Commander to replace them. Do you have any suggestions?'

Erund narrowed his eyes. He spoke in a loud confident tone so the nearest officers overheard. 'You don't need to look at anyone else for the position. I will not fail you like Vogran or Nefaro.'

Senetep stopped short, as if deflecting an insult, shocked to hear such an outspoken subordinate. Erund's disrespect bordered on treason. But every word was true. Maybe that's what he required now, a First Commander with the confidence to speak his mind and get the job done.

One of the crew yelled out in panic. 'Power crystals are eighty per cent fractured.'

Erund spoke up, directing his voice towards Senetep. 'That leaves us enough power for one light-speed jump. What do we do?'

Senetep marched between the crew, keeping his muscles moving while he considered their options. His affliction was distracting him from his duties. He needed a solution. Now. Their predicament had provided the perfect opportunity to test his enthusiastic candidate. He rounded on Erund. 'Do you have any suggestions?'

'We return to Akanae and attack the Empire's orbiting space docks. Emperor Neberun's fleets have only just come out of cryogenic sleep. The docks won't be fully operational yet. We steal a new vessel capable of infinite light-speed jumps and destroy the docks. Neberun won't be expecting the attack. That gives us the element of surprise.

It also hinders the Empire's ability to come after us.'

Senetep grunted with satisfaction. 'Coordinate the attack. If your performance pleases me, I'll promote you to First Commander.'

Erund grinned like a child.

'If you fail, I'll tear that pristine beard from your smiling face and eject you from the nearest airlock.'

'There is no room for failure,' Erund replied. 'The future of a pure Isharkute Empire relies on our actions today.'

Senetep folded his arms and nodded. Erund's attitude bordered on insolence, but his staunch determination set a high standard for the crew. He motioned for Erund to follow and marched into the centre of the bridge.

'Prepare a light-speed jump to Akanae. We will attack the space docks and claim what's rightfully ours. This new vessel will take us to the *Spearhead of Creation*. Erund will coordinate the attack from now on.'

Senetep took a seat in his command chair. He relaxed and casually stroked his beard, watching on in amusement.

Erund screamed orders at his subordinates and superiors with equal measure.

Senetep enjoyed the show. His finger caught in his beard and he accidentally pulled a clump of hair off his chin. He focused on the withered strands and gasped at the sight of his wrist. Black and purple bruises spoiled his forearm like rotten fruit. He sat upright, glancing around to see if anyone else noticed.

The affliction was advancing beyond his control. Constant rounds of cold therapy would do more harm than good at this late stage. The rate of cellular deterioration had sped up exponentially in the last 24 hours – ever since jumping through the wormhole to modern-day Earth. Human DNA provided a temporary cure, but he would die before injecting himself with their filthy genome. Cryogenic sleep was the only viable solution.

Erund stood in front of the bridge's sprawling viewscreen. The backdrop of space glistened with the ancient light of a billion stars. 'All stations prepare for light speed.' He turned and raised his hand towards Senetep. 'Awaiting your command.'

Senetep's stomach churned. It wasn't the affliction. His nausea was a reaction to something else. Apprehension. He was about to kill thousands of his own kind. His cause was justified. Purifying his species was paramount. But still, a part of him doubted his actions. He despised his weakness. Living among humans had made him soft.

He forced himself from the command chair and stood on wobbly legs.

The crew watched, curious, awaiting his command.

Senetep went to speak, but nothing came out. His mouth wouldn't open. His jaw muscles spasmed and clenched his teeth. His tongue flapped inside his mouth like a trapped animal. Muffled sounds gurgled from the back of his throat.

He collapsed against the balustrade around his command chair. His legs buckled, and he dropped to his knees, gasping. His lungs were heavy and unwilling to expand. His heart beat erratically. His vision blurred. As his consciousness faded, he had enough time for one final thought.

I won't die...not like this...

*   *   *

The darkness split apart with stark light. Senetep squinted into the glare, focusing on the stainless-steel wall of the annihilator's medical lab. He was lying on an operating table. Alive. He recalled his last moments on the bridge, collapsing in front of his crew.

The shrivelled carcass of a glutinous latchling sack lay next to him. Its singular tentacle rested on his chest, wet and glistening in the spotlight. Senetep wiped away the strings of saliva drooping between his chin and the tentacle. It had recently been pulled from his throat. There was only one reason it lay beside him: the creature had kept him breathing.

What had his scientists done to him?

Senetep shifted onto his elbows. The bruising on his forearms had faded. He was breathing easily and his heart beat with a steady thump. His mind was clear. Nearby, Erund was deep in conversation with two scientists.

Senetep flicked the latchling tentacle off his chest and sat up. His muscles were strong and responsive. This was the best he'd felt for a long time. 'What did you do to me?'

Erund and the scientists spun around, startled.

'You were dying; we needed to take emergency action to save you,' Erund said.

Senetep swung his legs off the table and placed his bare feet on the cool steel floor. The scientists took a nervous step backwards. 'What's wrong with you all?'

'To prevent a complete cellular collapse...I ordered these scientists to administer the only cure.'

Senetep's heart thumped hard against his ribs. 'Being what?'

'Human DNA. We injected you with a refined version of the cure, stripped of as much junk DNA that we could eliminate.'

Senetep leapt off the operating table and grabbed the nearest scientist by the neck. He snapped his vertebrae like chalk and flung the limp carcass across the lab. Senetep gazed down at his body, marvelling at his newfound strength. He felt decades younger. Invigorated with life. But it had come at a devastating cost.

His pure Isharkute blood had been spoiled by human DNA.

'ARGHH!' Senetep flipped over the operating table. He swiped all the medical equipment off the benches and tore the medical conduits draping from the ceiling. The severed ends whipped through the air, hissing like snakes, spewing gases and vapours into the lab.

'Stop!' Erund cried, backing up. 'Without the cure, you'd be dead.'

A squad of warriors rushed into the lab, staves drawn.

Senetep hurled items at them, blind with fury. 'Traitors! All of you!'

'Subdue him,' Erund ordered.

The warriors opened fire. Stun blasts erupted over Senetep's chest, forcing him across the lab. He collapsed against a trolley, fighting to stay conscious. The warriors hoisted him onto an operating table and strapped him down.

Erund leant over him and waved over the surviving scientist.

Senetep struggled to keep his eyes open.

'Can you erase his memories of this?' Erund said.

'I can try, but the results are unpredictable,' the scientist said. 'We can't isolate specific memories. We have to shock entire neural structures and hope we hit the right areas.'

'Do it.'

Senetep fought to remain lucid. His thoughts faded. Would he remember how Erund betrayed him? He buried the memory deep in his mind, hiding it amongst his earliest memories.

A dark emptiness followed.

*   *   *

Senetep awoke to find himself lying on an operating table in his scientist's labs. His mind was hazy, confused. The last thing he remembered was collapsing on the bridge. There was a gap in his memory. He sensed horrible dreams. Suffering.

Erund and a scientist approached. They looked anxious.

Senetep moved to sit up and found his arms strapped down. 'Why am I restrained?'

'For your own protection,' Erund said.

Senetep craned his neck around. The lab was in disarray. Equipment was strewn across the floor and an operating table lay on its side. 'What happened?'

'You don't remember?'

'No.'

Erund shared a subtle look with the scientist and stood aside, revealing a dead scientist on the floor behind them. 'You don't recall breaking his neck?'

Senetep tried to sit up again, grunting at the binds. 'No, I don't. Untie me.'

'We can't, not until you understand what happened.'

'Tell me!'

'You collapsed on the bridge and were immediately brought to this lab. Your cellular decay was killing you. In the panic and confusion, this scientist injected you with human DNA to save your life...an error I was unaware of until I arrived at the lab. If it had been my decision, I would have placed you in cryogenic stasis. I know your cause all along has been to avoid the human cure and find another way.'

Senetep felt a familiar rage building inside him.

'You have previously awoken to this knowledge. In your fury, you attacked and killed the scientist responsible. We subdued you for your own good. Not his.'

Senetep relaxed his fists and lay back. Being saved by the scourge of the galaxy was worse than dying. There was no escaping the filth that pumped through his veins. He was stuck in an eternal nightmare. Aside from nauseating disgust, he felt healthier and mentally sharper. Now calmer, he realised not all was lost. *The Spearhead of Creation* was still out there, waiting to be discovered. The Ancient vessel had the potential to cleanse his DNA and reset the Isharkute genome. He would put up with his tainted body until then.

'I understand,' Senetep said in a calm voice. 'Untie me. We need to return to our mission.'

Erund looked uncertain. He nodded to the warriors waiting in the background. They stepped forward and gingerly removed the restraints.

Senetep sat up and rubbed his wrists. The bruising from the affliction had almost disappeared. He felt stronger and sure of his body. His muscles held steady. No shakes. He hopped off the operating table and everyone took a step back. He must have torn the place apart to leave them this scared. Good! He snatched the surviving scientist by the neck.

'You should never have allowed your companion to infect me with human DNA,' Senetep growled. With a powerful twist, he snapped the scientist's neck and dropped his limp body in a crumpled heap.

The warriors drew their staves.

Senetep rounded on Erund. His sudden move caught the young Commander off-guard, making him jump in fright. Senetep smirked. 'Make sure their replacements are not imbeciles.' Erund nodded and exhaled a visible sigh of relief. 'Then meet me on the bridge for the attack on Akanae's space docks. Prove to me why I should promote you to First Commander.'

— CHAPTER 4 —

Dark Side Of The Moon

Bella trembled at the thought of travelling inside the Moon, an artificial sphere constructed by ancient aliens to incubate life on Earth. The revelation went against everything she was taught to believe. Where did her Catholic faith fit into all this? Even science had it wrong. The origins of life were more mysterious than she ever imagined. There was so much about the universe she didn't understand. Just thinking about it made her feel naïve and insignificant.

They were back aboard the luxurious royal transport, about to investigate the mysterious signal emanating from the Moon's core. The quick detour had delayed their journey to Akanae, the Isharkute homeworld.

Neberun and his team of science officers accompanied them. They stood around their consoles, examining holographic scans of the Moon. Neberun believed these artificial moons led to the *Spearhead of Creation*, like a trail of breadcrumbs scattered across the universe.

Bella sat with Sean and Nocao, picking at the odd alien delicacies being served up to them by Neberun's chefs. There was an antipasto-looking plate of yellow tentacles, purple fruit, and small black eggs. She wasn't game to put any near her mouth.

Nocao eagerly sampled everything on offer. He glanced up between mouthfuls. 'You two are missing out. I can't believe you aren't hungry.'

Bella shrugged. 'I liked your Isharkute drink. Not sure about your food.'

Sean toyed with one of the slimy tentacles. 'We should have got some takeaway before we left Earth.'

Bella placed a hand on her grumbling stomach. '*Si!* Pizza.'

Sean pointed to the clear-hull window. 'It's our last view of Earth before we fly around the dark side of the Moon.'

Bella glimpsed the vibrant blue orb. It seemed so tiny and vulnerable from this distance. Its sprawling continents showed no borders. No wars. No turmoil. It seemed so serene. She was overcome with emotion for her precious jewel of a home. Every human, and now every Isharkute, were lucky to share such an amazing place.

'It's called an Earthset,' Sean said. 'To see the Earth set behind the Moon like that.'

'It's so beautiful,' she whispered.

Earth's glow dimmed against the barren grey horizon and vanished. Bella shivered. The absence of her world against the eternal void of space made her feel isolated. Exposed. The bright lunar landscape transformed into a desert of dark, undulating shadows. Specks of light appeared in the distance, darting over the pockmarked landscape like fireflies. As they drew closer, Bella could see they were Isharkute vessels circling a gigantic crater.

A sizeable hologram of the Moon's surface shimmered to life in the middle of the cabin. Neberun manipulated the hologram with his long skeletal fingers, adjusting the angle and zoom to highlight the crater.

'Scans reveal this is the thinnest section of the Moon's outer crust. An advance squadron has blasted away the surface, revealing the inner structure.'

'Whoa! It looks like the inside of a cricket ball,' Sean said.

Bella tittered with astonishment. Sean's simple analogy was spot on. The Moon's rocky exterior hid a latticework of metallic beams, criss-crossing beneath the surface like the interwoven strings beneath the skin of a cricket ball.

'Ingenious structure,' Neberun remarked. 'The rings act like a gigantic flexible ball, designed to withstand an eternity of comet and asteroid strikes.'

They flew through the debris floating around the crater and down between the first intersection of colossal beams. The gleaming infrastructure was in pristine condition, undamaged by their energy blasts and impervious to the ravages of time.

'This is how the Moon looked in its original form,' Nocao said, gawking at the god-sized structure.

'Why did the Ancients hide the structure beneath the surface?' Bella asked.

'Maybe they didn't,' Sean said. 'The Moon may have collected its rocky surface after orbiting Earth for billions of years. These intersecting beams act like a giant net, catching all the debris headed to and from Earth.'

Nocao examined the data streaming alongside the hologram. 'You're correct, Sean. The Moon and Earth share similar isotopic ratios.'

'Sorry – I'm not a science nerd like you guys,' Bella said. 'What are isotopic ratios?'

'They're made up from the same type of rocks,' Sean jumped in. 'That doesn't happen anywhere else in the solar system. At least that we know about.'

'It's theoretically impossible,' Nocao added. 'For two planets to share the same rocks, they would have been one planet at some point. Then split in two.'

'Our scientists really have no idea how the Moon formed. For decades, they've based it on the "giant impact theory", where something the size of Mars hit our planet and spewed all the rocks into space. They said over time, all those rocks joined to make the Moon. It was their way of justifying why Earth shared the same rocks as the Moon.'

'Your scientists are half-correct,' Nocao said. 'An interstellar object must have hit the Earth somewhere in the past with enough force to send the debris into space.'

'Maybe it was the same asteroid that killed the dinosaurs,' Bella said, proud to add something to the conversation.

Sean glanced at her in astonishment. 'I never thought of it like that! Imagine if the dinosaurs looked up at the Moon the way the Ancients originally built it.'

Bella's confidence lifted. Adding to their conversation made her feel less out of her depth. It was intimidating being around such smart minds. Being an artist, she was on the back foot with all the science stuff.

Their vessel squeezed past the asteroids jammed among the beams, passing within metres of their jagged edges. Bella held her breath. Terrified but enthralled, she half-expected to see a bunch of dinosaur bones protruding from the stone. As they moved deeper inside the Moon, the beams became clean and devoid of stellar debris. Bella felt microscopic, like a mosquito flying through the girders of a skyscraper.

'Makes one feel somewhat insignificant,' Ramin remarked.

'Si, I was thinking the same thing.'

The beams parted to an inky black void.

'It's dark. Darker than space. It's like being sucked into a black hole.'

'Not really,' Nocao said. 'If you were sucked into a black hole, you would be stretched into a stream of atoms…or instantaneously incinerated.'

Bella rolled her eyes.

'At least the Ancients turned off the lights when they left,' Sean said.

'That's not entirely true,' Nocao said, joining the scientists to watch the incoming data. 'There's no other structure inside the Moon, but we've found the source of the signal.'

'Where's it coming from?' Neberun asked.

'Dead centre of the Moon.'

The colossal beams disappeared behind them, leaving them alone in the middle of a great void. A blue sphere appeared from the darkness, like a miniature planet spinning in the centre of a starless universe. Their vessel came to a stop and hovered before the sphere.

Bella stared, mesmerised by the beautiful glowing orb. It was twice the size of their vessel, and bright, without casting light.

'The orb is transmitting a signal,' a scientist announced.

'Show me,' Neberun said.

Alien glyphs projected overhead as a hologram. Bella studied the cascading columns of glyphs. 'They look like a cross between ancient Egyptian hieroglyphs and Japanese Kanji.'

'There's ten symbols,' Nocao confirmed. 'They appear to represent a base-10 number system. The same number system human beings use.'

'Can you decode it?' Sean asked.

Bella turned to Nocao. 'Base-10? What's that?'

'Humans predominantly use a base-10 number system,' Nocao replied, 'based on the fact you have ten fingers. This has been the primary counting system on Earth for thousands of years. On Akanae, we developed a base-24 because we have twelve fingers and twelve toes. Although we evolved on separate planets, our mathematics are founded on the same basic principles: fingers and toes.'

'Does that mean the Ancients have ten fingers like humans?'

'Don't be so presumptuous!' Neberun scoffed. 'The Ancients obviously left their base-10 code inside this Moon because they programmed your primates with ten fingers and toes. They expected you to decipher this message when you became advanced enough to discover it.'

'Sounds like the perfect explanation,' Ramin cut in, bowing nervously. 'Your incredible wisdom has solved the conundrum.'

Bella held back a laugh. Ramin's exaggerated praise for Emperor Neberun was verging on comical, but reminded her she was in the presence of royalty. She needed to show the same humility and respect.

'Isn't math the language of the universe?' Sean asked.

'Yes. Math is the logical method of universal communication,' Nocao said. 'Spoken languages evolve differently between species, but we live in the same physical universe, which means ratios, distances, and volumes will always be explained by math.'

'We have unscrambled the first permutation of code,' a scientist announced.

'Geez, that was quick!' Sean said.

A sprawling hologram of the universe materialised in place of the symbols, more detailed than any Isharkute map Bella had seen. Billions of glistening stars populated the luminous spiral-shaped galaxies. New symbols appeared over multiple galaxies. Bella pointed them out. 'What are those symbols?'

The scientist made some adjustments on his console.

Bella watched as the hologram zoomed in to their location in the Milky Way galaxy. A yellow line traced a path through the stars, weaving a wide circular arc, closing inwards towards the centre of their galaxy, creating a perfect spiral pattern. 'It's the Golden Ratio!'

'You know it?' Sean said, sounding surprised.

'Si! I studied it in art. I've used it in my paintings. It's a tool for composition, a way of achieving balance, harmony and beauty in art and design.'

Sean nodded, looking impressed. 'Here, that ratio shows the path the Spearhead took after it left Earth. It's the same map Senetep is using to find it.'

'Good!' Neberun said. 'Now we know where he's going.'

'We've deciphered a second permutation of code,' the scientist announced, peering up from his console.

A network of wavy blue lines appeared on the map, linking the outer and inner lines of the spiral.

'What are they?' Bella asked.

'Wormholes,' the scientist said, 'with stable entry and exit points.'

'Scusi me for asking so many questions, but what's a wormhole?'

'It's a shortcut through space,' Nocao said. 'It means we don't have to follow the path taken by the Spearhead. We can use the wormholes to jump instantaneously from one section of its trajectory to the next-'

'Senetep doesn't know about the wormholes,' Sean interjected. 'These weren't on his map. We can catch up to him!'

'We can do better than that. With this map, we can jump ahead of Senetep and beat him to the Spearhead. It will take months, even years, off our journey.'

The hologram zoomed out to display the entire universe. Bella gazed into the bright cluster of stars illuminating the core. 'What's that in the centre of the universe?'

'It might be the home of the Ancients,' Sean said.

The orb unexpectedly powered down, leaving their vessel in darkness.

'What happened?' Neberun asked.

'We finished deciphering the signal, and the sphere shut down,' a scientist said.

DONG!

A deep unsettling noise resonated through the void, as if someone had rung an incredibly loud bell. Bella covered her ears. The sonic wave passed through her body, vibrating her skull like a gong, making her dizzy. The noise gradually subsided.

'What happened?' Neberun said, swaying like a drunk man about to fall over.

'That was the Moon's inner structure,' a scientist called. 'The rings are shifting.'

'Fly us out. Now!'

The pilots spun the vessel about, aiming for the small patch of stars visible through the hole in the lunar crust. The gigantic rings criss-crossed over each other, dislodging the deep-seated rocks. A deadly asteroid field formed inside the void, thwarting their escape.

Bella covered her face and peeked between her fingers.

The colossal rings came at them from every angle, smashing into the rocks, kicking off shattered pieces in all directions. *BANG!* A hulking chunk bounced off the hull.

'*Mio Dio!*'

They zipped through the chaos like a fly avoiding a gigantic swat. They passed the inner rings and found the outside rings had remained stationary, keeping the surface of the moon intact. Their vessel shot out of the crater into space, chased by the deafening vibrations.

Neberun found his feet and shook his head. 'Why is the Moon still ringing?'

'It appears to be communicating,' a scientist replied.

'With what?'

The hologram of the universe reappeared overhead. The signal emanating from the Moon spread out across the Milky Way, passing the *Spearhead*, reaching beyond the edge of the galaxy. It repeated through the universe, tracing back to the bright cluster of stars in the core.

Neberun ambled around the holographic map, his light-blue eyes fixed on the centre. 'When your work is done, you will seek the source of the signal and contact the Ancients.'

Bella's stomach dropped. She was hurtling towards an uncertain future. Ready or not, all her questions about life and the universe were about to be answered.

— CHAPTER 5 —

The Dream

Sean was about to embark on a journey to unlock the secrets of life throughout the universe. It was incredible. Still, he couldn't shake one nagging worry. The pressure to tell Bella the truth was building. The longer he left it, the harder it was becoming. He wanted her by his side for the entire journey, but there was a major catch: if Bella travelled beyond Akanae, she would never see her family again. The time and distances were so vast her family would be long dead when she returned.

For now, he had time up his sleeve – time to keep Bella by his side a little longer.

After docking with Neberun's mothership, they transferred into a deep-space exploration vessel crewed by Isharkute scientists, pilots, warriors, and personnel. Emperor Neberun bid them farewell and remained on his mothership to oversee the Isharkute integration to Earth. With little fanfare, their vessel departed the docking bay and headed out to space.

Sean, Bella, Nocao and Ramin watched from the bridge. They travelled halfway between the Earth and Moon. The crew scanned and manipulated their holographic star maps, marking routes and preparing the jump to light speed. Sean smiled to himself. It was surreal, like he was living an episode of Star Trek.

'Our course is plotted,' the pilot announced.

'Initiate light speed,' Ramin said.

The stars stretched and curved around the viewscreen. There was a slight shudder through the polished alloy floor, and that was it – they were hurtling through the vastness of space at the speed of light.

'Wow!' Sean gasped.

'How long will it take to get to Akanae?' Bella asked.

'Twelve hours,' Ramin replied. 'Plenty of time to rest and recuperate. I've arranged private quarters for the three of you. After you've had time to rest, I'll brief you about your mission on Akanae.'

'Is it true there's only female Isharkute living on Akanae?'

'Females are the only permanent residents, but many lay in hibernation in the capital, struck down with the affliction after becoming life-bearers. We have an orbiting armada of space docks where a handful of males keep watch. They visit the planet daily, interacting as custodians rather than residents. They perform maintenance on the capitals and make sure our females are well-cared-for. Akanae is purposely kept as peaceful as possible. It's a nursery for our species. It's been this way for millennia, ever since the female Isharkute decided we should leave Akanae.'

'They told you to leave?'

'Yes. They consider males too hostile. Too warmongering. Not a good influence on the newborns.'

Bella smirked. 'Sounds like my kind of planet.'

Sean looked at her, surprised. 'Really?'

'I'm joking, *stupido!*' she said, playfully punching his arm.

Ramin laughed. 'Feisty! You will fit in well with our females. But first you must recuperate. Nocao will show you to your quarters.'

Nocao led Sean and Bella off the bridge and through a series of passages. Compared to Neberun's opulent royal vessel with its luxurious couches, alien finger food, and gold-appointed furniture, their new vessel was plain and functional.

'These are your quarters,' Nocao said, indicating two adjacent rooms. The cramped spaces contained a single sleeping pod, chair, table, crystal control panel, and not much else.

Bella stepped inside. 'What about privacy? There're no doors.'

'Just like school camp,' Sean said. 'No privacy.'

'Great!' Bella sighed. 'Now it's space camp without doors.'

Sean laughed, thinking she was joking.

She glared at him. 'I'm serious.'

Nocao entered and touched a panel next to the door frame. A dark shadow appeared in place of a door, closing her room to the passage.

Sean couldn't hear them at all. He knocked on the hard hologram. No answer. He raised his fist to knock harder, when the door suddenly dematerialised.

Bella stood there smiling, hands on her hips. 'Lonely?'

Sean sheepishly lowered his fist.

'Both quarters have holographic doors,' Nocao said.

'Why does everything have to be holograms with you guys?' Bella quipped.

'The technology reduces vessel mass and weight.'

'Makes sense.'

Nocao pressed a small panel above the sleeping pod and its door dematerialised, revealing a clear gelatinous mattress illuminated from beneath by a soft, inviting light. A transparent pillow sat at the head of the pod, three times longer than a normal pillow to support an Isharkute head.

Bella pressed her finger deep into the mattress. 'Feels squishy.'

'It will contour to the shape of your spine and protect you in case of a collision or sudden stop,' Nocao said. 'The pod will close once you lie down and automatically open when you wake. My quarters are down the hall. I'll see you at the briefing.'

'Wait!' Bella said. 'Aren't you forgetting something?'

Nocao regarded her with a puzzled expression.

'What about toilets?'

'Ah, of course! Humans frequent them far more than Isharkute.' Nocao placed his hand on a nearby panel and a section of the passage wall slid open. Sean and Bella peered inside to find the most Earthly-looking object on the ship.

'Wow, an alien toilet!' Bella remarked.

'At least it has a real door,' Sean added dryly.

'See you in a few hours,' Nocao said, shuffling off with a limp.

Sean watched him with concern. Nocao was doing his best to conceal his symptoms, but now they affected his legs. The sooner they reached Akanae and started the cure, the better.

'Is the affliction making him walk like that?' Bella asked.

'Yeah,' Sean said solemnly.

But that wasn't the only thing on his mind. He needed to tell Bella about the time effects of their mission beyond Akanae. It was the perfect moment. Just the two of them. Alone. He stared into her eyes, preparing to explain everything. A terrifying thought flashed through his mind. What if Nocao died after Bella returned to Earth? He'd be on his own. His mouth froze, half open. The words he was about to speak vanished into a silent breath.

'What's wrong?' Bella asked.

'What?'

'You're just staring at me...not saying anything. It's a little weird.'

'Sorry, I was...I was just thinking about something.'

'What?'

'It's Nocao...I'm just worried about him,' Sean replied softly, disappointed with himself for chickening out.

Bella hugged him. 'He'll be all right.'

Sean placed his arms around her, unsure if he was meant to keep up the romantic side of their relationship. They had kissed before. What did that make them? Boyfriend and girlfriend? Their mutual attraction and affection made them closer than friends. But how were they meant to act around each other from now on? If his dad ended up marrying Carla, that would have made Bella his extended family. She almost became his stepsister. They weren't related at all, but Sean couldn't shake the weird feeling. It just complicated an already-complicated situation.

Bella kissed him on the cheek and slipped inside her quarters. 'See you when you wake up, Sean.'

The holographic door materialised, leaving Sean alone in the hall again. Her prompt departure was an easy out this time around. He still needed to tell her the truth.

Sean climbed into the sleeping pod with a yawn. A sudden

tiredness overwhelmed him. He couldn't remember his last proper sleep. It seemed like he'd been awake for days. He lay down on the mushy mattress and the holographic door materialised, sealing him inside. The glow beneath dimmed to near complete darkness. It was silent. He nestled his head into the enormous pillow, closed his eyes, and drifted off to sleep.

*   *   *

After a timeless period of nothing, Sean found himself drifting outside the pod, his mind separated from his body. He floated across the passage and discovered Bella asleep in her pod. He continued through the wall to find Nocao sitting in his quarters, applying cold compresses to his afflicted muscles.

Sean directed his consciousness through the ship, finding he controlled where he went by focusing his thoughts.

He floated past the Isharkute warriors in the common room between the scientists in their labs, all the way up to Ramin sitting in his command chair on the bridge.

This was more than a dream. His mind was alert, as if awake. He focused his thoughts away from the vessel and unexpectedly emerged on the outside of the hull.

He was hovering in space!

His vessel disappeared into the vibrant spiral of an alien galaxy, leaving him floating in the middle of nowhere - alone. There were no nearby planets. Distant stars twinkled amidst colourful streaks of nebulae. Sean admired the beauty of the universe. His momentary feeling of contentment transformed into panic. Why had he stopped moving? His thoughts were too clear, too alert for a dream. Had his consciousness permanently detached from his body? Was he doomed to float through space for eternity, never to be reunited with his physical self?

His chaotic thoughts sent him hurtling through space. He was lost. Grasping at distant stars with hands he didn't have. His dream had become a nightmare. He tried to wake himself up. But there was a void between his mind and physical body. The stars blurred. He was falling through the endless vacuum of space. How would he escape?

'*DAD!*'

The stars jolted back into focus.

His consciousness found direction. He shot through the galaxy, passing entire solar systems in seconds. The more he thought about his dad, the faster he went.

A distortion appeared ahead, like a hole punched through the fabric of the universe. The stars curved around its circumference, as if being stretched and sucked into the darkness. It was a black hole! The galactic killer had a gravitational pull so strong not even light could escape its invisible grasp.

Sean tried to close his eyes, but he had no eyelids. There was no way to avert being sucked in. He plummeted towards the interminable void until it was all he saw.

FLASH!

Dazzling lights exploded in front of him.

Suddenly he was back in space, orbiting Earth. His consciousness was drawn to the night side of the planet, down through the clouds, across a moonlit jungle towards a flickering pinprick of light on the side of a mountain. It was a campfire. Now he was in the middle of a small village. His dad stood near the fire, a centaur amongst a tribe of humans, sipping what appeared to be coffee from a carved wooden cup.

Sean's panic eased. Logical thought gradually returned. Was this a dream or a window to the past? The details seemed too real to be an illusion. Nesuk and Rootuk emerged from the shadows and joined his dad by the fire.

'We need to narrow down our choices for the next location,' Nesuk said.

'It's my fault.' Henry sighed. 'I should've realised the last site wasn't going to work.'

Sean was startled by his dad's sombre tone. His emotional pain sounded so real. He had never experienced a dream this vivid. He hovered over the fire like a ghost, caught between this window into an unseen past and his own tenuous future. Why did he arrive here now? Was he brought here for a reason?

'The blame cannot fall upon you alone,' Rootuk said, drawing Sean's attention back to their conversation. 'Every decision is complicated and affects the future in ways we are yet to discover.'

'I appreciate your candour, but it's still my fault,' Henry replied.

'Do you have any ideas about a new site?'

'I've been thinking about it since we returned. We can't build another pyramid on a forty-five-degree angle. They're too high and easily discovered. But we still need a pyramid with the capacity to store the vessels and weaponry we've collected...'

Sean could see where this was going. He was witnessing a pivotal moment in his dad's efforts to help humanity.

'...It has to be built upon by later generations, something so large that when it disappears beneath the jungle, people will think it's a mountain.'

'Are there any sites like this in your time?' Rootuk asked.

'There's only one site on Earth with the scope to accomplish this...the La Danta pyramid in El Mirador, Guatemala.'

Sean watched the scene with a growing sense of incredulity. It *was* the past, well after his dad left the caves on the South African coast. Yeesha joined Henry as Nesuk and Rootuk left. Sean was filled with joy upon seeing her again. The intense burst of emotion changed something – now he could feel the searing heat of the fire! Was he being pulled into their reality?

'DAD!' he cried.

Henry and Yeesha focused on him, eyes wide in disbelief.

FLASH!

Sean awoke with a jolt, hitting his head against the interior of the sleeping pod. 'Ouch!'

The holographic door dematerialised. Sean rubbed his head and glanced around. He was back on their vessel heading for Akanae. The steady hum of the light-speed engines filled his ears. He climbed out of the pod. His mind was racing. What just happened?

How did Yeesha and his dad see him? Did he just astral project his consciousness through a black hole and back in time?

Nocao appeared in the doorway. 'Trouble sleeping?'

'You could say that,' Sean sighed. He felt exhausted, like he hadn't slept at all. 'How long was I asleep?'

'Eight hours. Why?'

'Something weird just happened to me.'

Nocao narrowed his eyes. 'You look unwell considering your amount of rest. We should run some scans.'

*   *   *

Thirty minutes later, Sean found himself sitting on a cold metallic bench in the science lab. He'd been poked, prodded, and scanned multiple times. Nocao, with the help of three scientists, had run every test possible on him. The latest scans of his neural activity appeared in a row of holograms. Sean felt guilty being the centre of attention, considering his friend was deteriorating from the affliction faster than any Isharkute on board. Nocao's shakes were worse than ever, but he pushed on, ignoring his failing limbs. He should be the one receiving their undivided attention.

'Why don't you just make a cure for yourself now? You have the male and female DNA with me and Bella.'

'Emperor Neberun gave explicit instructions not to develop the cure until your DNA has been purified on Akanae.'

'But you need it.'

'I can wait. The slightest impurity in your DNA may not be evident straight away and could affect future generations of Isharkute with disastrous side effects. But we are here to focus on you. Please remain quiet while I finish the scans.'

Sean couldn't figure out why he felt so tired. It was like he'd run a marathon – not that he'd ever run one. But he imagined this is how it felt. He regretted telling them about his out-of-body experience. The more he thought about it, the more absurd it seemed, making this a big waste of everyone's time.

It was too late now. He felt his face going red at the thought of being told he was perfectly fine, and it was all a dream.

Nocao enlarged a hologram of Sean's neural activity and tilted his head with interest.

Sean hopped off the bench and peered over Nocao's shoulder. A huge portion of his brain was lit up like a thunderstorm. Neurons fired through his synapses like lightening.

'Did you find something?' Sean asked.

'Yes. An explanation for your physical exhaustion. Your brain's frontal lobes are more active than we've ever seen in a human being.'

'What does that mean?'

'The human brain is inefficient. It normally uses 20 per cent of your body's energy, taking valuable nutrients and oxygen to support itself. We see your brain was working at a higher capacity, more like 70 per cent, while you were sleeping.'

'It was a dream after all!'

Nocao shook his head. 'A dream wouldn't use that much energy.'

'What happened to me then? Do you think I really travelled somewhere?'

'I believe your consciousness did.'

'How?'

'If you remember, I took scans of your body when we were in the Svalbard Seed Vault. That was before you turned on the Yonaguni beacon. Comparing the scans between now and then, I can see your brain function has increased exponentially.'

'Why? What's causing it?'

'Your interaction with the beacon.'

Sean suddenly realised the truth. 'You're right! I should've known all along. When I touched the control panel, it took me out of my body. I saw myself standing there. Then I shot up into space and joined the Isharkute fleet. I thought it was a telepathic link. Maybe my consciousness travelled across the universe.'

'It's possible that experience triggered something in your brain, sped up an evolutionary step...awakened a power that's always been there.'

Sean trembled with astonishment. But at least he had an answer. 'Maybe my human brain isn't so inefficient after all.'

Nocao raised a dubious eyebrow and continued studying the scans.

Making light of his out-of-body experience didn't ease Sean's discomfort. The image of his dad and Yeesha was burnt into his mind like a photograph, as if he stood right in front of them. What drew him to that moment in time? Was he able to control where and when he went?

Sean was determined to find out.

— CHAPTER 6 —

Attack On Nu-Serak

Senetep stared at the bridge viewscreen, blind to the galaxies zooming by. His mind was consumed by the impossible reality – human DNA now coursed through his veins, polluting his body. He had become what he vowed to eliminate, a traitor to the purity of his species. The two incompetent scientists that infected him were dead. They saved his life, but condemned him to a life of shame. He no longer represented that for which he fought, a pure Isharkute lineage. Did the *Spearhead of Creation* hold the technology to purify himself from the primate filth? It was his only option. Nothing would stand in his way, even if it meant destroying the universe to find out.

'We're approaching Akanae now,' Erund called over the bridge.

Senetep broke his stare at the viewscreen and focused on his candidate for First Commander. Erund had ably stepped into his leadership role. He seemed suited to command, even though he was young for such a position of power.

But something about Erund didn't sit right with Senetep. He couldn't touch on the exact problem. It was more of a hunch than anything. As if he had forgotten something crucial about Erund.

A sharp pain shot up his forearm. He glanced down and found his hand clenched on the command chair. He relaxed his fingers, leaving dents in the panel. For some reason, he was anxious. It had to be the human DNA. He took a settling breath and stood.

'Overseer Senetep, we've scanned the Empire's twelve orbiting space docks,' Erund said. 'Only one is manned, with minimal personnel. We're expecting little resistance due to our unexpected arrival.'

'What about vessels?'

'Docking station Nu-Serak has a deep-space scout vessel called the *Ragarn*. This was the first vessel Emperor Neberun sent to the station after the fleet awakened from cryogenic sleep. It's well-armed, light-speed capable, and equipped to track the *Spearhead*. It's the perfect replacement for our annihilator.'

'Excellent. Time to show me what you can do.'

Erund gave an eager nod. 'Weapons stations prepare to fire. Hold until I give the command.'

Senetep stood back, giving his protégé the bridge.

Their vessel dropped out of light speed. Akanae filled the viewscreen, glowing like an orb of amethyst. The orange moon of Nek-Karani nestled on the night side of the planet. The sphere-shaped docking station Nu-Serak emerged from the shadows.

Erund paced the bridge. 'Take us close to the *Ragarn*. I want cannons at thirty per cent power. Target the docking clamps.'

Senetep realised where this was going. Erund wasn't going to steal the vessel by storming Nu-Serak, he was going to blast the *Ragarn* free from the station and steal it from space.

'This is a risky manoeuvre, Erund.'

'I understand, but the stations have been in limited operation for the last 10,000 years. The Capital Guardians were in cryogenic sleep, awakening every 500 years to check on Akanae's cities. Neberun sent minimal forces to assist them, not expecting an attack. Our arrival will catch them off-guard, ill-prepared to defend themselves. I'd like permission to take whatever course of action I deem necessary.'

Senetep eased back into his command chair. 'Fine, but you'll have one opportunity before the station retaliates, increasing the chances of damaging our new vessel.'

'Indeed. However, stealing the *Ragarn* mid-flight avoids a hands-on firefight inside the station – a distraction we don't have time for.'

'Hah! If your brazen mission looks like it's failing, I'll kill you where you stand and take over myself.'

Erund nodded with a defiant, almost arrogant confidence.

Senetep liked that. Finally, someone prepared to back their words with actions.

An incoming transmission appeared on the viewscreen, presenting an elderly Isharkute Commander. His long white beard hung heavy with beads of rank and service. 'This is Elite Commander Saras Varn, Capital Guardian of the Isharkute Empire. We were not advised of your arrival. State your purpose before we respond with force.'

'Commander Varn, surrender the *Ragarn* to Overseer Senetep or face the consequences.'

Varn glanced over Erund's shoulder. His eyes widened. 'Senetep! Traitor to the Empire. Prepare to–'

'Expired old fool!' Erund said, terminating the transmission. He shoved a crew member aside and took manual control of the annihilator's cannons. 'Accelerate to attack speed!'

Their annihilator swooped in over the *Ragarn*. Erund timed his six shots perfectly, obliterating the docking station clamps on the first pass. The vessel floated free from the station.

Senetep leant forward in his chair. This was becoming interesting.

'Now take out the station's surface cannons,' Erund said, handing the console back to the crew member. 'Pilots, take us in between the *Ragarn* and the station. Engage docking clamps and umbilicals. All non-essential crew, prepare to change vessels.'

They circled around and came to a stop, blocking the *Ragarn* from the docking station. The pilots and gunners remained at their posts while the rest of the crew left the bridge.

'Don't expect it to be that easy,' Senetep said.

'The *Ragarn* awaits your command,' Erund said, acknowledging the five stinger pilots entering the bridge. 'I'm taking a small squadron to deal with the inevitable retaliation. I'll join you when we're done.'

Senetep hesitated. He was about to place the future of his *Spearhead* mission in Erund's inexperienced hands. Nefaro and Vogran's failures had eroded his trust in First Commanders. But

Erund's youthful fervour and determination reminded him of Ranatar, the best Commander he ever employed. Maybe this up-and-coming Isharkute possessed the balance of brains and brawn he had been searching for since then.

'I'll give you until the crew is assembled on the *Ragarn*. If your performance pleases me, then I'll wait for you to return.'

'I won't disappoint you,' Erund said dutifully.

'Empty promises don't impress me. Your actions will determine your fate.'

Erund nodded and motioned to the door. 'Please evacuate the annihilator, I have some final orders for the bridge crew before I leave.'

Senetep waved over his elite guards and marched off the bridge. They assembled in the docking bay with the rest of the crew. Outside, the *Ragarn* was tethered to their vessel with clamps and evacuation umbilicals.

The first umbilical doors opened, revealing the sparse and underpowered crew of the *Ragarn*. Confronted by Senetep's elite guards, the crew threw aside their weapons and dropped to their knees.

Senetep marched by without a sideways glance. 'Kill them!'

Lethal energy blasts rang through the docking bay, following him into the umbilical. The sound of death gave him pleasure. There was no time for mercy or second chances now. It was a relief to bear no emotion; a human weakness he needed to be wary of now their DNA was a part of him. To act callously and without remorse helped to sever his uncomfortable ties to humanity.

Senetep entered the bridge of the *Ragarn*. It was modest compared to his annihilator, but just as functional. Erund had made the right choice. The vessel was powerful and well-armed, but small enough to remain highly manoeuvrable. He could travel into the depths of the universe on a tenth of the energy. Muted explosions resonated through the hull. What was Erund up to out there?

'Bring up the viewscreen.'

His crew promptly assumed their new posts and the screen

flickered to life. Unbridled destruction littered Akanae's orbit. Nu-Serak Station was half-destroyed. Erund and his stinger squadron wrought havoc on the station, blasting it into the upper atmosphere where it would be torn apart. At the same time, the *annihilator* fired missiles towards the eleven remaining stations.

Senetep watched the viewscreen with a pleased grin.

A distant burst of light turned into a glowing ball of fire. Another explosion followed it, then another, until every station was destroyed.

Erund had taken their mission one step further. He was leaving nothing behind.

Nu-Serak Station suddenly exploded. The shock wave buffeted their vessel. Half the structure burned up in the atmosphere and the rest showered into orbit. The annihilator barrelled through the fiery debris, straight into Akanae's atmosphere. It disappeared into the shadow of the planet, firing all thrusters straight down. Soon after, a blinding explosion erupted on Akanae's surface.

Senetep nodded to himself, excited to see the outcome. 'Show me the impact zone.'

A hologram of Akanae's surface appeared in the middle of the bridge.

Senetep strode around the projection, admiring the destruction. Akanae's capital lay in ruins. Erund had struck at the centre of the Isharkute Empire, silencing the barely beating heart of their civilisation. Thousands of Isharkute in hibernation had been instantaneously vaporised. The final six life-bearers, Emperor Neberun's last hope for a cure, were now ashes on the wind.

'Overseer Senetep, are we waiting for Erund to return?' asked the pilot.

Senetep stared at the carnage, content he had found his new First Commander. He nodded to the pilot.

Erund's squadron returned and docked with the *Ragarn*. A short time later, Erund strode onto the bridge, smugly confident of his upcoming promotion. Senetep wasn't going to make it that easy. The entire bridge crew watched Erund approach.

Senetep observed his protégé without a word.

Droplets of sweat formed across Erund's forehead. He shifted nervously.

Senetep backhanded the youth without warning. The force sent him sprawled across the floor. Erund remained hunched over and rubbed his jaw.

'Well done,' Senetep said with a grin.

Erund picked himself up, his brow furrowed with confusion.

'I expect my First Commanders to think and act for themselves... but there are limits. You acted outside the boundaries of your position today, but only because I gave you permission. Understand that. Remember your place and you will serve me well.'

Erund straightened his shoulders with pride and nodded.

Senetep waved over his lead elite guard and held out his hand. The warrior unsheathed a blade from his belt, then sliced through the lower third of his beard. Several gold beads dropped into his palm and he passed them to Senetep.

'Erund Griss, initiate to the Guild of Arms, I promote you to the rank of First Commander. Take these beads as a sign of obedience, commitment and servitude.'

Senetep dropped the beads into Erund's hand.

'I accept with the utmost respect and humility. I devote my life to serve you.'

Senetep nodded and strode into the centre of the bridge. 'Show me the map of the *Spearhead*.'

A hologram of the universe materialised before them. The path of the Ancient alien vessel wound through the stars in a spiral pattern. The line passed right beside Akanae and their current position. Senetep mused over the fact that millions of years ago, the *Spearhead* had passed by his homeworld, sowing the seeds of life that would eventually become his species.

Erund stood beside him. 'If the *Spearhead* starts its journey on the outside of the universe and travels back to the centre, then Earth was visited millions of years before Akanae. Why were the humans less advanced than us? They should have been populating other planets in their solar system long before we journeyed to their planet.'

Senetep glanced at his First Commander. 'Because without our DNA, they would never have evolved beyond primates.'

Erund nodded but didn't respond.

Senetep sensed his First Commander was smarter than he let on. It was true, Earth had been populated by life long before Akanae, but Earth had endured far more instability. Millions of years before the first primates, a species of giant lizards had dominated the planet. The humans called them dinosaurs. Such a species had never evolved on Akanae. The dinosaurs were brought to extinction from an asteroid strike, a catastrophe Akanae had luckily avoided. However, on Earth there were still hundreds of millions of unaccounted years before the dinosaurs, plenty of time for another humanoid species to flourish and advance. But that was so far in the past, any evidence of such a culture was long extinguished.

To consider the *Spearhead* an actual ship travelling through the universe was a new concept for his crew. It created questions about life in the universe the Isharkute had never asked before. But Senetep didn't want his subordinates thinking too much. It distracted them from their mission. Knowledge was power, and the less they understood, the better.

'Begin plotting the fastest course to catch the *Spearhead*,' Senetep said.

Erund worked with the navigators, calculating and recalculating their course. Senetep watched from his command chair as their projected course appeared on the hologram, then disappeared and readjusted along an alternative route. This happened multiple times. Senetep tired of their ineptitude.

'Is there a problem?'

'The most direct course is riddled with deadly nebulae and super black holes, preventing us from travelling at light speed.'

'Then calculate our journey in stages. Find the first light-speed jump and we can recalibrate once we've reached that position.'

Erund and the navigators input the revised information and

quickly came up with a new course. A fresh line appeared through the hologram, starting from their location and meeting up with the *Spearhead's* ancient trajectory.

'It took the *Spearhead* millions of years to loop around the universe to that location, but we can be there in a matter of hours.'

Senetep observed Akanae one last time. Their home planet seemed inconsequential now. There was no future here. It awaited them in an unexplored galaxy near the centre of the universe, not this desolate planet. He motioned for Erund to give the command for light speed, and in that instant, they were gone.

— CHAPTER 7 —

Akanae

Their vessel dropped out of light speed and into normal space. Sean stared at the purple-blue planet dominating the bridge viewscreen: Akanae, the Isharkute homeworld. Colossal continents and lush vegetation covered two-thirds of the planet, painting a boundless landscape of sumptuous flora. The verdant jungles and forests seemed ancient, untouched. Sean was sure he could see the outlines of gargantuan trees, tens of thousands of years old. Vibrant turquoise oceans separated the continents. Flecks of white clouds circled the planet, touching the snowy peaks. Akanae was just like Earth: unique, fragile, and precious.

'Your planet is beautiful,' Bella said. 'It's like Earth's twin.'

'Earth's big twin,' Nocao confirmed, just as enthralled. 'Twice the size.'

Sean realised this was the first time Nocao had ever seen his home planet up close. After his birth on Akanae, he would have moved to Earth, where he grew up with his adopted father Horumbut, studying the early human tribes on his path to joining the Isharkute Guild of Sciences. The same could be said for every Isharkute on board, even Ramin. Although they were born on Akanae, Earth was the only home they knew.

A blanket of destruction unfurled upon the beautiful backdrop. Remnants of shattered vessels floated by, littered with twisted metal and lifeless Isharkute corpses.

Sean looked around at the crew. 'What happened?'

'We're not receiving transmissions from any of the twelve space docks,' the communications officer announced.

'That's because they're destroyed,' Nocao said.

'Senetep!' Ramin boomed, rising from his command chair.

'*Mio Dio!* Look,' Bella said, pointing to the night side of the planet.

The glow from continent-wide fires illuminated the darkness. Gigantic plumes of smoke reached from the hellish landscape like evil tendrils, ensnaring the advancing daylight.

'Scan for vessels,' Ramin ordered.

A hologram of Akanae materialised in the middle of the bridge, showing the true scope of destruction. The obliterated space docks created a ring of debris around the planet. The scan radiated outwards from the planet, showing no vessels in the system.

'He's already left,' Sean said.

'Scan Akanae's capital,' Ramin said.

The hologram zoomed into the raging fires. There was no city, just an apocalyptic crater. Smouldering rubble lay strewn outwards in a catastrophic circle. Charred trees stood like splinters, stripped bare of foliage. Smoke rose from the scorched black soil. Roads, pathways, and stairs led to shattered buildings wiped from their foundations. The capital of the Isharkute Empire was no more.

Nocao pointed to the burning shell of a vessel deep inside the crater. 'That's the remains of Senetep's annihilator.'

'Maybe he crashed,' Bella said in a hopeful tone.

'I doubt it,' Sean said. 'This is deliberate. Senetep knew we were coming here to work on a cure. He would have done anything to stop us.'

'He may have succeeded,' Ramin said gravely. 'Our six most promising life-bearers were in the capital's hibernation chambers. We have to go down there. Search for survivors.'

Sean didn't see the point. It was clear from the scans that no-one could have survived the explosion, even if the hibernation chambers were located deep underground.

They passed through Akanae's upper atmosphere and flew into turbulent clouds choked with ash and glowing embers. Bella grabbed Sean's arm and flashed him a terrified glance.

The chaos finally cleared, revealing an extensive impact crater at least ten kilometres wide and several kilometres deep. The skeletal fuselage of Senetep's annihilator hull lay deep in the hole, still burning white-hot at the core.

'It's horrible,' Bella said. 'I don't understand. Why would Senetep want to destroy his own planet? Doesn't he want to save the Isharkute?'

'He doesn't want to save anything,' Nocao said. 'He's only concerned about himself. Immortalising his legacy.'

'He's insane!' Sean remarked.

'He's an imbecile!' Ramin said. 'Emperor Neberun should have made an example of him 10,000 years ago. His inaction has led to this – the genocide of our species.'

The pilots set their vessel down on the rim of the crater. The sensors scanned the debris field and projected the results across the hologram. All traces of life had been vaporized. Sean had never seen such complete devastation. It was impossible to picture the once-grand capital from the burnt landscape.

'I wish we'd got here sooner,' Bella said.

An alarm sounded through the bridge.

'What is it?' Sean asked.

'Proximity sensors,' Nocao said. 'There's a vessel approaching.'

The bridge viewscreen filled with Isharkute symbols.

'Is it Senetep?' Sean said, frustrated at not being able to read the message.

'There's an incoming transmission request. It's a capital-designated vessel.'

'Accept the request,' Ramin said.

The viewscreen switched channels to display an Isharkute Commander and his crew. Beads of service decorated their long white plaited beards, and they all shared the same tattoo in the middle of their foreheads. The Commander wore a pair of gold chains from his nostrils to his earlobes, both encrusted with purple gems. The same gemstones decorated his gold armour, a rank and designation Sean had never seen before.

'This is Ormar Trell, Elite Commander to the Capital Guardians. We've been expecting you.'

'What happened here?' Ramin asked.

'We're sending you coordinates to a new location. I'll explain everything when you arrive.'

The transmission ended and the vessel departed.

They lifted off the crater and flew into the smoke, ascending until they burst through the ashen clouds into a clear blue sky. With the incinerated landscape far behind them, they were now flying over a planet brimming with life. The dense jungles reminded Sean of the Amazon, but there were hints of an alien world. Dashes of blue and red flashed through the dominant purple canopy, hinting at the biodiversity hiding from view. Sean glimpsed several Isharkute structures concealed beneath the foliage, poking through the treetops like the Aztec and Mayan pyramids on Earth.

The low-lying jungles transformed into a mountainous region. Craggy windswept peaks dropped into deep shadowy gorges. Their vessel swerved around the cliff faces, keeping pace with the Capital Guardians vessel. Ancient trees and gigantic vines sprouted from every available crevice. They emerged from the shadow of a snow-covered peak to find an austere citadel of white stone and silver alloy nestled into the side of a mountain.

'Where are we?' Sean asked.

'I know nothing about this place,' Ramin said. 'None of us have visited Akanae since we were born.'

They landed beside the Guardians' vessel on one of the citadel's platforms. It jutted out over a sheer cliff that dropped into a passing cloud.

Ramin led everyone outside to greet Ormar Trell. The Commander was one of the tallest Isharkute Sean had ever seen, at least twelve inches higher than Ramin. Ormar was not as solid and muscular as Senetep. His lean and gangly body reminded Sean of an NBA basketballer.

'Ormar Trell, we appreciate you finding us. When we arrived at the Empire's capital, we feared the worst.'

'There is much to fear Ramin, but the destruction of our capital is the least of our worries. Fortunately, my squad and I were on the planet when Senetep attacked. If we had been on Nu-Serak or one of the other stations, we would have been killed. Elite Commander Saras Varn was killed in the attack, forcing me to take command. We're all that's left of Akanae's Guardians. We've been awaiting your arrival since Emperor Neberun informed us of the events on Earth.' Ormar glanced at Sean and Bella with a curious eye. 'So, these are the human beings selected to save our species from the affliction.'

'Yes, this is Sean Livingstone and Bella Bonaforte.'

Ormar moved closer and peered down his nose at them. 'Tiny, aren't they? I expected humans to be bigger.'

'They are considered children among their species.'

'*Scusi!*' Bella scoffed. 'We're not children. We're teenagers.'

Ormar regarded her with bemusement. 'Maybe. But you have the unbridled tongue of a child.'

Sean sensed a sudden hostility from the Commander and offered his hand. Ormar scrutinised his gesture with a frown of uncertainty.

'It's a human custom to shake hands when you formally greet someone,' Ramin said.

Ormar offered his hand. His blue hand was cool and powerful. 'Sean, we have heard all about your exploits on Earth. It's satisfying to know Senetep was bested twice by a human teenager. His humiliation within the Empire must be unparalleled. No wonder he unleashed his fury on Akanae.'

Sean nodded. He wasn't sure if Ormar was giving him a compliment or blaming him for the destruction of the capital.

Ormar moved his attention to Nocao. 'You are Nocao, son of Horumbut. I congratulate you on being the youngest initiate in the Guild of Sciences. Your father's work on alien species, particularly the human being, was held in the highest regard by our esteemed life-bearer, Hemket Naw. She awaits all of you now.'

Ormar gestured towards the entrance to the citadel.

'Who's Hemket Naw?' Bella whispered to Sean.

Sean shrugged his shoulders. They were about to meet a female Isharkute, something he never imagined possible. He understood when male Isharkute reached 400 years or more in age they entered hibernation and emerged as females, or 'life-bearers', as the males called them, and could only give birth once. These life-bearers would survive for centuries, living and serving on Akanae as custodians to later generations of life-bearers.

The interior of the structure was tall and cavernous. Vaulted ceilings reached high above like a cathedral, carved deep into the mountain. It was more like an ancient Egyptian temple than a modern, futuristic structure. Sweeping, clear-crystal panels gave them impressive vistas of Akanae's mountainous region.

Ormar and his squad led them deep inside the citadel. Their footfalls echoed along the empty stone halls and stairs.

'These halls feel like they've been empty for centuries,' Sean said.

'They have!' Ormar remarked.

'Ten thousand years was an extraordinarily long time to wait for Neberun's fleet,' Nocao said. 'How did the Capital Guardians survive and protect Akanae for so long?'

'Through long periods of cryogenic sleep. We awoke every 500 years to check on the female population and perform maintenance on the capital. The females slept in thousand-year cycles. They only awakened to check on the males stuck in mid-transformation.'

'You must have almost given up hope,' Bella said.

'It's our sworn duty to protect the future of the Isharkute Empire,' Ormar replied sternly. 'If that means waiting an eternity, then we will.'

The passages burrowed into the mountain bedrock like miner's shafts. After navigating a maze of darkness, they finally emerged from a long passage into dazzling sunshine.

Sean shielded his eyes and squinted about. They were in a secluded garden tucked deep into a mountain crevice. Sheer, 100-metre cliffs loomed overhead, straight up to an open blue sky. Dense ivy with uniquely patterned leaves draped off the stone. In the centre of the garden was a circular pond surrounded by ornamental trees bulging with pink, pear-shaped fruit.

Hemket Naw stood hunched over the water, her back to them. At first, Sean thought she was one of the trees. Hemket was at least twelve feet tall and towered over Ormar with her spindly, elongated body. She raised her head to the sound of their footsteps and turned. Her face was long and feminine, with high cheekbones and pale-blue skin. Her jawline was delicately pointed, unlike the harder, square jaws of Isharkute males. She had thin, dark-blue lips and piercing green eyes.

Bella's grip on Sean's hand tightened.

Sean felt the hairs on the back of his neck stand on end. Hemket had a laser-sharp stare that cut straight through them. Her eyes exuded an unnerving intelligence and perception that was far more intimidating than Emperor Neberun's wise-old gaze.

Ormar peered up. 'Hemket Naw, I bring you Ramin, Royal Consult to Emperor Neberun, Nocao of the Guild of Sciences, and humans Sean Livingstone and Bella Bonaforte.'

Hemket nodded. She spoke in a sharp, husky tone. 'Thank you, Ormar. Leave us.'

Ormar and his squad retreated from the garden.

Hemket took a step towards them. Her wispy-thin purple robe shimmered like silk over her bony figure. 'Nocao, you're in the later stages of the affliction. I've never seen it attack a young Isharkute so aggressively.' Hunched over, she grasped Nocao's hand and pulled it towards her, peeling back his sleeve with one long finger.

Sean was shocked. He hadn't seen the extent of Nocao's affliction since they were in the Svalbard Seed Vault. His forearm was covered in black and purple blotches, with more emerging over his bicep.

'Our species has precious time left,' Hemket said. 'Nocao, you will be the first to trial the cure. All of you, follow me.'

Hemket strode through the garden to the far wall. Each one of her long strides was worth several for everyone else. They all hustled to keep up. Hemket entered another hallway that hollowed deep into the mountain. Now Sean understood why the vaulted halls were so tall; Hemket's head was metres from touching the ceiling.

'I never expected Isharkute females to be so tall,' Sean said.

'You haven't seen one about to enter hibernation,' Ramin said in a hushed voice. 'They can stand as wide as they stand tall.'

'How big are their babies?' Bella asked.

'Similar in size to a human child,' Nocao said.

Bella grimaced. 'Ouch! I don't even want to imagine how painful that could be.'

'That's why our hibernation process is so important. The cellular changes from male to female take a huge toll on our bodies. They must reach a certain body mass to achieve the transformation. Our affliction has stunted the last stages of our cellular transformation.'

Hemket led them down a long hallway to a polished metallic wall. She placed her hand on the centre of the wall. A blue glow outlined her gangly hand and pulsed several times, then the entire wall ascended into the ceiling, presenting them with a vast set of stairs descending into the bedrock. Hemket moved on, gliding over the steps with her lanky stride.

Everybody picked up their pace to keep up with her. The stairs circled around twice and opened into a passage illuminated by six hibernation tanks filled with a semi-translucent blue liquid. Each tank held an Isharkute stuck in mid-transformation from male to female. Their skeletal bodies floated in the fluid, curled up like babies in a womb. The largest of the six, the closest to full female form, also appeared the oldest. Her life-saving fluid was cloudy, and a thin film of algae lined the glass. The unfortunate Isharkute appeared to have been in the hibernation chamber for centuries.

Hemket turned and loomed over them, her face obscured by the shadows cast across the ceiling. Her green eyes glistened intently through the gloom.

'Decades ago, I had Ormar move our healthiest six life-bearers here, away from the capital city.'

'A wise decision,' Ramin said.

'They have not changed in centuries. Their life signs are barely traceable, each of them frozen in a nightmare from which they might never awake.'

Hemket drew her attention to Ramin. She grasped his upper

cranium with her long spider-like fingers and closed her eyes as if meditating. Ramin gave everyone a concerned sideways glance as if to say *Help!*

Hemket removed her hand. 'Ramin, how old are you?'

'Almost 410 years.'

She nodded thoughtfully. 'I sense it. You're close to transformation, in good health and with minimal signs of the affliction. If this human cure is successful, you might be the first male Isharkute to complete a successful hibernation cycle in millennia.'

Ramin acknowledged Hemket with a disgruntled *humph*, not thrilled by the news.

Sean chuckled to himself. The thought of Ramin having a baby seemed absurd.

Hemket turned her attention to Sean and Bella.

Sean felt nervous butterflies rise from his stomach. His heart quickened. He was still holding hands with Bella, but couldn't tell whose palms were sweatier.

'Before we extract the cure, Sean and Bella must undergo the cleansing ceremony, just like any Isharkute before entering hibernation.'

Sean glanced at Bella. This was the first they were hearing about a cleansing ceremony. 'What's the cleansing ceremony?'

'It's a sacred rite of passage designed to purge dangerous toxins from your body and prepare you for hibernation.'

'But we're not entering hibernation. I don't see–'

'Your DNA will cure the Isharkute and repair our hibernation cycle. You must undergo the same purging and rid your body of all toxins.'

'Excuse me, Hemket,' Ramin interjected. 'Can't we replicate the process here in your labs where it's safer?'

'The leeches of the Helior River only work in their native environment.'

'Leeches?!' Bella shrieked.

'Yes. They secrete a peptide into your blood to stop it from clotting. It has the added advantage of cleansing your cerebrospinal fluid from dangerous contaminants, a necessary step for a successful transformation. This natural process can't be replicated in a lab. Isharkute males have taken part in this ceremony for millennia.'

'I appreciate that,' Ramin said, 'but I don't see how we have the time to send Sean and Bella off on a cleansing ceremony, placing their lives in danger.'

Hemket rounded on Ramin, pointing her bony finger like a dagger.

'Ramin! I doubt you truly appreciate the situation at all. Such is the reason our species suffer this affliction. We have waited over 10,000 years for your return, extending our lives in stasis. By a fortuitous stroke of luck, your male ancestors created the human being, a species capable of rectifying your tainted DNA. For too long, Isharkute males have carelessly experimented with life forms, taking them from their natural environments, manipulating them in their hybrid programs. You explored space and enhanced your bodies with any species that gave you a biological advantage. In the effort to extend your lives, you have only shortened them and doomed all of us. We must return to simpler, more natural ways of living with nature. The cleansing ceremony is the first step in this direction – even for these humans.'

Sean gulped down the lump of fear growing in his throat. There was no way to avoid the cleansing ceremony.

— CHAPTER 8 —

The Cleansing

A short time later, Sean and Bella were flying away from the citadel and across the mountains aboard Ormar Trell's vessel. Ramin and Nocao stayed behind to work alongside Hemket's scientists and prepare for their return. Sean and Bella enquired about the cleansing ceremony on the way to their hidden location.

Ormar Trell was well acquainted with the Isharkute rite of passage, even though he was yet to experience it himself.

'We're travelling to the sacred Helior River. Once there, you will wade upstream through the leech-infested waters to a waterfall. You must pass through the waterfall into a hidden cave. Inside, you will find a specially prepared elixir. The leeches and elixir purge your body and mind of accumulated toxins. All male Isharkute partake in this ceremony before changing into life-bearers. Once you've completed this process, we can extract your purified DNA and synthesise a cure for our affliction.'

'Purging our bodies might not be so bad,' Bella said in a hopeful voice.

Sean struggled to see an upside. 'You think so?'

'Si! Sounds like the ultimate detox diet.'

'This is no diet,' Ormar warned. 'The elixir makes you violently ill. Some Isharkute have stayed in the cave for days on end, wracked with pain.'

Bella sighed. 'Well, maybe not.'

'We can do the river. Put up with the leeches. But do we really have to drink the elixir?' Sean asked. 'We're not Isharkute. No human's ever drunk it before. What if it kills us?'

Bella gave a wholehearted nod. 'And I'm already female. I don't need to transform like a male. Why do I have to do it?'

Ormar assessed them with his penetrating light-blue eyes. They displayed a sense of compassion rare among Isharkute. 'The rite of passage is symbolic of spiritual change, rather than physical. The river journey represents your passage through life. Passing through the waterfall signifies crossing from one stage of your life to the next. For Isharkute, this represents a metamorphosis. Drinking the elixir symbolises the body's final supplication to this process, to emerge as a new individual, purged of your former burdens.'

Bella didn't seem convinced. 'Mmm. I still don't like the thought of being wracked in pain.'

'What's in the elixir?' Sean asked.

'It's a hallucinogen, designed to help you confront any lingering pain, grief, and guilt. You must deal with this before you can re-emerge into the world anew.'

'But I don't have any past issues,' Bella said. 'This won't help me.'

Ormar gave her an unsettling grin.

Sean was not as confident as Bella. His emotions raged like a turbulent storm on the horizon. He was still coming to terms with much of his past, including the death of his parents. He knew that one day, when all this was over, that storm would catch up with him.

Their vessel descended beneath the leafy canopy of 1,000-year-old trees. Filtered beams of sunlight created a magical environment filled with vibrant colours and exotic flora. The forest understory reminded Sean of the giant redwood forests on Earth. Humongous tree trunks stood wrapped in gigantic vines. Stark yellow spores protruded from the ancient bark like winding steps. Sprawling ferns, massive flowers, and a unique display of unearthly plants filled the spaces between. Pockets of sunlight highlighted the scarlet flora with tinges of pink and purple.

'Wow! This is incredible,' Bella said in astonishment, peering through the clear hull. 'It's like something from a dream.'

'Don't let the beauty of the forest fool you,' Ormar warned. 'Some of these plants are lethal to the touch.'

'Good thing we're in the river, then,' Sean said.

'The river is safer, but you need to move fast. The leeches can grow to the size of your forearm. Once filled with blood, they will quickly weigh you down. Keep your head above the water at all times. If you attract too many, they will climb up your neck for exposed skin and suffocate you.'

Bella covered her mouth. 'Yuck!'

'How do we get them off?' Sean asked.

'You can't. If you pull them off you will rip the veins from your body, attracting thousands more leeches. The only way to remove them is by drinking the elixir. They will fall off by themselves and return to the river.'

Bella's face went green. 'That's disgusting.'

Their vessel landed on a clearing covered in smooth river pebbles. Ormar directed them down the gangway to the river's edge. The forest air was humid and filled with insects, some as big as golf balls. They hummed and buzzed about, bouncing off the vessel's hull with a heavy pitter-patter. Majestic bird calls echoed through the towering tree line. Unseen creatures scratched, scurried, and slithered their way around the undergrowth. Every inch of the forest teemed with life.

Bella ducked, swiping at an oversized mosquito. 'Urgh! I hope they don't sting.'

Ormar stood by the edge of the river. 'Enter the water here and continue upstream until you reach the waterfall.'

Sean and Bella slipped off their shoes and stepped into the cool water. Small effervescent bubbles covered their submerged skin like sparkling water. Sean led the way, navigating the slippery pebbles until his feet found the soft riverbed mud.

'You must discard your clothes – become one with nature as you journey up the river.'

Sean and Bella stared at each other in shock and replied in unison, 'We're not taking off our clothes!'

Ormar's mouth twinged as if he was holding back a laugh.

Is he joking? Sean wondered. That wasn't usual for an Isharkute.

'Fine! Suit yourselves. I will see you both when you emerge from the waterfall.' Omar retreated up the gangway and the vessel departed.

Sean peered into the dark plum-coloured water, searching for leeches. He couldn't see anything deeper than his thighs. 'We should start moving.'

'Uh-huh!' Bella said, wading close behind him.

They pushed into the centre of the river. At the deepest point, the water remained waist high and gentle enough to walk against. Sean kept clear of the violet ferns draping over the water just in case they were lethal. They held their arms above the surface, hoping to stay leech-free as long as possible.

'Have you seen any leeches yet?' Bella asked.

'Nope.'

'That's weird. I expected the river to be full of them.'

'I think we'll feel them before we see them.'

'Urgh! What was that?' Bella squealed. 'I stood on something big and slimy.'

'Shh!'

'I wish I had wings like you. You could just fly out of here if you wanted to.'

'I can't. They're still growing back. Plus, I wouldn't leave you.'

'Sure you wouldn't.'

'I'm serious.'

'Even if we were covered in gigantic leeches?'

'Especially then.'

Bella half-laughed. 'We'll see.'

Sean glanced over his shoulder. Bella's expression was hard to read. He couldn't tell if she was being genuine or messing with him. After everything they had been through together, it wasn't as though he needed to prove himself. 'What's that supposed to mean?'

'It's just – I'm not used to having a boyfriend who keeps to his word.'

Sean's heart skipped a beat. Did she just say 'boyfriend'? He felt his face going red.

Bella waded faster and caught up. 'Sean Livingstone, are you embarrassed?'

'Huh? No. What are you talking about?'

'You weren't sure if we were boyfriend and girlfriend?'

'I'm not... I mean, I wasn't thinking about it.'

Bella gave him a cheeky smirk. 'You weren't?'

Sean became tongue-tied. Were they boyfriend and girlfriend? He wasn't sure. This conversation was awkward. He wasn't experienced with relationships and needed to divert Bella's attention away from his embarrassment. 'How many boyfriends have you had?'

'Why? Are you jealous?'

'No. I was just wondering. You don't have to tell–'

'Three. But the first two weren't great boyfriends,' she explained, as if waiting for the invitation all along. 'My first was Alessandro in primary school. I was ten, he was eleven. I didn't even like him that much. He asked me to be his girlfriend, and I just said yes because I didn't want to upset him. It lasted two days. My first real boyfriend was Dieter. I met him when I moved to Paris to study art. He was in the same dormitory building as me, studying music. He was fifteen, I was fourteen. We were the youngest students in the school, so it was only a matter of time before we ended up together. Dieter was the first boy I ever kissed. He moved back to Germany when his mum got sick. He said he'd keep in touch, but that didn't last long.'

'What about your third boyfriend? What was he like?'

Bella took a moment to answer. 'Smart. Brave. But a little awkward around people.'

'What happened to him? What did he do wrong?'

'Nothing yet.'

Sean was about to ask who *he* was before realising – it was him! A surge of relief and excitement flooded his chest. He tried to hold back his smile. Impossible. Bella glimpsed his reaction and smiled to herself. Now she was the one with flushed cheeks.

'Whoa!' Bella froze and pointed to his waist. 'I think it's a leech!'

Sean glimpsed a dark-purple leech that had slipped under his t-shirt. Its slimy leather-like skin had black spots surrounded by yellow rings.

Bella's eyes went wide. The leeches were all over her as well, sliding over each other to find bare skin beneath her clothes.

'I can't feel my feet!' she gasped.

Sean stomped his foot. A squishy mass shot out from beneath his sole. What he thought had been the soft silt of the riverbed was in fact leeches. 'That's because we're standing on them.'

They stared down in horror through the water. The leeches slithered over their legs and moved beneath their clothes. Sean's feet felt swollen and heavy. He was wearing the leeches like waterlogged shoes. He grabbed Bella's hand and pulled her along. 'Keep moving, don't think about it.'

Bella shrieked. 'They're moving up my back. Urgh!'

'We have to get to the waterfall.'

They approached a sharp bend in the river. The sound of tumbling water echoed through the giant trees. A fine mist drifted through the ferns and shrubs draping over the bend.

'Come on. We're almost there.'

Sean pushed harder. The leeches made his legs twice as heavy, like he was trying to swim in a waterlogged sumo wrestling costume. He dipped his free hand in the water and paddled to increase his speed.

'Sean, stop it! Don't put your hand in the water.'

It was dangerous, but he was eager to see the waterfall. He powered against the current, keen to rid himself of the ugly bloodsuckers. His foot disappeared into a pothole and he slipped under the water. Bella's hand slid from his grasp and he floundered for a moment in panic. His leech-laden feet found a rocky purchase, and he lurched out of the water with a gasp.

Bella steadied him, then squealed in horror.

Sean saw the slimy bulge from the corner of his eye. A giant leech stuck to his face. The weight of it pulled his cheek and eyebrow down on one side of his face. He instinctively reached for it, desperate to yank it off.

'Don't!' Bella shrieked. 'You'll pull your face off.'

Sean went to speak and slurred his words. His mouth wasn't moving properly. Half his face was numb. The leech sucked the blood from his face with such force it pulled his skin super taut.

Bella clawed at her collar. A leech slid out from under her top and squirmed up the bare skin of her neck. More bulges appeared beneath her clothes, squelching their way upward.

Sean dragged Bella around the bend.

The waterfall stood thirty metres away, on the far side of a deep-looking pool. He trudged on, dragging Bella, trying to ignore the slimy monstrosity devouring his face. The riverbed sloped downwards. Another step and they would be out of their depth.

He pointed to the waterfall, forcing his stretched lips to work. 'Wiim wor wiit!'

Bella nodded, comprehending his distorted *Swim for it!* If not for their dire situation, they would have laughed at his silly voice.

They dove forward and swam breaststroke across the pool, straining to keep their heads above the surface. Sean tired after several strokes. His vision dimmed. The leeches had sucked so much blood, he was losing consciousness. Their engorged bodies dragged him under the water. His heart raced. His desperate breaths became rapid and short. He craned his tight face around to Bella. Her complexion had turned a deathly grey, each stroke more laboured than the last.

We're not going to make it! he thought.

Sean swam on, one arm after another, his failing eyes focused on the waterfall. The water roared like an animal. A few more strokes and he was there. Bella overtook him and disappeared behind the whitewash of water. He took a breath and followed, only to be shoved underwater by the downward force of water. With no energy left to kick, his arms flailed like useless appendages. He held onto his last breath, unable to fight against the torrent.

Bella's hand shot through the churning water, grasped hold of his collar, and pulled him up.

Sean scrambled onto a rocky ledge hidden behind the waterfall and collapsed on his back, gasping.

Bella yanked his arm. 'Come on. We're almost there!'

Sean rolled onto his stomach and forced himself onto his knees. The moss-covered ledge sloped up to an enormous cave. They clambered up the slippery slope, squishing the leeches smothering their knees. At the top of the rise they found a crude stone pedestal marked with Isharkute glyphs. It appeared ancient. An iridescent purple moss smothered the stone.

A gold chalice sat atop the pedestal, gleaming like a precious relic.

Bella dragged herself up the stone and clutched the chalice. Without looking inside, she took a long swig and passed it on, hands trembling.

He placed the chalice to his lips as best he could, avoiding the bulbous leech blocking one side of his mouth. Most of the elixir ran down his face, but he gulped a meagre mouthful.

The precious amount that ran down his throat took instant effect.

A burning started deep in his oesophagus and radiated through his chest. The heat was intense, as if his body was set alight from within.

Bella clutched her chest, face contorted with agony. She collapsed from view on the far side of the pedestal.

Sean reached after her. But she might as well have been a world away. The sudden movement sent a searing explosion of heat down his arm. He collapsed against the pedestal and dropped the chalice. It clanged down the slope, spilling the remaining elixir over the moss and rolled into the water. The leech slid off his face and flopped onto the pedestal. More leeches squirmed out from under his clothes and slithered back to the water. He suddenly felt woozy. All around him, the cave spun. Faster and faster. Sean held onto the pedestal, fighting to remain conscious.

It was impossible.

*   *   *

Sean awoke facedown, face pressed into hard stone. He arose, waking slowly from his groggy state. He checked his body. Thankfully, he was free of leeches. He sat up and glanced around. Where was Bella? The pedestal and rough cave walls were gone, replaced by a chamber constructed from huge stone blocks. It resembled the interior of the Great Pyramid. Natural light spilled in from a passage behind him. Sean staggered to his feet and followed the light. The passage inclined towards an exit glaring with daylight. Was he back at the mountain citadel on Akanae?

He shielded his eyes and stepped into the blinding light.

A smear of blood marked the stone at his feet. His eyes adjusted and he found himself on an Isharkute building overlooking a lush green jungle.

He was back on Earth!

WHOOSH!

Sean raised his arms in defence and ducked.

An Isharkute hunter-craft flew overhead, close enough to see the faces of the warriors through the open side. The vessel descended upon a clearing at the base of the building.

Far below, humans and hybrids fought a vicious battle against the Isharkute. Bodies lay scattered across the clearing. In the middle of the chaos, a small group of human tribespeople huddled in terror. The Isharkute warriors surrounded them as more rappelled down from the hovering hunter-craft.

It was the turning point in the battle. The Isharkute were about to win.

Was this a dream or a vision? Sean couldn't tell.

He felt the sun burning down on his face, the cool breeze rising from the jungle. Had his consciousness travelled through time again? A commotion at the edge of the jungle drew his attention.

The perimeter trees burst apart. A centaur leapt free and galloped towards the warriors with a long, distinctive polearm. It was his dad!

Henry charged through the squad at full speed, catapulting two warriors high into the air. He swung his polearm in a wide arc, knocking the staves from several warriors.

'Go!' Henry screamed.

The human captives leapt to their feet and raced for the protection of the jungle. Henry covered them from behind as two more hybrids arrived to assist – Hesalbar the manticore and Kryos the seven-foot-tall cyclops.

Sean recognised them from the Great Arena.

Hesalbar was a formidable foe. His scorpion tail, lion's body, enormous leathery wings, and human head enabled him to swoop, sting, and swipe at the warriors with incredible speed. Kryos picked up the warriors like toys and hurled them across the battlefield.

The fight had suddenly turned in their favour.

It didn't last long. Another three hunter-craft flew overhead and circled the clearing. More warrior squads were about to drop into the battle.

Henry shielded the humans into the shadow of the tree line. Trailing energy blasts tore up the surrounding foliage.

Back in the clearing, Kryos cried out and crumpled to his knees, clutching his injured leg. Hesalbar returned to help and flew protective circles around his fallen comrade.

A hunter-craft landed and First Commanders Nefaro and Vogran leapt into the carnage.

Sean launched off the building in desperation, but rather than flying, his thoughts shifted his point of view to the part of the battle he wanted to focus on. *Wow!* Unlike his previous out-of-body ventures, his consciousness wasn't present in the moment. This was a vision of the past, like watching history in virtual reality.

Why was he drawn to this exact moment in time? It had to be an important event. Maybe it was a decisive battle between his dad and Senetep's Commanders.

The warriors trod over the crumpled bodies of Hesalbar and Kryos, directing every weapon on Henry and the escaping humans.

Sean followed his dad into the jungle.

The humans scrambled through the undergrowth, clawing

through the tangled roots and choking vines. Energy blasts decimated the jungle canopy. Shredded leaves rained down all around them. Henry stumbled through the dense greenery, falling behind. Jungles were no place for a horse.

The Isharkute fanned out, cutting down the undergrowth with their staves, closing in fast.

Sean watched. Helpless to do anything. If only he could warn them, but he was merely an observer.

An Isharkute scout vessel crash-landed through the trees, forging a life-saving path through the impenetrable wall of green. It came to rest on a bed of splintered tree trunks and broken branches. The gangway hissed open. Yeesha, Rootuk, and Nesuk jumped out and helped the exhausted escapees aboard.

Sean fist-pumped the air. 'Yeah!'

Henry held his position and fired at the warriors closing in around them, giving Yeesha time to help her tribe aboard. She finally jumped onto the gangway. 'Henry! Everyone's on board except for you. We have to go.'

Henry backed up and galloped towards the vessel. He leapt over a fallen tree trunk, only to be stopped midair and yanked down. *Thump!* His front and rear legs lay spread-eagled across the log, stranding him in a vulnerable position. Sean zoomed in beside his dad, finding the vines knotted around his rear left hoof.

Henry jabbed the knot with his polearm. The vines were stuck tight.

Sean tried to help. He pulled on the knot, but it was like stone. Although he could touch things, his presence had no effect. He couldn't alter the vision.

Henry gazed up at Yeesha. The sad, resolute look in his eyes said *Leave me.*

Sean and Yeesha screamed at the same time, 'No!'

Energy blasts exploded along the log, tearing up the bark. *Bam!* Henry took a direct hit on his horse flank. *Bam! Bam!* He took a hit on his human back, then another on his shoulder. His head slumped forward.

Sean screamed, but nobody could hear him.

Yeesha, Rootuk and Nesuk raced up the gangway as it closed, leaving his dad to the Isharkute.

'What are you doing?' Sean cried. 'You can't leave him!'

The scout vessel lifted, spun about, then hovered in place. Its canons exploded, cutting a swathe of energy through the jungle like a giant machete, halving trees and Isharkute in one godlike swipe. As the trees crashed to the ground, a stream of golden sunlight broke through the leafy canopy and spotlighted his dad, prone on the log. Dead.

Sean stared in disbelief. Did this actually happen?

Yeesha and her tribe returned for Henry's body. They removed the vines snagging his hoof, then picked him up and reverently carried him up the gangway. Yeesha collected his polearm and followed the procession inside. Nesuk and Rootuk observed from the top of the gangway, faces wracked with grief.

The gangway closed and Sean's vision blurred. He sensed his consciousness being drawn away. Snippets of memories entered his mind. The Helior River...the leeches...Bella pulling him through the waterfall... drinking the elixir.

That's it! The vision was part of the cleansing ceremony.

Like it or not, he was returning to his waking body.

— CHAPTER 9 —

Life-Bearers

Sean awoke with a gasp and sat upright. His heart pounded against his ribs like an animal desperate to escape. He remained still, eyes shut, and focused on slowing his breathing. It was a useful trick he'd learned from Nasir, the man-falcon hybrid who taught him to fly. Each measured breath helped rein in his erratic pulse, one steady beat after another. Sean took the peaceful moment to reflect on what he just witnessed. The sight of his dad's lifeless body being carried up the gangway remained raw and vivid. It felt as though he'd lived those final moments with his dad in the jungle. Is that how he died? Was it meant to give him a sense of closure? His heart had slowed but was hollow with loss.

Sean eased off a bed, squinting. Daylight streamed through the floor-to-ceiling window dominating his room. The vista overlooked Akanae's impressive snow-capped peaks. He was back in Hemket's citadel.

There was nobody else in the room, or much in the way of furniture. Isharkute architecture was sparse and simple. A set of gleaming metallic medical devices sat on a side table.

A joyous-sounding voice filled the space. 'Sean!'

Bella raced into the room and threw her arms around him. She squeezed tight, in true Bonaforte fashion. Sean hugged her back. His heart quickened, filling with life again. Their time together in Leech River had saved him from second-guessing how to treat her. There was no doubt in his mind now. Bella was his girlfriend – his first *real* girlfriend.

'I'm so glad you're awake,' she said. 'I thought you were going to sleep forever.'

'How long was I asleep?'

'Three days,' Nocao said, entering the room.

'Three days!' Sean remarked, glancing at Bella. 'How long have you been awake?'

'About a day or so.' Bella flicked his hair off his forehead affectionately. 'You still look tired. Are you okay?'

'I'm not sure,' Sean said. He rubbed his eyes, still slightly unsettled. Was the dream a window to past events or a construct of his imagination? 'Do you remember anything between drinking the elixir and waking up?'

'Not much, except for some crazy dreams. What about you?'

Sean realised he shouldn't have asked. He wasn't ready to share his experience. It was too fresh. Too personal. He needed time to deal with what he had seen.

Nocao took his arm and felt his pulse. 'Aside from an elevated heart rate, your vital signs appear normal.'

'You missed all the fun,' Bella said.

Sean was about to ask what he'd missed, then noticed Nocao's broad smile. He took hold of Nocao's forearm and turned it over. His pale-blue skin was bruise-free, but more than that, his complexion was healthier than it had been in ages. 'What happened to your affliction? Are you cured?'

'Thanks to both of you.'

Sean leapt off the bed. 'That's awesome! Why didn't you tell me?'

'I just did,' Nocao said matter-of-factly.

Sean shook his head. 'Hang on a minute, aren't you excited? You just saved your entire species from extinction!'

'Not yet. I'm the first successful test subject.'

'I can't believe I missed it. You should've woken me up.'

'We couldn't wait for you to regain consciousness. Ormar transported your bodies straight from the waterfall cave to the labs here. The leeches filtered all the unwanted toxins from your body and the elixir took care of removing them.'

'See? It *was* the ultimate detox diet,' Bella cut in. 'I feel great.'

'Upon your arrival at the citadel, we extracted your spinal fluids.'

Sean rubbed his lower back, remembering the giant needle inserted into his spine last time they took a sample.

'Don't worry, I've improved the technique,' Nocao said. 'It took me a day to isolate the remnants of Isharkute DNA hiding in your genome. Then I rebuilt the Isharkute genome sequence using your combined DNA. From that, I constructed an active serum that attached itself to our broken genome and patched the gaps. It began working straight away. Twelve hours later, I was free of the affliction.'

'That's unbelievable.'

'Not at all, it's science. We're synthesising it for the rest of the population now.'

'Your dad Horumbut would be proud of you!'

'His research into the human genome gave me a starting point. Without his work, I wouldn't have been able to isolate Isharkute DNA so quickly from human.'

'It's still unbelievable.' Sean smirked. 'Where's Ramin?'

'He's in the citadel's hibernation chambers with Hemket. They're preparing to administer the serum to our final six life-bearers. I asked them to wait for our return. Follow me.'

Nocao led them through the deserted citadel. His brisk pace increased with every step, and before long, they were jogging. For Nocao, it was his father's legacy, a life's work coming to fruition. His excitement was palpable. But Sean didn't want to miss the opportunity to see their cure in action either. They were about to save the final six life-bearers.

After several sharp turns, Nocao raced down a steep stairwell.

Bella overshot the last exit and bumped into Sean. 'Sorry! He's so quick. How does he know his way around this place? Every passage looks the same.'

'He has a photographic memory.'

Bella sped after Nocao. 'Lucky him. I wish I did.'

Ormar Trell and one of his warriors guarded the entrance to the hibernation chamber. They lowered their staves and stood aside.

Ormar gave Sean a nod of admiration as he passed.

The subtle gesture lifted Sean's spirits, proving the cleansing ceremony had earned him a new level of respect.

Inside, Ramin stood between Hemket and the female scientists, looking like a child amongst a group of adults. Hemket was hunched over a trolley in the middle of the gloomy chamber, analysing six canisters of serum. The blue glow emanating from the hibernation tanks gave her skin a luminous, ghostly quality.

Hemket straightened her gangly frame. 'Just in time, you three. You can all bear witness to the fruits of your labour.'

With great care, Hemket passed the canisters to her scientists, who attached them to the valves above each pod. The skeletal figures remained motionless in their embryotic fluid, curled up in foetal positions, unaware they were about to be awoken. Overhead holograms displayed their dwindling life signs – the only indication they were still alive.

Hemket reached out to Nocao. 'In honour of your father Horumbut and your dedication to saving our species, you may administer the first serum.'

Nocao nodded with pride and approached the first hibernation pod. He twisted the canister and a small green light illuminated above it. The serum injected into the embryotic fluid with a swirl of magenta. The scientists repeated the process across the five remaining pods.

Sean observed the gaunt faces, anxiously awaiting their reaction to the serum.

Time passed.

Their sunken eyes refused to open, their contorted fingers unwilling to relax. Seconds felt like minutes. The serum dissolved into the fluid and found its way through the umbilical cords secured to the life-bearer's mouths. They were digesting the cure.

'Is it working?' Bella asked, breaking the silence.

'I would have expected something by now,' Ramin said. 'Nocao, do you have any suggestions?'

Nocao held up a data pad and assessed the life-bearers vital signs.

Sean moved close to one of the pods, eager to witness the slightest movement, any sign that the serum was working. The bony figure jerked without warning, thumping her kneecap against the pod's interior. Sean recoiled and bumped into Bella.

Hemket observed the tank, frowning with concern.

The life-bearer convulsed and thrashed through the fluid. She spat the umbilical from her mouth and spluttered, as if drowning in the fluid. The other five life-bearers became distraught. Their frail bodies writhed into unnatural poses, pounding against the glass. Hemket's scientists darted between the pods, manipulating the holographic controls, attempting to stabilise the distressed occupants.

Nocao jumped in to assist. Nothing they did improved the situation.

Bella grabbed hold of Sean's hand. 'What's happening?'

'I don't know.'

Sean had never seen Nocao work so fast. His agile hands moved with blurring precision, outshining his best piloting manoeuvres.

Less than a minute later, all six life-bearers had stopped moving. Their mouths hung open, detached from their umbilical cords, and their pale-blue skin had faded to a dark-purple. Their dwindling vital signs no longer appeared on the holograms.

The life-bearers were dead.

*   *   *

Afterwards, Hemket and her scientists remained the hibernation chamber to analyse what went wrong. Nocao returned to his lab, determined to discover why the serum had cured himself but killed the life-bearers.

All Sean and Bella could do was sit back and watch Nocao toil over his holograms, rebuilding the genetic sequences with his hands, retesting, only to arrive at the same results. There was nothing they could say that would help. Nocao had shown little emotion, but Sean knew his friend was hiding incredible pain and disappointment.

This was a massive blow, not only to himself, but to the Isharkute Empire. Without the life-bearers, the Isharkute were doomed to their affliction. Nocao belonged to the last generation. Emperor Neberun was yet to learn of their failure, but Sean held the belief that Nocao would find a solution.

'How long will he keep this up?' Bella whispered.

'As long as it takes,' Sean replied.

'He should take a break. It might help him think clearer.'

Ramin strode into the lab. 'Nocao, you could work for years and still not find an answer.'

Nocao didn't look up from his hologram. 'I can't find anything wrong with the Isharkute genome sequence. I don't understand why it didn't work.'

'Hemket suggested your cure may only work on males yet to become females.'

Nocao stopped what he was doing and lifted his head, ready to listen.

'All six life-bearers had already transitioned into female form. Their bodies were stuck in hibernation for centuries. Their DNA had decayed further during that time. They were worn out, near death, and unable to cope with such last-minute genetic manipulation.'

Nocao gave a resigned nod. 'I hope you're right.'

'Don't give up hope. You're living proof the serum works.'

'But I'm centuries away from turning into a life-bearer. We can't wait that long to see if it works. At present, it's only half a cure. If my generation can't transform into life-bearers, then our species will die.'

'Then we test the serum on Isharkute near the age of transformation.'

'Who do you suggest?'

'Do I need to state the obvious?' Ramin huffed. 'I know my youthful appearance betray my true age, but I'm 410 years old and well within the range of transformation.'

'It's too dangerous. What if I'm the anomaly here? The serum cured me, but it might kill you at your age. You're so close to transforming. It's too risky without more research.'

'You're not an anomaly.'

'You don't know that.'

'In fact, I do.'

'How?'

'Because two hours ago I volunteered myself to be injected with the serum, and like you, I'm now free of the affliction and in perfect health. My body is in the prime age range, so we needed to act fast. You can consider me your–' Ramin regarded Sean and Bella. 'How do you say it in human terms? "I'm your pig"?'

Bella gave Sean a grossed out, confused look.

Sean laughed. 'You mean guinea pig!'

'Yes! Nocao, I am your guinea pig. But we can't afford to sit around on Akanae and wait for my transformation into life-bearer. We must embark on our quest for the *Spearhead of Creation* before Senetep finds it.'

'You should stay here in case the serum works.'

'Don't be so narrow-minded. I wasn't the only guinea pig foolish enough to sign up for this experiment. Several guards from Ormar Trell's squad were also near transformation age and have received the serum. They all survived.'

Nocao shut down his working hologram. 'Then it's not as bad as I thought.'

'Enough talk, we have much to do. Gather what you need from the labs; we leave this evening after the life-bearers' funeral ceremony.'

*   *   *

Ramin and Nocao spent the remainder of the afternoon arranging a new vessel for the *Spearhead* mission. Akanae's twelve space docks had been destroyed in Senetep's attack, leaving a slim selection of vessels in long-term storage hangars scattered across the planet. They settled on the *Heroke*, a deep-space warrior-class fighter designed for military defence and incursions. They upgraded the deep-space scanners, communications systems, and converted one of the onboard storage spaces into a lab with the scientific equipment needed for the mission.

Sean, Bella and Nocao left the citadel for the funeral ceremony just as the sun set on Akanae's horizon. Twenty minutes later, they landed on another continent, deep in the middle of a prehistoric jungle. Night had fallen, leaving an incandescent mist hovering amongst the treetops, obscuring the canopy from view. The twisting tree trunks emerged from the ethereal mist like the tails of giant lizards climbing into the heavens.

The vessel gangway opened onto a paved stone path. Hemket stood waiting for them. She motioned to a row of glowing lanterns hanging off a nearby tree.

Sean took the first lantern. It was almost weightless and swayed in the breeze. The paper casing was lit from within by a soft yellow light that danced and shimmered with a mind of its own.

Bella held her lantern up to her face. 'It looks like a fairy!'

'It's a firefly,' Nocao said.

Hemket led them along the path. The oppressive humidity coated the jungle flora in a glistening layer of moisture and made the stones slippery. After several paces, the path descended into a concealed ravine. Overhead, the broad blue leaves created a living ceiling to the rock walls. Roaring water, distant and powerful, echoed from somewhere below. Consumed by the shadows, the glowing lanterns became their only source of light.

The ravine opened onto a secluded river illuminated by glowing lanterns.

The floating lights followed the river current, gently winding between steep rock walls to vanish over a waterfall into a wide valley set beneath glistening stars.

It was the brightest night sky Sean had ever seen. He marvelled at the celestial brilliance. This was a sacred site. The stars reflected off the water just like an infinity pool, creating the illusion of the river flowing straight into the heavens. Sean had never seen such a divine connection between the land and heavens captured so seamlessly.

Bella gasped. 'It's beautiful.'

'I couldn't even dream of something so magical,' Sean whispered.

Female Isharkute filed along both sides of the riverbank, taking their places on the thin rock ledges. Some placed lanterns in the water; others had already done so and stood back to watch. Hemket knelt, placed her lantern in the water, and moved along the ledge.

Sean was next in line.

Bella pressed up behind him and whispered, 'Should we put ours in too?'

Sean returned a silent nod. He leant over the edge, lowered his lantern into the current and moved on. Bella, Nocao and Ramin followed suit. They stood on the ledges and watched their lanterns disappear off the edge of the waterfall.

Further upstream, a brilliant display of lanterns illuminated the murky ravine. The lights shimmered up the rocks to the jungle flora far above as the first casket emerged like a ship in the night, carried around the river bend by the current. All six life-bearers had been launched from a hidden location upstream, laid on woven caskets embedded with lanterns. Their arms lay crossed over their chests, their long elegant fingers finally relaxed. The soft light gave their ancient faces a serene quality, as if they were sleeping. After centuries of uncertain stasis, the life-bearers had at last found peace.

The Isharkute crowd bowed their heads as the caskets floated by.

Sean and Bella showed the same respect.

One by one, the luminous caskets drifted over the edge, taking the light with them. The ravine darkened, leaving the river to reflect the celestial curtain of stars.

Then, as if someone stoked a fire, a sumptuous swarm of fireflies arose from beyond the waterfall. Freed from their paper lanterns, they swirled through the fine spray and flew away, mingling with the cosmos.

Sean glanced at Bella. Her eyes glistened with tears, reminding him of the pain yet to come – they were about to say goodbye to each other. Perhaps forever.

The *Spearhead* mission would take them so far into space that

Bella could never return to her family in their lifetime. She would never see her parents, Arturo, or Aunt Carla again. And even if he found the *Spearhead*, there was no guarantee he would defeat Senetep and make it back to Earth himself. Bella had no choice. As much as it hurt him, she had to return to her family. He would miss her energetic spirit, sharp wit, and willingness to embrace the unknown. But their feelings for each other did not eclipse the needs of her family. Bella had played her part in creating the cure. Her mission was over. She had to return to Earth.

Sean took a deep breath, confident in his decision.

It was time to say goodbye.

— CHAPTER 10 —

Trail Of Destruction

The *Ragarn* dropped out of light speed into the shadow of a planet brimming with colour. Beneath swirls of grey clouds lay great expanses of green, ochre, and turquoise. Senetep assessed the holographic scans from his command chair. The planet was a similar size to Earth, with oceans, continents, and an oxygen-rich atmosphere. It was a younger, healthier version of the humans' spoiled planet.

Erund strode through the bridge. 'This planet and its moon share the same ratios in size and distance from one another as Akanae and Nek-Karani and the Earth and its Moon.'

'What about life forms?'

'We're scanning hundreds of thousands of species. The most advanced is an upright hominid, much like the primates of planet Earth around 80,000 years ago. There're hundreds of tribes across all the continents.'

'Show me one.'

Erund peered over the shoulder of the science officer. 'Focus your scanners on a tribe near the equator.'

A hologram depicting a camp of humanoids materialised in the middle of the bridge. The primitive group of hunter-gatherers consisted of several families. They dressed in animal skins and worked with basic flint tools and wooden implements. Their camp was positioned by a river and comprised several stick shelters.

Senetep groaned. He loathed the sight of their grubby humanoid faces. They reminded him of the scourge coursing through his veins.

'Another infected planet,' he grumbled.

'Their level of evolution does not account for the anomalous pyramid on the planet's equatorial line. It's perfectly aligned to the cardinal points.'

'What pyramid?'

The hologram transformed to show an enormous pyramid of polished white stone rising out of swampy marshland. The 45-degree sides were mirror-smooth, displaying a craftsmanship that rivalled the Isharkute Empire.

'None of our ancestor's records match this planet or solar system.'

'Of course they don't!' Senetep snapped. 'Our ancestors didn't build the pyramid. It was placed here by the *Spearhead*.'

Senetep stared at the mysterious gleaming structure. Stopping now to investigate would slow them down, but every piece of information left by the *Spearhead* was another clue to its power and purpose. The opportunity was too good to ignore.

'We've plotted coordinates for our next light-speed jump,' Erund said. He waited longer than usual for a response. 'Shall we initiate the jump?'

'No! Prepare a landing party.'

*   *   *

Senetep stepped off the *Ragarn's* gangway into the brackish, knee-deep water. There was no dry ground as far as the eye could see, just mud, reeds, and low-lying shrubs. The marsh was the meeting point of a giant inland estuary and the ocean. Straight ahead, the pyramid arose from the water in pristine condition. Layers of light-green algae ran around the lower third of the structure, showing the high tide level. A structure of this size would be difficult to build in such sodden, unstable conditions.

Erund jumped into the water beside him. 'A concealed passage is located ten metres up the face of the pyramid. We must destroy the casing stones to reveal it.'

'The less time we spend on this bog, the better.'

Six of Senetep's best warriors assembled behind them.

Senetep forged on through the watery landscape, stave activated, ready to obliterate the unexpected.

Scans showed the marsh was teeming with life, mainly fish and crustaceans, but larger amphibians lurked in the deeper pools. The overcast sky reflected off the water, making it impossible to see what lay beneath the surface. Gigantic prehistoric dragonflies zoomed in to inspect them with their bulbous eyes and moved on.

Senetep noticed a ripple several paces ahead and stopped. The disturbance continued underwater, encircling their group. He tracked the ripples with his stave, moving just ahead of the wake, targeting the creature's head.

CRACK! The blast punched a circular tunnel through the water, deep into the mud.

A scaly serpent shot from the swell, coiling around them from all sides. The giant snake rose to twice their height. A pair of evil yellow eyes glared down upon them. It hissed angrily, revealing four translucent fangs and a throat of rosy-pink flesh.

The warriors opened fire along its length of brown-orange scales.

Hiss! The serpent whipped its head from side to side and writhed about, churning up a wall of muddy water. It finally turned belly-up and bobbed lifelessly in the water.

Senetep pushed the limp head aside with his stave. 'With some enhancements, I could make use of this creature in my hybrid program.'

They forged on to the pyramid.

Senetep peered up at the apex, hundreds of feet above, wondering why the structure had been sealed. What awaited them inside? Was it meant to be opened?

'You should step back,' Erund warned him.

A warrior knelt in front of the group and positioned a heavy duty, eight-pronged stave over his shoulder. The crystals powered up with a hum and the prongs crackled with increasing energy.

Senetep stood his ground, undeterred by the impending explosion.

BOOM!

The blast lit up the entire pyramid and obliterated a section of casing stones midway up. Debris rolled down the slope and plopped into the water. The dust cloud dispersed, revealing a shadowy passage leading inside. A warrior fired a grappling hook into the entrance, leaving a dangling rope for everyone to climb.

Senetep slung his stave over his shoulder and moved first. 'Cover me.'

Erund watched on as the warriors took up a defensive stance.

Senetep powered through the 45-degree ascent and clambered over the rubble littering the entrance. Inside, the passage towered at least ten times his height. It appeared to be built for a race of giants. He ran his hand along the megalithic stone wall. The flawless white blocks sat in perfect alignment, continuing deep into the interior.

Erund stumbled inside and held up a scanner. Its blue light probed the passage, measuring the dimensions and composition of the stone. 'The stone blocks are quartzite, with medium levels of phengite.'

'Is the quartzite indigenous to this planet?'

'Yes. Our topography scans suggest it was quarried from a series of distant mountain ranges closer to the tectonic plates. Half a continent away.'

The warriors assembled behind them, ready to move. Senetep reactivated his stave and led the way. The passage inclined towards the centre of the pyramid on a gentler, 20-degree slope. After a long descent, it opened into a vast chamber. In the centre was a large circular pool bordered by a knee-high ledge. Their ignited weapons reflected off the still surface, creating ribbons of light up the chamber walls.

Senetep leant over the edge and found his reflection peering back at him. 'Is it water?'

Erund examined the results of his scans. 'No. It's liquid mercury!'

'Mercury?! How deep?'

'The pool finishes just below floor level. It's fed by a series of channels and reservoirs deep inside the pyramid.'

Senetep walked around the pool, noting three more cavernous passages leading from the chamber. They were spaced even distances apart, as if facing the cardinal points. 'Where do these passages lead?'

'Each one exits to a separate pyramid face, all finishing at different heights.'

Senetep deactivated his stave and slung it over his shoulder. There was no threat here. He observed the simple monolithic architecture. What was the purpose of this chamber? The pool of mercury appeared to be the focal point of the entire pyramid. No hint of advanced technology anywhere. It felt like a monument, a marker left behind by the *Spearhead*. 'Scan every block from the foundation to the apex. Collect a sample of the mercury.'

Erund nodded and set to work.

A warrior approached the mercury and scooped a sample into a small container, spilling a small amount on his hand. It stuck to him like a silver leech. He panicked and tried to flick it off, dropping the sample container into the pool.

'Fool!' Senetep growled. He glared at Erund. 'We needed scientists on this mission, not feeble-handed warriors.'

The warrior jumped back and flung the mercury off his hand. It splattered across the floor, reformed into one blob, and slithered back into the pool like a sentient creature. Moments later, the pool began swirling in a clockwise motion. Within seconds it became a turbulent whirlpool of living silver. Erund backed back up and the warriors scrambled towards the passage.

'Stand your ground!' Senetep commanded.

The warriors stopped a safe distance from the pool, weapons aimed.

Senetep glanced at Erund. 'Keep scanning.'

Erund fumbled his scanner into position, hands shaking.

The liquid metal swirled out of the pool like a silent tornado, rising into the chamber, leaving behind an empty pool of bare stone. The mercury morphed into hundreds of silver spheres, then separated again, forming smaller groups of spheres.

'It's stabilising,' Erund said. 'Rearranging itself into patterns.'

Senetep took a step closer, tilting his head to follow the rotating blobs. They morphed into each other and formed new shapes. 'These patterns represent the molecular building blocks for life. Sulphur, phosphorus, oxygen, nitrogen, carbon, and hydrogen.'

Erund glanced at his scanner. 'You're right! They're organic elements.'

Every drop of mercury morphed back into a central blob, elongated, and expanded to form a distinctive double-helix. It was a DNA strand! The display held for a moment, then split off into more strands of DNA.

'Life forms!' Erund gasped. 'Thousands of them.'

'It's an ancient data bank left by the *Spearhead*,' Senetep said. 'The information is encoded in the mercury.'

'What turned it on?'

Senetep eyeballed the warrior responsible. 'The mercury activated as soon as it encountered organic matter.'

The mercury rejoined to form a giant ball of glinting silver. Several smaller blobs detached from the main sphere and orbited it like planets around a sun.

Erund checked his scanner. 'That's Akanae and Nek-Karani.'

'It traced our DNA back to our native solar system, showing us where we've come from.'

Akanae, Nek-Karani and their star lined up in a solar eclipse. The mercury display held for a few seconds, then divided into millions of glistening spheres, swirling outwards, forming a gigantic spiral that filled the chamber.

'It's a map of our entire galaxy!' Erund said.

Thin lines of mercury spread across the sea of stars, converging to a point near the centre of the galaxy.

Senetep instantly recognised the location. He had been staring at the same alignment of stars on his galactic maps since their journey begun. 'It's showing alternate paths to the *Spearhead*. Make sure you record everything.'

Erund nodded eagerly and held his scanner up to the map. The mercury completed the display and hovered above their heads. After a short time, the mercury swirled together in a vortex and returned to the pool.

'Incredible!' Erund said, gawking at the results on his scanner. 'What does it all mean?'

Senetep thought about it for a long moment. 'We just witnessed evolution. From the first molecular elements to DNA to our origins on Akanae.'

'It knows where we come from!'

'And it knows where we're going. This is more than just an updated map, it's an invitation to join the *Spearhead*.'

A primal scream reverberated through the chamber.

Everyone spun around.

A hulking male primate lumbered up the passage. Thick mud caked his muscular physique and his heavy brow displayed a handprint made of crimson paint. He wore a necklace decorated with yellowed talons and a tattered animal fur around his waist. The savage held his spear aloft and rushed into the chamber, leading more of his clan. Their beady deep-set eyes remained obscured beneath terrifying portraits of mud, red war paint, and long straggly hair. Bloodcurdling battle cries echoed through the chamber.

The warriors engaged in a vicious, close-quarters fight.

CRACK! One savage bounced off the wall from an energy blast and slumped to the floor, dead. The warriors fended off the ferocious brutes. Staves clanged against wooden clubs. It was brutal and bloody. The warriors spread out, thinning the pack to take clear shots.

CRACK! The next blast sent another savage hurtling through the air.

CRACK! CRACK! Another two battle cries ended abruptly.

The warriors methodically gained the upper hand, picking off the brutes one by one, avoiding friendly fire. In desperation, the leader hurled his spear across the pool.

Erund dove out of the way and the spear caught Senetep's shoulder. He grasped the shaft and pulled it from his flesh with a grimace. The leader rushed him like a wild animal chasing the scent of blood. Erund unslung his stave and stepped in front of Senetep.

Senetep shoved him aside and snapped the spear over his knee, brandishing the splintered ends like a pair of daggers. 'I'll kill him with his own weapon.'

The leader whipped a stone flint knife out from beneath his animal fur. His lips curled back over stained teeth as he lunged, screaming.

Senetep arched back from the crude blade, sensing the air whoosh by his face. The brute was faster and more agile than he expected: a hunter-gatherer used to surviving the unforgiving marshlands.

The leader returned a backhanded swipe.

Senetep craned his neck at an unnatural angle to avoid being sliced from ear to ear. As the blade whistled by, he lashed out, plunging a broken spear end into the brute's rock-hard thigh. The savage screamed in agony and hobbled about for a half-hearted swipe. Senetep dodged it with a snicker. Too easy. The savage relied on brute force, lacking any real combat skills. The leader pounced again. Senetep leapt aside and the blade smashed into the floor, shattering into a dozen pieces.

Senetep dived in, secured the leader in a headlock, and stabbed the other spear shaft into his chest. The brute sighed heavily and slumped over the edge of the pool. Dead.

The battle was over.

His warriors reassembled, bruised and splattered with blood (none of it their own).

The corpse slipped further into the pool and triggered the mercury. It swirled into the chamber, restarting the sequence of molecular elements and DNA. But this time, instead of displaying Akanae as the planet of origin, the mercury displayed their current planet and solar system. A solar eclipse formed again, and the entire display finished with the map to the *Spearhead*.

Senetep pulled the leader's corpse off the edge.

'The mercury responds to whatever life form makes contact with it,' Senetep said. 'In this case, the local savage triggered a display showing this planet as their origin.'

'Why did both displays include a solar eclipse?'

Senetep wondered the same thing.

He observed the corpse at his feet, noting the circles of dark-blue ink beneath his blood- and mud-smeared chest. He knelt and wiped away the muck, finding a crude tattoo inked across the leader's chest. It contained a sequence of twelve symbols that started as a complete circle on his left shoulder, successively eclipsing into a crescent moon shape. By the sixth symbol in the centre of his chest, the circle was once again complete, but now displayed another circle inside it. The pattern repeated in reverse to his right shoulder.

Erund peered over his shoulder. 'Are they the phases of the moon?'

'No. It's a solar eclipse.'

'How do you know?'

'Because these savages have played their part in the *Spearhead's* grand design. Evolving exactly as they were predestined. This pool of mercury is a repeating message, left to explain the seeding of life to an awakening of higher thought.'

'These savages are far from intelligent.'

'As are any evolving species in their infancy. We must return to the *Ragarn*. I need to prove a theory.'

*   *   *

Soon they were back in orbit. Senetep observed the primitive blue planet from his command chair. He refused to use regenerative salves on his wounded shoulder. He liked the pain. It invigorated him, kept his focus razor sharp.

'The seismic probe is ready to launch,' Erund announced. 'How deep do you want to explore?'

Senetep brought up the nearby moon on the bridge's central hologram. 'Set the drilling depth to infinite.'

'There are quicker ways to burrow through an entire moon. I'd suggest a–'

'Indulge me.'

Erund supervised the crew as they deployed the probe. It took several minutes for the probe to reach the moon and burrow down. The returning data filled the hologram with a detailed modelling of the lunar surface and its subsurface composition. The incoming data stream went blank. Erund double-checked the readings. 'The probe has stopped working or penetrated some form of massive void.'

'Expand the probe's scanning range and overlay that data on the hologram.'

The moon's hollow interior overlaid on the hologram for all to see, showing a thin lunar surface hiding a structure of gigantic, artificial rings.

Every crewmember stared in astonishment.

Senetep smiled to himself. 'The *Spearhead* did more than just seed life on this planet; it created an environment for life to flourish and intelligence to evolve.'

'How?' Erund said, staring in fascination at the hologram of the hollow moon.

'By placing an artificial moon in orbit around this planet, perfectly sized to create a solar eclipse. When day turns to night, a developing species looks to the sky and questions their world, their place within the universe. The solar eclipse is a planned event designed to promote evolutionary thought. These savages have already seen it, awakened to the sign from the sky. It's a deliberate message orchestrated by the *Spearhead*. But this species isn't the first. The same evolutionary and intellectual steps have taken place before.'

Erund glanced up, his face pale with a sudden realisation. 'Just like the relationship between Earth and its Moon.'

'And Akanae and Nek-Karani.'

The crew muttered amongst themselves. A palpable air of uncertainty and discontent was growing.

Senetep chose his next words carefully, aware he was breaking down their Isharkute belief systems for a second time. First, he proved the *Spearhead* was real and not some ancient mythology. Now, he suggested that Akanae's moon, Nek-Karani, was constructed to awaken a higher intelligence – Isharkute intelligence.

'I understand it's hard for many of you to accept this new reality, but it's no coincidence that intelligent life has evolved and continues to evolve on planets with artificial moons. These moons are manufactured in the exact size and location to create a solar eclipse. The odds of three solar systems sharing these exact ratios by chance are incalculable, proving there is a greater power at work. This is not a random event, rather a planned seeding of life. The *Spearhead of Creation* is the creator, the bringer of life, throughout the universe. With its power, we can eradicate our affliction. Turn day into night. Control life. Evolution. Death. Even resurrection. The Isharkute Empire will endure and thrive. Generations to come will speak our names for all eternity.'

The murmurs of discontent had now transformed into cheers. The crew were back on his side and willing.

'Before leaving this system, we will exterminate the indigenous humanoids to prevent further infestation. Prepare a neurotoxin to detonate in the planet's atmosphere. Once we have control of the *Spearhead*, we can return to these cleansed planets and restart life in our image.'

The crew set to work and Senetep returned to his command chair.

Erund approached and spoke privately. 'Why does the *Spearhead* create life and move on, never staying to witness its creation?'

'To allow life to proliferate in any form, uninterrupted. Once a species matures, it can spread through the universe, repeating the same process. Perpetuating life.'

'Sounds like a process fraught with potential errors – like humanity.'

Senetep smirked, glad to hear Erund echo his ideals. 'But remember, humanity would not have evolved as far as they have without Isharkute intervention.'

'But they would have eventually; we just sped the process up.'

'A fatal mistake made by our ancestors.'

'One that won't be made twice. The savages we encountered on this planet are already showing signs of intellectual growth. Give them room to fester and they'll spread through the galaxy like a virus. Your decision to eliminate them now is a masterful stroke.' Erund spoke his next words with an air of caution. 'I'd also like to recommend a further course of action.'

Senetep relaxed into his chair. 'What is that?'

'We launch a web of undetectable probes to keep watch over this solar system. If Emperor Neberun's forces are tracking us, we need an early warning system. Something to alert us of their presence.'

'Hmm. See to it then,' Senetep grumbled. 'And before we leave, destroy the pyramid. If Neberun is coming after us, I don't want him to uncover what we found.'

Erund nodded and returned to the crew.

Senetep sighed, troubled by his own complacency. His focus wasn't so razor sharp after all. Why did Erund need to recommend a course of action that should have occurred naturally to him? He was being sloppy. Was his human DNA slowing his mind? Erund was right. Emperor Neberun's forces were bound to be coming after them.

He needed to set a trap, one so deadly and inescapable, he would never have to worry again.

— CHAPTER 11 —

One-Way Ticket

Bella spent the evening sketching poignant moments from the funeral. Her pencil flowed from one scene to the next: outlining, shading, a little smudging with her thumb. She wanted to capture the images while they were fresh in her mind. A floating parade of caskets and lanterns. The life-bearer's serene faces. Fireflies mingling with the cosmos. For a funeral, it was the most beautiful ceremony she had ever seen. The experience had ignited her creative flame. Of all the items she brought from Earth, she was glad she packed a sketch pad and pencils.

She finished shading the edges of the waterfall and stretched her fingers, wondering how much time had passed. Time disappeared when she was absorbed in her art.

Her makeshift studio overlooked Hemket's mountain citadel and the surrounding mountains. Akanae's heavenly pink moon, Nek-Karani, sat high and full in the night sky and gave the snow-capped peaks a luminous quality. While she had been sketching, Sean and Nocao were off making final preparations for the *Spearhead* mission.

Her stomach filled with butterflies at thought of what was to come. They were about to venture into deep space to find an alien vessel responsible for seeding life throughout the universe. Unknowns aside, it was unbelievable.

Sean poked his head around the doorway. 'We're heading up to the landing platform.'

'Okay, I'm ready.' Bella packed her things and chased after him.

Sean marched two steps ahead of her the entire time. He had been unusually distant and distracted since the funeral. Bella put it down to nerves. She felt for him. The survival of two species, possibly the entire universe, rested upon him. Who wouldn't feel uptight with that kind of pressure?

The last of the crew boarded the *Heroke* as they arrived on the platform. Nocao stood at the bottom of the gangway, waiting for them. Ormar Trell stood on the opposite side of the platform next to his own vessel.

'Who's Ormar waiting for?' Bella asked.

'He's on another mission.'

'What's that?'

Sean didn't answer. Bella waved, but Ormar didn't respond. He watched her with an unusual, unsettling stare. Something weird was going on. Nocao gave Sean a raised eyebrow as they arrived at the gangway.

'*Basta!* What are you two hiding?'

Sean put down his bags and faced her. He had that weird, bottled-up expression again, like he was about to say something he would regret.

'You two look guilty, like you've done something wrong.'

Sean spoke in a soft voice. 'Bella, I should have told you earlier.'

Bella felt her heart skip a beat. 'Told me what?'

Sean hesitated and glanced at Nocao before responding. 'You can't come with us.'

'Sure!' she replied, passing it off as a bad joke. No way was he serious. She nudged past him. 'Come on, we need to leave.'

'I'm serious.'

Bella rounded on him, frustration building. 'What are you talking about?'

'We're travelling thousands of light-years to find the *Spearhead*. To us, the journey might take weeks, but on Earth, it will be thousands of years.'

'I don't get what you're saying.'

'There's a side effect to travelling at the speed of light. Time moves at normal speed for us, but much faster for the rest of the universe.'

'How fast?'

'One week to us could be an entire year on Earth. That's why you can't leave your family...they won't be alive when you return.'

Bella froze, feeling as though all the air had been sucked from her lungs. Her eyes welled with tears, but she remained determined not to cry. This was unfair. Why didn't Sean tell her earlier? How could he be this thoughtless? Being told at the last second was inconsiderate. No, it was incomprehensible! Her fist tightened. Before she could stop herself, she punched his arm.

Sean took the hit in silence and resisted the urge to rub the aching corker.

'Why are you telling me now?'

'I didn't know how to say it. It was never the right time. I just... I just wanted you to come with me.'

Bella stared straight through his eyes, processing everything. Could she even return to Earth now? She loved her family more than anything, but if this mission failed, the entire universe was in danger. What if her presence meant the difference between success and failure? She wished she had more time to think about it. 'You're so selfish,' she whispered harshly.

Sean lowered his head. 'I'm sorry.'

Bella felt a tear run down her cheek. Sean motioned towards her as if to wipe it away. He glimpsed her white-knuckled fist and hesitated, wary of being punched again.

'Ormar Trell has agreed to take you back to Earth.'

Bella looked at Ormar, then back to Sean. 'I can't leave my family...I can't imagine never seeing them again.' She rubbed away her tears. 'You shouldn't have left it so late to tell me.'

'I didn't mean to. I didn't want to burden you with the decision.'

'There is no decision!' she snapped.

'I know. That's why I should've told you ages ago - not spring it on you now.'

Another tear raced down her cheek. Sean reached out and she

shrugged him off. 'It's not fair. You should've told me sooner.'

'I should have,' Sean mumbled. 'But I never expected you to say yes.'

Bella glared at him. His naivety was infuriating. 'Then you don't know me at all.'

'What do you mean?'

'*Stupido!* After everything we've been through, how could I say no?' She stormed up the gangway, leaving them with dumbfounded expressions. Their voices carried after her.

'That was unexpected,' Nocao said.

'I know,' Sean replied.

Bella stomped up the main passage and stormed onto the bridge. She slumped into Ramin's command chair with a huff, only then noticing she wasn't alone. Hemket worked over a schematic hologram of the *Heroke*, assessing something technical. Bella was ready to confront anyone – anyone except Hemket. The female elder was physically imposing, superintelligent, and downright intimidating.

'*Scusi*, I didn't mean to interrupt–'

Hemket raised her head to greet the impromptu visitor. 'I'm preparing the onboard hibernation chamber for Ramin's transformation.'

Bella squirmed, unsure if she should remove herself from the chair.

Hemket finished her work, closed the hologram, and straightened to full height. Her head nudged the ceiling. The *Heroke* was clearly built for Isharkute males. She regarded Bella with interest. 'Your impatient demeanour and flushed complexion show a troubled state of mind.'

'Ha! You could say that.'

'Are you concerned about your mission?'

'In a way.'

'Explain.'

'I'm angry at Sean...and Nocao...and Ramin, and whoever else knew.'

'Aside from you, I must be the only one who doesn't know then.'

'They want to send me back to Earth. They knew this whole time and didn't say a thing. They kept it a secret. It's so annoying. They left it to the very last second to tell me. I thought they were open and honest. Especially Sean.'

'They are males, after all.'

'They're annoying. No wonder you kicked them off your planet.'

'My ancestors had many reasons for removing males from Akanae, the greatest being their immaturity. Isharkute males are self-obsessed, ignorantly headstrong, and determined to outdo each other. They fight, deceive, and betray their own to gain superiority. That's why we sent them into the universe, to mature until they were ready to return for their next stage of life.'

'I wish I could do that: tell Sean to come back when he's grown up.'

'Unfortunately, the separation of Isharkute sexes has contributed to our downfall. The Isharkute males were unsupervised during their expansion into the universe, a mistake that resulted in our affliction. Where we failed, humanity succeeded. Your sexes have lived alongside each other for thousands of years without destroying each other.'

'Si, but it hasn't been easy...or fair.'

'Regardless, humanity has survived this long. Your wisdom as a species is well earned. Sean may be young in human terms, but of the billions living on Earth, he was chosen to represent humanity. His faults are part of what defines him as a human, and a male. They also show that he cares about you deeply.'

Bella finally relaxed her fist and took a deep breath. Her emotions simmered. Hemket made a valid point. Sean may not be perfect, but he kept the truth from her because he cared.

'What cheek!' Ramin bellowed, striding onto the bridge. 'The stowaway is sitting in the captain's chair.'

Bella jumped out of the chair.

Sean and Nocao entered.

'Bella is not a stowaway,' Nocao said. 'The decision to stay aboard or return to Earth is up to her.'

Sean wisely kept his mouth shut.

Bella was the centre of attention now. All eyes remained fixed on her, awaiting her response. 'I haven't changed my mind. I'm coming...just as I always was.'

'Good. It's settled then,' Ramin said, approaching Hemket. 'Hemket, we thank you for your hospitality, but must bid you farewell.'

Hemket bowed, then made the Isharkute sign of the cosmos.

Ramin, Nocao and Sean returned the gesture. Bella copied their action, joining the thumb on her right hand to the outstretched fingers of her left hand. Hemket left the bridge and Ramin assumed his *precious* position in the command chair. The bridge crew took up their posts, leaving few seats for onlookers. Bella reluctantly sat next to Sean.

'Are you sure about this?' Sean asked.

'*Sì!* And don't ask me again.'

Sean went quiet, like a child being told off.

Bella wasn't going to let him off the hook so easily. This was the biggest decision of her life. She might never see her family again, but it was her decision.

The *Heroke* lifted off the citadel platform with a gentle bump. The mountain ranges shrank below them, giving way to a cloudless night sky. Bands of orange-yellow heat shimmered over the front viewscreen as they passed through the upper atmosphere. The minor turbulence ceased the moment they entered Akanae's orbit.

A billion unexplored stars filled the main viewscreen.

Bella peered around. An unusual silence had befallen the bridge crew. Ramin, notorious for commending himself, remained oddly quiet. Sean and Nocao remained tight-lipped. The Isharkute crew kept busy, plotting their course into the holographic star maps.

'Coordinates to our first wormhole are plotted,' the navigation officer announced. 'Based on the data we retrieved from Earth's Moon, we have calculated the nearest entry point.'

Ramin leant forward in his chair. 'Initiate a light-speed jump to that location.'

Bella gripped the seat, heart pounding. There was no turning back now. Every light-speed jump distanced her further from her family.

The jump lasted less than a minute. As the stars came back into focus, so too did a circular distortion ahead of their vessel. It stretched the stars in a spiral anticlockwise pattern, just like white droplets being stirred into a can of black paint.

'Did the Ancients create these wormholes?' Bella asked.

'I doubt it,' Nocao said. 'The *Spearhead* must have mapped them as it travelled through the galaxy, then sent that information back to Earth's Moon.'

'The Moon is like a receiver then?'

'Yes. It's possible that all moons created by the *Spearhead* are receivers and repeaters, sending out updated information about the universe as it continues exploring.'

'Information for who?' Bella asked.

'Any species able to understand and follow.'

'We're about to take the first step on this path now,' Ramin said. 'Hold on to something – we're entering the wormhole.'

Bella reached for Sean's hand and stopped herself. She didn't need his support for every little thing. This was her decision. Her journey. She would be strong for herself.

All eyes turned to the viewscreen. The *Heroke* approached the event horizon, the border between normal space and a starless void. As they crossed over, the bridge elongated like a rubber band, merging with the stars stretching into the inky blackness. There was a sudden flash. Bella felt giddy. A wave of nausea washed over her. She thought she was falling forward, unable to stop herself. Then everything snapped back to normal. Vibrant stars repopulated the viewscreen. They appeared different from before.

'Is that it?' Ramin cried in astonishment.

The navigator assessed the holographic star maps. 'We just travelled 35,000 light-years away from Akanae.'

Ramin sprang from his chair. 'Incredible.'

'How did we travel so far so quick?' Bella asked.

'Jumping through a wormhole is different to travelling at light speed,' Sean said. 'When we travel at light speed, we're covering huge distances at almost 300,000 km a second. Wormholes create folds in space, so instead of travelling all the way from one point to another, we just skip from the start to the finish.'

'How does that work?'

Sean thought about it for a moment. 'Imagine a piece of paper with the letters of the alphabet written across it. In normal travel you would pass every letter to get from A to Z. Wormholes fold the paper, so A meets Z, skipping the letters in between.'

'I get it – I just don't understand how the wormhole does it.'

'One of the great mysteries of the universe,' Ramin said.

'We've arrived at our destination,' the navigator said. An Earthlike world appeared on the viewscreen. 'I'm registering thousands of life forms, including primitive hominids. I'm also detecting the aftermath of a massive explosion near the equator.'

A dirty brown ash cloud came into view, rising above the clouds in a mushroom-shaped plume.

'Is it a volcano?' Sean asked.

Nocao assessed the data from his own hologram. 'The atmosphere is highly ionised, but it's not from an eruption or lightning strike. There was a recent surge of energy. I've located the remains of a large stone structure...the epicentre of the explosion.'

Nocao projected his hologram into the bridge for all to see. A square footprint of stone was all that remained of the structure. Thousands of shattered blocks littered the surrounding marshland. The aftermath reminded Bella of the destruction at Giza, with the remnants of the Great Pyramid strewn all over Cairo.

'Based on the volume and composition of debris, it looks like the remains of a pyramid. There's a local humanoid tribe. Most are dead, but there's a group of survivors stuck in the area. Mainly women and children. Many are injured. I doubt they will make it to safety.'

'That's horrible,' Bella said.

'The residual energy signatures prove it was created by an

Isharkute weapon. Probably a tectonic missile.'

'Senetep!' Sean said.

'Shields up! Scan the system,' Ramin ordered. 'He might still be here.'

The navigation officer spun his hologram about, highlighting vast expanses of space by hand. 'There are no other vessels in the system.'

'We just missed him!' Sean said, sounding relieved.

'I'm tracking a foreign object passing through the planet's upper atmosphere,' Nocao said. 'It's not manned. Putting it on the bridge viewscreen now.'

The viewscreen displayed a projectile flying at supersonic speed through the clouds.

'Is it a tectonic missile?' Sean asked.

'No, it's too small. Scanning now.'

An X-ray view of the missile overlaid the screen, zooming in to highlight a canister housed within the missile. It pulsed with a red glow.

'Red always means something bad,' Bella said.

'It's armed with a neurotoxin, enough to kill every living thing on the planet ten times over. The missile has been circling the planet, releasing the toxin, but it's still inactive. Once the missile empties its tank, it will detonate, creating a chain reaction through the atmosphere activating the toxin all over the planet.'

'Can we stop it? There's a world full of life down there.'

'Our only chance is to destroy the missile before it completes the deployment. If we can, the inactive toxin will just disperse and break down in the atmosphere.'

'Do it!' Ramin ordered.

Nocao sprinted across the bridge and nudged the pilot from his seat. 'I'll take the *Heroke* from here.'

Ramin sat in his chair and gripped the arms. 'Nocao, this isn't a stinger. It won't have the same manoeuvrability as the smaller vessels you're used to flying.'

Nocao adjusted the holographic controls to his liking. 'Same principals apply. I've already calculated the differences in my head.'

Sean turned to Bella. 'I'd hold on to something if I was you.'

Bella gripped her seat as the *Heroke* nosedived towards the planet. Nocao powered through the planet's exosphere at full speed. Superheated air roiled ahead of their vessel, like flying into an explosion. Bella peered around, half-expecting the violent vibrations to break their vessel apart. The turbulence abated, and they descended into the clouds.

Nocao tracked the missile from above, mimicking its every move, gradually descending to the same altitude with short bursts of acceleration. He closed in, weaving left and right in a nauseating manner, aiming the nose of their vessel towards the missile.

Bella crossed her fingers on one hand and held her stomach with the other.

'Now!' Nocao called.

The tactical officer locked his targeting system on the missile and fired.

A flash erupted across the viewscreen. Two missiles whooshed ahead, homing in on Senetep's planet killer. Nocao pulled up to avoid the detonation. *BOOM!* The shock wave threw everyone not holding on to the floor.

Bella and Sean fell down beside each other. She jumped back to her feet before he offered to help.

'Well done, Nocao!' Ramin cried, pulling himself back into his chair. 'Your fancy flying just saved every living organism on this primordial swamp of a planet. Prepare the coordinates for our next wormhole jump. We need to get ahead of Senetep before he causes more irreparable damage.'

'Wait!' Bella said. 'What about the survivors? We can't just leave those women and children to die in the marsh. We have to help them.'

'We don't have time.'

'Bella's right. They don't deserve to die,' Sean jumped in. 'Senetep destroyed the pyramid and tried to kill everything on the planet. There must be something he didn't want us to find.'

'What do you expect to discover within a smouldering pile of rubble?'

'I was thinking more about the people he tried to murder.'

'They're a primitive species. I would temper your expectations if I was you.'

'That's not true,' Nocao cut in. 'If not for the primitive tribes on Earth, we might never have found the cure for our affliction. An evolving, unspoiled species like this could be invaluable. We should collect a sample of their DNA. It may prove to be an invaluable clue about the *Spearhead*.'

'Fine!' Ramin boomed. 'I'm clearly outvoted here. You have one hour.'

The *Heroke* landed on the outskirts of the pyramid explosion zone. Bella stepped off the gangway onto the alien marshland. The lukewarm water was ankle deep and filled with grassy reeds. Shattered pyramid blocks protruded from the mud like weird cake decorations. The humid air was contaminated with an acrid, burnt smell. A dark mushroom cloud loomed in the distance, tainting the sky with a hazy brown muck.

Nocao led the way, surrounded by a squad of armed warriors.

Sean hung behind and kept pace with Bella. 'I'm glad you said something to Ramin. You know...about helping these people.'

'It's the right thing to do.'

'Senetep has no respect for life. I saw how he treated our ancestors. It was brutal. We need to make sure he never has that kind of power again.'

Bella gave a subtle nod, but she wasn't ready to let Sean off the hook yet.

Nocao stopped, raised his hand, and pointed to the tribe hiding in a thicket of bushes ahead. Their matted hair and lean bodies were coated in mud, except for their lower legs where the water had washed them clean. Bella stared, unsettled by their pale skin. Beneath the crud, they were just like human beings. Most were bleeding and nursing fresh wounds. They all wore splashes of red paint across their faces. A trio of young boys, no older than twelve or thirteen, guarded the women and infants. There were no men.

The boys raised their spears, acting as the men of the tribe.

The warriors raised their staves.

'Stop!' Bella called, splashing through the water to Nocao. 'They're harmless. They're just defending the women and children.'

'Lower your weapons,' Nocao said.

The warriors obeyed.

One of the injured women slumped to her knees and collapsed facedown in the water. None of the tribe moved to help, too petrified by the odd-looking strangers. She was about to drown in less than a foot of water. Right in front of them.

Bella snatched a container of healing salve from Nocao's utility belt, unscrewed the lid, and pushed through the warriors. She scooped out a handful of the gelatinous burgundy salve and approached the tribe.

The boys held their ground, spears aloft, hands trembling.

Bella cautiously knelt beside the fallen woman and rolled her body over. The mud washed away, revealing the youthful face of a girl not much older than herself. Blood oozed from a deep gash near the base of her neck. Bella rubbed the salve into the wound. Within seconds it started working, knitting the skin together like magic.

The woman gasped and sat up, surprising everybody.

Bella fell back on all fours.

The woman clambered away and rejoined her tribe. The boys threw their spears aside and the entire tribe dropped to their knees, bowing with outstretched arms.

Bella picked herself up, shocked. Were they praying? To her? She just wanted to help the woman, not become a revered godlike healer.

'What do we do now?' Bella asked.

'Guide them to safety, with as little interaction as possible,' Nocao said. 'Your actions have profoundly influenced this tribe, and possibly the entire species.'

'Is that a bad thing?'

'Only time can answer that question.'

Bella doubted her actions. Had she done something wrong? Only one person had experience with something like this, Sean. He lived a similar situation on Earth 10,000 years ago, where every interaction with their human ancestors had untold repercussions on their future. He might be able to reassure her of her actions. But she wasn't ready to let him in yet. She inadvertently glanced in Sean's direction, finding his gaze filled with compassion and understanding.

Deep inside, she wanted to forgive him, but her scars of betrayal were yet to fade.

— CHAPTER 12 —

The Reptilians

The immense reptile crashed through the trees, snapping solid trunks like twigs. Each thunderous stomp shook the ravine. Senetep watched from a safe distance, high up on the edge of a cliff. He glanced at his data pad, comparing the creature below to information gleaned from humanity's internet. The beast resembled an allosaurus, a carnivorous giant that roamed Earth long before the human infestation. Human palaeontologists called them dinosaurs; a reptilian species wiped from existence 200 million years ago.

This new primordial planet was lush with life and crawling with the behemoths, just like Earth in the distant past.

The allosaurus moved in, attracted by the cries of an injured stegosaurus. It placed one giant foot on its plump torso, sniffed around, then crunched its head with one sickening bite.

Senetep peered over the cliff and smiled. Their bait had worked.

Erund Griss and a squad of warriors emerged from their hiding spots at the base of the ravine. They encircled the allosaurus and fired their staves, concentrating on its legs. The creature roared and spun about, snapping at the aggressors. Its immense tail felled trees, showering Erund and his team with leaves, vines, and broken branches. They looked like vulnerable insects compared to the creature.

The squad held their position and the barrage finally took its toll. The allosaurus gave a final roar and toppled right where they had planned.

THUD!

The impact trembled the walls of the ravine.

Senetep made his way down the steep rock face. From ground level, the fallen allosaurus was more intimidating than any hybrid he had created. Such a creature in the Great Arena would have been a formidable addition to his line-up. Senetep stood in front of its open mouth, admiring the terrifying rows of blood-soaked teeth. The allosaurus's great yellow eye focused on him. It gasped for each cavernous breath, moments from death.

Erund approached, reading off a data pad. 'I've just received a message from our crew on the *Ragarn*. Our surveillance probes have detected an Isharkute vessel on the previous planet.'

'On the planet?! What about the neurotoxin?'

'The missile was destroyed before completing its full deployment. This confirms what we suspected: we're being followed. I don't understand. How could Neberun's forces find us so fast without your map to the *Spearhead*?'

'Outside our crew, no Isharkute have seen the map.'

'How did they find us then?'

'Sean Livingstone,' Senetep groaned. 'He saw my *Spearhead* map before I condemned him to death in the labyrinth. I did not expect his immature brain to retain the information.'

'You did not expect him to live, either.'

The allosaurus sighed its final breath, sending a swirl of leaves into the air.

Erund slung his stave over his shoulder. 'We're done here. We can pull back and wait for the scavengers to emerge from the jungle. The reptilians won't be far behind.'

'Are the neural control shards ready?'

'Yes,' Erund said. His wrist bracer beeped. 'But the scavengers are converging quicker than expected.'

'They smell the blood. Retreat to the safety of the *Ragarn*.'

Senetep led the march out of the ravine, watching the jungle with a wary eye. The reptilian species they were hunting made him uneasy. The upright bi-pedal vertebrates remained unseen, leaving only the stripped white bones of unfortunate victims in their wake.

Tracking their heat signatures revealed the reptilians hunted in packs and were drawn to sites where dinosaurs congregated in a feeding frenzy. Their lean muscular physique, extended cranium, and long arms and fingers resembled something between a human and Isharkute.

Senetep returned to the *Ragarn's* bridge and observed the allosaurus carcass through the viewscreen.

Swarms of small two-legged dinosaurs scurried from the undergrowth and tore at the leathery wall of skin. The skinny scavengers squealed, screeched, and climbed over each other to feast on the bloody meat.

A larger species resembling velociraptors sprang from the trees. They landed on top of the distended ribcage and shredded the meat using their clawed toes.

Erund examined the incoming data. Each new dinosaur was being scanned and recorded into the *Ragarn's* crystalline memory banks. 'Strange... Many of these species resemble fossils of creatures indigenous to Earth. How is that possible?'

'It means the *Spearhead* is seeding planets with the same DNA blueprints, leaving evolution to decide what lives and what dies.'

'The reptilians have evolved at an unprecedented rate.'

'The same might have occurred on Earth if the dinosaurs weren't killed by an asteroid strike. That single event changed the course of evolution and gave rise to the hominid infestation.'

The allosaurus was suddenly cast into shadow. A gigantic reptilian bird with a long beak lined with razor-sharp teeth landed on the carcass, squawking the raptors away. The pack scattered, screeching at the winged intruder.

'That's a pterodactyl!' Erund said. He analysed the data with a growing enthusiasm. 'Its wingspan is longer than the allosaurus.'

'The reptilians are closing in,' Senetep said, eyeing the hologram of the ravine. The heat signatures converged, closing off the ravine from all angles, leaving no escape for the dinosaurs feasting on the allosaurus and stegosaurus.

'What if they don't take the bait?'

'They will,' Senetep replied with a twinge of excitement. He missed the thrill of a vicious kill. 'They can't resist. Their insatiable desire to feed is a primal, undeniable instinct.'

The first attack came with the speed and voracity of an energy blast. A green-yellow blur sent the pterodactyl sprawling down the far side of the allosaurus carcass. There was a dreadful squawk and a rigid wing extended skyward.

The velociraptors lifted their heads out of the bloody meat, sensed the danger, and sprinted for the trees.

The unseen attacker finished with the pterodactyl and crawled atop the allosaurus, sniffing the air with its forked tongue. The tall humanoid reptilian was covered in yellow scales that changed to olive green down its back, arms, and legs. It had a broad, snake-like head, with bulbous black eyes and a wide, flattened neck like that of a cobra. Two lean muscular arms ended with elongated hands and prolonged claws.

The rest of the pack joined the carnage with blurring speed, bounding enormous lengths in a single pounce. Their legs were digitigrade in form, like the hind legs of a cat, allowing them to run on their toes – a unique evolutionary quirk that accounted for their incredible speed and agility.

'Magnificent species,' Senetep said, admiring their graceful dance of death.

Evolution still had an edge over hybrid creation, something that couldn't be replicated in a lab no matter how many species he had to experiment with.

Erund moved his hand over the control panel, preparing to trigger the trap.

'Don't be so anxious,' Senetep said. 'Wait until they're closer together. We can't afford one reptilian to get free.'

The reptilians killed the troublesome velociraptors and left the smaller dinosaurs to scurry back into the jungle. They moved onto the allosaurus and tore the meat from its giant ribcage in long digestible strips. Unlike the previous scavengers, the reptilians were methodical and well-ordered. They collected the bloody strips in piles, leaving behind a wall of gleaming white ribs. Once finished, the reptilians gathered their haul and darted for the jungle.

'Now!' Senetep cried.

Erund slammed the holographic trigger.

CRACK!

The burst of energy boomed through the jungle like thunder. The reptilians went rigid, caught amidst a network of hidden electrical emitters. Waves of glowing energy crackled over their bodies, but they continued to move, clawing and clambering for the jungle.

'No creature can withstand that amount of energy,' Erund said. 'Double the output!'

The viewscreen dimmed and flickered as the bridge crew directed extra current from the *Ragarn's* power crystals.

BOOM!

The emitters exceeded their limits and exploded, showering the jungle in sparks. The reptilians succumbed to the sudden power spike and collapsed in smouldering heaps.

'Are they dead?'

Erund adjusted the scans. 'No. Judging by their physiology, their brain activity has dropped to the equivalent of a reptile in hibernation. They appear unconscious.'

'For how long?'

'Impossible to say.'

Senetep led the way off the bridge. 'We don't have time to waste standing around surmising.'

Erund and the squad followed him down the gangway, leaving the safety of the *Ragarn* behind. They marched into the ravine on high alert, weapons crackling at full power. The reptilians lay sprawled out like giant lizards basking in the sun. Their lidless gloss-black eyes reflected the world like a dark crystal ball, making it impossible to tell if they were unconscious.

'What if we're the ones being lured into a trap now?' Erund whispered. 'They look like they're playing dead, waiting to strike.'

'Quiet!' Senetep hissed. He stood back and watched from a safe distance.

The warriors spread out quietly among the serpentine bodies and placed the small crystalline control chips on the back of their heads. Even the brawniest warriors appeared puny and vulnerable next to the prehistoric predators.

The control chips were used for hybrid training. Without them, it would have been impossible to tame the species of the air and water.

The final warrior raised his hand, signalling they were done.

At that exact moment, a deep pounding sound reverberated through the ravine. Erund glanced at his scanner and pointed to the trees lining the ravine. 'There!'

The green canopy of leaves shook and separated, pushed aside by something from below. It blocked their path to the *Ragarn*. There was no time to escape. They aimed their weapons at the wall of foliage. The pounding sped up.

Senetep steeled his grip. The vibrations raced up his legs and threw off his aim. 'Hold your positions!' he called. 'Don't move. Wait for my signal to fire.'

With one almighty stomp, the creature burst from the jungle and stopped. It stood twenty feet high, covered in grey leathery skin. The beast eyed them, lowered its head and roared, showing off rows of massive teeth.

Senetep recognised the dinosaur from the human records. 'It's a tyrannosaur. On Earth, it was an apex predator.'

'Why isn't it attacking?'

'It's posturing, displaying its dominance.'

The tyrannosaur lumbered forward, nose close to the ground, and sniffed a reptilian.

'With a taste for our reptilians,' Erund said. 'We should kill it now, protect our catch.'

'No. I have a better idea. Activate the control chips. Test them against the tyrannosaur.'

'We haven't calibrated the chips to their synapses yet. It may not work.'

Senetep slung his stave over his shoulder and snatched the

control pad off Erund. 'There's only one way to find out.' He started the program.

The reptilians stirred and rose to their feet in a calm and orderly manner. Their deadly claws hung by their sides, still dripping with allosaurus blood. They stood silent and motionless. Lethal organic robots awaiting a command.

The tyrannosaur lumbered back a step, snorting and shaking its head, keeping a watchful eye on the reptilians.

Senetep grinned. 'It appears the tyrannosaur is not the apex predator after all.' He set the beast as the target and his serpentine soldiers sprang into action.

The tyrannosaur had no hope. It snapped its jaws and swiped its heavy tail, missing every time. The reptilians evaded and attacked in a blur of green-yellow scales. Glistening red slashes appeared over the tyrannosaur's body like magic, as if the mighty beast was fighting an army of invisible blades.

'Marvellous!' Senetep cried. 'I haven't been entertained like this since the Great Arena.'

The tyrannosaur stumbled against the ravine wall and collapsed, smearing blood down the grey stone. The reptilians pounced, slashing, and stripping away the tyrannosaur's tattered flesh. The beast let out a final whine and slumped to the ground.

The reptilians straightened and stood where they finished their gruesome business, idly awaiting their next command.

'I'd argue that was a successful test,' Erund said.

'Primordial brains are easy to control. Their neural patterns are advanced compared to other species on this planet, but they still depend on three primitive instincts: hunt, kill, and feed.' Senetep handed the control pad to Erund. 'We're ready to set the final stage of our trap.'

The Ancients' pyramid was only a short distance from the ravine. Its gleaming triangular tip jutted from the jungle like a precious jewel. It was a different design to the pyramid Senetep destroyed on the previous planet. The polished casing stones were quarried from a purple gemstone and the sides sloped on a gentler, 32.5-degree angle. A third of the way up the north face was a sealed entrance, outlined within a rectangle of gleaming gold blocks.

It appeared the *Spearhead* adapted its design with each subsequent planet.

Senetep watched from his command chair as the *Ragarn* landed in an overgrown gully between the pyramid and surrounding jungle. Once settled, he left the bridge to join Erund and the warriors.

The gangway descended to a gush of hot air.

Senetep led the troupe outside.

Distant roars resonated across the steamy landscape. The air was thick with humidity. A variety of dinosaurs foraged around the gully. A pod of stegosaurs chewed at the vines smothering the lower casing stones. Several iguanodons nibbled the foliage off low-lying branches. Short armoured dinosaurs with club-like tails and stumpy heads shuffled through the leafy detritus littering the gully.

Gigantic quadrupeds, distant cousins to the Earthly brontosaurus and diplodocus, thundered through the dense jungle. These plodding monoliths remained unseen until their tiny heads and long necks poked above the treetops.

The warriors trekked around the base of the pyramid, stopping every ten paces or so to bury a sonic emitter deep in the soil.

Senetep scaled the vines entangling the lower stonework. He jumped onto the casing stones and climbed the pyramid for a clear vantage point. Sweat dripped from his brow. It was much hotter on the jungle plateau compared to the ravine. The stifling damp reminded him of the lush jungles that once surrounded his old capital on Earth. At that time, his dominance had never been more complete. He reigned in the Great Arena, was feared by all, and was served by Ranatar, the greatest First Commander he ever employed.

Senetep sighed, longing for such prosperous times.

The thought unsettled him. It was a human weakness to dwell on the things he had lost. Was their DNA altering his thoughts? Their filthy genome had saved him, but it made him weak. Before now, he had never pined for anything. Or anyone.

His callous old self died the day he was cured of the affliction.

Senetep reached the sprawling rectangle of gold blocks. He tested them with his boot. Rock solid. Just as the Ancients laid them millennia ago. Scans revealed a concealed passage directly below that led to a central chamber. His decision to leave the pyramid intact and unopened was a necessary part of the trap.

Erund joined him, dripping in sweat. 'The sonic emitters are in place. Once we activate them, there won't be a living creature within sight. The frequencies will deter anything that's not human or Isharkute. From orbit, it will appear as if the pyramid is emitting the frequency.'

'Good. The bait is set. This pyramid will be impossible to resist.'

Erund handed him a data pad of topographical scans. 'We've located a cave system in the nearby mountains, deep enough to mask the *Ragarn* from our pursuers.'

Senetep glanced at the data and handed it back. 'Good. Make the necessary arrangements.'

Erund observed the gold blocks. 'Are you having second thoughts?'

'Not at all. Why?'

'These pyramids are valuable repositories of information. It's a risk, allowing Neberun's forces access.'

'They may get inside; in fact, I'm counting on it. But they will never leave.'

'This is the second planet we've visited seeded by the *Spearhead*. Both had pyramids located on the equatorial line, left by the Ancients as a kind of manufacturer's stamp. If Earth was visited by the *Spearhead*, what happened to its pyramid? It's never been found.'

Senetep grinned. 'That's because I built my capital on top of it.'

'What?'

'When Earth was claimed by the Empire and divided amongst the overseers, I petitioned hard to claim the area. It was the warmest, most temperate zone on the planet. Everyone was vying for control, but my wealth and influence won out in the end. When I began excavations for my capital, I found the remains of an ancient pyramid buried beneath the jungle. I kept it a secret from Emperor Neberun, knowing it would jeopardise my claim on the site. There was no pool of mercury, just a central room with an empty marble box. Human archaeologists called it the King's Chamber.'

'What was it used for then?'

'I don't know. The chamber might have contained a smaller amount of the liquid mercury deep in antiquity, but there was no sign of it when I discovered it.'

'What if our ancestors removed the mercury to keep the *Spearhead* a secret? To stop its power from being used.'

'I wouldn't put it past Neberun and his scheming predecessors.'

'Doddering old fools,' Erund said. 'Now you control the secret. You understand what needs to be done with such knowledge and power. Once you have rectified the mistakes of our ancestors, the Isharkute will enter a prosperous new age.'

Senetep nodded, but something about Erund still troubled him, as if his willingness to please masked some deep, dark secret. A gaping hole existed in his memory, the day he was cured of the affliction. Did Erund give the order to use human DNA? It seemed convenient that both scientists responsible for injecting him were dead. There was one way to find out.

If Erund was in any way responsible, he would pay for it.

— CHAPTER 13 —

Jurassic Planet

Sean admired Bella's bravery and compassion. She was the driving force behind moving the marshland tribe to safe ground and tending to their wounds – a brief interaction that had a profound effect. Upon leaving the planet, the tribe bowed and prayed to them as their divine saviours. Did Bella's simple act of kindness create the foundation for a new religion? Possibly. But when was kindness ever a bad thing? Should they have left the tribe to fend for themselves and not interfered in their natural development?

Either way, Sean didn't know.

Strangely, their actions echoed Earth's history. Humanity had been visited by the Isharkute for millennia. The ancient Sumerians, Assyrians and Babylonians had documented this relationship better than any other culture. They called them the Anunnaki, a race of wise and powerful beings that passed on their knowledge so humanity could flourish. This relationship became lost to time. Until recently, humanity believed they were the only intelligent species, when in fact they were a species with amnesia.

Back on the *Heroke*, the marsh planet was now several hours behind them.

Sean sat by himself on the bridge, reviewing the data from the decimated pyramid. Aside from high levels of mercury, there was nothing significant amongst the rubble. His thoughts drifted, making it difficult to concentrate. He felt left out.

The crew kept busy plotting a course to the next wormhole. Nocao was absorbed in his work, analysing DNA samples taken from the marsh tribe. Bella sat with Ramin, entertained by colourful tales detailing his meteoric rise from Overseer to Royal Consult. She enjoyed his company. Ramin's jovial nature and egotistical perspective often had her in fits of laughter. Ramin lapped up the attention.

Sean watched Bella from the corner of his eye. When was she going to forgive him? She had been giving him the cold-shoulder since they left Akanae. It seemed like forever, and it was bringing him down. *Fair enough*, he thought. He should have told her the truth earlier. Then again, he never expected her to say yes.

There was nothing he could do to improve the situation now. He needed to suck it up. Bella would come around in her own time.

His isolation gave him a chance to reflect on his unique new ability. Did his consciousness really reach across space and time to his dad? Could he use the power whenever he wanted? Right now, he needed a little support. A friendly, comforting face.

He closed his eyes, envisioning the camp where he last saw his dad...

The flickering firelight... the tribe eating their meal... his dad drinking from a carved wooden cup... Yeesha, Nesuk, and Rootuk staring into the fire.

Sean focused on the smallest of details, hoping sheer willpower might transport him there.

A voice broke his concentration. 'We're about to enter the next wormhole.'

Sean opened his eyes, deflated. Tapping into his ability with a conscious mind seemed impossible, like trying to force himself into a dream. Until now, it only happened when he was asleep or unconscious, not something he could conjure at will.

A hologram of the next wormhole projected in the middle of the bridge.

Sean glanced at Bella, then walked over to the hologram for a closer look. The wormholes offered instantaneous jumps across the universe; short-cuts mapped by the *Spearhead*. Each one shaved billions of kilometres off their journey, but they still needed to light-speed jump between exit and entry points. Each time they did, Bella moved further in time and distance from her family on Earth.

'This wormhole jump should put us close to Senetep,' Nocao said. 'After that, each successive wormhole will widen the gap, placing us closer to the *Spearhead*.'

'Won't Senetep find the wormholes if he's going the same way as us?' Bella asked.

'I doubt it. The entry points are light-years away from the *Spearhead's* route. The likelihood of him discovering them is low.'

'And if he did,' Ramin cut in, 'he wouldn't know where the exit point was. It would be too risky.'

'Unless he found the Ancients' map like we did,' Sean said.

'Don't be so negative,' Bella said sharply.

Sean flinched, as if physically stung by her spiteful tone. He was better off keeping his mouth shut for a while.

The wormhole's event horizon appeared on the viewscreen. Stars stretched around the rim like reflections in a pool of swirling water. A dense black void hung in the middle.

The *Heroke* shuddered, then instantaneously arrived in a new corner of the universe. The scanners constructed a holographic map of the neighbouring solar systems. Planets, moons, nebulae, asteroid belts, and stars materialised in a rich tapestry of stellar formations.

Sean's stomach tingled with excitement. Space was a never-ending canvas of unexplored beauty, reminding him what sparked his interest in astro-archaeology.

Ramin stood from his command chair. 'Scan for Senetep's vessel.'

The bridge remained silent as the navigation officer checked the system. 'Nothing. It appears we beat him here.'

Sean sighed with relief.

'I've found a planet seeded by the *Spearhead*,' Nocao said.

The hologram displayed a rich, Earthlike planet with deep green continents and bright turquoise oceans. The orbiting moon shared the unique ratios of size and distance to the planet as the artificial moons built by the ancient alien vessel.

'The land, air, and water are swarming with life.'

'What sort of life?' Bella asked.

'Scans show creatures similar to ones that roamed Earth 100 million years ago. I believe you called them dinosaurs.'

'What?!' Bella and Sean said in unison, acknowledging one another with subtle grins.

The hologram showed a bird's-eye view of a jungle thriving with dinosaurs. Giant herbivores lumbered across the prehistoric landscape, foraging in herds. Gigantic pterodactyls swooped over grassy plains, casting aeroplane-sized shadows.

Nocao put his scans on the viewscreen, comparing the creatures against fossilised remains found on Earth. 'Some species resemble the tyrannosaurus, triceratops, brontosaurus, stegosaurus.'

'Wow! It's *Jurassic Park* for real,' Sean said.

'Don't you mean *Jurassic Planet*?' Bella quipped.

Sean chuckled, feeling a burst of encouragement. Bella had dropped her icy guard for a moment to let him in. 'The planets are earlier in evolution the closer we get to the *Spearhead*. It's like travelling back in time.'

'Your analogy is correct,' Nocao said. 'As we approach the *Spearhead*, seeded planets will become more primordial. Environments will become less stable, with species devolving until the principal form of life will be cellular-sized organisms. Landing on these worlds will become increasingly dangerous.'

'I'm more concerned with our immediate safety,' Ramin said. 'Keep scanning for signs of Senetep's vessel. He could drop out of light speed at any moment.'

'Running continuous scans,' the navigations officer responded.

Nocao looked up from his holographic controls with excitement. 'I've located a pyramid on the planet's equatorial line. This one is untouched.'

Ramin stepped forward. 'Show me.'

The hologram focused on a gleaming pyramid, rising from the leafy jungle foliage like a polished amethyst. The smooth casing stones reflected the midday sun in a dazzling rainbow of reflected light.

'You can see it from space,' Sean said, pointing to the planet on the bridge viewscreen. The reflection glinted from the greenery like a remote lighthouse.

Ramin shook his head. 'Incredible. I've never seen anything like it.'

'Archaeologists say the Great Pyramid would have been visible from space when it was covered in the original white limestone.'

'Intriguing. These pyramids are almost like some kind of production code.'

'If that's true, where's Earth's pyramid? The Great Pyramid fits the criteria. It's on a precise equatorial line, aligned to the cardinal points, but I thought Senetep built it.'

'Maybe not,' Nocao said. 'It's too much of a coincidence. Senetep might have discovered the original pyramid and built his capital over the top.'

'Why would he do that?'

'If the Guild of Sciences found out about an ancient alien monument, they would have forced Senetep to hand his zone over to the Empire. He would have done anything to keep it a secret.'

'It's likely he kept it a secret!' Ramin interjected. 'Senetep had the power and influence to get away with it. He's the only Isharkute with an ego bigger than mine.'

'Does Akanae have a pyramid like this?' Sean asked.

'No, but Akanae has been geographically unstable,' Nocao said. 'Our tectonic plates experienced a catastrophic shift 50 million years ago. Many of the continents on our equatorial line moved, split apart, and sank into our oceans. If there was a pyramid, it was probably destroyed millions of years ago.'

'Maybe these artificial moons are more than aggregators for life,' Sean said. 'They might be the Ancients' backup plan.'

'What do you mean?' Ramin asked.

'The Ancients knew these planets would go through environmental changes, some more severe than others. Tectonic shifts, asteroid strikes, or volcanic eruptions...there's so many things that change the face of a planet. It happened on Akanae and Earth.

The pyramids are a wake-up call to a developing species, a sign of a higher purpose and design within the universe. But if they're destroyed, the Ancients needed something just as obvious.'

'A moon,' Bella said.

'That's right. It's the perfect backup. It sits in the night sky for millions, even billions of years. Once a civilisation figures out the ratios of the moon to their planet and the nearest star, they've unlocked the first clue to the Ancients and the *Spearhead*.'

'The Moon gave us a map to the *Spearhead*. Do you think the pyramid has the same information?'

'I don't know. But we should find out.'

'Sean's right,' Nocao said. 'Senetep destroyed the previous pyramid for a reason. He discovered something he didn't want us to know about. It could be a crucial clue in our race for the *Spearhead*.'

'Then we'll explore the pyramid,' Ramin announced, turning to the bridge crew. 'Stay vigilant. If Senetep arrives, we'll need to leave in a hurry.'

Sean was certain they made the right decision. This was more exciting than finding the message inside the Moon. A pyramid was designed for terrestrial beings, containing something tangible and easier to comprehend. He wondered, did the Great Pyramid trigger Senetep's interest in the *Spearhead* and the Ancients? What was inside it when he built over the top of it? The pyramid must have been empty, even when he discovered it all those millennia ago.

The *Heroke* burst through the upper atmosphere with a shudder. The clouds cleared, revealing an unspoiled continent of lush vegetation, like the Amazon rainforest on steroids. Ahead, the purple pyramid soared over the landscape, as if a heavenly-sized gemstone had just dropped into the middle of the world.

'It's the most beautiful pyramid in the entire universe,' Bella gasped. 'Pity it's surrounded by dinosaurs. I don't want to be on a T-rex's menu.'

'You won't be,' Nocao said, examining the incoming data. 'Life readings show the dinosaurs are not going anywhere near the pyramid. They're keeping a wide berth around it.'

'Why?' Sean asked.

'The structure is emitting a high-range frequency that's keeping them away.'

'Like a dog whistle. Instead of calling them, it's pushing them away.'

'The frequency is harmless and inaudible to human and Isharkute ears. The Ancients must have put it there to protect the pyramid.'

'Good, it makes our job a little easier,' Ramin said. 'Is there an entrance?'

'The pyramid's north face has a rectangular outline embedded in gold blocks.'

'Can't get more obvious than that,' Sean said. 'They're inviting us inside.'

'Land the *Heroke* in front of the north face,' Ramin instructed. 'I want two full squads of warriors to accompany you.'

'You're not coming with us?'

'I'll stay behind and guard the *Heroke*.'

'Fair enough,' Sean replied. His next thought was to ask Bella, but that wasn't as straightforward. She was still prickly towards him. Simple conversations were impossible.

He had no idea how to make things better between them. Should he apologise again? Was it better to leave the past alone and start acting normal? She wasn't giving him a sign either way. They shared fleeting eye contact, and whenever she spoke to him it was abrupt and laced with resentment. Why was she holding onto her bad feelings for so long? It was her decision to come on the *Spearhead* mission, so her grumpiness couldn't last forever. Just to rub salt into his wound, she acted fine with everyone else.

Thinking about it, her situation wasn't so different to his.

Sean understood what it felt like being hurt by someone you trusted. He was the last to learn about his dad's engagement to Carla. For a long time, that betrayal of trust made him feel like an outsider. But he had perspective on those emotions now, realising he was never angry about their engagement; he was angry with his dad for hiding the truth.

Sean sighed to himself. Pity he didn't apply this hard-earned life lesson sooner. If he told Bella the truth from the beginning, they could have avoided all this.

The *Heroke* landed in a gully between the pyramid and the jungle. Layers of entwined roots choked every inch of soil.

Nocao led the way off the bridge. 'Okay, let's go.'

Bella followed, cutting abruptly in front of Sean. She glared over her shoulder, as if to warn him against saying anything.

Ramin observed their interaction and chuckled with amusement. 'And I thought female Isharkute held a grudge!'

Sean shrugged. 'That's okay. I deserve it.'

'Stay focused. Look after each other. Don't let your emotions jeopardise the mission.'

Sean nodded. It wasn't up to him. Bella had their relationship in a chokehold. Things would only improve when she was ready.

The gangway opened with a hiss of pressurised air. An oppressive wall of humidity rushed into the *Heroke*. A distant rumble of thunder rolled over the jungle. Sean peered around. There were no storm clouds, just blue sky. The noise was something else, something living. He suddenly realised it was the pounding of a billion dinosaur feet, vibrating like the beating heart of the planet.

Sean, Bella and Nocao were armed with energy staves and surrounded by warriors. Even with all this protection, Sean was still nervous. He'd seen *Jurassic Park* enough times to know what a raptor or tyrannosaur was capable of.

Sean stepped off the gangway. The entire planet heaved under the weight of its prehistoric inhabitants. A titanic roar echoed over the treetops. Bella recoiled and bumped into him.

'Sorry,' she whispered, half-smiling.

Sean perked up. That was the nicest Bella had been to him in a while.

The warriors climbed over the first hurdle of roots and pointed out a path up to the outline of gold casing stones, thirty metres up the pyramid face.

'Sean, Bella, go ahead with the first squad,' Nocao said.

'Where are you going?' Sean asked.

'To investigate the signal repelling the dinosaurs. There's one close to here, emanating from the pyramid's foundation blocks.'

'We should stay together,' Bella said, sounding concerned.

'I'll be a few minutes behind you,' Nocao assured her. 'Go with the squad and work out how to open the pyramid.'

Nocao marched up the gully, taking two of the warriors for protection.

Sean peered up the face of the pyramid. The first squad pressed on without waiting. There was no time to question Nocao's decision. 'We'd better start climbing,' he said. 'Do you want to go first?'

Bella nodded and pressed on. She climbed fast, striding over the thick vines as though she was trying to run away from him. Athleticism was a Bonaforte family trait. Her aunt Carla was a professional rock climber and would be proud to see her niece now.

A piercing screech cut through the air.

Sean and Bella ducked and spun about. A kilometre away, a giant pterodactyl swooped over the jungle and jabbed its immense beak through the trees, throwing up a fountain of shredded foliage. It snatched up a human-sized hadrosaur and glided off.

'Mio Dio!' Bella said. 'We're easy targets up here.'

'They won't come anywhere near us as long as that signal stays on.'

'Si. I doubt even you could outfly one of those giants.'

Sean's shoulder blades tingled at the thought. His wings felt as if they had regrown to full size. He ruffled them under his shirt, surprised to feel a cool breeze down his back. The thought of flying on this planet made him nervous. He just wanted to get the job done and leave before Senetep arrived.

CHAPTER 14

Ancient Updates

Sean gazed down upon the prehistoric jungle. It had taken them ten minutes to climb a third of the way up the pyramid face. From here, he could see how the jungle was slowly devouring the monolithic structure with its unstoppable tendrils. Give nature another fifty years and the pyramid would be swallowed whole by the environment.

Even at this height, a layer of ivy clung to the purple casing stones, held in place by centuries of accumulated dirt and mulch.

The warriors knelt around the rectangular outline of gold casing blocks reflecting through the carpet of ivy. They scanned the blocks, working on a way to open the passage beneath their feet.

Bella climbed several paces higher. 'If this is a door, the Ancients must have been a race of giants.'

'Explains why they built everything so big,' Sean said, striding up to join her.

'We've found the mechanism,' a warrior said. 'Stand back.'

Sean and Bella stepped outside the golden rectangle. The warrior adjusted his handheld scanner. A low hum resonated from the gold blocks.

'What are you doing?' Bella asked.

The warrior ignored her.

Bella placed her hands on her hips and huffed. '*Che maleducato!*'

Sean agreed, the warrior came across as rude. But as a race, the Isharkute did not indulge in unnecessary questions and small talk, particularly the warrior class. The stone-faced warriors remained focused on opening the pyramid, not answering the questions of a human girl.

'What are they doing?'

Sean had rerouted enough Isharkute power conduits to recognise the glyphs streaming across the warrior's device. 'He's sending an electrical current into the gold blocks.'

'Why?'

'There's a mechanism behind them. Gold is the perfect electrical conductor. It doesn't corrode like other metals. If the Ancients wanted to show us a way inside, this is the most direct way.'

A deep rumble echoed from within the pyramid and the twelve casing stones inside the golden rectangle shifted, sending a shock wave up the slope.

Bella jumped back. 'Whoa!'

The blocks ripped away from the ivy and retracted into the pyramid. The ivy snapped and flicked back like broken rubber bands, showering everyone with leaves and loose soil. A rush of cool air escaped the interior. The blocks continued in, rotated, and retracted from view, leaving a gargantuan passage descending into darkness.

Sean and Bella shared an incredulous look.

The lead warrior moved inside and activated his stave, guided by the light from its glowing blue crystal. The warriors filed after him and marched down the passage.

'Do we follow them?' Bella asked.

Sean wasn't sure. He peered down the pyramid. Nocao had disappeared in the overgrown gully, searching for the mysterious signal repelling the dinosaurs. He stepped into the passage and called after the warriors. 'Should we wait for Nocao?'

There was no answer, just the echo of his voice within the pyramid.

'So, it's not just me,' Bella said. 'They don't like talking much, do they?'

'Not really.'

'What do we do? We can't wait here.'

'We should stick to the plan.' Sean unslung his stave and twisted the activator handle. The forks snapped open and bristled with energy. 'You go first; I'll cover you from behind.'

Bella unslung her stave and activated the handle in one slick move, like she had done it a thousand times before. 'Si, but who covers you?'

'I'll be all right. Nocao won't be far behind.'

The passage descended on a gentle slope, levelled out, then ascended at a sharp 40-degree angle into the centre of the pyramid. Daylight disappeared behind them. The smooth walls, mortarless joints, vaulted ceiling, and steep incline copied the Grand Gallery in Egypt's Great Pyramid. Except here, everything was scaled up, at least three times the size.

After an arduous climb, the passage levelled out again.

The warriors stopped to examine six large niches in the wall, three on each side of the passage. Each one housed a large rectangular box carved from a single block of polished black stone.

'They must be 100 tonnes each,' Sean said. 'Even more with their lids.'

'Are they coffins?' Bella asked.

'You mean sarcophagi,' he corrected her.

Bella regarded him, eyes blazing over the glow of her weapon. 'Are you trying to be annoying?'

Sean bit his lip. He didn't mean to sound condescending, even though his comment came across that way. It proved he wasn't in her good books yet.

'Well?' she said, nudging him for a response. 'What are they?'

'I'm not sure. They look like sarcophagi...I mean coffins.'

Bella sighed and rolled her eyes.

One of the warriors finished scanning the boxes with his crystal tablet. 'They're empty.'

'Just like Saqqara,' Sean whispered to himself.

Bella glared. 'What did you say?'

'Nothing.'

Further on, the passage opened into a large chamber dominated by a central circular pool. The warriors spread out, searching the shadowy alcoves and connecting passages.

Sean approached the pool. Their staves reflected across the inky black surface with perfect clarity.

'Is that water?' Bella asked.

Sean peered over the edge. His anxious face stared back at him. The surface lay perfect and still, more like a solid mirror than a liquid. He deactivated his stave, slung it over his shoulder and reached out.

'Hey!' Bella said. 'I don't think you should be doing that.'

Sean paused, hovering over his reflection. Bella was right. What was he thinking? A slight ripple appeared, like a pebble dropping into a still pond. The disturbance stretched outwards and suctioned to his fingertip for a second, then retracted back into the pool.

'Ugh! That's not water!' Bella shrieked. 'It's alive.'

Sean jumped back and shook his hand. 'What was that?'

The warriors stepped back and aimed their staves at the pool.

'It's liquid mercury,' one of them called, checking his scanner.

The mercury swirled and levitated high into the chamber, like a swimming pool of silver flipped upside down in zero gravity. The vortex separated into blobs, then organised itself into patterns.

'I'm not big on science,' Bella said. 'But they look like chemical elements.'

The patterns rotated over their heads, then split apart and formed into two long chains. They coiled around each other, joined by rungs resembling a twirling ladder.

'That's a double-helix.' Sean said.

'What's that?'

'A strand of DNA, the genetic blueprints for life.'

The strand disintegrated into millions of tiny spheres. At first it appeared random and messy, but there was something familiar about the dense clusters.

Sean pointed to a sphere with rings. 'It's a galactic map!'

Countless worlds swished over their heads, morphing and realigning, as if they were travelling through the stars. The planets became familiar. Uranus, Saturn, Jupiter, Mars, and then Earth. The mercury slowed down, aligning the Sun, Moon, and Earth in a solar eclipse.

'That's Earth!' Bella remarked.

'I think it sampled my DNA and traced me back to Earth,' Sean said, glancing at his finger.

The mercury then split into millions of minuscule spheres, some as tiny as a grain of sand. They swirled outwards, filling the chamber with a dense spiral pattern. It was a complete map of the galaxy, more detailed than any Isharkute hologram. Razor-thin lines of mercury traced their way between the specks of silver, glistening like a spider's web caught in torchlight.

'What's going on?' Bella asked.

'I think it's showing us how to find the *Spearhead* and get back to Earth. But there're way more wormholes. Some stretch all the way.'

Bella stared at him, eyes brimming with hope. 'A quicker way home?'

Sean was careful in his reply. He didn't want to get Bella's hopes up only to crush them later. 'I'm not sure, but it has way more information than the sphere we found inside Earth's Moon.' He regarded the warrior scanning the mercury. 'Make sure you record everything. We can add this data to our maps.'

Bella moved closer to Sean. 'Why is this map better than the one we found in the Moon?'

'I'm guessing the *Spearhead* maps the universe as it travels, then sends the new data back to the all the moons it constructed.'

'Like an update from the Ancients?'

'Exactly.'

'Why was the map inside our Moon so out of date?'

'One of the artificial moons between here and Earth could have been destroyed, interrupting the signal. Or maybe our pyramid was broken, and the Moon got stuck with an old update. The *Spearhead* left Earth billions of years ago. That's a long time for something to go wrong.'

'Why does the *Spearhead* send the updates?'

'Because it wants to be found. The moons act like antennas. They repeat that signal through the universe and download it to the liquid mercury inside the planet's pyramid.'

'That's why Senetep destroyed the last pyramid?'

Sean stomach went cold with the realisation. 'He found the updated map! He'll beat us to the *Spearhead*.'

The mercury swirled into a central vortex and returned to the empty pool. Sean watched it, wide-eyed, speechless, as though all his hope was being sucked into the dense liquid.

Hurried footsteps echoed up the passage. Nocao raced into chamber holding a crystal cube. 'We found this hidden in the roots! It's an Isharkute sonic emitter.'

'Senetep beat us here!' Sean said.

'As soon as we dug it up, the signal stopped. The pyramid wasn't responsible for repelling the dinosaurs, it was this! Senetep wanted us inside the pyramid.'

'It's a trap,' Bella said.

'The dinosaurs are returning from the jungle. We need to get back to the *Heroke* before it's too late.'

Nocao hustled everyone out of the chamber and led the sprint outside. Distant roars echoed along the passage, reverberating ominously through the pyramid.

They burst into the harsh daylight. A pterodactyl swooped overhead, casting a 747-sized shadow across the pyramid face. Far below, the trees bordering the gully swayed, cracked, and shook. Unseen behemoths approached, crashing paths through the foliage.

'Hurry up,' Nocao called out, racing down the casing stones. 'No time for sightseeing!'

Sean trailed Bella, watching over her and the sky. The pterodactyl could dive in at any moment and pluck one of them up for lunch. His wings tingled, eager to burst free and glide him to safety. They scrambled over the roots entangling the foundation blocks and raced up the gully.

One hundred metres away, Ramin stood on the *Heroke's* gangway, waving them on. 'Hurry up!'

Sean, Bella and Nocao raced neck and neck along the gully. The warriors kept pace, forming a defensive circle around them. The ground trembled, as if the world had been disturbed from a peaceful slumber.

The trees to their left burst apart in a shower of leaves.

Six black claws, as large as a forearm, emerged from the plants, followed by an enormous jaw filled with glistening teeth.

Sean thought it was a T-rex, until he saw the tall spined fan running along its scaly back. A spinosaurus! The creature stood eight metres tall, and that was stooped over. It thundered into the gully ahead, cutting them off from the *Heroke*. The spinosaurus walked on two powerful legs and sported a pair of muscular human-like arms adorned with giant claws.

Everyone stopped.

Bella screamed. Nocao covered her mouth. Too late. The spinosaurus turned on them and exhaled a deep raspy breath, tilting its head, focusing its beady green eyes on them.

Behind them, a second dinosaur lumbered from the jungle. It was half the height of the spinosaurus and built like a tank, with four stocky legs, an armoured back, and a club tail. It resembled an ankylosaurus. The dinosaurs roared at each other.

Sean and Bella covered their ears, blocking out the deafening noise. The ankylosaurus pounded the ground with its tail, rocking the gully, shaking loose leaves from the trees.

'We're the meat in the sandwich,' Sean said.

Bella glared at him. 'You think so?!'

'Sean's right,' Nocao said. 'It's a standoff. The winner gets us for lunch.'

Bella glanced in both directions. 'What do we do?'

'When they attack each other...run!'

The warriors closed around them in a defensive circle, weapons aimed in front and behind. The spinosaurus launched first, claws spread, mouth agape, wide enough to swallow a car. It split their group in two, knocking everyone aside as it charged the ankylosaurus. The warriors spun about and fired at its exposed underbelly. The spinosaurus flinched and kept running. The ankylosaurus turned sideways and clubbed the spinosaurus in the flank with its huge tail. The carnivore screeched in pain and collapsed against the pyramid. With the spinosaurus down, there was a clear path to the *Heroke*.

'RUN!' Nocao screamed.

Everyone burst into a life-saving sprint for the gangway. The titanic tussle behind them sounded like it was tearing the world apart.

Sean didn't dare turn around. He made sure Bella kept pace with him the entire way. Forty metres to go, thirty-five...

Just then, an Isharkute vessel emerged from the far side of the pyramid and hovered in place, canons aimed at the *Heroke*. Senetep!

Ramin waved them onto the gangway, oblivious to the impending danger.

Nocao waved back, screaming at the top of his lungs. 'Get out of there!'

Sean grabbed Bella and Nocao by the arms and pulled them towards a clump of log-sized roots next to the pyramid, diving for cover as...

BOOM!

A blinding white light went off like a flash bang. Superheated air blasted over their heads, searing the exposed roots. The three of them huddled tight as the world burned around them. Chunks of the *Heroke* smashed into the pyramid and slid down the side, tearing the vines and foliage off the casing blocks.

The heatwave passed and Sean poked his head over the smouldering roots.

The *Heroke* was gone. Spot fires raged throughout the jungle. The spinosaurus lay on its side, half its body charred and smoking. The ankylosaurus floundered on its back, pounding the ground with its clubbed tail, trying to right itself. There was no sign of Ramin or the warriors.

Senetep's vessel shifted position, recharging its canons, poised to pick off any survivors brave enough to emerge from the carnage.

Sean ducked out of sight. 'We have to get inside the pyramid.'

'How?' Nocao said. 'Those canons will wipe us out with one blast.'

Bella pointed skyward. '*Guarda!*'

A flock of pterodactyls swooped onto Senetep's vessel, attracted to the hum of the engines. They clung to the hull, smashing and sawing their immense beaks over the metal, attempting to crack it open like a giant egg.

'Now's our chance!' Sean said. 'We run back down the gully, climb the pyramid using the path we took before. It's the easiest way through the roots.'

'Go, lead the way!' Nocao said.

They sprinted through the gully, dodging the flames and white-hot hunks of metal. Four warriors stumbled from the debris, battered and bleeding but alive.

'Follow us!' Bella called.

To their right, the spinosaurus staggered to its feet. Blackened skin cracked and flaked off the roasted side of its body. It stood on the helpless ankylosaurus and slashed the exposed skin of its pale belly wide open.

Sean reached the gap in the roots and began the climb.

The spinosaurus spun around, attracted to the movement.

'Climb as fast as you can!' Sean cried.

Monstrous footsteps thundered up behind them, shaking the casing stones. The spinosaurus snapped up the warrior at the back of their group. It flipped him into the air, opened its jaws, and caught his body with a sickening crunch.

'Hide!' Nocao shrieked.

Everyone dived into the roots and vegetation growing over the blocks. The spinosaurus ripped off the vines with its teeth and burrowed its snout amongst the roots, sniffing for the next tasty morsel.

RIP! The warrior beside Bella was torn from his hiding spot by one leg. He dangled upside down from the creature's mouth, firing his stave. *BOOM! BOOM! BOOM!* The spinosaurus flung the warrior half a kilometre away over the jungle and clambered sideways, slipping awkwardly as the roots ripped off the casing stones. It shoved its head into a clump of roots and came eye to eye with Bella. Her mouth dropped open in a silent scream.

Sean watched, petrified, unable to move.

The spinosaurus bared its bloodstained teeth and exhaled, blasting her hair with a gust of hot stinky breath. It paused, made a strange whimpering sound, and withdrew its head from the roots. The monster clambered down the pyramid.

Bella remained frozen in position.

Sean peeked through the roots. The spinosaurus stood in the gully, facing the jungle. It lowered its head and swayed from side to side, cowering to something. Sean poked his head clear and saw a group of humanoid reptilians standing amongst the trees. Their lithe upright bodies were covered in yellow and dark-green scales. They had huge black eyes, flared necks like a cobra, and lethal, metre-long claws.

The spinosaurus skulked off, head down, tail dragging on the ground in a show of submission. It had little effect. The reptilians attacked the carnivore from all sides, savaging its mighty body with blistering speed.

Sean crawled over to Bella and grabbed her hand. She flinched in terror.

'You're okay,' Sean whispered. 'Keep climbing!'

They reached the gold-framed passage and spun around. The spinosaurus made a horrible gurgling sound and collapsed, shredded of skin like a carcass in an abattoir. The reptilians emerged from the carnage, claws glistening with fresh blood.

'Get inside, close the door!' Nocao shouted, pushing Sean inside.

'I don't know how.'

'Get to the central chamber, we'll figure it out from there.'

The reptilians leapt over the roots, clearing multiple casing stones in a single pounce, on a straight line for the entrance. Senetep's vessel swung into view and hovered over the jungle, aiming at the passage. BOOM! BOOM! The onboard cannons blasted the pterodactyls off the hull.

Sean turned and sprinted down the passage. A chilling sensation filled the pit of his stomach. With no weapons, no escape vessel, and no way to close the pyramid; they were running towards certain death.

— CHAPTER 15 —

Deadly Reunion

Bella raced after Nocao, stumbling over his heels in panic and desperation. Sean kept pace behind her, followed by the last two warriors. Their heavy breathing and footfalls echoed through the pyramid, enhancing the claustrophobic terror. They raced past the stone boxes, up the passage, and emerged in the main chamber.

The warriors stood guard, weapons aimed back the way they came. 'Is there a way to close this chamber?' one of them said.

Sean raced around the chamber, running his hands along the stone walls. 'There might be a hidden passage. If we can find–'

'We don't have time for that,' Nocao said. 'Think of something else.'

'Like what?' Bella said. She backed up to the mercury pool, accidentally kicking something across the floor. It was the sonic emitter Nocao dropped earlier. She picked up the crystalline cube and handed it to Nocao. 'Senetep used this to keep the dinosaurs away. Can you turn it on? It might turn those lizard people away.'

Sean stopped what he was doing and rushed over. 'Great idea!'

Nocao placed the emitter on the floor and knelt over it, unclipping the handheld scanner from his belt. A sequence of glyphs appeared across the screen. 'It's encrypted. I need time to break it. I don't know if–'

'Just try,' Bella said. 'It's all we've got.'

Nocao started typing over the glyphs, changing the order.

Bella held her breath and crossed her fingers. Everyone went quiet. All she could hear was her pounding heart, hammering like a fist inside her chest. The emitter glowed bright blue for a second and deactivated.

'Ugh! I almost had it,' Nocao groaned. He continued typing fresh sequences of glyphs into the scanner. His fingers moved so fast they became a blur.

'Hurry up!' Sean whispered.

'Shh!' Bella hissed. 'He's doing his best. Let him concentrate.'

A grating sound filled the chamber, like fingernails down a blackboard. Bella clenched her teeth.

Sean looked at her, horrified. 'Those creatures are inside the pyramid.'

'How do you know?'

'I know that sound. It's talons on stone.'

The emitter glowed to life, then died again. Nocao shook his head and sighed in exasperation. 'I can't break the encryption.'

The warriors opened fire, illuminating the gloomy passage with energy blasts. The boom and crackle reverberated through the chamber, amplified in the enclosed space.

Bella covered her ringing ears.

The reptilians struck so fast it appeared the warriors fell apart for no reason. Their severed arms dropped to the floor, still gripping their staves.

Bella turned away in horror.

Sean grabbed her arm and rushed around to the far side of the pool. Nocao grabbed the emitter and followed, head down, using every second to crack the encryption.

The eight-foot-tall reptilians entered, stepping over the gory remains. Their taloned feet clanged across the stone floor. They passed the blood-splattered walls and encircled the pool, coming at them from both sides, cold and robotic. The black vertical pupils of their reptilian eyes were devoid of emotion. They resembled mindless killing automatons.

Bella's legs trembled hard. She glimpsed the devastating, blood-soaked talons protruding from their scaly fingers. One swipe would cleave all three of them straight through. This was it. They were about to die.

Sean edged in front of her and whispered, 'Close your eyes.'

In that moment, Bella realised her terrible mistake. She should have forgiven Sean sooner. He only kept the truth from her because he cared. Now, in their final moments, he was showing his true self – placing his life before hers.

'I'm sorry,' Bella whispered in his ear. She felt his body relax. With seconds to live, at least she had given him some comfort. The knot inside her chest eased a little. She covered his eyes with her hands and buried her face into his shoulder. 'Don't look.'

The clang of talons closed in.

Bella pictured her family. With Sean in her arms and her family in her mind, she would not die alone. She held her breath, waiting for the inevitable. Nothing. No searing pain. No noise. Had it happened? Was she already dead? Her pounding heart was the only sign she was still alive.

A slow and deliberate clap echoed through the chamber.

Sean gently removed her hands from his face.

Bella opened her eyes. The reptilians stood in a semicircle around them, claws by their sides, dead still, as if flicked off by a switch. A tall, physically imposing Isharkute strode in front of the blank reptilians, clapping in a slow and unsettling rhythm. Behind him, a squad of warriors lined up around the chamber.

'Senetep!' Sean whispered over his shoulder.

'We would've been better off dead,' Nocao muttered, pushing the emitter out of sight with his heel.

Bella had never seen the heinous Overseer in the flesh. Senetep's muscular stature and imposing height enhanced his menacing presence. He stopped, glaring down over his white gemstone-braided beard.

'Sean Livingstone,' Senetep said, crossing his arms. 'You never fail to entertain.'

'I do my best,' Sean said dryly.

Bella pulled Sean closer. His trembling body undermined his bravado.

Senetep acknowledged Nocao. 'Pity you sided with Sean and

his useless species. You could have been a valuable addition to my science team. Given a chance, you might have atoned for your father's misguided research.'

'I'm glad to disappoint you,' Nocao said.

Senetep sneered at Bella and focused on Sean. 'Last time we met, I clipped your wings. By sheer luck and chance, you prevailed. This time...I will finish the job myself.'

Bella glanced at Nocao, desperate for a glimmer of hope. Nocao stood hard against the wall, hiding the emitter behind his boot.

'But you're cured!' Sean said. 'Last time we met, your arms were covered in bruises. You were sick with the affliction.'

'How's that possible?' Nocao cut in. 'Human DNA holds the only known cure. You would never...'

Senetep narrowed his eyes. Bella sensed his growing contempt, rising to boiling point beneath his cool blue facade.

'Maybe humans aren't useless after all,' Sean said. 'It proves we're all connected. We're all part of the same biological blueprint left behind by the Ancients. Our DNA might be different, but deep down, we're the same.'

Senetep's calculating eyes flickered with recognition. 'An error on behalf of the Ancients. Once I control the *Spearhead*, I'll wipe the universe clean. Rewrite life as I please, starting with your precious Earth.'

Sean drew breath to speak, then–

Whack! A powerful backhand ripped Sean from Bella's arm and sent him sprawling.

Bella stood, exposed and trembling before the Overseer. Sean slumped against the wall, his back to her. His back heaved like he was sobbing, but he was silent.

'We've been playing this game for too long,' Senetep said. 'Erund, spin him around to face me.'

One of the Isharkute stepped forward and grabbed Sean by the collar.

'Erund Griss?!' Nocao scoffed. 'Couldn't you have found a better First Commander? I guess you don't have the power and connections you once had.'

'Silence him!' Senetep barked.

A warrior smashed Nocao in the stomach with his stave. Nocao dropped to his knees, doubled over and gasping for breath.

Erund wrenched Sean away from the wall.

Bella shrieked. Sean had a gaping cut across his brow and his face was wet with fresh blood. His eye was swollen shut and purple. He swayed, delirious and confused. Senetep struck him again, sending him crashing into her. Sean collapsed at her feet, hunched on all fours.

'Stop it!' Bella cried.

'Silence the female,' Senetep said.

Bella leant over Sean's crumpled body. Erund heaved her aside. She rolled across the floor and bumped into the cold scaly leg of a reptilian. She scrambled away.

Senetep kicked Sean in the ribs with so much force it lifted him off the floor. Sean landed facedown, flat on the stone, barely moving. Senetep kicked him again and again. Crunching, cracking his ribs. The sickening thuds were unbearable. Sean's gasps became less frequent. He was being beaten to death.

Bella looked askance at Nocao, desperate for action. He remained crouched where he fell, head down, fixated on cracking the emitter's encryption.

Bella clung to a sliver of hope. They had one chance, no matter how small. Nocao was already figuring a way out of this.

Senetep kicked Sean against the wall of the pool.

Bella turned away. She couldn't watch any more cruelty. Nocao waved at her and pointed to floor. His message was clear. *Get down!* Bella nodded. The emitter turned bright blue, drawing everyone's attention.

Senetep spun around, his confounded expression highlighted by the glowing cube. 'Destroy that emitter!'

The device created a piercing, high-pitched whistle, then exploded in a storm of sparks and electrical forks. The reptilians swayed on their feet, then sprang to life, flicking their serpentine heads about. They hissed over forked tongues, claws and talons poised to strike.

'The reptilians control chips have short-circuited!' Erund squealed.

'Kill them!' Senetep screamed.

The warriors turned their weapons on the reptilians and fired point-blank, killing two of the creatures instantly. The pack split, striking down the warriors with their claws. Senetep and Erund dashed for the exit.

Nocao scrambled over to Sean's crumpled body. 'Help me get him into the pool.'

'That's not water. It's liquid mercury,' Bella said.

'Then hold your breath,' Nocao said, dragging Sean up to the edge. 'This fight will be over in seconds. It's the only place to hide.'

Bella peeked over the edge of the pool wall. The one-sided battle was almost over. Senetep's warriors were being decimated. Their training and advanced weapons were no match for the primitive species. Once the warriors were dead, they were next.

Nocao pinched Sean's nose and mouth shut, then plunged backwards into the pool.

Bella closed her eyes, pinched her nose, and followed.

The liquid mercury suctioned to her body, heavy and dense, like she dropped into a vat of viscous oil. Her instinct was to swim for the surface, but something unexpected happened. The cool metal lowered her to the bottom of the pool, forming a breathable pocket of air around her body. Her bubble joined with Sean and Nocao's bubble. The surrounding wall of silver distorted their astonished expressions into comical faces, just like an amusement park mirror.

The mercury parted, leaving them sitting on the bare stone blocks at the bottom of the pool. It gathered and swirled over their heads. The upside down vortex resembled water emptying from a bath. Soon there was enough space to sit up. The mercury rose above the pool wall and kept rising.

Nocao craned his head around. 'What's going on?'

'We started the sequence.'

'What sequence?'

'The mercury is like your holograms. This whole pool will be empty in a few seconds.'

Nocao pointed to a square chute in the middle of the pool. 'There! Help me.'

Bella helped drag Sean across the stone. He moaned something unintelligible through his battered face. She hated seeing him like this, but at least he was still alive.

Nocao peered inside the chute, then dropped inside. His voice echoed up from below. 'Lower Sean over the side.'

Bella manoeuvred Sean's legs over the edge and assisted him down. The mercury was now a metre above the pool wall.

Hissss!

Bella glimpsed a set of bloodied claws. Without hesitation, she slipped feet first into the darkness and landed on her backside with a thud.

Nocao switched on a small work light, illuminating the space with a soft white glow. They were inside a small circular chamber. Dark holes in the wall led to a pyramid pipe system, too small to climb through. There was no escape.

Bella tended to Sean. His skin was deathly pale in the dim light. 'Sean, can you hear me?' She leant close to his face and listened for his breath. Nothing. 'I can't tell if he's breathing.'

Nocao rolled Sean onto his back, pulled back his t-shirt and examined his chest. Bruises gathered under his skin like ominous storm clouds. Nocao examined his ribs one by one, working up his neck. Sean's chest didn't appear to be moving. If he was breathing, it was too shallow to see.

'What's wrong with him?' Bella asked.

'He has multiple broken ribs, a crushed lung and internal bleeding. Without urgent treatment, he will not survive.'

'Use your healing ointment.'

Nocao reached for his utility belt and groaned. 'I must've dropped it somewhere.'

Bella shivered, terrified at the thought of losing Sean. She needed to stay strong, think of a way to save him. She whispered in his ear. 'Hold on, we'll figure something out.' She kissed him on the forehead and sat up, ready for action. 'What about our ship? There must be something we can salvage from the wreckage.'

'I doubt it. The *Heroke* was incinerated.'

'What about Senetep's warriors? One of them might have been carrying a tub of your magical healing stuff.'

'Yes, but how will you deal with the reptilians?'

'I don't know! We can't just wait here and hope for a miracle. We need help. If we act now, we can still save Sean. Can't you just turn that emitter thing back on?'

'No, but you just gave me an idea!' Nocao said, taking out his scanner device. 'If I adjust my scanner to emit the same frequency as the emitter, it will drive them away.'

'Perfect!'

Nocao typed the frequency into the device. 'Yes, but this scanner only has enough power for a couple of hours.'

'Don't worry, we won't be that long.'

'The range is limited, but it will give you time.'

'Me?! Aren't we doing this together?'

'I can't leave Sean like this. If he goes into cardiac arrest, he will need ongoing resuscitation.'

Bella took a deep breath and steadied herself. 'You're right...I have to do this by myself. Is the signal working?'

Nocao nodded and passed her the scanner.

The slim crystalline scanner was no bigger than a phone. Bella slipped the card in her back jeans pocket and peered up through the chute. The mercury had just completed its cycle of organic elements, DNA strands, star systems, and returned to the pool. 'Here, help me up.'

Nocao boosted her up through the chute.

Bella reached for the mercury, triggering the sequence again. She hauled herself onto the stone and crouched, waiting as the liquid metal swirled higher into the chamber, then crab-crawled over to the edge of the pool. She leant against the wall, held her breath, and listened.

The chamber was quiet except for an electrical hum.

Bella peered over the edge. Abandoned staves littered the floor. Their power crystals were still active and vibrating on the stone, creating the noise. There was no sign of life. Or death. Every corpse had been removed. The reptilians were nowhere in sight. She slipped over the edge as the mercury descended back into the pool and scooped up the nearest stave.

She edged along the pool, stepping over the shredded Isharkute armour. There were no containers of healing salves. Nothing to help Sean. All blood smears led to the passage. The reptilians had taken their kills back to the jungle.

Bella started down the passage. Her shoes squelched in the half-dried plasma. She felt the scanner in her back pocket to double-check it was there – her only protection from the reptilians. The mere thought of them made her want to turn around and run back.

She gritted her teeth, gripped the stave with firm hands, and pushed on.

Bella reached the end of the passage and stepped into the late afternoon light. The setting sun glinted off the casing stones in picturesque rays of pink and purple. Below, the remains of the *Heroke* lay scattered amongst the jungle, burning and smouldering. Plumes of black smoke tainted the peach-coloured sky. There was no sign of Senetep, his warriors, or the reptilians.

Bella gazed upon the alien horizon and shuddered.

She was stranded on a prehistoric world billions of light-years from home. The indigenous residents roared and screeched from the jungle, intent to devour her the moment her scanner stopped working.

'Thank goodness, my child!' boomed a voice from below.

Bella jolted backwards in shock and stumbled against the entrance, almost toppling down the face of the pyramid. She aimed her stave in the voice's direction. Halfway down the slope to the gully, Ramin and a band of battered and scorched warriors ascended towards her. Ramin raised his arms in mock surrender and called out. 'Not the welcoming I was expecting.'

Bella lowered her weapon and burst into tears of relief.

'Aren't you going to invite us in?' Ramin said. His beaming smile cut through the gloom and despair like a beacon of hope.

Bella blurted out a laugh that sounded more like a cry. She had never been so pleased to see another living soul.

— CHAPTER 16 —

Living Message

Senetep sat alone in his quarters aboard the *Ragarn*, strapping and tending to his injuries. He had barely escaped the pyramid with Erund and a handful of warriors. With no weapons or technology, the reptilians had carved up his squads with lethal efficiency. He admired them for it. They were a species worth studying further. Rather than obliterate the pyramid, he left it to the indigenous reptilians. The stench of blood would attract dinosaurs from all over the jungle, creating the perfect hunting ground.

The simple pleasure of extinguishing Sean Livingstone's last breath had escaped him once again. It was unfathomable. How was an insignificant human child able to cause so much trouble for so long? Humans weren't that smart, especially children.

Senetep squeezed the gash on his thigh together and stemmed the flow of blood. Instead of healing the wound with a regenerative salve, he bound it, content to live with the scar. The searing pain reminded him of his goal. It kept him alert. Gave him clarity.

He tightened the bind and grimaced.

It was clear why Sean escaped him multiple times. His First Commanders were to blame. First Ranatar, then Nefaro and Vogran, and now Erund Griss.

Erund should have created a resistance field to protect the reptilian's control chips from overloading. That simple oversight allowed Nocao to reconfigure their own emitter against them, setting the reptilians free to attack. How could Erund have overlooked such a detail? It almost seemed deliberate - just like the injection of human DNA that saved him from the affliction.

Was Erund responsible? There was one way to find out.

Senetep activated his holographic control panel and sifted through the onboard logs, tracing back to the exact date and time when he awoke inside the lab. The visual recording logs from that time had been erased. A chill of betrayal raced through his veins.

Erund erased the logs to hide the truth!

His First Commander had given the order to administer the cure, saving him from the affliction but spoiling his pure Isharkute bloodline.

He launched out of the chair and returned to the bridge. The crew kept to their business, plotting coordinates and scanning systems, deliberately avoiding eye contact. Erund was nowhere to be seen.

'Where is Erund Griss?' Senetep demanded.

'Medical bay,' the security officer replied.

Senetep stormed off the bridge. He marched down the passage, toying with every conceivable way to kill his traitorous Commander.

Senetep entered the medical bay and found Erund on an operating table, grimacing, clutching a deep gash stretching from his shoulder to elbow.

The lead scientist hastily approached, data pad in hand. 'Overseer Senetep! You require an antibacterial injection straight away.'

'What's going on?'

'The reptilian claws were laced with a prehistoric bacterium. Once it enters your nervous system, there's no stopping it.'

Senetep noticed two deceased warriors nearby. They lay in fixed contorted poses, faces locked in anguish, lips curled back over clenched teeth. Both warriors had been sliced open by the reptilian's claws during their escape. Senetep glanced down at his thigh. His wound was nowhere as severe, but he felt the heat radiating through the bandages. The bacteria were already marching through his tissue and muscles, preparing to launch an attack on his nervous system.

He snatched the data pad off the scientist and examined the magnified sample of bacteria. The microscopic spirals darted about like tadpoles, drilling into healthy cells, shredding them into genetic gunk.

The scientist ushered Senetep over to the operating table opposite Erund. He loaded a vial of serum into an injection gun and knelt to administer the injection.

'What about Erund? Will he survive?' Senetep asked.

'Yes. We thought he may lose his arm, but–'

'See that he does.'

The scientist paused in shock. 'But we can save it.'

'Save it, and you'll lose your own arm.'

The scientist gave an enthusiastic nod and injected the serum into his thigh.

Senetep enjoyed watching his First Commander writhe in pain. Erund would pay for his transgressions, beginning with an arm. In the long run, taking Erund apart piece by piece would give him more pleasure than killing him outright. Erund would understand what it felt like to be a lesser, incomplete version of himself.

Senetep rubbed his thigh. The heat dissipated from his wound as the antibacterial serum took effect.

The lead scientist moved over to Erund. 'Strap him. Prepare to amputate his arm.'

'What?!' Erund groaned. 'You said I'd keep it.'

Senetep helped the scientists hold him down. 'Don't fight it. I need you to return to duty as soon as possible.'

Erund glowered at him, tears of pain streaming from his eyes. He fell silent. With a chiselled look of determination, he laid back, willing to accept his fate.

Senetep concealed his surprise, not expecting such resilience from his youthful Commander. It troubled him on a deeper level. Had he finally met his match? His successor? His usurper? Erund displayed a level of fortitude not seen in Nefaro or Vogran, or even Ranatar.

The scientists strapped Erund's ankles, wrists, and waist to the table. One of them placed a life-support organism beside his head and stretched out the slimy tentacle.

Erund turned his head away. 'No! I want to remain conscious.'

'What about the pain?' asked the scientist.

Erund made deliberate eye contact with Senetep. 'I can tolerate it.'

The scientists laid out a selection of shiny knives and saws. One of them pulled Erund's injured arm over the edge of the table, positioning it to amputate.

Senetep watched on, wondering if it was better to have Erund die on the operating table. This show of power was dangerous. Erund was intent to prove his strength in front of the crew. What was Erund's long-term goal? Was he planning a mutiny, or gaining favour? He had never second-guessed his Commanders before. Were these suspicions irrational or justified? Senetep couldn't tell. His thoughts lacked the resolve of his old self – before his cure. The human DNA tainting his genes explained his paranoia.

The scientists set to work, slicing down through skin, muscle, and bone. Erund gritted his teeth and swallowed his scream.

Senetep smirked. Suspicions aside, it was hard not to be impressed by Erund's resilience. The hologram displaying Erund's vital signs drew his attention. In their microscopic realm, the invading bacteria moved in tiny spiral-shaped patterns, mirroring the path taken by the *Spearhead* through the universe.

Interesting. This simple spiral pattern linked the smallest and largest things in the universe. Was it a message from the Ancients? One designed to hide in plain sight?

The thought sparked an idea.

Senetep returned to the bridge and begun investigating the holographic star maps. He rotated the hologram 90 degrees, so the *Spearhead's* spiral trajectory stood vertical.

Sean Livingstone once said the spiral represented something humans called the Golden Ratio, the number 1.618. It was true. Every planet they visited was consistent with the number. The pyramids left by the Ancients carried the same dimensions – the surface of the four sides divided by the base equalled 1.618. A pattern mirrored in plants, flowers, shells, ocean waves, storm clouds, cyclones, anatomy – even the proportions of his own face.

All life presented the pattern in some form, be it the size of a spiral galaxy or a deadly bacterium. It was no fluke. This was a well-executed master plan to proliferate and advertise life. The symmetry represented something greater than a map to the *Spearhead*.

Was there a hidden message encoded in all forms of life? If so, this might be the ultimate key to the *Spearhead*. With their recent discoveries, he had enough data to test his theory.

Senetep activated a new hologram. 'Compare ten per cent of catalogued DNA samples taken from Akanae, Earth, and our previous two destinations. Isolate similarities.'

Billions of double-helix formations flashed through the hologram, moving so fast they blurred into one homogenous strand of DNA. Data streamed down both sides of the hologram. In every DNA sequence there was a large portion of random genetic material with no defined purpose.

In humans, this comprised 98 per cent of their DNA, something they called 'junk DNA'. Their ignorance and immaturity were laughable. Evolution was too well designed to waste such valuable space. This DNA was not junk. The Ancients left it for a purpose.

'Extract the genome sequences unique to each species.'

Billions of nucleotides, the blueprints for each life form, disappeared from the equation. Stripped of their individual genetic information, the double-helix formations resembled broken ladders with missing rungs.

'Now remove evolutionary markers.'

Billions more nucleotides vanished from the hologram, disappearing like grains of sand in a gust of wind.

'Overlap the remaining DNA from sampled species.'

The fragmented strands fit together like a puzzle, each filling a gap in the other. Senetep sat forward. 'That's it!'

The stripped back and reassembled DNA created the blueprint for a new, undiscovered form of life. Was he looking at the DNA of the Ancients, the creators of the *Spearhead*?

His elation turned to disappointment, then anger.

Sean Livingstone was right after all! Every living organism in the universe was connected; a single piece in one giant puzzle.

He detested the notion, but there was no denying it. The Isharkute were not a perfect master race, but a chance variation of life's original blueprint. The search for the *Spearhead* had evolved beyond his search for pure Isharkute DNA, it had become a search for the perfect expression of life.

If he could find it, he could do more than cure his species, he could rewrite their entire genetic sequence and create the perfect Isharkute. He would create a flawless, invincible, eternal version of himself. A living god!

There was one problem. The mysterious double-helix was incomplete. A gap in the top section of the spiral meant there was one more piece to the puzzle. Life in its most primordial form, from which any species could evolve.

DNA so young could only be found on a planet where life was yet to evolve beyond single-celled organisms.

Senetep zoomed the hologram into the *Spearhead's* recently visited solar systems, focusing on the nearest habitable planets. Three planets fit the criteria. According to the calculations, the nearest of these worlds was visited 100,000 years ago, just enough time for the single-celled organisms to flourish. Within this embryonic landscape lived the last piece of the puzzle.

Erund returned to the bridge.

Senetep ended the hologram and greeted his Commander. Erund appeared pale and exhausted, but eager to prove his worth. His right arm was gone, the stump already sealed with a healing salve. The crew continued their duties, sneaking sideways glances at their First Commander.

'Reporting for duty,' Erund said.

'Good,' Senetep said. 'I've plotted the remaining course: three more light-speed jumps and we should reach the *Spearhead*.'

Erund nodded, then paused, face shadowed in a pensive expression.

'Is there something wrong?'

Erund stood a little straighter. 'Permission to speak openly.'

'What is it?' Senetep said, rising from his chair. His concern infused with uncomfortable anticipation. What was Erund up to?

'Have you considered what we will do when we engage the *Spearhead*? I doubt the original species still pilot the vessel. It will have a self-defence mechanism to protect itself from intruders. I fail to see how we can board it without resistance. We are one ship against a vessel that has been roaming the universe for billions of years.'

'You're right, Erund, and I have given this much thought,' Senetep replied, pleased to be asked the question. Erund's timing could not have been better. If the crew reserved any doubt about their mission, they were about to be reassured. 'Keep your eye on the main viewscreen.'

Erund gave him a confused look, then faced the screen.

On cue, a squadron of fifteen Isharkute vessels appeared from nowhere, dropping out of light speed in front of the *Ragarn*. Senetep smiled to himself.

'Shields up!' Erund called. 'Prepare cannons.'

'Stand down,' Senetep ordered, striding to the front of the bridge to face his crew. 'This fleet belongs to me. Eighteen months have passed on Earth since we left. Over this time my loyal supporters remained hidden, preparing for this day. They are joining us on the last leg of our journey, to claim the *Spearhead* for the Isharkute Empire. Soon, we will control the universe as we were meant to.'

A cheer erupted across the bridge.

The chants echoed through the *Ragarn*. 'Sen-e-tep! Sen-e-tep! Sen-e-tep!' The communications channels from the other vessels filtered through the bridge, echoing the same support.

Senetep raised his hands to quiet the voices. 'We have one more world to visit before we take the *Spearhead*. I have uncovered an ancient message, one encoded within all living things. It was left for us, to lead us towards our destiny. You are all a part of this journey, a historic moment for our species. The Isharkute Empire will be more powerful than ever.'

Erund started the chant again. 'Sen-e-tep! Sen-e-tep! Sen-e-tep!'

Senetep crossed his arms and soaked up the adulation. He was close to his end goal. Nothing could stop him now.

CHAPTER 17

Universal Network

Sean hovered above the pyramid, or at least his mind did. He gazed upon the prehistoric sunset, the smouldering fragments of the *Heroke* scattered through the jungle below. The excruciating pain was gone. His lungs were relieved of the crushing pressure; yet, he didn't breathe in this spectral state. Senetep had kicked him to the edge of existence. If not for his previous out-of-body experiences, he would assume he was dead. But he wasn't. Not yet. His battered body lay below, deep inside the pyramid with Nocao. Senetep had left the planet, chased off by the deadly reptilians. His bird's-eye view showed Bella, Ramin, and a group of warriors rushing inside the pyramid to save him.

That meant he had limited time in this state, with the ability to visit any time and place in the universe.

This might be the last opportunity to revisit his dad. Their previous connection over the campfire lasted seconds. Sean needed to see him now, more than anything. The thought pulled him away from the planet, back through time and space.

Stars and galaxies rolled past quickly, out of control.

Without focus, his consciousness might spin off into a forgotten corner of the universe, lost for eternity.

He pictured his dad constructing the Yonaguni beacon, a target he could not miss – the device that started all his out-of-body experiences.

His consciousness found direction, bouncing through the Ancients' galactic network of artificial moons and pyramids. He barrelled down on Earth, through the clouds, over the ocean, and towards the shoreline. There it was! The tip of the Yonaguni beacon glinted like a lighthouse, guiding him in. He passed through the stone walls into the main control chamber. Henry stood there, half-man and half-horse, working in front of the main control pedestal.

Sean settled on the opposite side of the pedestal. 'Dad!'

Henry reared up in fright, hooves clanging across the stone. He took a moment to gather his thoughts and speak. 'Sean?'

'Yeah. It's me.'

Henry rubbed his eyes and spoke to himself. 'I've been working too hard.'

'No you haven't. I'm really here...well, my consciousness is.'

Henry cantered around the pedestal with an incredulous gaze. He reached out with a trembling hand. His eyes were filled with wonder, but his expression remained fragile and full of doubt. His hand passed straight through Sean's face. 'You're really here, like a ghost.'

'I am,' Sean said warmly, longing to touch his dad for real. 'But I'm not dead yet. At least I hope not.'

'How are you doing this?'

'Astral projection, I think. I've been able to do it since I activated this beacon.'

Henry smiled. 'So it worked! You contacted Neberun's fleet?'

'Yeah, we did. I–'

Henry raised his hand. 'Don't tell me anything else. I shouldn't learn too much about the future. It might jeopardise the outcome.' He eyed Sean up and down. 'This wasn't part of the plan. The beacon is a high-powered transmitter, it wasn't supposed to have any long-term effect on you.'

'I can't explain it, but it did. Now I can travel anywhere, to any point in time.'

'Amazing!' His elation turned serious. 'I wish I could ask why you're here, but... I'm thinking it's not a casual visit.'

'I just wanted to see you,' Sean in a soft voice. 'I miss you.'

Henry smiled. 'Sean, I miss you too. But whatever's happened, whatever ability you've gained, it's a misuse of that power to come back for personal reasons. You risk changing everything we've accomplished. Your life exists in the future. Not the past. You don't need to visit me, as long as you hold on to me in your heart. I'll always be with you.'

'I love you, Dad.'

'I love you too, Sean. But don't let the memory of me hold you back. If you have something important to do, then focus on that. The past is already set. Secure your future.'

Sean gave a pensive nod and waved goodbye. Henry waved back, eyes glistening with tears. They shared a parting smile.

Sean left the beacon and shot into Earth's orbit. His dad was right, he shouldn't waste this opportunity. If he could go anywhere, see anything, he needed to see how close Senetep was to finding the *Spearhead*.

Sean focused on those cruel, pale-blue eyes. His consciousness pulled away from Earth and rocketed through the universe after Senetep.

His journey felt safer this time, more focused; the sensation of spiralling out of control eliminated. Purpose guided him, not unruly emotions. His mind rebounded through a grid of planets, pyramids, and moons, repeating him across vast distances of space like a radio signal.

The blur of stars slowed to a stop and sharpened.

He travelled alongside Senetep's vessel. Fifteen more trailed behind, making a formidable squad. Where did Senetep find help? It was impossible to tell how close they were to the *Spearhead*. He needed to discover for himself.

His mind shot ahead of the squad and stopped in orbit before a serene, Earthlike world.

A gigantic vessel rotated into view on the far side of the planet, silhouetted by the glare of the nearest star. The triangular craft stretched hundreds of kilometres from tip to tip. It was the *Spearhead of Creation*!

The vessel resembled a pyramid floating in space until it rolled over, revealing a flat design, just several kilometres in height. It was a literal arrowhead, thrown billions of years ago by a mysterious race of Ancients.

A stream of tiny craft formed a chain between the *Spearhead* and the planet. At this distance, they were ants compared to the mammoth vessel. What were they? Sean pushed in, close enough to touch them. These strange automatons were the size of a person, with diamond-shaped bodies and long triple-jointed appendages that dangled below them like jellyfish tentacles. They descended in thousands to the planet's surface.

Sean wanted to follow, but something made him pause.

A voice had entered his mind, distant and unclear, like an echo. There was more than one. Their warm, reassuring tones eased his mind. Was it the probes? The *Spearhead*? No.

It was the Ancients!

They beckoned, drawing his focus away from the *Spearhead*. Their incomprehensible language comforted him, like a parent cradling a baby. He relaxed, allowing himself to be guided.

The universe whooshed by in an instant, and he left the *Spearhead* millions of light-years behind. He stopped in a magical place awash with celestial brilliance. Here, the space between the stars was not black, but painted in a heavenly rainbow of muted colours. Stunning nebulae, billions of kilometres wide, swept across the infinite backdrop. Clouds of interstellar dust glowed with radiation and solar flares.

This was the oldest part of the universe: its living core, where life began.

A planet emerged from the pastel backdrop. Its surface glinted with an organised symmetry of gold and silver, the traces of an advanced culture. Immense cities covered the landmasses and extended over the oceans in an intricate web of structures. He zoomed down to the surface and travelled with incredible speed between the crystalline cities. Sean didn't have to think about where he was going. The Ancients were guiding him through their long-abandoned civilisation.

A pyramid appeared on the horizon.

It gradually became the focal point of the city, with every road, bridge and building propagating out from its four sides. The structure stood thousands of storeys tall. He passed through a vast opening, up a grand flight of steps to a central chamber built around a circular portal. The portal's metallic rim rippled with blue light, sending waves of energy into its centre. Where did it lead?

The glowing portal attracted his consciousness like a magnet.

Stop! The Ancients warned him not to approach.

Sean couldn't help himself. The mesmerising energy was hard to resist. The voices became stern. Forceful. Now he sensed the danger. He should not enter the portal, not while his consciousness was disconnected from his body. They told him it was time to leave and return to his body. He had seen what they wanted him to see.

He cleared his mind and pictured Bella's face.

She was billions of light-years away, nursing his injured body. He visualised her brown eyes, dark hair, and soft ruby lips. A bright light filled the edge of his vision...

Sean sat upright with a deep, life-saving gasp. He was back in the pyramid, surrounded by a crowd of concerned faces. Bella, Nocao and Ramin crouched over him. Behind them stood the battered and scorched warriors from the *Heroke*.

Bella threw her arms around him. '*Grazie Dio!*'

'We thought you had left us for good that time,' Ramin said.

Nocao helped Sean to his feet. 'How do you feel?'

'Okay, I think,' Sean said, touching his ribs. There was a mild discomfort when he breathed in, but considering the brutal beating, he was surprisingly good. 'What happened?'

'You were dead–'

'For several minutes,' Bella exclaimed. 'Nocao resuscitated you.'

Sean inadvertently wiped his lips.

Nocao raised an eyebrow, mildly offended.

Bella laughed. 'It was quite intimate.' Sean and Nocao glared at her in unison. She raised her hands. '*Sto scherzando!* Don't you understand a joke? After that, he used a healing salve on your broken ribs.'

Sean observed the chamber. The liquid mercury had settled back in the pool and a stash of salvaged weapons leant against the wall. Splashes of dried blood and deep scratches marred the chamber walls. 'Seems I missed a big fight.'

Bella shook her head. 'You have no idea. It was insane.'

'What do we do now?' Ramin said. 'We're stranded on this planet with plagues of overgrown lizards. The *Heroke* is destroyed, along with any chance of communicating with Akanae or Earth.'

Sean knew that wasn't true. The Ancients had just shown him the way, by transmitting his consciousness across the universe via the network of pyramids and moons. 'The *Spearhead* left us a way to communicate.'

'How?' Nocao asked.

'Touch the mercury and I'll show you.'

Nocao dipped his finger in the pool. The liquid mercury swirled and levitated into the centre of the chamber and cycled through its encoded information.

'The mercury is more than just a databank, it's an interface to send and receive messages through the moons.'

'Like a telephone?' Bella asked.

'Exactly. If you think of it that way, the pyramids are phones, designed to send and receive calls. But they won't work without the moons. These artificial moons are the cellular network, responsible for sending the signal between planets seeded by the *Spearhead*.'

The mercury completed its display of DNA sequences and split into millions of tiny specks, creating a map of the universe. Sean walked through the map, swishing his hands through thousands of solar systems. The tiny blobs rippled aside like water and reformed once he passed. 'This is an updated map of the universe, showing the exact location of the *Spearhead* in relation to all the planets and wormholes it's discovered since leaving this system.'

'But the data we downloaded from Earth's Moon wasn't updated,' Nocao said.

'That's right.'

'So Earth's in a dead zone,' Bella added. 'Why weren't we getting the signal?'

'The Moon was receiving the signal, but it had nowhere to send the information. It's basically an antenna, not designed to store endless amounts of data.'

'That makes sense,' Nocao said. 'I believe your Moon was storing its last received signal, which was thousands, possibly millions of years old. When we scanned the orb, it downloaded the data to our vessel, thinking we were the pyramid, re-establishing contact.'

'Yes. And when the Moon started ringing, it was re-establishing a connection in the network. Trying to access the latest updates from the *Spearhead*.'

'But any new data will bottleneck until it has somewhere to download.'

'Who broke our phone?' Bella said. 'Why don't we have a pyramid like this to collect the info?'

Sean smiled. Bella looked proud to be keeping up with the *sciencey stuff*, as she called it. 'We don't know. The only pyramid I know about on Earth that has liquid mercury is the Pyramid of the Feathered Serpent.'

'What's that?'

'It's the third largest pyramid in Teotihuacan, Mexico.'

Bella shook her head. 'How do you know so much about everything?'

'I read a lot,' Sean said defensively. 'The chamber was discovered a couple of years ago. I was all over it because they used a robot like my dad's.'

'It's possible the mercury was moved from the Great Pyramid in Egypt to Mexico at some point in your history,' Nocao said.

'Or it could be natural mercury. Which means the Maya were just imitating the original function of the Great Pyramid.'

'Either way, there seems to be a missing chapter of history between the fall of the dinosaurs and the Isharkute arrival on Earth.'

'None of this solves our problem,' Bella cut in. 'It's obvious we can't call Earth. Can we call Akanae instead? It was seeded by the *Spearhead,* which means it should have a pyramid with mercury. Right?'

Sean nodded. 'Nocao, do you have a pyramid like this on Akanae?'

'Not that I'm aware of.'

'Unless such a pyramid has been kept a secret by Hemket and Emperor Neberun,' Ramin said. 'We should make the call. See if anyone answers.'

Sean regarded Nocao. 'Can you do it?'

'I need communications equipment.'

'Can we salvage anything from the *Heroke?*'

'Several sections are still intact,' Ramin said. 'You might find enough components to make this work. But you need to move fast. We reactivated Senetep's sonic emitters to keep the lizards away, but they are running out of power.'

Nocao held his scanner over the pool. 'I'll stay behind and start working on the interface.'

Sean would have preferred Nocao to come. He was an excellent shot with a stave, but he was their only hope of making the technical stuff work. Nobody else had a clue. They collected as many weapons as they could carry and left the chamber.

Outside, the horizon was aglow with the setting sun. The fires had died, leaving the *Heroke* as piles of smouldering shrapnel. The warriors led the way down the pyramid slope to the jungle floor.

The hum of giant mosquitos filled the evening air. They buzzed past, brandishing their frightening proboscis needles used to pierce tough dinosaur skin. Their engorged bodies were as big as Sean's fist and filled with dinosaur blood.

'That's one helluva mozzie bite!' Sean remarked.

'Not funny,' Bella said, ducking as one flew over her head.

'Don't worry. I think they're ignoring us. We're too small.'

'I hope so.'

'Through here,' Ramin said, heading towards a V-shaped divide in the jungle. Further in, a massive forward section of the *Heroke's* hull rested in a clump of fallen trees. 'Any salvageable communications equipment will be in there.'

Sean followed Bella, swiping away any mosquitos that came too close.

She glanced over her shoulder and smiled. 'Thanks.'

'No problem.'

'I'm so glad you're okay.'

'Me too.'

'You know, you were dead for minutes. It felt like hours. I thought you weren't going to make it. I don't know what I'd do without you.'

'You're a survivor – you would have found a way.'

Sean helped Bella over a fallen log. She waited for him, then asked another question. 'What do you remember about dying?'

'Why?'

'I think I died after the minotaur attack...but I'm not sure. There was no light. Nothing at all. Just darkness. I'm Catholic. My parents brought me up to believe in God...I expected something to happen when I died.'

'Maybe it wasn't your time to die.'

'That doesn't change what I experienced. How do my beliefs fit into all of this?'

'I'm not religious, so I'm not the best person to ask.'

'That makes you the perfect person to ask. You're not biased.'

'I guess so,' Sean said. 'My dad told me something that makes sense. Every myth and legend, even religions, stem from a shred of truth. The Isharkute believed the *Spearhead* was a myth until Senetep proved it was real.'

'What does that mean for me?'

'It means there's an answer. It might differ from what you expected, but that doesn't mean you should change. Isn't being Catholic more than just believing in God and heaven? It's supposed to guide you towards a positive and fulfilling life.'

'For someone who's not religious, you understand it. What happened when you died? Was it the same as me, nothing?'

'Not exactly.'

Bella spun around, eyes wide with shock. 'Why? What did you see?'

'It's not what you think. When I activated the Yonaguni Monument, something happened to me. Nocao said it changed the way my brain works, or something. Ever since, I've been able to leave my body and travel anywhere in time and space.'

Bella shoved his shoulder. '*Stai scherzando?*'

'I'm not joking.'

'So where did you go?'

'I think I travelled to the Ancients' homeworld. They guided me to a doorway or portal in the middle of their city.'

'Fascinating story,' Ramin interrupted, 'but we are lacking a more immediate door. One of us needs to climb up there!'

Sean peered up at the wreckage. The nose of the *Heroke* had landed vertically, with the opening several storeys above. Beyond that, stars appeared in the deep purple sky. Night was fast encroaching. The ravenous roars and stomping sounded closer than ever.

'I can fly up there,' Sean said. 'What am I looking for?'

Ramin handed him a small crystalline data pad. It projected a hologram showing the location of several crystal control shards on the *Heroke's* bridge.

Sean memorised the location and put the data pad in his back pocket.

His wings tingled like crazy, itching to take flight. He pulled down the back of his t-shirt and they shot free, blasting Bella's hair back over her shoulders. 'Sorry about that.'

Bella admired his shiny new wings. 'They seem different.'

Their paper-thin translucent film glistened in the dim light and stretched on either side of him, twice the length of his arms.

Sean handed his stave to Ramin. 'Here. I won't be able to carry this.'

'Good luck,' Bella said. 'And be careful.'

Sean eyed the opening and took off. With two strong flaps he shot higher than the trees and stared down into the broken hull. It was great to be flying again. He had missed the freedom and exhilaration. These newly grown wings felt more responsive than his previous, grafted-on ones.

Squaaaaaaawk!

Sean instinctively ducked.

A pterodactyl swooped over the jungle canopy not far away, a stark reminder they had limited time before the emitters stopped working.

Sean dove inside the wreck, avoiding the red-hot sections of broken hull. This was trickier than he thought. Every passage was a vertical shaft and a potential death trap. He descended through plumes of acrid smoke and dropped into a large void illuminated by several fires – the remains of the bridge.

Sean double-checked his hologram for directions and flew over to the communications console. He popped the compartment open and pulled out the shards, tucking the card-sized crystals into his pockets.

He squinted, tears running down his cheeks. The smoke stung his eyes. He couldn't breathe in this smoke for much longer. If he blacked out here, he would suffocate before the others could reach him.

Sean pulled the last control shard free, shoved it in his pocket, and peered up through stinging eyes. He flapped his wings and zipped through the shafts, smoke curling into eddies beneath his wings. Lungs bursting, he shot clear of the hull and sucked in the fresh air. He hovered over jungle, gasping, coughing, and sucking as much air as he could.

CRACK!

An energy blast rang over his head.

Sean dove aside and glanced down. His friends were gone. He flew a little higher and spotted them running full steam ahead towards the pyramid. The warrior responsible for the warning shot waved desperately at him, then raced after the others.

What was going on?

He didn't notice at first, but his wings were buzzing, stronger than ever. His sixth sense had kicked in. And it meant one thing. Danger!

Sean felt the push of air from behind. Something was coming up fast. At this height, it could only be one thing; the pterodactyl!

He plummeted into the leafy treetops as the branches snapped and cracked around him, throwing up a ferocious gust of shredded leaves. The pterodactyl ripped through the canopy with its long beak, trying to scoop him up. It created the wind shear of a jet airliner, almost sucking him into its slipstream.

This could only mean one thing. The sonic emitters had run out of energy and the dinosaurs were closing in, searching for a meal before bedtime.

Sean flew straight for the pyramid's gold-framed entrance, glancing over his shoulder at the pterodactyl. It circled behind him in a sweeping arc, lining up for another pass. Sean flapped as hard as he could, then angled his wings, diving for the entrance. His companions passed beneath. At the last second, he spread his wings and braked, landing inside the passage at running speed.

Nocao sprinted down the passage and threw him a stave. 'Here, take this!'

They ran to the opening and aimed at the incoming pterodactyl. It was silent, like a giant glider. Sean glanced down at his friends. They were easy pickings on the side of the pyramid.

'Shoot!' Nocao said.

BOOM! BOOM! BOOM!

They let the pterodactyl have it. Multiple blasts erupted across its wings, so big they were impossible to miss. One impacted high on its cranium, making it screech. The pterodactyl swerved hard and flapped off towards the sunset, shaking its head and screeching.

'Yes!' Sean said. 'He'll have a headache tonight.'

Bella reached the entrance first, followed by Ramin and the warriors. At that exact moment, a tyrannosaur burst from the jungle and stomped along the gully. It climbed up the roots strangling the foundation blocks and peered up, fixing its beady eyes upon them.

ROOOOAAAAR!

'Whoa! I think that's a T-rex?' Sean cried in exhilaration. 'Unbelievable!'

'Get inside,' Nocao said.

The tyrannosaur took a step in their direction and stopped. It lumbered off the pyramid and turned about, facing something in the encroaching shadows. The jungle went quiet.

'Oh no!' Bella whispered. 'They're back.'

Glossy black eyes glinted through the foliage, reflecting the dying reams of daylight. The reptilians had returned. The tyrannosaur dropped its head and growled, swishing its mighty tail from side to side, ripping vines and roots off the pyramid.

'Get inside!' Nocao said in a hushed voice.

The reptilians pounced from the jungle and slashed the tyrannosaur, sending a fountain of crimson high into the air. This fight would be over in seconds. Sean stumbled backwards and tripped over Bella's feet. They both fell, tangled up, just metres from the opening.

'What are you doing?' Nocao said, herding them back. 'Get up, keep moving!'

Sean helped Bella to her feet and pulled her along. Ramin and the warriors raced ahead to the main chamber. Twenty paces in, Nocao stopped, put down his stave and started doing something to the passage wall.

'What are you doing?' Sean called over his shoulder.

'Closing the door.'

'LOOK OUT!' Bella screamed.

Nocao was unaware he had been followed inside. The ten-foot-tall reptilian loomed behind him, claws scraping along the wall. *HISSSSS!* One swipe, and it would be over.

For all of them.

— CHAPTER 18 —

Orion Taskforce

Sean launched high into the passage and fired his stave. The reptilian leapt backwards, avoiding the blast. The energy bolt ricocheted off the stone blocks, throwing up bits of pulverised stone and choking the exit with dust.

Nocao crawled from the haze and pressed a button on his bracer. Four enormous blocks ejected from both sides of the passage wall. He rolled aside, narrowly avoiding being sandwiched. The blocks joined, sealing the passage from floor to ceiling, then slid towards the outer wall of the pyramid, locking the reptilian outside with a thunderous *clunk*.

Sean flew down to Nocao. 'That was close!'

'Too close.' Nocao stood, dusting himself off. 'I accessed the pyramid's control systems while you were gone. The main door was one of them.'

'Just in time. We won't be able to open it until we have a way off this planet.'

'*Cominciamo!*' Bella said. 'I don't like being locked in here.'

They returned to the main chamber, finding Nocao had made progress interfacing with the mercury pool. A thin sliver of silver extended over the edge of the pool and formed an Isharkute control panel, working just like a hologram, but made of mercury. Nocao's scanner protruded from the centre of the panel.

Sean rushed over. Up close, he noticed the Isharkute glyphs indented in the silver. 'Wow! You hacked the mercury!'

'Not in the human sense of the word. I interfaced my scanner with the mercury. I'm starting to understand how it works.'

'Looks like it's starting to understand how we work!'

'Yes. The mercury responds to different frequencies, both biological and technological. For instance, when our bare skin touches the mercury it triggers a scan of our physiological state, assessing our pulse, respiratory system, neural activity, and other bodily processes. These infrasonic waves, or frequencies, are unique to every species. The mercury shares this data back to us in three-dimensional displays, like you saw before, breaking down our biology, DNA, and place of origin in the universe.'

'Sounds like its way of saying hello.'

'Once the mercury has acknowledged us, it displays a map of the universe, showing us how to get from here to the *Spearhead*.'

'And all the way to the Ancients' planet.'

'Yes.'

Bella peered over the edge of the pool. 'Clever liquid. Sounds like it's alive.'

'If you mean sentient, no. The mercury stores information, just like a computer. It can operate as a collective or split off into independent shapes and sizes with no loss of function.'

'Does that mean each drop works on its own?' Sean said.

'Correct, and can store infinite amounts of information. When I scanned pool, the mercury responded by forming this panel. It's a replica of the panel my scanner interfaced with on the *Heroke*.'

'How did it do that?'

'The mercury must have analysed the last interface used by the scanner and replicated it.'

'This technology is trying everything to communicate with us.'

'But the *Heroke* is destroyed.' Bella said. 'What good is the panel?'

'This interface can control the pyramid.'

'Wow! That's awesome.'

'Watch this,' Nocao said, typing a command into the silvery glyphs.

The centre of the pool stretched up, separated into a large blob, and formed a three-dimensional schematic of the pyramid.

It hovered in place, glistening like a hologram made of quicksilver.

Sean noticed three chambers above theirs, hidden within thousands of tonnes of stone. A series of smaller shafts dissected the pyramid on diagonal angles, starting from their chamber, reaching all the way out to the exterior. 'Those shafts look like the ones inside the Great Pyramid on Earth.'

'What's in the chambers above this?' Ramin asked.

Nocao typed more commands into the silver and the schematic zoomed into the first empty chamber. 'Nothing, they're empty.'

'What about the shafts?' Sean said.

Nocao zoomed the schematic out to a full view. 'Judging by their antenna-like configuration, I believe they're part of the communications system between this pyramid and the orbiting moon.'

Bella pointed out the large black sarcophagi in the entrance passage. 'What about these? Aren't they coffins for the Ancients–' she looked askance at Sean. 'Oh *scusi*, I meant sarcophagi?'

Sean chuckled, relieved to see her sense of humour returning.

'No,' Nocao said, pointing out a network of channels running beneath their chamber. 'The mercury uses these shafts to move from the chamber beneath us into the boxes.'

'What for?'

'Their proximity to the outer door suggests–'

'Yes, yes,' Ramin huffed, throwing his hands up in the air. 'This is all very fascinating. But unless we tell this silver metal how to contact someone, we will slowly suffocate inside this pyramid. I do not intend to spend my final breath marvelling at such discoveries. Do what you set out to. Send the call for help.'

Sean dug into his pockets and handed over the crystal cards salvaged from the *Heroke*.

Nocao placed them on the panel of mercury. Tiny strands of silver formed around the edges of the cards and spread across the surface like the roots of a tree.

'How do you know what you're doing?' Bella asked.

Nocao adjusted the mercury, sliding the raised indentations of silver as if he was using an audio mixing console. 'I'm using the panel as I would on the *Heroke,* programming it to send our signal. If I'm right, the mercury should interpret my commands and send a distress call to Akanae, then on to Earth.'

'Are you sure it will work?'

'No.'

'No?!'

'It's what you call *a hunch.*'

'Bah!' Ramin stormed off around the pool. 'Our lives depend on guesswork.'

The mercury spilled over the edge of the pool in four streams and raced outwards in opposite directions. Ramin jumped out of the way. The streams reached the adjacent walls, climbed high into the chamber, then channelled into four small voids. The entire pool emptied, leaving just enough mercury to maintain the control panel.

'Where's it going?' Bella asked.

'Filling the upper shafts,' Nocao said. 'Creating the antenna to send the signal.'

Ramin rushed over. 'It worked?'

The *Heroke's* communication shards illuminated. A low frequency resonated through the pyramid. Sean felt the hairs on his arm stand on end. The noise grew to an uncomfortable crescendo and suddenly ended. The shards went dark.

The mercury drained from the shafts and down the walls.

Sean watched the mercury return to the pool, stomach churning with excitement. The age-old mystery surrounding the purpose of Egypt's Great Pyramid was finally solved. It made sense why the shafts and chambers were empty. There were never any Pharaohs or undiscovered treasure buried within its walls. It had been home to an ancient technology in the form of liquid mercury, removed thousands of years before Senetep and the Isharkute even arrived on Earth.

Nocao checked his scanner. 'The message is sent. I altered the wavelength so Akanae's moon, Nek-Karani, will transmit the message on a monitored frequency. Hemket should discover the message within minutes.'

Bella raised her hand and high-fived Nocao. '*Grande!* Well done, team. How long do we have to wait?'

'Considering how long it took to get here, a few days.'

'Very well then,' Ramin said. 'I suggest we eat and sleep, conserve our energy. We could be here a while.'

Nocao continued working on the mercury while everyone settled in for the evening. Ramin passed everyone a ration, a small square wobbly substance resembling raspberry jelly. Sean and tested it with his tongue, expecting something sweet. He recoiled, scrunching his face at the strong peppery flavour.

'It's not about taste, it's about survival,' Ramin said. 'One ration will keep you hydrated for days.'

Sean swallowed it whole, trying not to gag on the pungent aroma.

Bella forced hers down with a grimace. '*Grazie Dio.* I couldn't eat another if I tried.'

Ramin snickered and savoured his portion, nibbling off tiny amounts.

The warriors marched up and down the passage, making sure nothing worked its way inside. Sean thought they would be better off conserving their energy, but their patrols helped him relax. Maybe get some sleep. Bella sat against the edge of the pool. Sean joined her.

Bella remained quiet for a long time. 'How much time do you think has passed on Earth since we left?'

'A few months, maybe a bit more.'

Bella placed her hand on the floor between them and opened it to him. Sean slipped his fingers between hers and squeezed gently. She smiled and rested her head on his shoulder.

Sean took a deep breath and eased back. His body relaxed, feeling like it could sink into the hard stone. All his troubles faded away, and for that moment, it felt as though their connection could ward off anything the universe might throw at them. He closed his eyes and drifted off into a dreamless sleep.

*   *   *

Sean awoke to the sound of grinding stone echoing from the passage. He felt the deep vibrations coming up through the chamber floor.

Bella stirred and sat forward, rubbing her eyes. 'What's that noise?'

'I don't know, stay here with Ramin.'

Sean leapt to his feet, grabbed his stave, and chased Nocao down the passage. 'What's happening?'

'Something activated the pyramid door from the outside.'

They raced up the ascending passage to exit and found their warriors retreating from the inward moving stone wall. The blocks parted and stark daylight spilled into the passage. A tall spindly silhouette loomed in the entrance, casting a terrifying shadow down the length of the passage.

Sean squinted into the light, heart pounding. 'It's a reptilian!'

Nocao lowered his stave. 'Hold your fire!'

Ramin's booming voice echoed from behind. 'Hemket! You should learn how to knock.'

Bella raced up to Sean and Nocao, brimming with excitement. 'We're saved!'

Hemket strode through the entrance, slow and elegant like a giraffe. Her robe billowed in the warm breeze blowing inside. A platoon of warriors marched behind her.

Sean led the way back to the main chamber. His spirits lifted. There was a hustle in his step and his wings tingled with excitement. He felt more awake now, realising how groggy he had been when he raced down to confront their surprise guests.

'Your timing is impeccable,' Ramin said. 'It's been less than twelve hours since we sent the distress call. We were ambushed by Senetep and set upon by the indigenous species – a giant bloodthirsty lot.'

The warriors assembled around the pool and stood guard.

Hemket strode around the chamber with an inquisitive gaze. She stopped in front of the mercury panel interfacing with Nocao's scanner. 'Fascinating technology. How does it work?'

'It's liquid mercury,' Nocao said, stepping up to the panel. 'Every lifeform the Ancients created, every planet they visited, is encoded within each drop. It's a database, continuously updated by the *Spearhead* through a universal network of pyramids and moons.'

'We received your distress call. At first, we discovered the signal was being transmitted from Nek-Karani. Then we discovered our moon was acting as a repeater and communicating with an undiscovered pyramid deep in the Ultarek Ocean.'

'It's not an Isharkute pyramid,' Nocao said. 'It will be just like this one, built by the same race of Ancients who built the *Spearhead*.'

'Where is Senetep now?'

'Closer to the *Spearhead* than us,' Sean cut in, sounding more desperate than he intended.

'We lost our advantage over Senetep,' Ramin added in a more measured tone. 'He has the same map to the *Spearhead* as us, showing all the wormholes that shortcut across the universe. We need a new vessel and crew if we are to catch him.'

'Your request was answered months ago.' Hemket motioned to the passage. 'Emperor Neberun has sent you reinforcements from Earth.'

Sean had to look twice to believe his eyes. Commander Hazim El-Amin entered the chamber with a broad smile and open arms. His black hair was longer and swept back behind his ears under a navy beret. His bristly five o'clock shadow made him appear older and wiser. 'Sean, Bella, Nocao! It's been far too long.'

The four of them laughed with joy and embraced like old friends.

'How long have we been gone?' Sean asked.

'Eighteen months,' Hazim said, facing Bella. 'And before you ask, your family is fine and doing well. They send their love, along with plenty of videos and letters. They miss you terribly and can't wait for you to return.'

Bella seized Hazim in a crushing hug. He gasped, eyes bulging with surprise.

Sean smiled to himself, all too familiar with Bella's superhuman hugging power.

A squad of human and Isharkute soldiers filed into the chamber, all dressed in the same navy uniform as Hazim. The blend of fabric and Isharkute armour resembled a bulletproof vest, but not as bulky. Sean noticed the circular emblem embroidered on their chests, displaying an open human hand overlaid with a sixth finger representing the Isharkute. Three stars decorated the palm of the hand, signifying the Belt of Orion, the link between human and Isharkute civilisations.

'What regiment is this?' Nocao asked. 'I don't recognise the uniforms.'

'I'm in charge of the Orion Taskforce. It's the first special-ops division combining human and Isharkute military forces. I've been preparing this partnership for the last year, while Admiral Powell's been taking care of the politics with Emperor Neberun.'

'Admiral?' Sean exclaimed. 'He got a promotion.'

'Yes, much has changed since you left. But aside from the obvious teething issues, the Isharkute integration to Earth has gone well. Thanks to you and Bella, Hemket's scientists have delivered the cure to the Isharkute living on Earth.'

'We cannot call it a cure yet,' Hemket intervened. 'The treatment eliminates the affliction, but we are still yet to see a male successfully transform into a life-bearer. Ramin is one of the few males in the right age range, on the verge of transformation.'

Bella sidled up to Ramin and put an affectionate arm around him. 'Sí. He's having a tiny blue *bambino!*"

'There's nothing tiny about them,' Ramin grumbled.

'You're expecting?!' Hazim blurted out. 'Congratulations.'

Sean laughed. It was great to feel normal for a change, but he knew it couldn't last. Their mission was more urgent than ever. 'I hate to spoil the fun, but we need to catch Senetep. He's close to the *Spearhead.*'

Hazim put his hand on Sean's back. 'And we arrived just in time to help.'

'How did you get here so quick? It took eighteen months of Earth time for us to travel here. Why didn't it take the same for you?'

'Nocao's distress signal included the revised map of wormholes. Space is riddled with them. It's like Swiss cheese out there. We shortcut our way across the universe with minimal light-speed jumps between wormholes. It took us four hours to complete the journey, but on this planet, like Earth and Akanae, only one day has passed.'

Bella's voice burst with excitement. 'That means I can get home!'

'I can organise transport to Earth if you want to return.'

'No, but thanks for the offer.' She looked at Sean, eyes bursting with hope. 'We need to finish what we started.'

Sean smiled and nodded, confident that all the hurtful things between them were ancient history. They could move on. No regrets.

Hazim led them outside into the light of a new dawn. The morning breeze blew across the face of the pyramid, warm and thick with humidity. The roars were a distant echo, and the air hummed with overgrown prehistoric insects.

'Incredible world,' Hazim said. 'Just like Earth millions of years ago.'

'I call it Jurassic Planet,' Bella said.

Hazim laughed. 'We scanned hundreds of dinosaurs on our approach, but that's barely scraped the surface. There's an abundance of the life on this planet – and I thought I'd seen it all when I landed on Akanae for the first time.'

Below, two vessels sat parked on the edge of the jungle. Four more hovered overhead. Hazim directed them down the pyramid slope to the gully. 'We reactivated the emitters to keep the dinosaurs away.'

'There's a reptilian species that makes the dinosaurs look like puppies,' Bella said.

Sean chuckled. 'Without the emitters, it would be impossible to get close enough to this pyramid to rescue us.'

'This is more than a rescue mission,' Hazim said. 'We're here to assist you on the rest of your journey.'

'Marvellous!' Ramin called from the back of the line. 'I would never say it to him, but I always believed our esteemed Emperor sent us off a little underpowered.'

'He spared what he could at the time. But in hindsight, it's lucky he didn't send all his forces out at once. We needed to deal with the rising threat.'

'What's that?' Sean asked.

'Six months after you left, there was an uprising of Senetep's supporters on Earth. They attacked several installations, including the pyramid at El Mirador, and stole a squadron of vessels. We expect his forces will combine to capture and defend the *Spearhead*.'

They jumped off the lower blocks and cut across the scorched gully, weaving around the remains of the *Heroke*. Their new vessel was twice the size and heavily armed – more like a military vessel than one designed for exploration.

Hazim directed them up the gangway. 'The crew will show you to your quarters. We'll meet on the bridge after you've all cleaned up and had something to eat.'

Ramin wiped the mud off his boot on the side of the gangway. 'Finally, we can feel civilised again.'

Hazim pulled Sean aside. 'I need to talk to you about a personal matter.'

Sean's heart quickened. What could Hazim be talking about? Bella overheard and stopped to wait for him. 'Don't worry, I'll catch up,' Sean said.

Bella cast him a concerned eye and walked off.

Sean waited until they were alone. 'What is it?'

'Not long after you left, your aunt Janine and uncle Steve contacted us from Australia. They saw you on the global telecast–'

'Are they okay?'

'Yes, they're fine. But they sounded worried, wondering why you hadn't contacted them.'

Sean lost his breath. It felt like someone had just punched him in the gut, taking all the wind out of him. He felt sick with guilt. It's not like he had forgotten about his aunt and uncle, but he'd spent so much time away and the world had changed so fast. He should have contacted them, just to let them know he was okay. They deserved that. It was immature and selfish of him not to consider their emotions. They would have been worried sick about him.

He'd always treated living with them as a punishment, never allowing himself to get as close as he could have. It always felt like a temporary arrangement. But now, after everything he had been through, he understood the error of his ways. Steve and Janine had given up their freedom to care for him. He owed them so much.

'Sean, are you okay?'

Sean snapped back into the moment, realising he had been staring vacantly. 'Yeah, I'm okay. Did they say anything else?'

'They recorded a video message for you. When you're ready, you can watch it.'

Sean nodded, nervous about what they might say.

— CHAPTER 19 —

The Spearhead

Senetep took his first step onto the primordial landscape, a barren, stormy world covered in vast volcanic continents and turbulent oceans. The planet was still in its infancy, incubating the cellular-sized life forms that would populate the world for millions, potentially billions of years to come. The *Spearhead* had sown the seeds of life here 100,000 years before – a mere grain of sand on the beach of time.

Senetep strode across the black gravel. It crunched under his boots.

The incoming tide dominated the horizon like a mountain range. The whitecaps could be mistaken for snow-covered peaks if not for the titanic columns of water ejecting into the sky. On this world, oceans swamped the continents on a daily cycle, churning up rocks, sand, and soil, creating a fertile playground for life. The epic tides resulted from the artificial moon. It hung full and bright in the daytime sky, poking through the clouds like a dim star, drawing forward a thousand-foot wall of water that threatened everything in its path.

Behind him, the *Ragarn* glistened like quicksilver against the outcropping of gloomy grey rocks. His new squad of fifteen vessels had landed nearby. Several kilometres to his right, the Ancients' pyramid towered over a plateau of smooth stone, positioned on the planet's equatorial line and aligned to the cardinal points.

But he wasn't here to investigate the pyramid. The last clue to taking control of the *Spearhead* lay in the puddles ahead.

Senetep knelt beside one of the deeper pools. In his shadow, the pristine water became invisible against the gravel. He focused on the minuscule flecks darting through the pool, barely perceptible to the naked eye. These infinitesimal expressions of life were about to unlock the greatest power in the universe.

Senetep unscrewed a crystal container and scooped a sample of water. He held it up to the light. There were thousands of them, darting about the container as if inside another universe altogether. He replaced the lid and returned to the *Ragarn*.

The warriors assembled outside their vessels in military formation. He recognised many of the hardened faces. They stared ahead, determined and devoted to his cause. These followers represented a fraction of his former capital, but combined with the budding life forms in his hand, they had the potential to achieve anything.

Erund Griss stood front and centre of the *Ragarn's* crew, proudly holding his stave with a single arm.

Senetep held the container for all to see. 'I'm holding the purest expression of life in the universe. This untainted DNA is the key to the *Spearhead*. It can put an end to our affliction and purify us of the imperfections passed on by our ancestors. With this power, we can unlock the secrets of life and build worlds as we desire.'

Erund raised his stave. 'Sen-e-tep! Sen-e-tep!'

The warriors joined in, punching their staves at the stormy sky. Their raucous chants followed him up the gangway into the *Ragarn*.

*   *   *

Senetep observed the tidal shift from the safety of his command chair. By the time they returned to orbit, their previous landing area was consumed by a devastating wave, leaving just the tip of the pyramid poking through the tumultuous ocean.

Erund entered the bridge. 'The scientists are ready for you.'

Senetep closed the hologram and followed Erund to the *Ragarn's* science lab. The scientists stood around a central examination station, working on holographic models of multiple DNA strands.

The lead scientist greeted them. 'We've finished analysing the microbial life forms and are ready to integrate them with your research.'

Senetep nodded, keeping a calm, cool composure. On the inside, an unstoppable tide of excitement and apprehension raced through his body. All his plans hinged on this.

The holographic DNA strands converged to form a new double-helix. The coil of nucleic acid sprouted from the bottom, growing into a spiral chain, combining all the life forms they had ever encountered. The double-helix climbed to full height and completed the final rung.

Senetep drew a silent breath of relief.

'The sequence is complete,' the scientist said. 'This represents a new, undiscovered life form.'

'This DNA sequence isn't new. It's been around for billions of years, scattered and encoded in life forms throughout the universe.'

'What is it?' Erund asked.

'You're looking at an Ancient, the species responsible for the *Spearhead*.'

'What do we do with it?' the scientist asked.

'Synthesise a live sample, but only at the cellular level. We don't want to resurrect these Ancient aliens from extinction. They had their time. We are the rightful successors to their knowledge and technology now.'

'How do you know they're extinct?' Erund said.

'It's no accident their DNA spread across the universe. It was meant to be found long after they were gone.'

'Like a test?'

'Exactly. Now that we have passed their test, we possess the power to control the *Spearhead*.'

'We will inform you when the sample is complete,' the scientist said.

Senetep returned to the bridge to await confirmation. Once the sample was ready, his squadron would make the final jump and intercept the legendary vessel. He sat on the edge of his command chair, stomach churning with excitement and trepidation as he analysed the galactic maps. Their journey had delivered them close to the centre of the spiral-shaped course taken by the *Spearhead*. It was a strange coincidence that their rendezvous with the *Spearhead* was near the completion of its inward spiral. Had the Ancients calculated this time frame into its course? Did they expect their earliest seeded life forms to evolve and advance sufficiently to catch the vessel near the end of its journey? It was an interesting thought, one that made the universe seem planned, as though it worked to some grand timetable.

The scientist appeared over the comms hologram. 'Overseer Senetep, we've successfully synthesised a living sample of the Ancients' DNA.'

'Good. Replicate multiple samples and encase them in crystal slides.' Senetep ended the hologram and stood. 'What's our position?'

'We're approaching the wormhole's event horizon,' Erund replied. 'It will deliver us within visual range of the *Spearhead*.'

'Onscreen.'

The bridge viewscreen shimmered to life with a million pinpricks of light. Straight ahead, a dense circle of black hung in the middle of space. Stars stretched around its perimeter, the only hint of the invisible forces bending time and space.

'The squadron awaits your command,' Erund continued.

'Take us in,' Senetep said.

The void filled their viewscreen, eclipsing the stars. There was a sudden jolt, and a vibrant new solar system replaced the emptiness. They had arrived.

Senetep arose from his chair as the *Ragarn* completed a 180-degree turn, revealing a fresh blue planet. He froze, enthralled by the glorious sight. The *Spearhead* emerged from the far side of the planet, sunlight flaring behind it like the flames of creation. He stepped forward, heart racing. 'Clear all UV light and enhance.'

The viewscreen zoomed in, eliminating the glare obscuring their view. The *Spearhead* was triangular in design, several hundred kilometres from tip to tip. The flat, nondescript surface had a rough texture resembling stone. An opening in the underside released a stream of drones to the planet, like worker bees leaving their nest. A bright, craterless moon orbited in the background. They had arrived in the last stages of the *Spearhead's* process. With the lunar construction complete, the planet was undergoing the final seeding of life.

Senetep had never experienced such awe and humility. He felt small and inconsequential in the face of perfection. That was a first! But this vessel had toiled for billions of years without its masters, leaving a universe full of life in its wake. He forced the distraction from his mind: a moment of humility in the face of creation was nothing to be ashamed of.

'Scan the planet.'

A hologram materialised in the middle of the bridge, showing the action on the planet's surface. The insect-like drones swarmed over a mountain range, systematically carving square blocks from the face of a cliff in neat rows. Glowing red lasers sliced through the stone in seconds. Once the blocks had cooled, the drones picked them up with their mechanical appendages and joined the train flying across the landscape. They deposited the blocks atop a pyramid amid construction.

'Everything is automated,' Erund said. 'What are your orders?'

'Approach the *Spearhead,* but keep the squad at this position.'

Erund relayed the orders.

Senetep moved to the front of the bridge as the *Ragarn* flew over the top of the Ancient vessel. He held his breath, hoping their presence didn't trigger a self-defence mechanism. A circle of light appeared directly ahead, streaming out of the alien hull, casting a beam of light into space.

'Target weapons systems,' Erund cried. 'Shields at maximum!'

Senetep spun around. 'Stop! Cancel that order. Hold our position.'

The *Ragarn* came to a gentle stop. The crew ceased what they were doing and watched the viewscreen. A featureless pyramid, hundreds of time bigger than their vessel, emerged from the *Spearhead's* hull, spinning slowly as it ascended through the column of light.

'Is it a weapon?' Erund asked.

'I doubt it. If the *Spearhead* was threatened by our presence, it would have obliterated us by now. It appears to be some form of probe. Disengage all weapons and lower shields.'

The crew obeyed his command. The pyramid came to a measured stop, then tilted upwards, rolling backwards so the underside faced their vessel. Its grey metallic surface glinted in the light. There were no markings or panels, nothing to inform its construction.

Erund moved a step closer to the tactical officer. 'Be ready for anything.'

The triangular face held still, as if watching them.

'What's it doing?' Erund said.

'Awaiting contact. Transmit the Ancients' DNA code.'

'Transmitting now,' replied the communications officer.

Nothing. Senetep edged forward, anxiously awaiting a response. The pyramid hung there, glistening like a celestial pendant in the white light. A niggle of panic set in. Was their method of communication too unsophisticated for the probe? 'Transmit the code on a continuous cycle.'

'Repeating the transmission.'

Senetep raised his hand. 'Wait!'

An iris opened in the centre of the triangle. A red glow emanated from within and bathed the *Ragarn*. Their vessel shot towards the triangular face and its imposing red eye.

'Why are we moving towards it?'

Erund pushed the pilots aside and double-checked the navigational holograms. 'The probe is pulling us in. Shall we reverse thrust?'

'No! Don't do anything.'

The pyramid inhaled their vessel with ease, like a black hole devouring a star. They passed through the gigantic iris into a cavernous void suffused by red light. The iris closed behind them, cutting off all communication and isolating them from the squadron. The disorienting wash of red disappeared, and the *Ragarn* lost power. Every holographic control dematerialised and the bridge viewscreen went blank. The vessel shuddered and became weightless for a second, then jolted to a stop, throwing everyone forward.

CLANG!

Vibrations rang through the ship and dissipated, leaving them in a deathly silence. They had landed on a solid surface. The emergency lighting shimmered to life and illuminated the bridge with a dim blue hue.

A scratching sound emerged outside the hull, then turned into a tapping that sounded like their vessel was being probed by the beaks of giant birds.

'Stand by your posts. Erund, join me in the lab.'

The tapping transformed into a crackling electrical sound. It reverberated through the darkened passages.

Senetep and Erund ran out of the bridge, through the winding passages and into the lab. The scientists scrambled around in the dim light, trying to reactivate the vessels power crystals.

'Where's the DNA sample?' Senetep shouted.

'Here!' The lead scientist rushed over with a clear tablet. 'There's a culture of live cells encased within the crystal.'

A loud clunk echoed through the vessel.

'Sounds like they've breached the hull,' Erund said.

Red light burst from the passage, casting a monstrous parade of alien silhouettes across the lab walls. Senetep stepped back. Shadows of spindly mechanical arms and bulbous shells stretched over the lab worktables. The probes floated into the lab, one after another, their singular red eyes ablaze. These Ancient machines were an odd assortment of shapes and sizes, with multi-jointed arms, claws, pincers, and bizarre appendages. They whirred and clunked about, sounding like machines that had been running for billions of years. The probes hovered over the worktables, casting swathes of scarlet light across everything.

A warrior raced into the lab, weapon drawn.

The nearest probe spun about and pinned him to the wall. A hose protruded from its metallic shell and squirted a translucent resin over his exposed face and neck. His mouth half-opened and went rigid in a silent scream. There was a wisp of vapour, then a chemical reaction. The resin ate through skin, muscle, and bone, dissolving any trace of organic matter from his head to his toes. The probe withdrew its arm and spun about, leaving the empty armour to *clang* across the floor.

Three more warriors raced down the passage. More probes clunked and whined across the lab to confront them.

'Drop your weapons!' Senetep hollered.

The warriors deactivated their staves and threw them down. The probes approached the weapons, scanned them, and pinned the warriors against the wall.

Senetep felt a rush of air to his left. A large probe with six arms lurched over the worktable, drawn by the sound of his voice. He attempted to hold up the tablet containing the DNA sample, but the cold metal pincers immobilised him in place.

The probe's glowing eye projected ribbons of red light down his body.

Senetep was helpless. His arms, legs, and head were secured in a vice grip. He peered down. In the edge of his vision, he noticed the red light intensifying on his tablet.

The machine whistled a distorted tune and its red eye switched to white. The probes whistled in response and the horde of angry eyes changed to white. They glided out of the lab in an orderly file and the *Ragarn's* power systems came back online.

'What happened?' Erund asked.

Senetep help up the tablet. 'We have permission to board the *Spearhead*.'

*   *   *

Senetep led Erund and three scientists down the gangway and into the superstructure of the *Spearhead*. Gravity and oxygen were normal. The *Ragarn* had been deposited in the middle of a vast bridge stretching from the outer hull to the central core, a gigantic spire composed of towers and pyramids. Senetep paused and marvelled at the incredible scale. The alien spire soared overhead like a million buildings stacked on top of each other, fading into a haze of atmosphere.

The immense pyramid that deposited them here ascended high into the spire and disappeared amongst the structure.

Senetep peered over the bridge into the barren expanse. The void was home to the millions of probes working on the planet. Some probes still inhabited the space. They darted by, motors humming, guided by their white glowing eyes.

A probe resembling a giant mosquito turned in their direction, eye turning red. It flew over to the bridge and hovered in front of them, spreading its imposing metal arms and pincers.

Senetep held out the sample of Ancients' DNA. The probe scanned the tablet and gave a distorted whistle. Its eye flashed to white. The machine lowered its arms, whirred about, and floated towards the spire.

Senetep marched after the probe.

'Why walk when we can fly?' Erund said. 'We restored the *Ragarn* to full power. At least it offers us some protection.'

'We were left on this bridge for a reason. I don't want to risk triggering any self-defence mechanisms.'

Erund gave a reluctant nod and fell in line. He had been resistant to disarming the warriors and leaving them on the *Ragarn*, but Senetep remained convinced this was a science mission, not a tactical one. One probe had proven a lethal force, and they were walking through a nest, home to millions more.

It took an hour walking at full pace to reach the outskirts of the spire. The probe led them through an avenue of metallic towers that twisted up into the spire like the roots of some colossal mechanical tree.

The probe passed beneath a sprawling arch, hundreds of metres high, and floated down a descending passage of waist-high steps. Senetep sprinted to catch up. He used his hands to lower himself down each step, racing to keep pace with the probe. The architecture was designed for gigantic legs with a massive gait.

Erund puffed and panted from the back of the line, a full step behind the scientists, and clambering to make do with his missing arm. 'The Ancients were a race of giants!'

'Or we're a race of midgets,' Senetep called back.

The passage spiralled around, completing one full turn before opening into a hall of epic proportions. Senetep leapt down the last step and rushed forward, quickly catching his breath. Overhead, the sweeping walls melded into the spire's internal structure. The infinite ceiling reflected in a lake of liquid mercury. It was as wide as the pool in the Great Arena, with enough space to house a fully grown kraken.

The probe whistled, then ascended into the spire. Its glowing eye became a distant pinprick of light and the machine disappeared altogether.

Senetep stood at the edge of the sprawling pool, gazing upon the flawless quicksilver. The scientists stood beside him and scanned the mercury. Erund finally joined them, sweating and puffing.

Senetep held out his hand to the lead scientist. 'Spray a synthesised sample of the Ancients DNA on my fingertip.'

The scientist unclipped a small canister from his utility belt and coated Senetep's fingertip with a clear spray.

Senetep knelt and placed his fingertip upon the mercury. The silver suctioned to his skin then sucked back into the pool. The entire lake begun swirling like a whirlpool, dipping in the centre while rising above the edges of the pool.

Erund and the scientists took a step backwards.

The mercury sped up and levitated into the chamber, separating into thousands of spinning blobs. They divided further, into millions, then billions of glistening droplets.

'They're planets, stars, solar systems,' the lead scientist said. 'Every galaxy in the universe!'

Senetep walked about, head up, enthralled by the dizzying spectacle. There were uncountable clusters of galaxies.

The mercury had now split into trillions of reflective specks, spreading from wall to wall and high into the spire, forming a complete map of the universe.

Tiny spirals of light formed inside the miniature galaxies, starting in the centre of the map and spreading out to the fringes of the universe. It was replaying the seeds of creation, blossoming like fields of incandescent flowers throughout a fertile universe. Each unique spiral represented another *Spearhead*, seeding life in another galaxy.

'This isn't the only *Spearhead!*' Senetep gasped.

'There're millions of them,' Erund whispered. 'Seeding the galaxies.'

The creeping paths of light merged, creating an intergalactic network of paths and wormholes back to the core. As the connections solidified, the centre of the map brightened, shining like a beacon to every *Spearhead*.

'What's that light in the centre?' Erund asked.

'The home of the Ancients, the birthplace of creation. Our ultimate destination.'

'What's our next course of action?'

'We stay in this chamber until we figure out how to access and control the *Spearhead's* command systems.'

'And once we do?'

'We recall the drones and steer this vessel through the nearest wormhole back to Earth. After the drones have eradicated every living organism on that pitiful planet, we travel to Akanae and repeat the process. Then we set a course for the home of the Ancients. From there, we can take control of every *Spearhead* and rewrite the universe.'

— CHAPTER 20 —

Primeval Puzzle

It was rare for Sean to have privacy these days. But for the last hour, that's exactly what Hazim had ordered. The break gave him a chance to clean up, rest, and eat something before the upcoming briefing. They were safely aboard their new vessel, the *Alnitak*, named after one of three stars in Orion's Belt. It was General Hazim's command vessel, the flagship of the Orion Taskforce, representing the first military partnership between humanity and the Isharkute. Another two identical vessels, the *Alnilam* and *Mintaka*, completed the squadron.

His quarters looked like any Isharkute military vessel, sparsely appointed and designed for the warrior class. Warriors required little in the way of comforts. Items Sean took for granted, such as soap, shampoo, and toothpaste, were a rare commodity. Some human influences had made their way aboard. At the foot of his bed was a green military case with a towel, a neatly pressed taskforce uniform, and a few extras to make him feel normal again.

Sean finished some dry biscuits and cheese from the army rations. He gulped down a full bottle of water, hoping the rehydration might shake his headache. The dull ache had persisted in the back of his skull since Yonaguni.

Sean rummaged through the case and found what he was searching for - a bottle of aspirin. It was nice to have something familiar for a change. He cracked open a fresh bottle of water, swallowed two, and sat at the hologram terminal.

Hazim had cued up his aunt and uncle's message to play.

Sean closed his eyes and rubbed his temples. He took a deep breath and waited for his thoughts slow. He couldn't avoid Steve and Janine any longer.

Being alone exacerbated his guilt. He should have contacted them before leaving Earth, but in the chaos, it was the furthest thing from his mind.

Sean opened his eyes, took a deep breath, and activated the message.

Steve and Janine appeared in a three-dimensional holographic projection. Their sad smiles reminded him of the day they dropped him at the airport. They were sitting in his bedroom. It looked just as he'd left it months before. Astronomy posters plastered the walls. Hard drives and cables cluttered his computer desk. Well-worn books on space, history, and ancient civilisations packed his overflowing bookshelf.

It was a surprising snapshot into how nerdy he was.

Steve leant forward and tapped the lens. 'Hi, Sean. We've never used one of these Isharkute recording spheres before. It took us a long time to find out how to contact you, but once we found General Powell, things moved quickly.'

'We saw you on the television. That's when we knew how to find you,' Janine said.

'After everything in Egypt, we feared the worst,' Steve cut in. 'We're so relieved to see you're okay–'

Janine leant close to the sphere and smiled, eyes glistening with tears. 'You're doing more than okay, Sean...you're saving the world.'

'We're so proud of you.'

'We just wanted to let you know we're okay. You probably had trouble finding us after Senetep's invasion. The army moved us out. We had no phones, no internet for weeks. Food was scarce. We weren't sure if we'd ever make it back here. But things are slowly returning to normal.' Janine's expression became solemn. 'A few months after you left, we had a funeral for your dad. We know you would have liked to have been there, but we needed closure.'

'Sean, it may not be possible, but we'd love to hear from you, just to know you're okay.'

The door to Sean's quarters slid open, and he paused the hologram. Bella stood in the doorway, glancing at the hologram, dressed in the Orion Taskforce uniform. 'Sorry, I didn't mean to interrupt.'

'Don't worry, you're not interrupting.'

'Is that your aunt and uncle?'

'Yeah, it's my dad's sister Janine and her husband Steve.'

Bella stepped into the room. 'Are they okay?'

Sean turned off the hologram and stood, forcing a smile. He wasn't ready to explain the situation. Not while he was dealing with it himself. 'They're fine.'

'Are you okay?'

'Yeah, let's go,' he said, brushing past her into the hall.

A human soldier from the taskforce escorted them to the *Alnitak's* bridge. The human and Isharkute crew worked alongside each other in teams of two across all the stations. Sean had not expected to see their cultures integrate so soon, but more time had passed on Earth than it had for himself, allowing plenty of time for change.

Nocao and Hazim stood at the navigation station, observing a holographic map of the surrounding galaxies. They were busy tracking and highlighting the trajectory of Senetep's squadron.

'Nocao, did you even have a break?' Sean asked.

'A few minutes,' Nocao responded, engrossed in the hologram. He enlarged a section, focusing on a distant solar system.

'He disobeyed a direct order to rest,' Hazim said.

'And with good reason. I was concerned we have run out of time... and my assumptions are correct. Senetep's squadron has intercepted a vessel of unknown origin orbiting this planet. We can't visualise the vessel from this distance, but it's on the *Spearhead's* trajectory.'

The flashing dots representing Senetep's squadron had stopped in front of a huge flashing dot, comparable in size to the nearby planet.

A terrible sinking sensation filled Sean's stomach. 'He beat us there!'

'His squadron is keeping a distance from the *Spearhead* for now.'

'How did you find him?'

'We've been tracing the power signatures of the stolen vessels,' Hazim said. 'Each power crystal emits a unique frequency. We've been tracking them since they left Earth. The problem is, one vessel is unaccounted for.'

'It's Senetep's flagship, the *Ragarn*.' Nocao said. 'The same one that attacked us on Jurassic Planet.'

'He stole it during his attack on Akanae,' Hazim said. 'We isolated its power signature from the squadron and tracked it all the way to this location, then it vanished.'

'It's inside the *Spearhead*,' Sean said. 'It has to be. We should attack now. Before it's too late!'

'Not so fast,' Nocao said. 'Senetep's squadron made one stop before intercepting the *Spearhead*.' He changed the hologram to focus on a grey-blue world in another solar system. 'We've traced their power signals back to this planet. They spent a short amount of time on the equator, several kilometres from the pyramid.'

'Senetep would only stop there if it was necessary.'

Hazim nodded. 'Nocao and I were discussing that when you walked in.'

'It's obvious, isn't it?' Bella cut in. 'He needed something to get in the *Spearhead*.'

Sean touched the hologram, magnifying the desolate grey landscape surrounding the pyramid. 'What makes this planet different to the ones we visited?'

'The *Spearhead* recently seeded this world,' Nocao said.

'How recent?'

'100,000 years.'

Bella chuckled. 'You call that recent?'

Nocao raised his eyebrow at her. 'Yes, compared to the age of the universe.' Bella gave an innocent shrug and Nocao continued.

'The first signs of life will be forming on the surface, giving valuable clues about the Ancient vessel and how it works. Time is against us, but we should investigate. If not, Senetep might be one crucial step ahead of us.'

After a sobering pause, Sean spoke up. 'It might be the difference between getting aboard the *Spearhead* or not. We don't have a choice.'

'Our thoughts exactly,' Hazim said, 'but we have limited time. You'll have an hour on the surface at most. After that, we leave to intercept Senetep's squadron.'

'What's the plan?'

Hazim took control of the hologram, adjusting it to display every vessel in the Orion Taskforce. 'We have a dozen stinger squadrons spread across the fleet – 100 vessels in all, ready to launch. Our pilots have been training for this incursion for the last year.'

'I'm more than experienced in this type of combat,' Nocao said. 'I'll pilot one of the stingers.'

'I appreciate your enthusiasm, Nocao, but you need to sit this battle out. Stay focused on getting aboard the *Spearhead*. Our first attack will distract Senetep's squadron, giving you two the opportunity to sneak aboard the Ancient vessel.'

'We don't even know how to get inside yet,' Sean said.

'Neither did Senetep,' Nocao said. 'Yet, it appears he succeeded. By following his footsteps, the answer should become apparent.'

Bella raised her hands. 'Fingers crossed!'

Hazim passed on the new coordinates to the crew. The *Alnitak* adjusted course and jumped into light speed. There was a slight shudder through the bridge and the stars streaked across the main viewscreen.

Hazim glanced at Sean. 'Impressive, huh?'

Sean gave a distracted nod, more impressed by the multi-lingual, multi-species crew. They shared workstations without a hint of prejudice. Humanity had adapted to the alien technology in record speed. 'I can't believe how well they work together. Who came up with the Orion Taskforce?'

'I did,' Hazim said, modest as ever.

'It's a brilliant idea.'

'I was inspired after seeing the way you and Nocao worked together. It was a natural step to bring our species together, forget our differences, and work to achieve a common goal.'

'Thanks to Senetep,' Nocao said. 'His intention was to divide us and enslave humanity, but he only brought us together.'

'And sped up humanity's journey into the space,' Sean said.

Hazim nodded. 'A journey that humans have been longing to make since we first gazed upon the heavens.'

'Why is that?' Bella asked. 'Why are we drawn to leave the safety of our home?'

'Like us, you question your existence,' Nocao said. 'You look to the stars, questioning your place in the universe. You desire to be more than you are. To understand your purpose.'

'That's true, Nocao,' Hazim said. 'My ancient Egyptian ancestors dreamt of a journey like this, thousands of years before space travel existed. They even constructed solar boats made from wood to emulate the journey. Most of those vessels never sailed on water, built purely to signify a greater belief. We've found many throughout my country, the most famous being Khufu's ship near the Great Pyramid.'

'I know it well,' Bella said. 'I jumped aboard it to escape General Maddock.'

'I don't blame you,' Hazim said with a grin. 'In Egyptian mythology, Ra's solar boat was called the *Mandjet*, or the *Boat of Millions of Years*. He used it to travel across the sky, giving light to the Earth during the day. Throughout the night, Ra defended his boat against Apep, a gigantic snake intent on devouring the boat and creating eternal darkness. Every night, Ra succeeded, reappearing as the sunrise on the eastern horizon. This eternal cycle represented growth, decline, death, and resurrection.'

'The *Boat of Millions of Years* could be a reinterpretation of the *Spearhead*,' Sean said.

'I thought the same thing. Every time the *Spearhead* visits a planet, it brings life to the light, then fights off the eternal night by constructing a moon.'

'And the boat's journey through the night sky might represent the *Spearhead's* journey through space. The great snake Apep could be an astronomical phenomenon like a black hole or wormhole, threatening to devour it.'

'Interesting, I hadn't thought of it that way,' Hazim said. 'I'm not sure how my ancestors came so close to the truth.'

'It makes sense that our cultures developed mythologies around the *Spearhead*,' Nocao said. 'We're all born from the same distant ancestors. Their history resides in all of us, encoded within our DNA.'

Sean noticed Nocao's comment draw a few sideways glances from the Isharkute crew. It was still a hard truth for many of them to accept.

Bella looked around the bridge. 'Where's Ramin? Why didn't he join us?'

'I haven't heard from him since we boarded,' Sean said.

'He is experiencing the first symptoms of prehibernation,' Hemket said. Her lanky body emerged from a shadowy corner of the bridge. She had been listening and watching the entire time.

'Is he okay?' Bella asked.

'His body is about to undergo metamorphosis into female form. It can be an excruciating experience and this vessel is ill-prepared to cater for him. I would prefer to return him to the forests of Akanae for a traditional, more natural birth. But there isn't time. We shall make do aboard this cold, hard vessel. I have reserved a private space for him in one of the empty cargo holds. Ramin will remain there until he's fully transformed.'

'Can we see him?'

'If he is still conscious.'

Sean, Bella and Nocao followed Hemket down through the lower decks and into a dimly lit cargo hold. The large bay doors closed behind them, sealing them inside the expansive space. A strong floral fragrance hung heavy in the air.

Sean remained still, waiting for his eyes to adjust to the dim light.

An orange glow illuminated the murkiness, flickering across their faces like a candle in the breeze. Hemket strode ahead, seeing perfectly in the dark. Sean took Bella's hand and shuffled ahead, unable to see the floor.

His eyes slowly adjusted. Female Isharkute watched them from the alcoves. Their long gangly forms were accentuated by their shimmering gowns, hovering like spectres in the night.

They rounded a corner to find a translucent screen shimmering with warm light. Hemket drew the material aside and motioned them inside.

Sean mindfully navigated the intimate space, stepping around the arrangement of waist-high candles. Their luminous wax stems twisted about like gnarled tree trunks, creating the appearance of a glowing forest. Wide bowls of liquid set between the candles glistened like miniature lakes, and there were canisters overflowing with exotic herbs and flowers.

'It smells like the forest on Akanae,' Bella whispered.

In the middle of the phosphorous landscape, curled up on the floor, lay Ramin. A white silky material gathered around him like a peeled back cocoon.

He craned his head to look at them and spoke in a weak voice. 'I'm afraid you're not seeing me at my best.'

'That's okay,' Sean whispered. He felt like he was visiting a relative in hospital, unsure of what to say next, trying to avoid the fact they were sick. Ramin had always been proud and vain. To see him like this was unsettling.

Ramin reached out.

Sean helped him into a sitting position. Ramin's fingers were long and bony and he nursed his bloated stomach with a hand that nearly wrapped around his entire waist. His hands and fingers had extended to over twice their original length.

'It feels like every part of my body is being stretched over hot coals,' Ramin said, glancing at Bella. 'Consider yourself lucky. Human pregnancies are not as painful as this.'

Bella smiled, fighting back the tears in her eyes.

'Fear not, young Bella. Hemket's midwives are doing an excellent job. I'm their first patient in decades.'

'Is there anything we can do to help?' Sean asked.

Ramin grimaced and lay back. He strained to speak this time. 'Make the universe a safe place for my unborn child.'

Sean nodded.

Ramin curled over and clutched his stomach, muttering incoherently. His eyes rolled back and he slipped into a semi-conscious state. Two midwives loped gracefully through the candles and knelt beside him, tending to his needs.

'That's enough,' Hemket said. 'Ramin must conserve his energy for the metamorphosis.'

The midwives wrapped the white material around Ramin's body, humming what sounded like a hymn, gently folding layer upon layer, until his face was hidden from view. It reminded Sean of the Egyptian mummification process.

Ramin moaned through the wrappings.

One midwife poured a decanter of oil over the material and it suctioned to Ramin's body, emphasising his curled-up foetal position. His glistening, pulsating form resembled a giant caterpillar shifting about inside a cocoon. The midwives laid dried herbs and flowers over his shell and retreated through the sea of candles.

Hemket directed Sean, Bella and Nocao out of the cargo hold and into the passage. 'You are the first outsiders to witness our hibernation ceremony.'

'How long will he be like that?' Bella asked.

'Some transformations take days, others, weeks. But Ramin is experiencing a rare condition where his transformation and pregnancy are happening at the same time. When he emerges from his cocoon, he will have given birth.'

Hemket left them and returned to assist the midwives.

*　　*　　*

The *Alnitak* dropped out of light speed and landed on the primordial planet, their last stop before engaging the *Spearhead* and Senetep's squadron. The *Alnilam* and *Mintaka* remained in orbit to protect them against any surprise attacks. Sean, Bella and Nocao joined Hazim and the landing party in the departure area.

'We're within walking distance of the pyramid,' Hazim said. 'Nocao, there are several pools where you can take samples. Sean and Bella, you're with me. We'll explore the pyramid. But remember, we have one hour. Move fast.'

'That's not enough time to open the pyramid,' Sean said.

'I don't believe we need to. Our scans show the pyramid remains unopened. Whatever Senetep found, it wasn't inside.'

'How do you know?'

'There's a daily tide that sweeps across the planet. It's left a thin layer of barnacles across the casing stones. The barnacles are undisturbed. We don't expect to encounter any life forms bigger than a tadpole...but take a weapon just in case.'

Sean's wings tingled as he took a stave from the rack. He hoped Hazim was right. Each new world had presented them with unexpected problems. What did this one hold in store?

The *Alnitak* touched down with a gentle nudge. The exterior door opened, allowing a burst of cold salty air into the bay.

Sean followed the squad down the gangway onto the crunchy black gravel. The bleak surface stretched all the way to a horizon littered with storm clouds. To their right, the Ancients' pyramid arose from the battered landscape. Its glossy black casing stones were only visible at the tip, while the rest of the structure was carpeted in greenish barnacles.

Nocao held his scanner up to the landscape. 'The tides are 3,000 kilometres away. At their current speed, they'll be here in eighty minutes.'

'Don't worry, we'll be long gone,' Hazim said.

Sean trembled. They weren't clouds in the distance, but the crests of gigantic waves. These unstoppable tsunamis raged across the planet, covering entire continents in a day. It was a world inside a washing machine, churning up the building blocks for life to flourish. All this was made possible because of the artificial moon and its proximity to the planet. Over billions of years it would travel outwards, inch by inch, decreasing its gravitational pull, leaving a more stable environment. This relationship copied the Earth and Moon, Akanae and Nek-Karani; a billion-year process that encouraged life to evolve.

Nocao scanned the nearby pools as Hazim and the squad marched towards the pyramid. Sean hesitated. A spark of an idea formed in his mind. Everything suddenly fell into place. He just needed a moment process what it meant.

Bella turned around. 'What's wrong?'

'It's a waste of time.'

'What is?'

He understood the reason they were here. Sean was too excited to answer. He spun around and sprinted back to Nocao. Bella chased after him, shoes crunching across the gravel. Nocao scooped a sample of water and paused, looking with concern at the crazy person running towards him.

Sean skidded to a stop, kicking up a wave of gravel. 'I just figured it out.'

Nocao rose to his feet, screwing the lid on the sample container. Bella caught up, followed by Hazim. The squad spread out behind them, weapons directed at the bleak terrain.

Hazim glanced around, as if expecting something to attack them out of thin air. 'Sean, what's going on?'

'I figured it out.'

'You already said that!'

Sean took a deep breath and gathered his thoughts. 'The pyramids are just repositories for information. Nothing more. They don't hide any special instructions about how to control the *Spearhead*.'

'So why did Senetep come here?'

'To sample life in its earliest, purest form. The organisms on this planet are just starting to evolve beyond single-celled organisms into more complex life forms.' Sean snatched Nocao's sample and held it up to the sunlight, illuminating the specks darting through the water. '*Life* is the key to the *Spearhead*.'

Nocao snatched back his sample. 'How?'

'Like you said before, we all share the same ancestors. Traces of the Ancients live inside all of us, encoded in our DNA. They left clues in every living thing, like a trail of breadcrumbs through the universe. What if every strand of DNA is part of a bigger picture?'

'Like pieces of a puzzle,' Nocao said, catching on to his train of thought.

'Yeah, we could rebuild the puzzle.'

'If we compared the DNA from every known species, starting with this one, we might find a pattern. Something to link it all together.'

'Yes! You could rebuild the Ancients' DNA.'

'What good is that?' Hazim asked.

'It's a key – a genetic key to access the *Spearhead*.'

Hazim slung his stave over his shoulder. 'You two don't disappoint. Sounds like our work here is done. Nocao, can you figure this out before we reach Senetep's squadron?'

Nocao eyed the sample. His cool blue complexion turned pallid. 'I can try.'

Sean had never seen his Isharkute friend look so terrified.

— CHAPTER 21 —

Interface

Sean watched the tide race across the barren grey landscape from the safety of the *Alnitak's* command bridge. The first wave smashed into the pyramid with devastating power, throwing a plume of water hundreds of metres high. How long could the pyramid withstand this constant beating? One thousand years? One hundred thousand? Tumultuous events like this might explain why Egypt's Great Pyramid emerged from antiquity in such bad shape.

'We have three hours before we reach Senetep's squadron,' Hazim said. 'I'll assemble a taskforce to infiltrate the *Spearhead*. In the meantime, you and Bella head down to the science lab and help Nocao.'

'Good idea,' Sean said.

'Not that he needs our help. He's probably come up with a solution already,' Bella said. 'He's the smartest person I know.' She cocked her head at Sean. 'No offence.'

Sean headed off with a laugh.

Down in the lab, Nocao paced anxiously around a floor-to-ceiling hologram of a double-helix. Every scientist in the fleet had transferred aboard to assist. They rushed about the lab, manipulating small holographic DNA models projected from their data pads, comparing results.

'How's it going?' Sean asked.

'We solved it!'

Bella elbowed Sean in the ribs. 'See? I told you!'

Nocao stopped in front of the rotating hologram. 'This double-helix is a complete reconstruction of the Ancients' DNA.'

'That was fast!' Sean said.

'It was simple – no wonder Senetep figured it out. We compared the genetic sequences of every species on record, stripped away all evolutionary markers and unique traits, then overlapped the remaining nucleotides. It fit together perfectly, like a puzzle. The microbial sample we took from the planet was the first base pair in the sequence, the piece that brought it all together.'

'How do we use it to get inside the *Spearhead*?'

'We can transmit the DNA as data or present it in physical form. We've already started synthesising a sample, but I have another idea.' Nocao narrowed his eyes at Sean. 'If this works, it will put us one step ahead of Senetep.'

'What's that?' Sean said dubiously.

'By harnessing the power of your brain.'

'My brain? I don't like the sound of that.'

'Don't worry, it's completely safe.'

'When you say that, it sounds even more dangerous.'

Bella nudged him in the ribs. 'Let Nocao explain.'

'Okay.'

'The Yonaguni beacon transmitted your consciousness across the universe to Neberun's fleet. Since then, you've repeated this ability with limited success. With my help, I believe we can link you into the Ancients' communication network and transmit your consciousness inside the *Spearhead*. You could spy on Senetep. Find out everything he knows before we arrive. It would be a huge tactical advantage.'

'It sounds risky. Are you sure you can access their network?'

'I've already done it – when I sent the distress call from the dinosaur pyramid. But in that case, my scanner physically interfaced with the mercury. Since we left, I hadn't been able to access the Ancients' signal.' Nocao typed across his data pad and stood back from the hologram. 'Until now.'

A distorted sine wave appeared inside Ancients' double-helix. The turbulent waves settled into a harmonious rhythm, sitting perfectly in the twisting backbone of DNA.

'What's that?' Bella asked.

'It's a sine wave,' Sean jumped in. 'Showing us the amplitude and frequency of the *Spearhead's* signal.'

Bella turned to Nocao. 'And you hacked into it with their DNA!'

'Not hacked. The Ancients' DNA acts like a filter, clearing away the galactic noise. The *Spearhead* is constantly transmitting data into our galaxy. Now we can access this signal and trace it back to the source.'

'You just unlocked the Ancients' wi-fi password.'

'I have access to their network, but I don't have time to decipher their systems.'

'Hold on,' Sean interjected. 'You want to upload my consciousness to the *Spearhead* so I can spy on Senetep?'

'Exactly. You can direct your consciousness at will, go anywhere you want inside the *Spearhead*. It's the perfect interface.'

'I don't have much luck when I try to force it.'

'I can assist you. A mild sedative should help you establish the link.'

Bella took his hand. 'You can do it.'

Sean didn't have much time to think it over. They were hours away from confronting Senetep's fleet, with no idea how much control the Overseer had over the Ancient vessel. They stared at him, eagerly expecting an answer.

'All right, I'll try. But this won't do my headache any good.'

'What headache?' Nocao said.

'I've had it for days now. Could be a migraine. I think it's getting worse. I had some aspirin, but–'

Nocao guided him to an examination table. 'Sit here, I'll examine you.'

'It's not that bad, we can get on with–'

'Stop talking.' Nocao said, pressing a hand between his shoulder blades to straighten his back. He wasn't taking no for an answer.

'I thought it might be my new wings.'

'Please, stop talking,' Nocao said. He worked up Sean's spine, firmly examining every vertebrae and muscle with his fingers.

'You've never complained of migraines. How long have you been having them?'

'They started after we left Earth. Last time you scanned me you said the Yonaguni beacon changed my brain's chemistry, that it was working harder than any human brain you'd ever seen.'

'Yes, but you'd just experienced your first out-of-body experience. It appeared to be a natural side effect.'

'Where did you go the first time?' Bella said.

'He visited his father, 10,000 years ago.'

'*Che cosa!*' Bella cried. 'You travelled through time? I thought you only travelled to the Ancients homeworld... You never told me about your dad.'

'The Ancients' homeworld!' Nocao said. 'You didn't tell me that.'

Sean sighed. He had some explaining to do.

'It's all been happening so fast. I'm struggling to understand it myself. These things sound crazy. More like dreams and hallucinations. I'm not comfortable talking about them when I don't really understand them myself. There's one thing I know for sure: the migraines are getting worse.'

Nocao held a scanner to Sean's head and observed his neural activity on a data pad. 'Your mind is functioning at twice the normal human capacity right now.'

'Probably since I started hearing the voices.'

Nocao and Bella glared at him, blurting in unison. 'What voices?!'

'I think it's the Ancients.'

'What are they saying?' Nocao asked.

'Nothing I can understand. It's more like a feeling. Like they're calling to me.'

Nocao eyed the scan, deep in thought, then looked over to the hologram showing the Ancients' DNA entwined with the *Spearhead's* signal. 'I believe there's a logical explanation.'

'What's that?'

'Your brain is acting like a receiver, picking up a signal being relayed through the *Spearhead*. You weren't born with this ability; it was awakened after the Yonaguni beacon beamed your consciousness across the galaxy. The Ancients picked up your thoughts like a radio signal and locked onto you. This could be part of the *Spearhead's* mission, to seed life, then alert the Ancients when a life form evolves beyond the confines of their physical body.'

'If the Ancients evolved beyond their mortal bodies, that would explain why their planet is deserted.'

'Where did they go? Another dimension or something?' Bella asked.

'Another plane of existence – one that Sean can communicate with.'

'You make him sound like a radio.'

'Correct. In fact, we all are. Consciousness is not easily explained, even among the Isharkute. We don't completely understand where it comes from. We're all just organic beings made from the same cellular material. What defines our consciousness? Where does a thought come from? Where does our personality and sense of purpose come from?'

'Our soul,' Bella said. 'That's what makes us unique.'

'Call it what you will,' Nocao said, 'but is that soul or conscious thought created in your physical body? Or are we receivers, drawing our consciousness from elsewhere in the universe?'

'That makes sense,' Sean said. 'It would explain a lot of things, like reincarnation and people who remember past lives. People with multiple personalities might be like broken radios, picking up too many signals at once. Consciousness could be a force, floating around the universe, waiting for a host. When the host body dies, it moves on to the next.'

'Most importantly,' Nocao said, 'it would explain your ability to astral project your mind outside of your body.'

'We're running out of time,' Sean said. He swung his legs onto the table and lay back, ready for action. 'How do I do this?'

Nocao pushed his head to the side and stuck small electrodes behind his ears. 'I'll transmit the *Spearhead's* signal straight into your organic translators. Once you have untethered your mind from your body, focus your thoughts on the signal. It should sound like a gentle hum.'

'Okay. Got it.'

Bella leant over him. 'Be careful.'

'I'm not going anywhere...not physically, anyway,' Sean said.

'Don't get lost out there.'

Sean took hold of her hand. 'I've got you to guide me home.'

Bella kissed him on the lips. Sean gave her a confident smile. The anchor between his mind and physical body could not be stronger.

Nocao placed a syringe gun to his neck. 'I'll monitor your vital signs. If anything strange happens, I'll wake you up.'

Sean gave an apprehensive nod. There was a brief pain in his neck. The stark overhead lights blurred into shifting blobs, and the lab's bustling sounds became a distant echo.

Sean floated upwards, through his eyelids, towards the glowing splotches. He felt the moment of separation from his body, as if drawn out by a magnet. His vision cleared. He was now floating over his body, peering down upon Nocao and Bella. His peripheral vision warped around him like a wide-angle lens, showing the breadth of the busy lab.

Sean hovered over his body. It was a disconcerting sensation, like looking in a mirror, except his eyes were closed. His body seemed like someone else altogether. He felt too close, like he was intruding into his own personal space.

He concentrated on the electrodes feeding his ears.

The hum appeared from nothing and resonated through his consciousness, tingling like static electricity, giving his thoughts weight and form.

CRACK!

His mind was suddenly wrenched into a powerful stream of energy. He zoomed outside the hull of the *Alnitak*. He glimpsed the other two vessels in their fleet, the *Alnilam* and *Mintaka*, then shot light-years ahead. Stars, solar systems, and galaxies flashed by in a celestial blur. It was easier this time. He didn't need to focus on a destination, as the *Spearhead's* signal guided him in on autopilot.

He sensed the Ancient vessel getting closer, but he wanted to see it.

The twisting tunnel of light flashed into sharp focus.

Sean found himself in a new solar system, the *Spearhead* directly ahead, orbiting a vibrant young planet.

Senetep's squadron was in a holding pattern a safe distance away. Sean moved past the squad and onto the *Spearhead*. The expansive grey hull consumed his view. He travelled into the cavernous interior, over a sprawling bridge, past Senetep's flagship, the *Ragarn*, speeding towards a central spire of colossal towers and pyramids.

He spiralled through an epic archway, down an equally impressive set of stairs, and into the central chamber. Senetep and his scientists stood before an immense liquid mercury map of the universe.

Senetep's voice echoed through the space. 'Recall the drones, set a course for the nearest wormhole.'

Sean panicked. Was he too late? Where was Senetep sending the *Spearhead*?

That thought pulled him into the map, shrinking his perspective down to match the scale of this mercury-made universe. A river of silver shot past him, like a comet hurtling through space. He focused on the river and his point of view merged with the stream, following a course being plotted by the scientists. The entire universe was recreated with microscopic specks of mercury, with more detail than the naked eye could distinguish at normal size. He whizzed past planets, solar systems, and entire galaxies glistening in quicksilver, finally coming to a stop in front of a planet. Even without colour, the continents embossed upon its reflective surface were unmistakable. It was Earth!

The *Spearhead* was being redirected to his home planet!

Sean pulled out of the map and returned to his bird's-eye view of the chamber, desperate for more details. 'Reconfigure the drones for a planetwide erasure of Earth...then Akanae.'

Sean had heard enough. He focused on Bella's hand, desperate to get back to her.

But instead of being pulled towards his body, he was being drawn in another direction, down through the *Spearhead's* superstructure. The disorienting blur of metal cleared, and he flew into a dim chamber dominated by a circular platform pulsing with three concentric rings of energy.

Why was he here? The voices answered: The Ancients brought him here for a reason.

The luminous rings drew him near, ebbing with a warm, inviting energy. He was close enough to touch the amber-coloured rings. If only he had hands. *That's it! That's what the Ancients want me to do. They want me to touch the rings.* His realisation acted like a reset button.

CRACK! A flash of light snapped him back into his mortal body onboard the *Alnitak*. He jolted upright, gulping a lungful of air.

'Are you all right?' Bella said.

Sean looked down. They were still holding hands. Their connection seemed unbreakable. His heart felt stronger, invincible, even. He stared into her eyes. 'As long as I'm with you.'

Bella squeezed him tight.

Nocao cleared his throat. 'I hate to break up your romantic interlude, but we have a strict schedule if we are to save the universe.'

Sean laughed, then became serious. 'We have less time than I thought we did... I need to speak to Hazim.'

Soon after, they were all on the bridge and Sean finished explaining everything. Hazim found his out-of-body adventures hard to believe at first, but Nocao backed him up with the science of it all. There was too much evidence to pass it off as a hallucination.

'And you believe Senetep is turning the *Spearhead* around, to take it through a wormhole back to Earth.'

'Yes. He could be there within a day,' Sean said. 'Akanae is after that.'

'How does he intend to use it?'

'The *Spearhead* carries millions of drones, they're like worker bees. But instead of using them to create life, he's reconfiguring them to wipe out every living cell–'

'Like a giant pest exterminator.'

'Yeah, but he's not stopping there. He has the entire universe in his sights.'

'Let me get this straight. You want to infiltrate the *Spearhead* and do what?'

'I don't know exactly,' Sean admitted. 'The Ancients showed me a platform with glowing rings for a reason. I trust their instincts. I'm not sure why, but they trust me. That's why they're reaching out to me.'

'Ancient voices communicating through a universal network of moons and pyramids!' Hazim exclaimed. 'Do you have any idea how far-fetched that sounds?'

'No more far-fetched than any of this,' Sean said, looking around.

Hazim smiled. 'You have a point.' He waved over a youthful Isharkute with intelligent eyes and a clean white beard braided with beads of the Guild of Arms. 'This is Commander Tukuil Ekar. He's leading the taskforce into the *Spearhead*.'

Tukuil acknowledged the three of them with a respectful nod. 'It's an honour to serve with you all.'

Sean, Bella and Nocao regarded each other with a mutual recognition. Like it or not, they had become war heroes in this fight for the universe.

'We have one more light-speed jump before we meet Senetep's fleet,' Hazim said. 'I want you three to go over the mission details with Tukuil. Your objective is simple: get aboard, and do whatever's necessary to take control of the *Spearhead* before Senetep takes it through the wormhole.'

— CHAPTER 22 —

Incursion

The *Alnitak*, *Alnilam*, and *Mintaka* dropped out of light speed right behind Senetep's squadron. Sean had seen the *Spearhead* in his mind, but even so, he was not prepared for the actual scale of the Ancient vessel. He stared at the bridge viewscreen in awe, frozen in place, butterflies raging through his stomach. Senetep's vessels were specks against the monolith. The *Spearhead* blocked out the stars, and this was just the side view. From the top, the flat triangular vessel was big enough to hide a planet. Sean glanced over his shoulder. The crew stood silently at their posts, mouths agape, staring in wonder at their creator. It was hard to comprehend.

'*Mio Dio!*' Bella whispered to herself.

'Shields at 100 per cent,' Hazim ordered. 'Weapons ready.'

The crew sprang into action and prepared for battle.

Sean pointed to the swarm of probes leaving the planet and streaming into the underside of the *Spearhead's* hull. 'That's an entry point for our dropship!'

Hazim rounded on them. 'You need to leave. Once the first wave of stingers have completed their pass, I'll give you the signal to launch.'

'Good luck!' Sean said, shaking hands with Hazim.

Bella gave Hazim a quick goodbye hug. Nocao made the sign of the cosmos. Hazim returned the gesture and faced Tukuil. 'Look after these three. They're our best hope.'

Tukuil nodded. 'They can look after themselves.'

Hazim smiled. 'Of that, I'm sure.'

Tukuil led the charge down to the docking bay. Sean had never seen the passages so busy. The crew rushed by them, nodding in admiration. Their eyes showed fear, but their faces were set with determination. A palpable tension filled the air. It was war!

They entered the docking bay as a squad of stingers launched into space.

Tukuil directed them over to an armour-plated vessel resembling a cross between an army tank and an Isharkute transport. Inside, it was standing room only. A squad of human and Isharkute soldiers shared the cramped space. They had Isharkute staves slung over their backs and Beretta M-9s in their hip holsters. The squad moved aside and gave them room, tipping their navy berets in respect.

Sean, Bella and Nocao squeezed aboard.

Flashes of light erupted across the front windscreen, drawing everyone's attention to the cockpit. The battle had begun. Tukuil activated a hologram showing the skirmish outside. Squads of stingers swept across Senetep's vessels, showering their hulls in energy blasts. The *Alnitak, Alnilam,* and *Mintaka* hung back, firing from a distance. The first defensive stingers emerged from Senetep's vessels. They didn't stand a chance. A barrage of fire obliterated them moments after appearing.

Nocao peered into the cockpit, looking eager to slip into the pilot's seat.

Sean gave him a friendly nudge. 'You're meant to sit this one out. Remember?'

Nocao grumbled.

A hologram of Hazim appeared over the cockpit controls. 'The first wave has completed their run. We're in place to give you covering fire.'

'Launch!' Tukuil called from the back of the cabin.

Sean grasped the overhead rail as the dropship lurched out of the docking bay. They left the safety of the *Alnitak* behind and plunged into space. There was a moment of nausea-inducing weightlessness, like riding a rollercoaster. They swerved, plunged, and banked hard through the relentless crossfire. In space, there was no up or down, just unpredictable turns. It took incredible effort just to hang on. Bella's panic-stricken face took on a sickly green tinge.

BOOM!

An explosion rolled across their windscreen, sending violent vibrations through the cabin. Sean clutched the overhead rail with his both hands. That was too close for comfort.

Nocao shook his head. 'Our pilots aren't reacting fast enough.'

Sean glowered at him to be quiet, hoping the pilots hadn't heard the comment. He didn't want them to lose confidence.

They flew under Senetep's fleet, drawing the attention of several stingers from Senetep's defences. The pilots accelerated towards the *Spearhead* as the stingers opened fire.

'Hold on tight!' Sean called through the cabin.

The pilots banked hard to avoid the attack. Energy blasts flashed by their left side and erupted across the *Spearhead's* hull. They went into a disorienting barrel roll, skimming down the side of the gigantic vessel. The wall of grey blurred by the windscreen, like they were falling down the side of an endless cliff.

Sean glanced over at Bella. Her eyes were shut tight, teeth clenched. She rocked about, clutching the rail with everything she had.

They cleared the hull, swerved left, and flew head-on into the swarm of probes. The pilots reacted, sending their dropship into a dive for the planet. The returning probes diverted from the *Spearhead* and attacked the fleet.

Tukuil worked his way forward to the cockpit. 'What's happening?'

'Senetep's turning the probes against our fleet,' Sean said.

The probes swarmed the *Mintaka* like voracious insects. They teemed over every square inch of the vessel in a nightmarish horde of mechanical legs and flaming red eyes. They peeled off sections of the hull like paper and poured inside.

Bella opened her eyes and gasped. 'Urgh! What are they doing?'

The Isharkute captain of the *Mintaka* appeared on the comms hologram, his face wracked with panic and desperation. 'The probes have breached the hull. They're decimating my crew.' Behind him, a group of survivors furiously welded the bridge doors shut. 'We can't keep them back any longer!'

The probes ripped the doors open and rushed inside. The bridge went dark. Distorted screams came through the hologram. Muzzle flashes and energy blasts erupted like fireworks, illuminating a new horror. The probes unleashed deadly hoses from their armoured shells. They writhed about like snakes, spitting acid over the crew, dissolving them where they stood.

Bella turned away. 'That's horrible!'

Sean watched in shock, unable to draw his eyes away. By the time the emergency lighting kicked in, the *Mintaka's* bridge was devoid of life. Crumpled uniforms lay in heaps over empty boots. The probes had erased every trace of organic matter, proving they were as efficient at eradicating life as creating it.

'Hazim, turn your ship around!' Sean said. 'Get the fleet out of here.'

'Not until you're inside the *Spearhead*.'

Sean peered through the dropship windscreen. The probes returning from the planet were now diverting to the *Mintaka*, leaving the hole into the *Spearhead* open. They had a chance to get inside.

'Why aren't the probes attacking us?' Bella asked.

'I don't know,' Sean shot back.

'They're working as a hive mind,' Nocao said. 'Attacking one vessel at a time. Senetep can't control them individually.'

'Good,' Tukuil said. 'That gives us time.'

Fresh energy blasts exploded ahead of them, jolting them off course, throwing everyone to one side of the cabin. Nocao caught Bella with one arm and steadied her onto the overhead rails.

'There's two stingers on our tail and Senetep's fleet is firing at us,' cried one of the pilots. 'We won't make it.'

Tukuil scrambled over the tangle of fallen bodies into the cockpit entrance. 'Take evasive action.'

Nocao squeezed past him. 'No! Aim for the entry point. We won't get another chance.'

Tukuil pushed him back, blocking the doorway. 'Ignore that.

Dive for the planet. We'll lose them in the atmosphere and return for another pass.'

Nocao huffed in frustration and pounded the cabin wall.

The dropship suddenly plummeted towards the planet's exosphere. The hull rattled and shook. Explosions pounded them from every side. Superheated waves of atmospheric gases heaved across the windscreen.

Sean white-knuckled the rails, feeling like he was about to fall forward onto the cockpit windscreen.

As they cleared the upper atmosphere the blasts subsided, the dropship settled into a smoother flight. The pilots followed the train of drones down to the continent, flying in the opposite direction.

Sean eyed the stingers on the navigational hologram. They were still in hot pursuit and following them down to the planet's surface. 'We're not out of trouble yet.'

They descended into the shadow of a mountain range and followed the probes through a deep ravine. The dark-grey cliffs closed in around them. Gusts of wind sent them dangerously close to the unforgiving stone, just metres from the probes. One wrong manoeuvre and it was all over. The gap tightened. Sean held his breath. The ravine suddenly parted, bathing the cockpit in sunlight. They shot across a sprawling rocky plateau.

'Wow!' Sean blurted with relief and excitement.

A near-complete pyramid arose from the landscape, pristine and gleaming in a polished dark-grey stone. The last few probes lowered the final casing stones into place, completing the pyramid. Sean never expected to arrive on a planet in time to see the *Spearhead* complete its work.

The cockpit flashed with warning holograms, showing the stingers emerging from the ravine behind them.

'Our pilots should have stuck to the ravines,' Nocao grumbled. 'This vessel is too slow to outrun the stingers in a normal atmosphere.'

The stingers passed overhead, bombarding them with energy blasts.

Tukuil spun around and waved Nocao forward. 'Fine. Show us what you can do.'

Nocao pushed through and took the first pilot's seat.

Sean gave Bella a hopeful smile. They were in safe hands now. His friend had flown them away from tectonic missiles, underground lava lakes, and an erupting volcano.

Nocao glanced at the holographic map while flying straight at the pyramid, passing metres below the probes. Far ahead, the stingers circled around for another pass, preparing to attack them head-on. Nocao skimmed beneath the line of probes, diving for the pyramid, close enough to pick out each individual block.

'Hold on!' Nocao hollered, yanking hard on the controls.

The dropship suddenly veered skyward, cutting a sharp line beside the probes. The stingers opened fire, tearing divots of stone off the plateau and up the pyramid, obliterating chunks of freshly laid blocks. The probes scattered like wasps defending a disturbed nest and chased down the stingers. They latched onto the vessels, tore them open, and melted the pilots in their seats. The empty stingers crashed upon the plateau, and the probes returned to repair the damaged pyramid.

'Hah! Just what I thought,' Nocao cried. 'The *Spearhead* has a great self-defence mechanism; its probes behave like blood cells fighting off an infection.'

'As long as they don't turn on us,' Bella said.

'They won't, as long as we don't pose a threat.'

'Clever,' Sean said, suddenly realising the weight of Nocao's analogy. He hadn't thought of it that way. The *Spearhead*, probes, and host planet acted as one giant organism while the seeding took place. Any threat, no matter how small, was swiftly eliminated.

Unfortunately, the deadliest virus had already slipped through the *Spearhead's* defences and infected the system. Senetep. If they could convince the *Spearhead* that Senetep was an infection, the drones would turn on him.

Nocao slipped their dropship into the stream of probes, like blood cells racing back to the beating heart. They passed through the atmosphere and into space. Their situation had not improved. The *Mintaka* drifted helplessly as the drones infiltrated the *Alnilam*.

The *Spearhead* had pushed further into space, on course to the wormhole back to Earth.

'How long until the *Spearhead* reaches the wormhole?' Sean asked.

Nocao brought up the nearest wormhole on the holographic map. 'Fifteen minutes. We can't waste any more time, we're going in!'

Hazim's hologram reappeared. 'Good to see you back, we'll cover you as long as we can.'

'You can't do any more,' Sean said. 'Get out of here!'

The transmission broke up and turned to static.

Sean peered out the windscreen. The probes swarmed over the *Alnitak*, their last flagship in the Orion Taskforce. Hazim and his crew were minutes away from being dissolved. The *Spearhead* eclipsed his view of the besieged ship; a grim premonition he might never see Hazim again.

Nocao accelerated for the opening, merging with the returning probes.

The expansive hull filled their view, and in the next instant, they were flying through a dark circular shaft crammed with probes. Their luminous white eyes criss-crossed the tunnel walls like car headlights, then scattered, becoming distant pinpricks of light in an infinite haze.

'We're inside the *Spearhead*!' Sean said.

A central spire dominated the centre of the void, like a thousand cities all stacked together. The gigantic outer walls created an all-encompassing gloom, with no clear beginning or end.

'Unbelievable!' Tukuil said, leaning into the cockpit to peer through the windscreen. 'A small moon could sit between the spire and hull without touching either.'

Nocao checked the environmental scans. 'It has breathable atmosphere and regular gravity.' A thin line materialised from the atmospheric haze above the dropship. Nocao saw it and adjusted their course to intercept. 'That's a bridge. I'm picking up readings from Senetep's vessel, the *Ragarn*.'

Tukuil seemed ready to pounce on the controls. 'Destroy it. Now! While we have the chance.'

'It's too risky,' Sean said. 'It might set the drones against us.'

'You're right – they'll perceive it as an attack.' Nocao said, glancing over his shoulder to Sean. 'It's up to you now. Where do we set down?'

'Scan the spire for openings beneath the bridge.'

Nocao's co-pilot adjusted the hologram scanner. The lower section of the spire resembled an upside down collection of skyscrapers, tapering off to a fine point that touched the outer hull kilometres below.

Without thinking, Sean pointed to an area on the hologram. 'That's it! Land there.'

'You sure?'

Sean nodded, unnerved by his subconscious knowledge. He knew exactly where to go, as if the Ancients had implanted the answer in his mind.

Nocao flew the dropship in and landed on an open platform set in front of a towering archway. A gang of probes swooped in, swathing the hull with their ominous red eyes. *Clunk! Tap, tap, tap!* Their spidery arms prodded the hull.

Bella clutched onto Sean. 'They want to melt us!'

Nocao rushed out of the cockpit, back through the cabin, and opened his case of scientific equipment.

'What are you doing?' Tukuil said.

Nocao held up a small vial of clear liquid. 'They're looking for this.'

'What is it?'

'A synthesised version of the Ancients' DNA, the alien race that built the *Spearhead*.' Nocao edged past the soldiers to the exterior door. 'Once the probes verify this genome, they should leave us alone.'

'Should?!' Tukuil responded, sounding less than convinced.

Nocao attached the vial into a tiny pump and sprayed a sample over his hand. He opened the exterior door. Red light flooded the cabin. A spindly set of mechanical legs stretched inside and unfurled around the opening, followed by a blazing red eye.

Sean shielded his face. It was like being hit in the eyes by a high-powered laser.

Nocao squinted and held up his hand.

The probe narrowed its eye beam into an intense ribbon of scarlet light. It scanned his hand, gave a distorted whistle, and flew off, drawing the other probes with it.

Nocao breathed a sigh of relief. 'We're in.'

Sean led everyone outside and sprinted through the main arch. He intuitively knew the way even though he had never been here before. They raced down passageways left deserted for billions of years. Soaring walls and vaulted ceilings loomed over them in god-sized scale. Their footsteps echoed through the lonely space.

They arrived in a circular chamber; the same one Sean visited in his vision. A raised circular platform, roughly 10 metres wide, dominated the centre area. Three concentric rings of liquid mercury were embedded around its outer circumference.

The taskforce set up defensive positions around the chamber.

Nocao walked up the steps to the platform, scanning the area with his handheld data recorder. Sean paused on the top step. His inner voice warned him not to step inside the rings. Bella peered over his shoulder as he knelt for a closer inspection. Mercury flowed through the rings in a steady clockwise motion.

Sean pulled back his sleeve, mesmerised by the flow of silver. Deep in his subconscious, he knew he had to touch it.

'What are you doing?' Nocao said.

'I'm meant to activate this.'

Tukuil marched up the steps, stave charged and ready for action. 'What is this device?'

'I'm not sure,' Sean replied. The need to touch the rings raged inside him, spreading like an out-of-control bushfire. It was urgent. The Ancients were screaming at him. *Do it now!* He glanced at Bella. She gave him a subtle, reaffirming nod and he looked at Tukuil. 'This is what we came here to do. I know it's right.'

'Okay, we'll cover you,' Tukuil said. He returned to the bottom step and aimed at the entrance to the chamber.

Sean took a deep breath and lowered his hand over the outermost ring of silver. The cool slivers of mercury stretched out and enveloped his fingers, then his hand. He closed his eyes, submitting himself to the Ancients' technology. *Yes! This is what they wanted.*

A brilliant light flashed through his mind's eye, extinguishing the urgency. The Ancients finally became quiet.

Sean opened his eyes. The platform inside the rings had transformed into a horizontal pool of energy, casting ripples of amber light up the chamber walls.

Nocao assessed the readings on his scanner with bewilderment. 'You just opened a portal!'

'It looks an upside down world,' Bella said, leaning precariously over the edge. 'I can see another room. There's some kind of opening or doorway on the other side. That gold light...it's a sunset on another planet.'

'It's the Ancients' planet,' Sean said, realising he just linked the *Spearhead's* portal to one on their homeworld.

Nocao's scanner beeped loudly.

'What's that?'

'Our dropship shields have been compromised. It's under attack from–'

BOOM! An explosion rumbled down the passage, followed by a blast of superheated air. A wall of flames rolled into the chamber, incinerating the squad members near the entrance.

A second blast wave surged through the chamber, lifting Sean off his feet, throwing him backwards over the portal. His wings instinctively shot out, gliding him to safety high in the chamber. Everything else appeared to happen in slow motion.

The force had thrown Bella and Nocao straight into the portal.

Sean watched in horror as their bodies dematerialised atom by atom, like grains of sand washed away by a wave. Suddenly, they were gone. He shielded his face from the searing heat. The air was too hot to dive after them.

A line of drones flew into the chamber and formed a defensive circle around the portal. More drones mopped up the carnage, dissolving the scorched corpses.

The flames and smoke cleared.

Tukuil was the only one still moving. He dragged his smoking body up the stairs to the portal. His charred black flesh cracked apart, exposing the raw pink flesh beneath. With a grimace, he stretched for the portal's golden light. The hovering drone sprayed him. There was a sudden searing sound, like a piece of meat being thrown on a hot grill, and he was gone too.

Sean hovered, numb with shock. He was the last one left. His vacant stare was drawn to the lone figure descending the passage.

Senetep peered up at him and narrowed his icy-blue eyes, smug with satisfaction. That evil expression could extinguish life itself.

— CHAPTER 23 —

Armageddon

Senetep entered the chamber, drones swarming over him in a protective circle. Erund Griss, his one-armed Commander, led the way, kicking aside the trail of smouldering uniforms. These grim reminders were the only evidence the Orion Taskforce ever existed.

Sean eyed the portal from his elevated position. It was still active. He could dive for it if he wasn't surrounded by drones. A squad of warriors marched around the portal, weapons trained on him. There was no way out of this. He would have been better off falling through the portal with Nocao and Bella. They were millions of light-years away in the centre of the universe. Stranded, alone, and helpless without him.

Senetep strolled around the portal, peering up at him. 'You can't stay up there forever.'

Sean noticed the group of scientists following close behind. They monitored handheld tablets, making constant adjustments to the displays. *Is that how they control the drones?*

'Come down before I shoot you down.'

Sean cast a hopeful eye around the chamber, searching for a crack in the defences. He had to reach the portal. It was his only escape. The drones closed in around him. Their deadly hoses whipped about like angry, poison-spitting asps. One wrong move and he would dissolve in midair, leaving his empty uniform to fall away.

Sean landed with his hands raised in the air. He kept an eye on the scientists and their control tablets, noting how the drones responded to their commands.

'Don't look so despondent,' Senetep said. 'Consider your allies lucky. Between Earth and Akanae, there are billions more lives to eradicate. Not all will be as quick and painless as theirs.'

Sean wanted to retort with something scathing. He bit his lip and swallowed his insults. It was more effective to keep quiet and deny Senetep any satisfaction.

Senetep brushed past him, smirking with cruel pleasure.

Sean's stomach twinged. Not from nerves, but rather muscle memory. Their last brutal encounter was hardwired into his body.

'I should have guessed I'd find you down here,' Senetep mused, strolling back into view. He acted calm and in control, like his old self from 10,000 years ago. 'It appears our fates are entwined, destined to see this to the end.'

Sean kept his mouth shut, swallowing the insults.

Senetep walked up the steps up to the portal. The scientists typed into their data pads and two of the drones floated aside, giving him access. Senetep stood on the top step and leant over, admiring the ripples of golden energy. 'Where does this portal lead?'

'I don't know,' Sean muttered.

Senetep glowered over his shoulder. 'What did you say?'

Sean squared his shoulders and found his voice. 'I said I don't know.'

Senetep returned a cold, calculating gaze. 'The *Spearhead* is hundreds of kilometres square in diameter, yet you bypassed the main control centre and came straight here. Your taskforce knew exactly what they were doing.'

Sean kept silent. He wasn't being asked a question. Senetep liked the sound of his own voice, and judging from their past encounters, would eventually give up his intentions. If the Overseer had one weakness, it was his self-obsession. Overconfidence had its pitfalls.

'I'll tell you what I think,' Senetep continued. 'I believe you've opened a portal. You know, like I do, whoever gets to the Ancients' homeworld first can control the millions of *Spearheads* roaming the universe, seeding infinite expressions of life.'

Sean suppressed a grin. *No, I didn't know that. But thanks for telling me!*

Senetep stormed down the steps and loomed over him. 'Where does the portal lead?'

Sean shrugged, waiting for the inevitable strike. Standing in the Overseer's shadow, he felt like an ant about to be stomped on.

'Tell me where it goes. Or I'll subject you to the worst fate imaginable.'

It can't get worse than this. Sean wanted to collapse in a trembling mess. He steeled himself against his nerves, clenched his teeth, and kept silent, determined not to give Senetep a moment of satisfaction.

'I'll force you to watch the death of your precious planet. It would be a mercy to die, a fate I may grant you...if you tell me where this portal goes.'

Sean dug in, committed to keeping his silence. He was nauseous with fear, as if he had jumped off a cliff.

'I can make you suffer for eternity, extend your life for centuries; millennia longer than your frail carcass was designed to endure. You will live in a state of constant pain and suffering, carrying the memories of your species' demise.'

Sean tried to block out what he was hearing. It couldn't end like this, not after everything he had sacrificed and fought for.

'Or you can be the next to die, taking comfort in the thought there was nothing you could do to save the billions after you.'

Sean trembled, too terrified to think straight. He had run out of options. It was down to survival now. Staying alive gave him a chance, even when that chance seemed infinitesimal. He dropped his head in mock defeat. 'I wish I knew, but I don't know where the portal goes.'

'See it your way,' Senetep said in a grave tone. 'You can begin your eternity of anguish by witnessing the demise of your fleet.'

The scientists projected a hologram of the carnage outside. There was no battle. The *Alnilam* and *Mintaka* drifted towards the planet, wiped clean of life. The crew of the *Alnitak* put up a valiant fight against the seething horde of drones. Explosions erupted across the ship, ejecting batches of drones into space. The machines turned around, flew straight back into the hull, and continued their methodical eradication.

Sean struggled to watch, knowing that within the chaos, hundreds of lives were being erased. Hazim should have warped out of there the moment the *Alnilam* was overrun.

BOOM!

The hologram went bright white, then dimmed, revealing a flaming carcass of twisted metal. The *Alnitak* had just exploded, spewing thousands of white-hot drones into space. Their glowing shells cooled quickly in the vacuum of space, and the drones returned to the *Spearhead*. The battle was over. Hazim, Hemket, Ramin and his unborn child, the entire crew: all gone.

Senetep laughed. 'Your captain was overwhelmed. He just overloaded the power crystals and triggered a self-destruct. Let me guess, he was human.'

Sean stared at the devastation. A tingling sensation shot through his wings. He tightened his fists, fear shifting into rage.

The explosion forced the *Alnilam* and *Mintaka* into the planet's exosphere. They spiralled out of control and disintegrated into brilliant fireballs. The drones streamed from the planet and moon in their millions, filling the *Spearhead's* internal void.

The scientists set up a life-size holographic link to their companions, hundreds of levels above in the *Spearhead's* main control chamber. Their devices were patched into the mercury the same way Nocao had done in the pyramid. Senetep and Erund were now preoccupied with redirecting the *Spearhead* towards the wormhole.

Sean considered his options. The portal remained active but could switch off at any moment. He was two flaps away. His wings were ready. But he was surrounded. The drones encircled the portal in a protective wall and more hovered overhead, ready to exterminate him. A pair of warriors stood behind him, prodding their staves into his back. He needed to create a distraction.

A *really big* distraction.

A second or two was all he needed, enough to fly through the portal. If he joined Bella and Nocao on the Ancients' planet, they might could override the *Spearhead* before it reached Earth, or better yet, shut it down completely.

Sean watched their journey through the hologram.

The destroyed fleet vanished from view and the planet they were orbiting was now a distant pinprick of light against a backdrop of stars. For a vessel that took billions of years to travel the galaxy, the *Spearhead* also moved exceptionally fast.

The view spun about to confront the distinctive black void of a wormhole. Stars stretched around its event horizon. There was a moment of weightlessness followed by a shudder. The hologram glitched, disappeared, and reappeared to reveal a new region of space. They had passed through the wormhole and were picking up speed. Stars whooshed by, then a large planet with rings. The next planet was covered in swirling clouds and a gigantic red spot.

Sean recognised it straight away. Jupiter! They shot past Mars and the *Spearhead* slowed down to orbit a magnificent blue orb. Earth.

'Release the drones!' Senetep commanded.

Sean tensed all over. His chest constricted like a vice, turning each breath into a sharp, painful gasp. It felt like he was having a heart attack. The faces of all the people he ever knew flashed through his mind. His aunt and uncle. His friends from school. Bella's family. Her brother Arturo. Carla. They were all about to die. He couldn't stand still any longer.

Sean lunged forward. 'STOP!'

The drones dropped in front of him and unleashed their deadly hoses. The warriors backed off, steering well clear of the danger.

'Wait!' Senetep stormed through the hologram of Earth, straight for Sean.

The scientists typed across their data pads and the drones ascended out of Senetep's way. He grabbed Sean by the collar and hurled him in front of the hologram. 'You have a front-row seat to Armageddon.'

Sean tried to stand. Senetep kicked him down and ground his

face against the floor with the sole of his boot, forcing him to watch. Sean closed his eyes.

Senetep dug his sole in. 'Open your eyes or I'll remove your eyelids.'

Sean grimaced through squished cheeks and reluctantly opened his eyes to the nightmare.

Millions of drones descended upon Earth in spiralling tornados of death. Emperor Neberun's orbiting fleet of motherships were no match for the endless hordes. They put up no defences, caught completely off-guard by the attack.

Senetep grunted with satisfaction. 'Show me the surface.'

The hologram split into a carousel of scenes showing the drones descending upon on capital cities. New York. Mumbai. London. Beijing. Sydney. Cairo. Rome. Cities in daylight fell into shadow while those at night were shrouded in a sea of glowing red eyes. The drones eradicated those outside first. After that, they attached to buildings, cars, planes, boats; anything concealing signs of life. Driverless cars ploughed into each other. Planes dropped from the sky. Bicycles and scooters continued without their riders for a second and fell over. Playgrounds filled with children were left empty, swings swaying in the air.

But it wasn't just human beings and Isharkute being eradicated, it was plants and animals too. Entire ecosystems were being erased. Earth was being wiped clean as though any form of life was a bacterium.

Sean squirmed, desperate to avert his gaze. He couldn't take it any longer. The destruction was too much to process. He closed his eyes.

Senetep twisted his heel. 'Open your eyes!'

Sean squinted even tighter.

'OPEN THEM!'

The pressure was excruciating. He couldn't breathe. It felt like his skull was about to crack and explode. But he dug in deeper, drawing upon everything to keep his eyes shut.

Senetep removed his heel and Sean gulped in a lungful of air.

Something hard rolled him over and pinned his arms and legs to the floor. Small metallic pincers slipped beneath his eyelids and pulled them open, bringing him face-to-face with a drone. The glowing red eye scrutinised him. A mechanical finger extruded from the drone's shell. The outer tip unfolded, revealing a shiny scalpel.

Sean squirmed and writhed under its metal grip. 'NO!'

His right hand somehow slipped free. He clutched the mechanical scalpel, slicing his finger. It moved for his eyelid. Sean pushed back on the finger, but it was too strong.

The appendage rotated into position, preparing to sever his eyelid. He watched a droplet of his blood run down the blade and disappear into the joint. The drone shuddered. Its red eye flickered like it was malfunctioning, then focused into his, sending pulses of scarlet light into his retina.

The blazing red softened to pink, then white.

Sean's entire body was overcome with a buzzing sensation. It moved through him in waves, in time with the drone's pulsing white eye. He had connected with the drone. Deeper in his mind, he felt something else. It was the Ancients! They were speaking to him through the drone, sowing their suggestions in his subconscious. Suddenly, he knew what to do. He stared into the luminous eye and directed his thoughts into the machine, forcing the drone to ignore him and lock onto a new target.

Senetep...Senetep...Senetep...

The drone gave a distorted whistle. The pincers suddenly retracted from his eyelids and the drone shot up high into the chamber. Sean rubbed his eyes and stood, focusing on his telepathic connection to the machine. The drones circled around their rogue counterpart, screeching and whining like confused and broken automatons. Sean fixated on his drone, using sheer willpower to send his thoughts through its metal casing.

'What's happening?' Senetep said.

The scientists fumbled about with their devices, panicking. 'The drone is malfunctioning!' one of them cried.

'We've lost control,' called another.

Sean closed his eyes, slowed his breathing, and created a mental image of Senetep.

Senetep...Senetep...Senetep...

Sen...e...tep...Sen...e...tep...

S...e...n...e...t...e...p...

There was a ghostly flicker and Sean was suddenly looking through the drone's eye. The view was warped and distorted, like a fisheye lens. He was connected to the drone on a telepathic level, with full control. He trained the mechanical eye on Senetep and the drone zipped across the chamber. At that exact moment, every other drone froze in position.

Senetep moved backwards, stumbling over his own feet. 'Get control of it.'

'We can't...they're all malfunctioning,' a scientist cried.

'Destroy it!'

Sean positioned the drone in front of Senetep, his prime directive now crystal clear. *Kill...Kill...Kill...* The drone ejected its deadly hose.

Senetep fell backwards, arms crossed over his face in terror. 'NOW!'

The warriors unleashed a barrage of energy blasts. Senetep scurried away as the drone went into a defensive spin, deflecting shots all over the chamber.

Sean's consciousness was thrown back into his body. He opened his eyes and found himself alone, unguarded, and free to jump through the portal. The nearby hologram showed the drones had stopped their global assault. His interruption caused their hive minds to malfunction, crippling them like a computer virus.

Sean flapped his wings and zipped across the chamber, keeping low to the floor, away from the ricocheting energy blasts.

'Stop him!' Senetep bellowed.

Sean dove into the portal, leaving his devastated world behind.

CHAPTER 24

Hall Of The Ancients

Sean phased through vibrant kaleidoscopes of light, his physical body broken down into weightless bits of information. His consciousness remained intact. Stars, solar systems, and galaxies roared by like he was sitting on the nose of a rocket traversing billions of light-years.

An iris of intense energy appeared directly ahead, siphoning his scattered form into a tunnel of blinding light.

FWOOSH!

Sean was thrust forward with a thunderous crackle of energy, instantaneously assembled back into his flesh-and-blood body. His wings shot out to give him a soft landing. He was in a new chamber, crouched in the middle of a circular platform encircled by three rings of mercury. Straight ahead, the exit led to open skies. Heavenly clouds of pink and peach drifted across a horizon aglow with golden light.

Behind him, a disc of energy rippled like a vertical swimming pool, showing a distorted view of the chamber he just escaped. The portal was still open. Senetep and his warriors could jump through at any moment.

Sean raced over to the rings, desperate to close the connection.

He crouched over the outer ring and dipped his hand into the cool silver, closed his eyes, and merged his mind with the technology. There were no controls. No instructions. *How am I meant to do this? I'm thinking too hard.* Sean cleared his mind and slowed his breathing. He created a mental image of the portal stretching across the universe like a piece of string, then a gigantic pair of scissors flying in like a starship. *SNIP!*

A burst of energy washed over him.

Sean opened his eyes to find the portal closed. He withdrew his hand from the mercury and rubbed it, thinking about what he achieved. His mental image of scissors cutting string was enough to close the portal. In theory, anyone who interfaced with the mercury could achieve the same result, even Bella and Nocao.

With the hum of the portal gone, the chamber was dead quiet.

The silence enveloped Sean, bringing unimaginable horrors. Millions of lives had been vaporised in the blink of an eye, wiping three-quarters of Earth clean of life. How would he explain that to Bella? Or Nocao? Untold Isharkute perished in the attack, pushing them closer to extinction. Could he have done more? Prevented it somehow?

Dwelling on what *could have been* didn't help. He concentrated on what he *could* achieve: finding his friends and saving the millions still in peril.

Sean searched for any sign that Bella and Nocao had been here. If they arrived through the same portal, they were long gone. Heading outside, he found a message on the alloy wall. His heart leapt. The chunky letters were written in a thick black substance – Bella's mascara!

Sean, we are alive and well. We waited for hours. You didn't come through. We are heading into the city for food, water, anything to help. Find us!! We will keep a lookout for you and return later. Hope to see you soon! Bella and Nocao. XXOO

His heart was pounding as he finished reading. He dashed outside and found himself on the edge of an aerial platform, deep in the heart of a soaring alien metropolis.

Immense buildings, towers, and spires were linked in a labyrinth of bridges and walkways, all built thousands of metres above the planet surface. Smooth alloy surfaces blended seamlessly with clear crystalline panels, as if moulded by a giant hand. The city glimmered like a diamond in the encroaching twilight, reflecting rays of pastel light between the structures.

Three moons hung in the violet sky overhead, dwarfed from behind by a massive planet with three outer rings. For a second, he forgot all his troubles. He was in a magical place. Like something from a dream.

A warm breeze blew across the platform, making his wings twinge.

Sean leapt off the edge and glided over the walkway linking the platform to the city, keeping an eye out for his friends. The light was fading fast, casting vast areas of the city into shadow.

Bella and Nocao said they waited for hours, yet only thirty minutes had passed for him on the *Spearhead*. Moving through the wormhole to Earth while the portal was open must have created a time dilation between the *Spearhead* and the Ancients' planet.

Hopefully, it was only a difference of hours. Not days or months.

Sean thought he heard an echo of distant voices between the buildings. It was hard to hear over the rush of wind. He circled around, swooping through the growing shadows. Did he imagine it? Were the Ancients trying to communicate? It made sense. He was closer to them than ever before.

'SEAN!' Screamed a pair of desperate voices.

Sean flapped his wings and shot higher, checking the myriad of walkways and bridges. He spotted two figures jumping about and waving wildly. Bella and Nocao! He dove with excitement, almost overshooting the walkway.

'You made it!' Bella screamed, throwing her arms around him. '*Grazie Dio!*'

Nocao nudged between them and gave Sean a welcoming embrace. 'How long have you been here?'

'A few minutes.'

'What happened?'

'Senetep destroyed the dropship and killed our squad.'

'I thought as much,' Nocao said, disheartened. 'Did he follow you through?'

'No. I closed the portal.'

Bella stared at him, eyes wide with shock. '*Aspettare*... Can we still get back to Earth?'

Sean went to speak, but no words came out. What could he say? There was no Earth to go back to. The drones had erased millions of innocent people. Men. Women. Children. Isharkute. Even the plants and animals. The barren landscapes flashed through his mind, a burden he could no longer bear his own. Tears welled in his eyes. He wiped them away, struggling to hold back the torrent of emotions rising from deep inside him. His body felt fragile. The mental and physical exhaustion had finally caught up to him.

Nocao and Bella helped him sit.

His body was shaking all over now. He couldn't look them in the eyes.

Sean pulled up his knees and buried his face. He sobbed. His friends held tight, refusing to let go. They asked no questions. Their comfort gradually gave him some relief. The uncontrollable storm of emotions had passed.

He raised his head, still unable to look his friends in the eye. 'I was too late. Senetep took the *Spearhead* to Earth. He forced me to watch the attack.'

There was a long, uncomfortable moment of silence.

'What about Neberun's fleet?' Nocao said. 'Did they fight back?'

'There wasn't time. The wormhole dropped the *Spearhead* right outside Earth's solar system. By the time we arrived, the drones were everywhere. Millions of them.'

'What about Earth?' Bella asked in a trembling voice.

Sean shook his head and finally looked at her. 'It was bad. I don't know how much is left.'

Bella's eyes shimmered with tears. She put on a brave face and remained silent. Sean was glad she didn't want to go into details.

'How did you get away?' Nocao asked.

Sean held up his hand, revealing the cut on his finger. 'I cut my finger on a drone. It sampled my blood, activating a telepathic connection. I took control of it and escaped. The Ancients are reaching out to me through their technology. I think they recognise Senetep as a threat.'

'Then this battle isn't over. There are thousands of humans living on Akanae and other bases throughout the galaxy. Although we suffered catastrophic losses today, we can still save those left.' Nocao stood and offered his hand to Sean. 'Are you ready?'

Sean perked up. They were far from home, but far from alone. By working together, anything was possible. With that shred of hope, he took Nocao's hand and stood. 'I'm ready.'

Sean reached out to Bella.

She took his hand, stood up, and steeled herself with a deep breath. 'I'm ready too.'

'Senetep said he could control every *Spearhead* in the universe from the Ancients' planet,' Sean said. 'But we don't need to control all of them. Just his.'

'He'll be coming after us with everything he has,' Nocao said. 'How do we control the *Spearhead*?'

'There's a building in the centre of the city–'

'You mean that!' Nocao said, pointing out a unique spiral-shaped tower nestled between the darkening spires. 'That appears to be the focal point of the entire city.'

'That's ages away,' Bella said. 'It would take hours to walk there.'

'Approximately eighty-seven minutes,' Nocao said, checking his scanner.

'How long have you been walking?' Sean asked.

'Forty-five minutes, but we waited three hours before leaving. How long after us did you enter the portal?'

'About half an hour.'

'That means there's a time dilation of about three hours across the portal.'

'If Senetep can't activate the *Spearhead* portal, he'll need to jump through multiple wormholes just to get here. That puts us hours ahead of him.'

Bella forged ahead. '*Sbrigati!* What are you waiting for then?'

Sean and Nocao hustled after her. They jogged for a bit, walked to catch their breath, then jogged again. Normally Sean would fly ahead, but he didn't like the idea of being alone right now. None of them did. They spurred each other on, but mostly kept to themselves during the journey. Bella was dealing with the uncertainty better than Sean expected. She had no idea if her family were still alive. Her strength and resilience inspired him to succeed.

The sun was setting as they ran across the final bridge. Above, the spiral building captured the dying rays of sunlight, dispersing a rainbow of luminous rays throughout the surrounding crystalline towers.

Sean stopped to catch his breath, taking in the view. 'Wow! It looks like Asgard.'

'What is Asgard?' Nocao said.

'It's one of the Nine Worlds from Norse mythology.'

Bella pushed between them. 'Which is connected to Midgard, the world of humanity, by a rainbow bridge called the Bifröst.'

Sean regarded her with surprise. 'Did you study Norse mythology?'

'No, I just like the *Thor* movie.'

'Ah, another one of your cultural references.' Nocao sighed. 'I am disadvantaged until I watch these pre-recorded performances.'

'Bella's onto something, though,' Sean said. 'There's a definite symbolic connection. Asgard was meant to exist in the sky, just like this city. The Bifröst is a bridge that links faraway places, just like the portal we used. The streaks of light we saw inside it could be interpreted as the rainbow bridge.'

'You think humans once used this portal?'

'Possibly, way back in antiquity. Maybe the Ancients' technology inspired Norse mythology. It could have been their way of interpreting something beyond their comprehension. I bet most gods and mythologies link back to the Ancients in some way.'

'Similar to the way Isharkute mythology explains the *Spearhead of Creation*,' Nocao said.

They sprinted across the bridge and passed beneath a gigantic arch. There were no doors or gates anywhere, as if the Ancients left their city open for visitors. The sweeping entrance spiralled up into the building with an arduous mountain of metre-high steps.

Bella stopped at the first step and sighed. '*Mio Dio!* That's a big climb! The Ancients must have been titans.'

'I'll fly up to the turn, let you know how far it goes.'

'Don't wait for us,' Nocao said. 'We'll catch up, eventually. You can interface with the Ancients' technology. Start without us.'

'All right, call out if you need help.'

Sean launched over half-a-dozen stairs with a single flap. By the next flap he was around the bend, his friends out of sight. He followed the cyclical incline, counting two complete rotations before the staircase opened into a towering hall.

Sean landed and stared up in awe.

Soaring crystalline panels captured the rich ochre sunset, dispersing rays of colour like stained-glass windows. It resembled a gothic cathedral with its high vaulted ceilings and wide-open spaces. Immense pillars arose from the corners of the hall and disappeared into the shadows far above. An upright metallic ring, ten metres high and wide, stood in the middle of the hall atop a high platform. It was wide enough to drive a truck through.

It was the portal from his vision, the one the Ancients warned him not to enter. Was he supposed to turn it on? How were they meant to control the *Spearhead* from here? There were no pools of liquid mercury. No way to interface with the Ancients' technology. They must have missed something.

It was hard to see everything from his position. If the Ancients were a race of giants, then clues might be higher up. He flew above the crystal windows for a bird's-eye view. Looking down, he discovered the portal stood atop a layered platform, spiral in shape.

Then he realised, the ornate pillars were the feet of gigantic statues. Sean spun around. An icy shiver shot down his spine. Four mammoth faces hung in the gloom, watching him with an eerie silence.

The elongated faces, wide brows, and thin lips uncannily resembled the moai from Easter Island. They faced the centre of the hall, guarding the portal.

It's the hall of the Ancients!

Sean felt compelled to touch the face of his most distant ancestor.

He flew over and placed a hand on the cool alloy. A warm tingling transferred up his arm and flowed through his body, filling him with a profound sense of peace and harmony. He closed his eyes. His stress and anxiety faded. The alien consciousness reached deep into his soul, absolving him of guilt, assuring him that his sacrifices and selfless acts were not in vain.

But he already knew that; the Ancients just cleared the noise.

These ancient beings did more than just ignite the first spark of life, they were universal guardians, constantly on watch, waiting for their creations to seek them out and complete the circle of life.

Sean wanted to warn them. Senetep threatened their master plan for the universe. But the Ancients already knew – they were reading his memories.

Their imminent response rumbled through the hall.

Far below, a river of mercury streamed from the feet of each statue. The silver raced through indentations forming in the floor and pooled around the portal platform.

A sudden, shooting pain struck Sean through his temples. He took his hand off the statue and clutched his head. Lights flashed before his eyes, distorting his vision. His wings fluttered erratically. He zigzagged about and plummeted towards the floor. Incomprehensible amounts of information bombarded his mind. The Ancients were telepathically downloading everything he needed to beat Senetep into his memories.

It's too much! Too fast!

Sean hit the floor hard and collapsed to his knees, holding his head. The more he resisted, the more it hurt. *Don't resist*, said a voice. That's it! He opened his mind and it was over in a second. He stayed hunched, collecting his thoughts. The next thing he knew, Bella and Nocao helped him to his feet, both red-faced and puffing hard.

Nocao grabbed his shoulders. 'Are you okay?'

Sean came out of his daze, confident and ready for anything. 'I know how to defeat Senetep once and for all.'

CHAPTER 25

Losing Control

The attacking drone deactivated and *clunked* to the floor at Senetep's feet. Its red eye faded and disappeared. Senetep jumped up and raced over to the portal where Sean just dematerialised. He teetered on the edge, fighting the urge to jump after the teenager. It was too risky. The portal could drop him anywhere, isolating him from the fleet.

Senetep pointed to the nearest warrior. 'You! Go after him.'

The warrior stepped up to the portal and peered cautiously over the edge, reluctant to take the plunge. 'Where does it go?'

Erund came up from behind and shoved him into the portal. 'Don't question your orders!'

The warrior tumbled into the rippling energy, arms flailing. The portal suddenly closed, melding his half-dematerialised body with the alloy floor.

Senetep rounded on his scientists, fuming. 'Reactivate the portal.'

The throng of scientists stood in a stunned silence, staring wide-eyed at the corpse sticking out of the floor.

Erund marched down the steps and unslung his stave with one arm. 'You heard your Overseer. Get to work!'

The scientists snapped to attention and scurried around their holograms.

Erund watched over them, then returned to Senetep. 'We need a contingency plan. Sean infiltrated the *Spearhead* without us knowing, then turned a drone against us. With this portal, he poses a legitimate threat.'

'He's still just a child,' Senetep scoffed. 'One with an extraordinary amount of luck.'

'Regardless, he should not be underestimated.'

Senetep tightened his fist, resisting the impulse to strike Erund for his insolence. Unfortunately, he needed his subordinates for a while longer. He let his rage pass and glanced at the deactivated drone. 'Assign a team of scientists to examine the drone. Find out how Sean was able to turn it against me.'

Erund nodded dutifully, but didn't leave.

'Is there something else?'

'We've all seen the power of this vessel. It erased life on Earth within minutes. If that force turns against us, we will be powerless to stop it.'

'What are you suggesting?'

'We should temporarily evacuate the *Spearhead* and return to our fleet. Once we're certain we're in control, we can return.'

'Your logical approach sounds like cowardice.'

'I'm only protecting your interests.'

Senetep regarded Erund with a dubious eye. 'We didn't come this far to abandon the *Spearhead* at the first sign of danger. We are rewriting the universe: billions of years' worth of evolution. The stakes will never be higher. If you feel compelled to run from this vessel, then I'll take a leg to compliment your missing arm.'

Erund straightened his shoulders. 'Of course, you're right. If the need arises, I'll be the last to leave this ship.'

'I may take you up on that offer.'

Erund nodded and joined the scientists.

Senetep wandered over to the fallen drone. Its deadly hose hung lifelessly from its shell, showing just how close he had come to being dissolved. His stomach churned at the thought. Anxiety was a human weakness, inherited from human DNA, not his own failing. He nudged the drone with his boot, wondering how Sean was able to override its programming. A multi-jointed appendage flopped out of its armoured shell. On the end was a small blade. A bead of scarlet raced down the edge and dripped onto the floor. Senetep knelt, inspecting the droplet. Was there something in Sean's blood that made the drone malfunction?

Two scientists joined him, ready to examine the drone.

'Start by sampling this blood,' Senetep said.

The lead scientist rushed over, proudly holding up his data pad. 'Overseer Senetep, we've analysed the data recorded while the portal was active. Its power signature leads to the centre of the universe, the home planet of the Ancients.'

'Can you open it?'

'We are still working on it.'

Senetep sighed in exasperation. 'We control this entire vessel and its fleet of drones. Why can't we access a simple portal?'

'We're dealing with a long-lost technology. We don't fully understand how–'

'How what?! How a child is able to sneak aboard this ship and activate the portal, yet you have only just discovered where it leads?'

Senetep marched between the scientists. 'If this portal is not active within five minutes, one of you will die. Then another five minutes after that. I will kill every one of you if need be.'

The scientists worked feverishly over their holographic panels.

One scientist rushed over to the mercury. He tripped on the top step and landed with one hand in the outermost ring of mercury. His scanner slid across the face of the portal and came to a stop beside the corpse jutting from the surface.

'Incompetent fool!' Senetep hollered. He unsheathed his blade and stormed over, ready to make an example of the blundering buffoon.

The scientist panicked and withdrew his hand from the mercury, stretching out a long glob of silver. The portal momentarily shimmered to life, dematerialising the scanner and the corpse. As the scientist crawled away the mercury pulled off his hand and the portal closed.

Senetep sheathed his blade and shoved the scientist aside, kneeling to examine the rings of mercury.

Erund rushed over. 'What just happened?'

'The answer has been in front of us the entire time. It's the mercury. We've been accessing it all wrong.'

'What do you mean?'

'Our first interaction with this technology was triggered by one of our warriors. He touched the pool of mercury in the first pyramid we visited, activating the display of elements and star maps. Since then, we've using our machines to talk to machines. It works, but it's not efficient. Not the way this technology was designed. The mercury is an interface between the biological and the technological, linking the minds of sentient beings with machines.'

Senetep glared at the scientist cowering beside him. 'This fool had one intention. To open the portal. He achieved that with his touch. The power of his thought.'

'That's why we can control the *Spearhead* but struggle to open the portal,' Erund added excitedly. 'Our technology has nothing like this, nothing to compare it to.'

'It explains how Sean activated the portal.'

Senetep placed his fingertips in the mercury. The metal slid over his fingers and covered his hand like a silver glove. He raised his hand, admiring the elegant and sophisticated connection. He closed his eyes and concentrated on opening the portal.

The mercury suddenly peeled off his hand and returned to the ring. He opened his eyes. The portal remained closed.

Something had gone drastically wrong.

The scientists scrambled about, calling in panicked voices, 'We've lost control of the Spearhead...'

'...all navigation controls are gone...'

'The drones are being recalled...'

The deactivated drone honked and whistled. Its eye blazed to life and the machine lurched upright, *clunking* across the floor.

Senetep unslung his stave and jumped back, aiming at the reanimated machine.

The drone's eye flicked from white to red, then settled on white. It launched high into the chamber and joined the circling ring of drones. They departed single file up the exiting passage.

Senetep turned his attention to the hologram of Earth. The drones vacated the cities in gigantic plumes. They swirled through the sky and returned to orbit, swarming inside the *Spearhead* like insects returning to their hive. 'What's happening?'

'The *Spearhead* is receiving new commands,' Erund said, 'overriding ours.'

'Sean Livingstone,' Senetep seethed. The cunning child had taken control of the *Spearhead* from the Ancients' homeworld.

'Evacuate to the *Ragarn!*' Senetep cried, leading the charge up the passage.

He returned to the vessel and headed straight to the bridge. The pilots launched and navigated through the swarms of returning drones. The autonomous machines whipped past and stacked neatly against each other in their millions, filling up the *Spearhead's* internal void. Senetep clambered over to his command chair and held on as the *Ragarn* barrel-rolled through the exit tunnel and shot into space. A giant mechanical orifice closed behind them, sealing the drones inside the *Spearhead*.

Planet Earth filled their viewscreen. Emperor Neberun's motherships hung in orbit, devoid of crews.

Erund scrambled onto the bridge and sheepishly straightened his uniform. He approached the main viewscreen. 'Give me a status report.'

One of the scientists stepped forward. 'We've lost control of the *Spearhead*, but gained the entire Isharkute fleet. Every vessel Emperor Neberun possessed is now yours.'

Senetep hated the confident tone in his voice. He shot out of his chair and marched over. The scientist stepped back, face wracked with fear. Senetep gripped the imbecile by the neck and forced him to his knees.

'Fool! Neberun's fleet is nothing compared to the *Spearhead of Creation.*'

He tightened his grip, cracking vertebrae. The scientist's eyes bulged as his windpipe collapsed. He gurgled his last breath and his head lolled to the side.

Senetep flung the lifeless body aside and faced his crew. 'Move our fleet out of here before the *Spearhead* turns on us. Calculate coordinates to the centre of the universe using the Ancients' database. We won't stop until we reach our destination.'

Erund nodded and waved over two crew members to remove the corpse.

'Stop!' Senetep ordered. 'Leave him there as a reminder.'

The crew returned to their posts.

Senetep retreated to his private quarters for the safety of his crew. If not, there wouldn't be a soul left to pilot the *Ragarn*.

He paced his quarters, stewing over his failure. How could he lose the *Spearhead* to a human teenager? He was on the verge of eradicating their species forever, but this one outlier remained – Sean Livingstone. His name invoked pure rage. Next time they met, there would be no small talk, no chance of keeping him alive. The boy would die. Instantly. By his own hands.

Senetep caught his reflection in the wall and punched it with all his might. 'AARGH!'

His fist created a divot in the gleaming alloy panel. It felt good. Satisfying.

THUMP! THUMP! THUMP!

He lashed out, over and over. Bloody knuckle prints smeared the panel. He couldn't stop, punching harder with each strike. An unruly scream bellowed from his chest. The panel buckled off the wall and crashed to the floor.

Panting heavily, Senetep caught his reflection in the damaged panel. The distorted face reflected his inner turmoil. He kicked the panel across the room and sat down with a container of healing salve. A holographic map of their journey appeared beside him. He watched their progress while tending to his shattered knuckles, visualising every way he might kill Sean. The gruesome thoughts settled his mind.

Hours passed, along with millions of light-years. The map finally flashed with their destination. After thirty-seven consecutive wormhole jumps, they had arrived at the Ancients' homeworld.

Senetep returned to the bridge, calm and focused. He rubbed his knuckles, noting the purple blemish of recently healed skin.

The viewscreen revealed a metallic planet bathed in golden light. Immense buildings, spires, bridges, and highways were visible from orbit. The surface of the planet was an endless city.

'We're scanning structures throughout the core,' Erund said. 'The planet is completely manufactured. We've located three life forms, two human and one Isharkute.'

'Target their position and alert the fleet.'

'Are we going to strike from orbit?'

'No. Land at their position. I will take care of this personally. Nobody kills Sean Livingstone except me.'

The crew shared furtive glances.

Senetep sensed a subtle shift in their demeanour. They appeared uncertain and anxious, as if they doubted his leadership. Was there dissension brewing among the ranks, or worse, mutiny?

Erund acknowledged several crew members and spoke. 'Permission to speak openly.'

Senetep narrowed his gaze. *Where is this going? If Erund contradicts my orders, he will die where he stands.* He placed a hand on the hilt of his blade. Ready for anything.

'Speak.'

'Our journey took hours, but on this planet, that translates to a few days, giving Sean a head start with the Ancients' technology. It would be safer to obliterate that section of the planet, pick up the pieces, and move on.'

Senetep caressed the hilt with his thumb, keen to silence such cowardice. But he was so close to finishing the mission, he needed to maintain order and obedience a short while longer. He moved his hand off the hilt.

'A careless scattershot attack might set off a chain reaction that destroys the entire planet. This mission requires a delicate touch, like removing a brain tumour. One wrong move and we severely incapacitate or kill the host. Should we succeed, we will control the ultimate power in the universe.'

'Understood,' Erund said, bowing and backing off.

There was no elation or cheers of support. The crew remained by their posts, motivated by fear, not support for his cause.

Senetep saw his last chance approaching. If this mission failed, his crew would abandon him. It was win or die.

The *Ragarn* landed on the main bridge leading to the spiral-shaped building where Sean's life signs were located. Senetep unslung his customised polearm and twisted the activator. The octagonal arrangement of forks shot open and buzzed with energy. Drawing on four supersized crystals, his stave had enough firepower to take down a stinger or hunter-craft.

He was taking no chances this time.

The gangway lowered, filling the *Ragarn's* loading bay with warm morning light.

Senetep led his squad outside and into the alien building, monitoring the scanner attached to his wrist bracer. Strangely, Sean's life signs were faint and hard to pinpoint, making it impossible to tell if he was conscious, injured, or near death.

They marched through the arched entrance and trudged up the giant steps. The passage wound up the inside of the building, with no end in sight. Senetep set a fierce pace, bounding up each step, keeping one hand on his stave the entire time.

The arduous climb led them into a grand hall. Dawn light spilled in through windows set high above, spotlighting an upright metallic ring atop a large platform. He peered up through the glare, using his enhanced eyesight to unscramble the hazy shadows beyond. Four colossal statues loomed over the ring from each corner of the hall.

'It's another portal!' Erund said.

Senetep glared at him to be quiet and checked his scanner. They were right on top of the life readings. He surveyed the hall. Nothing. No signs of life. It made little sense.

He edged inside. Something caught his eye, and he spun around, polearm aimed into the shadows at the foot of a statue.

Sean, Nocao and Bella walked out with their hands raised in

surrender. Sean stepped into the light. His complexion looked waxy and unnatural, but more surprising, he was grinning madly.

Senetep suddenly realised his mistake. His impatience had led them into a trap. He pulled the trigger, but it was already too late.

CHAPTER 26

Zodiac Attack

Sean watched the energy blast pass straight through his body and obliterate the foot of the statue. The dust settled. He remained in the same spot, unscathed by the explosion. Bella and Nocao stood beside him, hands raised in the air. All three of them gave the intruders a cheeky smile.

Senetep and Erund shared expressions of disbelief.

Far above, in the safety of his pod, Sean smiled to himself.

Over the last two days they had unlocked an amazing new technology. The three of them hovered inside their own oblong pods, hundreds of metres above Senetep. These protective shells were once used by the Ancients to travel their cities. The liquid mercury cores kept them protected within a bubble of oxygen while they controlled their liquid mercury avatars below.

Nocao and Bella had adapted to the Ancient technology quicker than Sean expected, perfecting their symbiotic relationship with the mercury. Like himself, they could now control the mercury with their minds. Their pods communicated with the pool in the centre of the hall, which drew its liquid mercury from the planet's core. This endless resource could manifest anything they could imagine, creating the ultimate defence.

Sean lowered his arms. His avatar mimicked the movement. 'You missed,' he said, drawing a deliberate grin.

'Hey, *bruto!*' Bella said, putting her hands on her hips. 'Is that all you've got?'

Senetep changed his aim to her and fired. The blast tore a gaping hole through Bella's avatar torso, splattering liquid mercury across the floor. Within seconds, the globules reformed and raced back to fill in her disfigured body.

Senetep was snap-frozen in place with a stupid, gobsmacked expression stamped into his face.

Nocao laughed. 'Your weapons can't hurt us now.'

'Cowards!' Senetep shrieked, looking around the hall. 'Show yourselves!'

'I think it's time to release our special powers,' Bella said, turning to Sean and Nocao. 'What do you say?'

Sean winked. 'Give the order.'

Bella pointed at Senetep and cried out, 'Unleash the ZODIAC ATTACK!'

Sean laughed. She was loving this. It was Bella's idea to use the signs of the zodiac as their defence. Her birthday was April 21, which made her star sign Taurus, the Bull – a perfect fit given her tough physical nature. Nocao had no Earthly zodiac sign, but chose Sagittarius, the Hunter, a mythical human figure representing his home constellation of Orion.

Sean's zodiac sign was Leo, the great Lion. Ironically, the monster that had stalked his nightmares was now his creature of power. He conjured up an image of a lion. His avatar transformed into a gigantic version of the beast, drawing extra mercury from the pool.

Senetep and his awe-struck entourage gawked at his incredible transformation. Mouths agape. Speechless.

Inside the pod, Sean leant forward into a crawling position, ready to control his lion avatar. Bella's avatar transformed into a hulking bull, four times the size of an elephant. Nocao grew several storeys tall, taking on the form of an ancient Isharkute hunter, complete with spear and shield. They towered over the puny intruders, glinting in brilliant silver: zodiac guardians to the hall of Ancients.

Two warriors backed up in fear and fled down the passage.

'Hold your positions!' Senetep growled.

Sean smiled to himself. Cracks appeared in Senetep's ranks. Even First Commander Erund Griss seemed ready to flee. Sean was surprised it had taken this long. Senetep's insane plan to erase all life in the universe, including his homeworld of Akanae, showed his distorted view of reality. They supported a lunatic.

Sean screamed inside his pod. His lion avatar recreated the roar with thunderous force, quaking the foundations of the hall. Bella stomped her enormous hoof and tilted her silver horns at Senetep, preparing to charge.

'Open fire!' Senetep screamed.

Bella's bull charged forward. Her mercury body swallowed the energy blasts, instantly filling in the holes. She carved a path through Senetep's group, catapulting several unlucky warriors across the hall.

'Woo-hoo!' Bella cheered.

Nocao's hunter swung his spear, collecting half the squad in one hit. The warriors collapsed in piles on top of each other, scrambling to pick up their weapons.

Sean focused on Senetep, the last figure standing. It had come down to the two of them. His lion growled and took a giant pawstep forward.

Senetep advanced, frowning with determination, firing shot after useless shot. CRACK! CRACK! CRACK! CRACK!

Sean shook his head, taking the impacts across his lion's mane, absorbing the energy.

Senetep stopped and looked about. His warriors lay scattered about the hall, injured, unconscious, or clambering for the exit.

'Hah, hah! Look at them run,' Bella cheered. 'We won!'

Senetep gazed up at the three silver giants, finally fixating on Sean's lion. His scowl twisted into one of panic.

Sean glared down at his nemesis. For the first time in 10,000 years, he had the upper hand. He stepped forward, swiping the polearm from Senetep's grasp. His adrenalin surged. He growled hungrily. This is it! He was about to avenge the deaths of every unfortunate victim. Finally end Senetep's reign of terror. Sean raised his head and screamed in a mix of victory and pain.

His lion avatar roared and crouched on its hind legs, preparing to pounce. One massive bite would finish it all.

'Their life signs are coming from up there!' screamed a desperate voice.

Sean glanced over to find Erund slumped by the pool, eyeing his scanner, pointing up at their pods. Senetep's gaze shifted from his lion avatar up to his protective pod, hovering in the shadows high in the hall. An icy shiver shot down Sean's back, as if the Overseer saw him through the pod.

'Target our position and fire!' Senetep screamed into his wrist bracer, sprinting for the passage.

Sean froze in shock. Their situation was about to become disastrous.

'What's going on?' Bella called.

'He ordered an aerial strike!' Nocao cried.

'Descend, descend, descend!' Sean yelled.

BOOM!

Sean glimpsed the aerial strike through the eyes of his avatar. The first wave of missiles struck the outside of the hall, right above their pods, shattering the crystalline panels with a ruinous fireball.

The shock wave resonated through Sean's protective bubble of mercury like a bell. The ear-splitting noise broke his concentration and disconnected him from his avatar, leaving him blind and out of control. His pod bounced through the hall like a ping-pong ball. Disoriented and stunned, he floated about in his pod, unable to tell up from down. The roar of the explosion died, and his pod settled.

Sean lay there in his muted shell, wondering what was happening outside. Everything had become quiet. 'Bella? Nocao? Can you hear me?'

No answer.

Disconnected from his avatar, his eyes to the outside world switched off. He needed to know what was going on.

With that thought, the pod fell open, dropping Sean into thick choking smoke. The protective liquid mercury gushed across the floor and slid back to the pool. He was sitting on the floor of the hall. Burning debris lay all around. More crashed down around him. High above, the crystal panels cracked and crumbled from their frames. The opening sucked out plumes of smoke like an extraction fan. At floor level, the portal and pool of liquid mercury remained intact.

The smoke cleared, revealing two battered pods on the far side of the hall.

Bella and Nocao!

Firm hands suddenly yanked him to his feet. The warriors stood aside as an ominous, familiar figure emerged from the whirling smoke. Senetep. Erund limped after him, half his face burnt and blackened.

Senetep loomed over Sean, polearm in hand. 'An entire planet of technology at your disposal and you toyed with it like children. Was that the best you could come up with?'

Sean stood there, tongue-tied with shock. He couldn't believe how quickly the tables had turned. He eyed the portal. *Why didn't I open it when I had the chance?* Now it was his only chance. He needed to unleash the power the Ancients warned him to avoid. Even if it killed him.

Senetep sighed in frustration and lashed out.

Sean copped the punch right in the stomach and fell backwards across the floor, clutching his ribs and struggling to breathe.

'I asked you a question,' Senetep grumbled. 'Was that the best you could come up with?'

Sean forced himself to stand. Drawing on his winded lungs, he spoke in a breathless voice. 'The Ancients are peaceful. They don't have weapons or defence systems.'

Senetep eyed the portal curiously. 'You talk about them as if they still exist.'

'They do, but not like us.'

'Where are they?'

'They don't live in our universe. They evolved past their physical form into a higher state of consciousness.'

Senetep laughed. 'Sounds like an evolutionary blunder to me. A higher state of consciousness that has no influence on the universe. I believe in what's real. What I can touch. What I can control. The

Ancients made the fatal mistake of leaving their knowledge behind.'

'They expected us to be ready to embrace their knowledge, not misuse the power.'

Senetep snickered. 'Their last mistake.'

Sean breathed deeper and flinched, like a knife was stuck between his ribs. 'They created life to repeat the cycle of evolution, hoping one day their offspring would join them.'

'If you believe humanity is part of the Ancients' grand plan, you're overestimating your own importance. Humanity is an accident. It should never have happened.'

'If we hadn't, you'd be dead from the affliction.'

Senetep mouth twitched. His brow furrowed, and he swung his polearm around.

Sean took the hit across his upper arm. The impact threw him to floor. He grasped his burning arm, feeling the broken bones beneath the flesh. Senetep stormed over, face glaring with rage. Sean curled up as Senetep ploughed his boot into him, kicking him like a soccer ball.

Senetep marched after him, ice-blue eyes glistening with deadly intent.

'Humans are the descendants of a shrew, an insignificant marsupial that lived 100 million years ago under the feet of the dinosaurs. If not for the asteroid that wiped out that superior reptilian species, you would have never evolved beyond a rodent.'

'But we did,' Sean gasped. 'All life deserves a chance.'

Senetep snarled and kicked again.

The force lifted Sean off the floor. His ribs cracked. He landed on his back next to the pool of mercury, craning around to look at the portal.

'You're still rodents,' Senetep said, pressing his boot into Sean's face. 'You don't have the right to share anything. When I rebuild the universe, I'll crush such worthless scum beneath my heel.' Senetep removed his heel. 'But not you.'

Sean rolled his head back and sucked hard for air. His broken chest wheezed and gurgled. He couldn't move.

Senetep loomed over him, evil glee spread across his face. He raised his polearm in preparation to strike. 'I want you to see your death coming.'

Sean braced himself for the inevitable.

He gave up on breathing.

His vision dimmed.

On the edge of conscious thought, the Ancients spoke to him. Their voices echoed through his mind, louder and clearer than ever before. *Open the portal!*

Sean closed his eyes and put his dying energy into making one final connection. His fingers crept across the floor, searching for the mercury. He felt the edge of the pool and dipped his fingers into the cool liquid metal.

On the verge of death, he pictured the portal opening – and it happened.

VROOM!

Then silence.

Sean opened his eyes to a wondrous sight.

The portal glowed brighter than the sun. Strangely, the light didn't hurt his eyes. Then it vanished, leaving behind an eerie blue glow. Elongated humanoid shadows emerged from the portal, filling the hall, phasing in and out of view like ghosts. Their opaque forms lacked definition.

Senetep and his warriors moved in extreme slow motion compared to the ghostly entities, as if different dimensions and speeds overlaid each other.

A shadow enveloped Erund. His expression twisted with confusion, awe, and horror. The shadow suddenly radiated a magnificent prism of light. One by one, the spectral forms attached to the warriors like shadowy leeches and illuminated in kaleidoscopes of colour.

Sean watched the luminous display, wondering what they were doing.

He began to distinguish shapes in the glow. Golden humanoid forms, radiant with heavenly light. It was the Ancients! He lay there, frozen in time, admiring their ethereal beauty. Their divine appearance resembled angels.

Opening the portal allowed them a moment of influence in the physical universe, a moment to correct millennia of mistakes.

Senetep's mouth dropped open in terror as the shadow enveloped him. Ethereal lights bathed his face, locking in his scowl of disbelief and realisation. In that nanosecond, the Ancient entity deconstructed him atom by atom, telepathically informing Sean that the Overseer would suffer an eternity of agony in a timeless plane of existence.

Senetep's body phased out of existence and the hall returned to a bluish twilight colour. The portal remained open.

Sean couldn't move, still caught in this endless second of time. Was he doomed to an eternity of limbo, entombed between two planes of existence? This must be why the Ancients told him not to cross the portal.

The Ancients materialised and hovered overhead, observing him, bathing his mortal body with their warm, luminous aura. He sensed their good intentions, realising if they had faces, they would be smiling. A sense of wellbeing pervaded his consciousness, infusing his body with warmth and restoring it to full health. A new message entered his mind. *Thank you.*

With a sudden burst of light, the Ancients vanished.

The portal had closed.

— CHAPTER 27 —

Understanding

Sean lay on the floor, thinking about his close encounter with the Ancients. Senetep was dead. It was hard to believe. A journey that begun millennia ago had finally come full circle. He had lived several lifetimes in just a few months. It was incredible, too insane to be real. Sean gingerly picked himself up, touching his ribs. He took a deep breath and relaxed. No pain. The Ancients had revived him from the brink of death. Senetep's polearm lay before him, the only trace the Overseer ever existed. Sean kicked it aside and smiled to himself.

Bella's ecstatic scream broke the silence. 'Sean!'

Sean lifted his head. Nocao and Bella raced over, weaving between the smouldering debris.

Bella hugged him and looked around. 'Where did they go?'

'Why? What did you see?'

'The warriors pulled us out of the pods, then vanished. Right in front of us.'

Sean glanced up at the portal. 'It happened so fast you never saw it.'

'You opened the portal,' Nocao said.

Bella gave Sean a friendly shove. 'Wait! I thought you weren't meant to.'

'I wasn't...at least until then,' Sean said. It was like a fog lifted from his mind. The intentions of the Ancients became clear. 'They've been communicating with me since Yonaguni. Guiding me to this place. At this exact point in time. All along, they were preparing me to open the portal, to stop Senetep.'

'Where did he go?'

'The Ancients took him. They exist in another dimension, outside our universe. He's being deconstructed one atom at a time, suffering an eternity of agony.'

'*Grazie Dio!* Sounds like hell to me.'

Nocao nodded. 'Sounds like a just punishment for his transgressions against humanity, the Isharkute, and every species that suffered under his rule.'

'Including our families,' Sean said thoughtfully.

They became quiet. The silence brought a moment of reflection. Saving the universe had come at a terrible cost. Millions had died. Earth was a barren, lifeless world. Sean and Bella, along with a handful of humans on Akanae, represented the last of humanity. With the Isharkute decimated in equal measure, both species now made the universe's endangered list.

Nocao finally broke the silence. 'We should return to Akanae, inform the survivors of everything's that's happened.'

'You're right,' Sean said, perking up. 'We need to rebuild our planets.'

Bella shook her head. 'Why are you both giving up so easily? If the Ancients are so powerful, why don't we ask them to fix Earth? Put it back the way it was.'

'How?'

'You said they exist outside our time and space.'

'Yeah, but-'

'Don't you see? That means they're not locked into our universe or our time. They can go anywhere, do anything.'

'Not really. If they have that kind of freedom, they could have stopped Senetep without my help.'

'Wait, Bella may be onto something here,' Nocao said. 'That portal is more than just a teleporter, it accesses dimensions outside ours. Time might act differently over there. It may not be linear.'

'*Si!* You could contact the Ancients through the portal. Tell them to go back and kill Senetep before he destroys Earth.'

Nocao rubbed his beard, impressed. 'Mmm...your plan might be possible.'

'See, I'm getting used to this sciencey stuff.'

'But the Ancients have limited access to this universe. That's why they led me here, to open the portal so they could cross over. They would have stopped Senetep before now if it was possible.'

Bella thought about it for a moment. 'Then we use the portal to send ourselves back in time.'

'You have taken your sciencey aspirations to a new level,' Nocao said. 'We could stop Senetep before he attacks the Earth.'

'*Si!* Or kill him as a baby.'

Sean laughed. 'That would be easier.'

'I would advise against such extreme jumps,' Nocao said. 'It will change too much history. The results would become exponentially unpredictable. We need to keep the time frame as tight as possible. A couple of days shouldn't disrupt our universe too much.'

'Aside from saving a few billion lives,' Sean added.

'This wasn't meant to happen,' Bella said. Emotion filled her voice. 'We have to make things right.'

'Nocao, you're right. This portal is different to the one that brought us here. The Ancients used it to leave this universe, to move into a dimension where time and space don't apply. That's why they warned me not to enter. If I'd crossed over while separated from my body, my consciousness would have been stuck there, with no way of getting back.'

Bella sighed. 'So, it's impossible then?'

'No, that's what makes it possible. This portal doesn't need a physical portal on the receiving end; it has enough power to generate its own exit point. We just need to give it coordinates and a time.'

Bella shook her head with disbelief. 'How do you know all this?'

'I'm not sure. If I think about the Ancients' technology or ask a question, the answer just comes to me. It feels like the information has been put inside my mind – not in my direct consciousness, but in the background. Like a computer backup. Stored away until I need it.'

'It explains his increased brain activity,' Nocao said.

Sean rubbed his temple. 'And my headaches.'

'Your connection to the Ancients is more involved than I first believed. They have been seeding you with knowledge.'

'Why you?' Bella asked.

'It could have been anyone. But I was the one who activated the Yonaguni beacon. The moment I did, the Ancients locked onto my consciousness and started communicating.'

'If you tuned this portal onto the *Spearhead* before he attacks Earth,' Nocao said. 'We could jump straight into the control room, catch Senetep off-guard and kill him.'

Sean went cold with a terrible realisation. 'You realise what that means?'

'We can save Earth!' Bella exclaimed.

'It means we're bringing Senetep back to life. If we fail, he has another chance to destroy the universe.'

'Eight billion lives are worth the risk,' Bella said with unflinching determination.

'But we'll be risking billions, maybe trillions more.'

'I share your concern,' Nocao said. 'But Senetep upset the natural balance of evolution in the universe. I believe that's why the Ancients reached out to you, to stop him from destroying their work.'

'And we have. He's dead.'

'Yes. And now we need to correct his mistakes.'

Sean wasn't convinced. He searched his mind for the answer. Nothing came. For now, the Ancients remained quiet. Deep down, he knew the Ancients would not persuade him either way. They had given him the tools and knowledge to make his own decisions. The moral responsibility had fallen upon him.

Nocao approached the mercury pool. 'Everything you need is right here.'

'We have to try,' Bella said.

Sean caught her desperate gaze, shuddering at the thought of resurrecting Senetep. The risk was incalculable. The consequences unimaginable. Yet... Could he ignore the chance to reverse the apocalypse? No way.

'Okay, what do I do?' Sean said, looking to Nocao.

'Start by establishing a link between the portal and the *Spearhead*.'

Sean knelt beside the pool, dipped his hand in the mercury, and concentrated on the Ancients' network of portals. The mercury levitated into the centre of the hall, spinning and separating into a glistening display of stars, solar systems, and galaxies. Thousands of silver strands reached through the miniature universe, creating a meticulous web of portals linking the Ancients home planet to every *Spearhead* roaming the stars.

'There's so many of them!' Bella exclaimed.

'Concentrate on our *Spearhead*,' Nocao said. 'See if you can make a connection.'

Sean immediately thought of Earth, the *Spearhead's* last location. The miniature blobs of mercury pulled together and formed larger blobs, changing the map, creating a zoomed-in view of Earth. A sliver of mercury representing the link to the portal pierced the map and connected with the *Spearhead*.

'Well done. But you're looking through the portal in a linear path,' Nocao said. 'Try to connect to the *Spearhead* at an earlier point in time.'

Sean eyed Nocao, frustrated. 'Easier said than done.'

Bella rubbed his shoulder. 'You can do it.'

Sean took a deep breath and stared at the map, forcing the connection to change. Nothing happened. How was he supposed to change time? It was like searching for a door in a pitch-black room. He couldn't see the handle, let alone reach for it.

'I don't know how to do this.' Sean sighed.

'Trust yourself,' Bella said in a soothing voice. 'Think...you've done something similar.'

'When?'

'You reached out to your dad, found him across thousands of years.'

'You're right!'

He connected to his dad through emotions. Those feelings acted like an anchor, pulling him through time. But how would he connect with the *Spearhead* at a specific point in time? There was nobody aboard he shared an emotional bond with. Maybe it didn't need to be a friendship. A ludicrous idea struck him; one so dangerous it might just work.

He shared a link with someone in the correct moment in time – Senetep!

A mutual hatred and loathing tethered their bond. His wings twinged at the memory of being severed. He opened his mind to the horrors Senetep inflicted upon him, his dad, and the billions of innocent souls. Hatred swelled into his chest. The intense emotion emanated from him like a beacon, solidifying the connection. Sean pictured the moment they intercepted Senetep's fleet at the *Spearhead*.

The map suddenly changed. Earth's solar system disappeared. The mercury morphed into a different layout of planets, displaying the *Spearhead*, Senetep's squadron, and the three vessels from the Orion Taskforce fleet.

'You've done it!' Nocao said. 'We're looking back in time at the *Spearhead*.'

Behind them, the portal crackled to life. A ghostly blue light shimmered within the giant ring.

'The portal's opening,' Bella hollered.

A deep hum reverberated through the hall. Lightning bolts erupted across the ring, thundering through the hall like an encroaching storm.

The sound filled Sean with dread. He pictured those ice-blue eyes. Senetep's penetrating stare broke his concentration. Phantom pains shot through his ribs. He doubled over, gasping for air. The disruption severed his connection to the mercury and the portal powered down.

Bella spun around. 'Why did you stop?'

Sean remained hunched over. He caught his breath. 'We can't take the risk. Not until we have a foolproof plan.'

Nocao gave a pensive nod. 'You're right.'

'We have a time machine,' Bella said. 'That gives us all the time in the world to figure it out. Right?'

'Not exactly. I only have enough rations for two days. After that, we must search for food and water.'

'We have two days to figure it out then,' Sean said.

They left the hall and found an open-air room atop a nearby tower overlooking the city. Sean watched the maintenance drones repair the portal hall from the balcony. The Ancients had been gone for billions of years, but their city remained a living thing unto itself.

Over the next few hours, every crazy idea to kill Senetep was thrown into the mix. They considered arriving at different points in time, trying to figure out when Senetep was most vulnerable. Nothing was certain. It was all becoming too far-fetched and complicated. The more they discussed it, the more uncertain the plan seemed.

Sean figured it was time for a break when they considered dropping a T-rex through the portal. He fought off a yawn. It was late in the day and everyone looked tired. 'We should sleep on it.'

'Yes. A couple of hours should be enough,' Nocao said.

'I was hoping for a bit longer than that,' Bella said, fighting off a yawn.

'Your human brains require significant downtime compared to mine.'

'I find that a little surprising.'

'How so?'

Bella cocked an eyebrow at Nocao's forehead. 'Isn't it obvious?'

'Oh! I see. You're referring to the size of my cranium.' Nocao touched his head. 'My brain may be twice the size, but it's twice as efficient.'

Bella chuckled. 'Sure it is!'

'I'll run data on several of our less fanciful ideas after some rest.' Nocao laid back and closed his eyes. Within seconds, he was perfectly still and breathing steadily.

'Is he asleep already?' Bella whispered.

'Apparently he's also efficient at falling asleep.'

Sharing a quiet laugh, they tiptoed to the other side of the room. They sat on the edge of an open balcony and watched the dwindling reams of sunlight flicker over the alien horizon.

'It's funny. Even here, a sunset looks the same as it does on Earth,' Bella said. 'Makes you wonder.'

'Wonder what?'

'If humans really are special. After everything I've seen, it makes me question everything I was taught to believe. I was brought up a Catholic, but I don't see how God fits into any of this.'

Sean shook his head. 'You know what's even stranger?'

Bella gave him a quizzical look.

'I'm starting to feel the opposite. I wasn't brought up to believe in anything other than myself. That's what my dad always taught me. Religion was never a thing in my family. My dad had too many questions. He didn't take things for granted. He believed in things he could prove. Things he could dig up out of the ground. He wanted to be in control, to direct the course of his own life, not leave it up to fate, something he couldn't see for himself.'

'So, what's changed for you?'

'I saw something that made me reconsider.'

'Like what?'

'I saw an Ancient.'

Bella's eyes widened. 'What did it look like?'

Sean paused, careful with his choice of words. It was hard to deny his first impression, but there was only one way to describe what he saw. 'The Ancients look like angels.'

Bella bumped his shoulder with hers. 'Are you serious?'

'Yeah. They were beautiful. Radiant, like the sun. But it didn't hurt to look at them. Don't give up believing what you were taught. After seeing them, and what they could do, I realise how little we know. We're only starting to understand how life was created. After that, there's a whole other dimension that's a complete mystery.'

'Do you think they've become gods and angels?'

'I don't know, but they have that kind of omnipotent power. They've left their mortal bodies and moved on to a higher form of existence.'

'Life after death is the foundation for every religion.'

'Yeah. This might explain why all human religions share the same belief. That there's a better place waiting for us after we die. The Ancients might have encoded this deep inside our DNA, driving us to search for a higher form of life.'

'Makes sense. We're descendants of the Ancients, after all.'

'It seems the more we learn, the less we know. We have just as many questions as before, maybe more.'

They watched the sun disappear behind the horizon of alien structures. The amber-coloured light tapered off to a violet sky populated by unfamiliar stars. It reminded Sean of the countless hours spent sitting on his aunt and uncle's back deck late at night, peering up through his $100 telescope. Alpha Centauri, Omega Centauri, the Southern Cross, the Magellanic Clouds, and the magnificent Jewel Box cluster. He longed to see them again from the Earth he remembered, not the desolate wasteland it had become.

'I miss my family,' Bella said sombrely. 'We have to figure this out.'

Sean stared into her eyes, determined to find a foolproof plan before morning.

— CHAPTER 28 —

Silver Bullet

Sean awoke in the middle of the night, heart drumming against his chest, mind buzzing with the answer. The solution to their problem lay in the hall. It had been in front of them the entire time. He crawled over to Bella and gently roused her.

'What is it?' she murmured.

'I figured it out!'

Bella lay there for a second, half-asleep, then shot up. 'What?'

'Come with me.'

Nocao stood nearby, busily calculating their odds of success into a glowing hologram. He paused his work and looked up. 'Did you think of something?'

'Yeah! The Ancients erased every trace of Senetep, Erund, and the warriors, except for one thing – Senetep's weapon.'

Bella yawned, bleary-eyed and unimpressed. 'What? Are we meant to shoot him with it?'

'In a way, but it's not the weapon. It's what's on it. His DNA. The Ancients deliberately left a sample of his DNA. We can take it back in time with us–'

'For what purpose?' Nocao asked.

'We upload Senetep's DNA into the mercury on the *Spearhead* and tell the drones to eradicate any trace of it. We don't need to defeat his entire fleet, just Senetep. It's perfect. We turn the very thing he's been chasing against him. He doesn't stand a chance. Once he's dead, Erund and the others will surrender.'

Nocao rubbed his beard in consternation, nodding. 'You're right.'

'If we time our arrival with the Orion Taskforce, we can hit Senetep with everything at once–'

'And stop the *Spearhead* from destroying Earth?' Bella cut in.

'Yes. We can stop it before it even travels through the wormhole.'

Nocao ended the hologram and raced for the exit. 'You'd better hope those drones repairing the hall didn't do too good of a job.'

Sean chased after him. 'Oh no! I never thought of that.'

The repair drones had finished their flawless restoration by the time they returned. Beams of moonlight streamed through the new crystal panels, illuminating the portal in a pale-blue glow. Every scrap of debris had been removed, and the architecture returned to pristine condition. There was no sign of the previous battle except for Senetep's polearm. It lay exactly where Sean kicked it, beside the pool of mercury.

The three of them stood around the weapon, reluctant to touch it.

'The fact the repair drones didn't remove the weapon validates your plan,' Nocao said, activating his handheld scanner. 'There are traces of Senetep's DNA all over the handle. I can take a sample and upload it to the mercury.'

Sean knelt over the polearm. 'No need. I can interface with the mercury and upload the sample directly.'

'It's freaky how you know all this,' Bella said.

Nocao put his scanner away. 'I must admit, I'm surprised how easily you're adapting to your implanted knowledge.'

'*Sí!* This is more magic than science.'

'That's Arthur C. Clarke's Third Law!' Sean said brightly, excited to hear Bella echo one of his favourite science fiction authors.

'*Any sufficiently advanced technology is indistinguishable from magic,*' Nocao added with an air of pride.

Sean looked at him in shock. 'You know Arthur C. Clarke?'

'During the journey from Earth to Akanae, I familiarised myself with notable human scientists. Charles Darwin, Albert Einstein, and Stephen Hawking, along with writers, leaders, theologians, inventors and futurists. I studied human history for a broader perspective on our voyage. Clarke was one of the "Big Three" writers of science fiction. His work *2001: A Space Odyssey* shared similar themes to our quest for the *Spearhead*.'

'I'm impressed.'

Bella rolled her eyes. 'You two are such nerds.'

'I'll take that as a compliment,' Sean chuckled. 'But you should see the film, Nocao. It's as good as the book.'

'To do so, we must return Earth to the way it was.'

Sean leant over the pool and dipped his fingers into the mercury. The liquid metal enveloped his hand like a glove. He focused on Senetep's polearm, picturing the remnants of microscopic DNA on the handle. A rivulet of silver slithered across the floor and wrapped itself around the weapon, probing and sampling the handle with fluid-like fingers. Sean sensed multiple traces of DNA from all the hands that previously touched the weapon. He closed his eyes and concentrated on isolating Senetep's DNA. The mercury did the rest.

Sean finally opened his eyes and the mercury returned to the pool. 'It's done.'

'How do we transfer that information into the *Spearhead*?' Nocao asked.

Sean turned over his hand, revealing a droplet of quivering mercury in his palm. 'We take this back in time and add it to the mercury pool in the *Spearhead's* main control room. It will instruct the drones to kill Senetep.'

'How long will it take?'

'It should be instant.'

'What if there're no drones in the control room?'

Sean shrugged. 'We survive until they get there.'

'If that works, we still have to convince Erund not to shoot us on the spot.'

'This still sounds risky,' Bella said. 'I thought the plan was foolproof.'

'No plan is 100 per cent foolproof. But I've seen Senetep's crew. Their obedience is motivated by fear of death. He's been killing pilots and scientists for the slightest mistakes. It won't take much to make them turn. They've lost faith in him. They know he's insane. Problem is, none of them are brave enough to stand up to him. Erund Griss looks ready to jump ship. I'm pretty sure I can convince him to surrender once Senetep's dead.'

Nocao sighed heavily. '"Pretty sure" will have to do, I guess.'

'I can do it.'

'Why do we need to take such an unnecessary risk?' Bella said. 'We have a time machine! Just go further back in time, before Senetep even reaches the control room.'

'Going back further leaves too much room for error. It gives him a chance to escape. We can't risk it. We need him in the control room, exposed. It's the safest way.'

'What's our plan of attack then?' Bella asked.

'It's impossible to predict where Senetep will be at any point in time. To be safe, I'll open the portal just outside the main control room, fly in and add the mercury before they know what's happened. That keeps you two out of danger.'

'We respect your concern,' Nocao said. 'But if something happens to you, our entire plan fails.'

'*Si!* Friends don't leave each other in the middle of a fight. We're in this together.'

Sean nodded, glad to have such steadfast friends. Together, he was confident they could rise to any challenge.

'All right. I'll drop all of us in the control room, out of sight.' He glanced down at the tiny drop of mercury. He closed his hand and looked to his friends. 'You ready?'

'I'm ready!' Bella responded.

'Let's finish this for the last time,' Nocao said.

Sean held his hand over the pool and fixated on creating a link with the *Spearhead*. A sliver of mercury spiralled out of the pool and covered his hand. Seconds later, the entire pool levitated into the air, spinning like a whirlpool. The mercury exploded into a million silver blobs and reformed to show the *Spearhead* in orbit around Earth.

The first part was done. He was getting a lot quicker at this. Now came the hard part. Changing the arrival time; a connection that required him to unleash his dreaded, most suppressed memories.

Sean took a deep breath, cleared his thoughts, and lowered his emotional guard.

He allowed his earliest memories of Senetep to poison his mind... *Being forced against the slitherquill's cage...Horumbut's brutal death... the destruction of the Arc de Triomphe...the Isharkute invasion...Senetep severing his wings and tossing them aside...kicked and beaten to the brink of death...Earth's destruction...billions of lives ending, without mercy...*

Months of pent-up emotions swelled through his body. Tears streamed down his cheeks. He fixated on those icy-blue eyes. Senetep's hatred and loathing sucked him in like a black hole, solidifying their connection across time and space.

Sean pushed through the anguish and focused on the *Spearhead*, homing in to open the portal moments before the Orion Taskforce arrived.

The portal erupted with light and thundered through the hall. A luminous wave of blue light stabilised inside the ring, creating a vertical wall of shimmering energy.

Sean slumped forward, exhausted.

Bella placed her arm around him. 'Are you okay?'

Sean mustered a nod. It was all he could manage. Creating the link had taken a huge mental and physical toll. He straightened, self-consciously wiping the tears from his cheeks.

Bella kissed his cheek and embraced him. 'I'm proud of you.'

Sean took a deep breath and peered up to the shimmering portal, ready to face Senetep one last time. The pool of mercury parted, opening a path to the portal platform between walls of glossy silver. They crossed over and followed the spiral-shaped platform to the top.

Sean paused, peering up in awe. The energised portal ring stood several storeys high, casting a soft blue light throughout the hall. Inside the portal, a kaleidoscope of stars spiralled into a bright core.

'*È bellissimo!*' Bella gasped.

Sean's stomach turned with a rush of butterflies. They were

about to step into the unknown. He grasped Bella's hand, and she gripped Nocao's hand.

Sean led them to the edge. The hairs on his arm stood on end and leaned towards the portal, charged with static electricity. A curious tingling flowed through his body. He turned to his friends. Their faces reflected his wonder and terror.

He nodded.

They nodded back.

Sean faced the portal and glanced down at the drop of mercury in his hand. He made a fist, securing it in his grasp. Billions of lives depended on it.

He stepped forward. His knee touched the energy first. It buzzed up his leg like pins and needles, then overwhelmed him, yanking him forward.

BOOM!

His body dematerialised into atom-sized electrons, but his consciousness remained, hurtling through space and time at unfathomable speeds. Trillions of heavenly lights flew around him. Was this the realm of the Ancients? An eternity passed in the blink of an eye, then...

BOOM!

Sean stepped out of thin air onto a metal floor, Bella and Nocao behind him, all three of them still holding hands.

They were deep inside the *Spearhead's* control chamber, hidden behind a row of columns from Senetep and his entourage of scientists and warriors. Nobody noticed their arrival. The centre of the chamber was dominated by a pool of mercury the size of a small lake, above which hovered an immense map of the universe.

Senetep's voice boomed across the chamber. 'This isn't the only *Spearhead!*'

Sean was tempted to spring into action straight away.

'There're millions of them,' Erund whispered. 'Seeding the galaxies.' The middle of the map grew brighter, highlighting the centre of the universe and a shimmering golden planet. 'What's that light in the centre?'

'The home of the Ancients, the birthplace of creation. Our ultimate destination.'

'What's our next course of action?'

'We stay in this chamber until we figure out how to access and control the *Spearhead's* command systems.'

'And once we do?'

'We recall the drones and steer this vessel through the nearest wormhole back to Earth. After the drones have eradicated every living organism on that pitiful planet, we travel to Akanae and repeat the process. Then we set a course for the home of the Ancients. From there, we can take control of every *Spearhead* and rewrite the universe.'

Sean realised the importance of this moment. His timing couldn't have been better. He opened his hand. The droplet quivered in his palm like a living bullet.

'What now?' Bella whispered.

'I'll fly over there. Throw this in the mercury and trigger the drones.'

'What are you waiting for?' Nocao cut in. 'Senetep is unarmed. There are no warriors. Your timing was perfect.'

Sean closed his fist. 'Stay out of sight. This is easier than we thought.'

Bella pulled him close and kissed him. 'Don't get too confident.'

Sean nodded.

He darted ahead and crouched in the shadows, pulling his top down to slip his paper-thin wings over his collar.

'Sean!' Bella whispered desperately.

Sean stopped and turned to see what was wrong. Bella pointed to the far side of the chamber with a panic-stricken expression. A squad of fully armed warriors filed down the steps and assembled around Senetep. *Damn!*

Bella and Nocao shook their heads and waved him back.

Sean felt the urgency rise inside him. He couldn't wait. *I've got this!* he mouthed, turning around before they could convince him otherwise.

He bolted behind the rows of columns, spread his wings, and took off, sailing silently through the chamber recesses. Nobody had seen him. Zipping out from the shadows, he came up on the far side of the mercury pool, at least fifty metres away from Senetep and his warriors. He flapped hard and shot upwards, high over the mercury map and pool. It was impossible to miss from here.

'LOOK!' Erund screamed.

Senetep glanced up and did a double-take, eyes like saucers. 'How did he get in here? Shoot him down!'

Sean threw the encoded drop of mercury straight down into the silver and shot away, avoiding the crossfire of staves. He circled around the pool, descending to shoulder-height, directing the warriors to fire towards each other.

Senetep roared like an animal and snatched a stave from a warrior.

Sean kept an eye on him, flying blindly at a blistering speed. The Overseer took aim, tracking ahead of his flight path with rock-solid precision. Sean panicked, feeling like he was being reeled in like a fish. He needed to change direction before the final strike...

CRACK!

Excruciating pain tore through his left shoulder and his wing exploded in flames. Sean glimpsed over his smouldering shoulder. The tattered remains of his wing flapped about uselessly. He crash-landed and tumbled across the floor.

Dazed, Sean sat up and found himself surrounded by crackling staves. He clutched his injured shoulder with grazed hands.

Senetep marched over. A furious but concerned glare filled his eyes. 'Where did you come from?'

Sean didn't answer. He bottled up his pain with a grimace. It felt like his entire back was on fire. How long until the drones reacted?

The Overseer paced around him, agitated, peering anxiously around the chamber. 'Who else is with you?'

Sean curled over and held his breath, hoping he could hold out until the drones arrived.

'Answer me!' Senetep barked, jabbing him in the back with

his stave. 'I can make you suffer for eternity, extend your life for centuries; millennia longer than your frail carcass was designed to endure. You will live in a state of constant pain and suffering, carrying the memories of your species' demise.'

'You made that threat once before,' Sean said, raising his head. 'Word for word.'

Senetep looked confused, then drove the electrified forks into his side like a taser.

Sean rolled across the floor, gnashing his teeth, holding onto the hope of what was about to happen. The rampant energy dissipated. His muscles relaxed. Sean took a deep breath and craned his neck to meet Senetep's eyes. 'You keep making the same mistakes.'

Senetep snarled and took aim, fingers tightening on the trigger.

Sean had run out of time. *This is it!*

'He's not alone!' Nocao called across the chamber.

Senetep froze. His uncertain eyes glanced aside. Nocao and Bella walked out from behind the columns, hands raised in surrender.

'Bring them here!' Senetep ordered. 'They can all die together.'

Sean nodded to his friends and forced a smile. They smiled back as the warriors forced them to kneel beside him.

'We have control of the drones,' called a scientist as a line of drones flew into the chamber.

'We don't need these anymore,' Senetep said, tossing the stave aside. He raised his arms to the drones circling overhead. 'I now control the greatest force in the universe.'

A drone descended in front of Bella and centred its pulsing red eye upon her. Its front panel slid open and a deadly proboscis unfurled.

Sean suddenly doubted his plan. Had the drop of mercury worked? Why was the drone targeting Bella and not Senetep?

Senetep stood over Sean. 'Tell me how you got here. Or watch your friends die one at a time.'

The red eye flickered, then settled. The drone gave a distorted beep and rotated with a noisy whir of Ancient motors. Senetep backed away from the advancing machine, almost tripping over his own feet. More drones descended, forming a circle around him.

'What's going on?' Senetep cried, looking desperately to his scientists. 'Why are they targeting me? Deactivate them!'

The scientists scrambled over their holograms. 'We've lost control,' one called.

'Something else has taken control of the system,' said another.

Senetep fell backwards and clambered across the floor towards his discarded weapon. 'Stop them! Destroy them!'

Sean pulled himself to his feet and limped after Senetep, determined to face his nemesis one last time. Erund and the warriors watched on, torn between acting and doing nothing.

Senetep moved within hold of his stave and Erund stepped in, kicking it out of reach. He scowled at his First Commander. 'Traitor!'

The drones unleashed their dissolving hoses and closed in for the kill.

Sean approached the circle. A drone floated aside, allowing him to step through. Bella and Nocao joined him. Sean ignored the pain and straightened his shoulders, standing proudly over his fallen enemy. 'Now we control the greatest force in the universe.'

Senetep growled like a cornered animal, glancing about for help. None was coming.

'I just wanted you to know it was us who beat you.'

Sean stepped back and the drones released their life-dissolving liquid.

Senetep screamed in agony as his body was vaporised from the feet up. Skin, muscle, and bone dissolved layer by layer, in the most excruciating way possible. His contorted face finally sizzled away and evaporated. The Overseer's empty armour clanged to the floor in a swirl of vapour and the drones ascended out of sight. Job done.

'Throw down your weapons!' Erund said, tossing his weapon aside. 'This is over. We're surrendering to the Empire.'

The surrounding warriors regarded each other with subtle nods and lowered their staves.

Sean was glad to see they needed little convincing.

'Three vessels just dropped out of light speed within range of the *Spearhead*,' a scientist announced.

'It's the Orion Taskforce!' Nocao said.

Sean looked down at the empty armour and breathed a sigh of relief. They had accomplished the impossible.

— CHAPTER 29 —

Unexpected Delivery

Several hours later, Sean, Bella and Nocao were back aboard the *Alnitak* with Hazim, having a private meeting in his ready room. Hazim was ecstatic to find them alive after they inexplicably vanished off the bridge, but wanted an explanation. They all sat around a large desk embedded with glowing control panels. Nocao used holograms to demonstrate his theory, explaining how copies of themselves could not occupy the same time line and that such a conundrum could unbalance the fabric of space and time within the universe.

Sean took it to mean the universe had corrected itself by shifting them from the *Alnitak* to the *Spearhead* the instant they jumped through time. That meant they returned to their original time line, not a parallel universe with a different outcome. If so, he was the only witness to Earth's annihilation: a nightmare he would burden for every living soul.

Bella yawned multiple times during the lengthy debriefing, looking like she might fall asleep in her chair.

Sean fought back his yawns, happy to let Nocao do the talking. He was too exhausted to explain everything right now. When queried by Hazim for his side of the story, he kept it short and simple, saying they had travelled back from a disastrous future.

Meanwhile, Erund Griss had surrendered Senetep's fleet, avoiding an unnecessary battle. Erund seemed relieved to concede, as if punishment by the Isharkute Empire was salvation compared to serving Senetep. He was now under guard in the *Alnitak's* docking bay, along with Senetep's senior officers, scientists, and warriors.

'What do we do with the *Spearhead*?' Hazim asked.

'Nothing,' Sean said. 'The drones will finish building the moon and prepare the planet for life. Once it's finished, it will move on to the next habitable planet. It's been doing this for billions of years. The best thing we can do is leave it alone and return home.'

'I'm not sure our superiors will feel the same way. The portal that brought you back from the future is a dangerous technology. In the wrong hands, it could undo everything we have achieved.'

'That's why the Ancients gave me a way to contact them, no matter where we are in the universe.'

'I've assigned three full squads to guard the canister of mercury you brought back from the *Spearhead's* control room. Nobody gets in or out of our secure cargo hold without my permission. It's the most valuable sample of liquid mercury in the universe.'

'It needs to be kept a secret.'

'I agree. Nobody outside the Orion Taskforce knows about it, not even Senetep's supporters. Still, they present a considerable risk travelling on the same vessel. As a precaution, I'll move them aboard the *Alnilam* and *Mintaka* for the voyage home.'

'What happens when we get to Earth?'

'Expect a full debriefing. Those in command will want to know what they're dealing with.'

'I'll brief them. But I'm worried. The Ancients entrusted me with the mercury. I don't want to betray that trust by handing it over to someone else.'

Hazim nodded, brow furrowed with concern. 'Unfortunately, we don't make those decisions.'

Sean looked at his friends and back to Hazim, doubting they should take the mercury back at all. The Ancients reached out to him moments before he left the *Spearhead*, instructing him to take the mercury as a safeguard. It was his responsibility. 'I'm worried. I don't think our species are ready to control such power.'

Nobody argued the point. They regarded each other with the same uneasy silence.

The door slid open and Hemket ducked her lanky body through the doorway, acknowledging everyone with a hasty nod. 'We must return to Akanae at once!'

Nocao stood sharply. 'What's wrong?'

'Ramin's cocoon is deteriorating. He urgently requires a natural environment to survive his metamorphosis. The forests of Akanae are imbued with healing powers that cannot be replicated within the walls of this vessel.'

'Fine,' Hazim said, rising from his chair. 'I'll inform the fleet. We will detour via Akanae on our return to Earth.'

Sean, Bella and Nocao followed Hemket down to the *Alnitak's* cargo bay. Bella bombarded Hemket with questions about Ramin, sounding like an anxious family member. Her concern displayed how close they had all become.

They entered the dimly lit cargo hold. Candlelight flickered through the draped-off birthing space. The midwives knelt in a circle around Ramin's withered cocoon, pouring oils and fluids over the glistening surface. His emaciated outline suddenly spasmed. Beside him, the skinny outline of a smaller figure quivered in response.

'*Mio Dio!*" Bella whispered in awe. 'It's a *bambino!*'

But it was no baby. The newborn was about the size of a ten-year-old child. A thick umbilical cord protruded from the sagging cocoon, linking their stomachs. Slow-moving fluids passed through the translucent umbilical.

'Nocao, it may not look like it, but your cure has worked,' Hemket said. 'This is the closest we have come to a successful birth in centuries. But Ramin and her offspring are fighting a rare disorder that affects a small percentage of births.'

'What is that?' Nocao said.

'The child was born early, while Ramin was in the last stages of metamorphosis. Her offspring is taking a heavy toll.'

Bella knelt beside a midwife and helped pour the ointment. 'It's a premature birth.'

Nocao waved his scanner over the cocoon. 'The amniotic fluid is not regenerating fast enough. The child is taking what it needs to survive.'

'Will they live?' Bella asked.

'Not in this state.'

'Can you synthesise more amniotic fluid?' Sean said.

'I don't know. But I doubt the healing power of Akanae's forests can replenish them from such a depleted state. We need to find a scientific cure instead of pinning our hopes on a holistic solution.'

'There's no time,' Hemket said. 'Our safest option is to return to Akanae. We can be there before the end of the day.'

'I can find a solution before then.'

'I appreciate your enthusiasm, Nocao, but you cannot solve this in one day. The condition has affected our species since the beginning of Isharkute civilisation. The Guild of Sciences has never developed a viable treatment. I'm afraid this is out of our hands.'

Sean stared at Hemket. Her comment sparked an idea. 'Maybe not.'

'What do you mean?'

Sean turned to Nocao. 'You can interface with the mercury I brought back from the *Spearhead* and communicate with the Ancients. They might be able to help.'

'How? You're the only one who's been able to speak with them.'

'I can guide you.'

Nocao holstered his scanner and nodded.

Bella passed another bowl of oil to the midwife. 'I'll stay with Ramin.'

A few minutes later, Sean and Nocao met Hazim outside the heavily guarded cargo hold several decks below. The guards stepped aside, allowing them entry. Sean led Nocao and Hazim inside. A tall metallic cylinder stood in the centre of the empty space.

Sean placed his hand on the side of the cylinder, and it parted in the middle, revealing a column of liquid mercury hovering in midair.

Hazim approached, enthralled by the silver. 'Incredible! And this communicates with the *Spearhead*?'

'Yes. It's also a direct link into the Ancients database. Every form of life the *Spearhead* created is stored within the mercury. It holds the blueprints for all life in the universe.'

Hazim shook his head. 'Unbelievable. How do you use it?'

'By touch at first. Once the connection is strong enough, it becomes telepathic. My ability isn't unique. Any sentient life form can communicate with it.'

Nocao stepped forward. 'Show me how.'

'I'll be outside,' Hazim said, heading for the exit. 'I'll make sure nobody distracts your work.'

Sean and Nocao waited for the door to close.

Silence enveloped them.

'Okay, clear your mind,' Sean said in a soft voice. 'Close your eyes if it helps. Focus on what you need. What you want to learn.'

Nocao fixated on the silver.

Sean spoke softly, mindful not to disturb Nocao's concentration. 'When you're ready, reach out. Touch the mercury.'

Nocao closed his eyes and reached out. A sliver of mercury extracted from the column and connected with the tips of his fingers.

Sean whispered, 'You'll sense a presence, like someone sharing your thoughts. Don't fight it. Let them in.'

Nocao remained still for a long moment, then shuddered. His eyelids stayed shut while his eyes continued moving beneath. It gave the appearance he was dreaming, when in fact he was processing huge amounts of information.

Sean tiptoed across the room and slumped down beside the wall, keeping an eye on his friend. This could last minutes or hours. His tiredness was hard to fight. He sat up straighter, forcing his eyes to stay open. Easier said than done. He should have remained standing. Sitting down just invited sleep. His head lolled forward. Closing his eyes for a few seconds would make a world of difference. A one-minute power nap couldn't hurt...

Sean awoke with a start.

He was lying on the floor. Nocao crouched over him and shook his body. Perspiration glistened up his long blue forehead and his pale-blue eyes looked shell shocked, like someone had blasted his mind with information. Sean knew the feeling.

He clambered to his feet. 'Are you okay? How long was I asleep?'

'I need to get to the lab!'

Sean chased him into the outside, past the waiting guards. Hazim joined the pursuit through the *Alnitak's* winding maze of corridors. Nocao kept a frantic pace, muttering and gesticulating to himself.

'Is he okay?' Hazim said.

'I've never seen him like this.'

They rushed into the lab. Hemket and a team of Isharkute scientists stood waiting, ready to help. Nocao accessed a holographic terminal and brought up the Ancients' DNA sequence. He zoomed into the double-helix, cross-referencing the nucleotides with an Isharkute double-helix. Hemket approached, data pad in hand, eager to help. Nocao ignored her, working as if he was the only person in the lab.

Hemket craned her head around to Sean, waiting for an explanation.

Sean shrugged. 'Just let him go. He knows what he's doing.'

Nocao brought up an endless list of double-helixes and overlaid them on the Ancients' genome sequence. He worked possessed, as if channelling the wisdom of the Ancients. Nocao spun around and begun typing on another holographic terminal, laughing to himself.

Hazim raised an eyebrow. 'Are you sure he's okay?'

'I think so. I've hardly seen him laugh.'

Nocao finished typing and stood back from the terminal. He exhaled a deep, satisfied breath and watched his new code process millions of DNA sequences against the Ancients' genome. 'The Ancients' genome solves everything. It's so simple. So perfect.'

'Does it help Ramin and his offspring?' Hemket asked.

Nocao met her alarmed expression with a wondrous gaze. 'It's a cure for everything. Every illness. For any species.'

'How is this possible?'

'All life is based on the Ancients' genome. We've been handed the blueprints for all forms of life. A guide to creation!'

Sean stared in awe at the beautiful spiral.

*   *   *

Rays of sunshine filtered through the canopy of purple foliage, creating a warm pocket of light between the gargantuan trees. Ramin's cocoon lay on a bed of ferns, glistening in the radiance. Six hours had passed since Nocao administered Ramin with a cure. Over that time the cocoon had rejuvenated into a healthy pulsating sac. Aside from the occasional elbow or knee pressing against the outer wall, Ramin and his offspring were no longer visible within the sac.

Sean stood with Nocao and Bella, surrounded by Hemket and the midwives. They waited in silence, enveloped by the forest ambience. Melodic bird calls echoed through the treetops. Curious insects hovered to inspect the cocoon. Bella promptly waved them off. Distant animals roared and bellowed. Instead of feeling threatened, the wild, natural setting embraced them with living energy like no lab or vessel could. Returning to Akanae was the right thing to do. Humans and Isharkute had relied on technology for too long, forgetting their links to nature.

'I feel like a parent expecting my first child,' Nocao whispered.

'I know what you mean,' Sean said.

'This baby is our responsibility too,' Bella said softly. 'We should care for him like he's our own.'

Nocao smiled. 'We will.'

A ripping sound cut between them and the cocoon split down the centre. Long, glistening, spider-like fingers curled over the edges of the sac. Clear amniotic fluid oozed from the slit and seeped into the forest floor. The fingers pulled open the cocoon, revealing a tall blue head covered in ooze. Ramin wiped the fluid from her transformed face and opened her eyes. Her features had thinned and elongated into an elegant female form. She looked up at them and smiled.

Sean could still see the mischievous gleam of his old friend behind the fresh face. Ramin hadn't changed a bit.

Ramin peeled back the rest of the cocoon, revealing a glistening body curled up in a foetal position. The child was fully formed and sleeping peacefully.

'Unbelievable!' Sean whispered.

Ramin stroked her child's head and cleared away the amniotic film from his face. The child's eyes fluttered open, revealing the most striking blue eyes Sean had ever seen. The newborn peered up to Ramin and reached out. They held each other in a loving embrace.

Sean had come to learn this was an important bonding, for within days, they would be separated for life. Ramin would remain on Akanae, preparing for a new generation of life-bearers, while her child moved off-world to begin life with his surrogate father.

Hemket knelt beside them. 'Ramin, you must name your child.'

Ramin nodded and turned to Nocao. 'I name him Horum, in honour of your father Horumbut.'

A tear rolled down Nocao's cheek.

Until now, Sean had no idea the Isharkute could even cry. The momentous occasion brought tears to his own eyes. Bella took his hand and squeezed it gently, smiling. She was crying tears of joy too. Sean felt a warmth swell up inside him. He was surrounded by family, one sprawling family that stretched beyond human and Isharkute existence, reaching into the furthest corners of the universe.

His journey was complete. It was time to go home.

— CHAPTER 30 —

Earthrise

The *Alnitak* dropped out of light speed and entered Earth's solar system. Sean watched from the bridge, enjoying a local sightseeing trip past Neptune, Uranus, Saturn, Jupiter, and Mars, making their final approach to Earth from the dark side of the Moon.

Hazim gave Sean a smile and nodded. His course was deliberate, to showcase the perfect Earthrise. The fragile blue orb appeared over the Moon's grey horizon, just like the famous *Earthrise* photograph taken in 1968 during the Apollo 8 mission.

Sean had a poster of the photo stuck to the ceiling in his old bedroom. He used to lie in complete darkness and illuminate Earth with his torch, creating the illusion he was flying through space.

His imagination had become reality.

Sean was anxious about returning. Not because of the inevitable press conferences and media attention, or the meetings with Emperor Neberun and new world leaders; it was returning to face his aunt and uncle. He felt guilty for not contacting them. There was no excuse. It was time to be honest with himself, about his mistakes, and apologise.

Bella came up and stood beside him. 'You look nervous.'

Sean realised he'd been making fists. He relaxed his hands and rubbed his sweaty palms on his pants. 'Is it that obvious?'

'Don't worry, I am too. If we thought we were famous before we left, that's nothing compared to what it'll be like this time.'

Sean gave a half-hearted nod.

Bella glanced sideways at him. 'Is something else bothering you?'

Sean didn't want to burden her with his own problems. This was his mistake. His responsibility. He would deal with it himself.

'I'm okay. Just nervous about seeing everyone again.'

To avoid the onslaught of media attention, Hazim had arranged for the *Alnitak* to dock with Emperor Neberun's mothership, where they could reunite with friends and family in private before returning to Earth. The gigantic silver disc emerged from the dark of Earth's night side. Its tip gleamed as it caught the sunlight.

'What are we waiting here for? *Andiamo!*' Bella called, dragging Sean off the bridge.

She jogged through the passages down to the main gangway. The *Alnitak* shuddered gently as it touched down inside the mothership. Everyone assembled in the departure area, eager to disembark. Bella paced about, too excited to stand still. The gangway lowered with a hiss of escaping oxygen.

'BELLA!' cried a familiar voice.

'Arty!' Bella screamed, rushing down the gangway. She leapt into Arturo's arms. They hugged tight, tears streaming down their cheeks. Her parents, Marco and Francesca, joined the embrace, overwhelmed with joy and relief.

Sean tentatively followed, peering around the expansive docking bay for his aunt and uncle. Strangely, they were nowhere to be seen – just Isharkute and human personnel attending to their duties.

'Sean!' Carla called, jumping out of a transport vessel that just landed.

Her comforting smile and open arms eased his apprehension. They gave each other a warm hug. Carla looked the same, albeit a little older and wiser. Nearly two years had passed on Earth since his departure, giving her time to come to terms with Henry's death.

Carla caressed his cheek, eyes full of compassion. 'How are you?'

'Glad to be home.'

Bella smiled, looking like she had a million more questions. 'If you're wondering, your aunt and uncle came with me.'

Sean's heart skipped a beat. 'They did?'

'*Si*. I've come to know them well since you've been gone. Janine's told me plenty of things about your dad from their childhood. I feel like I know him better than ever before.'

'Where are they?'

'Right there,' Carla said, nodding over his shoulder.

Sean's heart skipped a beat. He turned around. His aunt and uncle stepped into the docking bay, awed by the mothership. Steve looked like he'd just stepped out of a university lecture. His close-trimmed auburn beard, bald head and black-rimmed spectacles complimented his casual navy blazer and chequered shirt. Janine was more corporate in her business pants, woollen sweater, and fancy scarf. She was always well-dressed and presentable, even on lazy weekends. Sean loved their normality.

Sean didn't even realise he was walking towards them and suddenly found himself wrapped in their embrace. All his worries faded away. Family bonds could never be broken. Sean stood back, determined to say everything he needed to right now.

'I'm sorry I didn't contact you.'

Janine tenderly touched his cheek. 'It's okay, Sean. We're just relieved to see you alive and well.'

'It's not okay. I mean, I just wanted to–'

'It's okay, Sean,' Steve cut in. 'We understand. We don't blame you. You were under immense pressure. Saving the planet is no easy feat.'

'Thanks, but what I'm also trying to say is–' Sean paused. 'I'm sorry for taking you for granted. You sacrificed a lot to care for me when mum died. All those years, I resented not having a regular family. I took it out on you. Blamed you for keeping me away from Dad. I'm sorry.'

'We understand,' Janine said. 'Your feelings were natural.'

Steve smiled and placed a hand on Sean's shoulder. 'The kid I dropped off at the airport has come home a man.'

Sean felt a massive weight lift off his shoulders. For the first time in his life, he was free of the emotional burden.

'Thought you could get away without a proper Bonaforte hug?' boomed a voice from behind. Sean spun around to find himself caught in Arturo's inescapable grasp. His arms seemed twice as muscular and strong as before. '*Grazie* for saving the world, but more importantly, for bringing Bella home.'

Sean acknowledged his navy suit and emblem. 'You're in the Orion Taskforce!'

'*Sì!* I signed up three months ago, hoping I'd qualify in time for the rescue mission to save you guys.'

'Don't worry, there'll be plenty more missions.'

'*Che cosa!* Where are you going this time?'

'Nowhere. But I'm sure you will be.'

Arturo looked towards the *Alnitak's* gangway. 'Where's Nocao? I wanted to thank him.'

'He's preparing to meet with Emperor Neberun.'

'Then I'll catch up with him later.'

'Sean Livingstone, come here!' Francesca hollered, cutting between them. She hugged Sean and kissed him on the cheek. '*Grazie, grazie* for bringing my Bella home.'

'And for saving the world,' Marco said, taking over hugging duties.

Sean joined in the jubilation. Hugging, laughing, and appreciating the joyous reunion with his extended family. In that moment, he experienced what they had fought so hard to protect. The most powerful force in the universe transcended time and space, preventing anyone from ever being truly alone.

Love.

*   *   *

Sean and Bella stood alone in Emperor Neberun's opulent private chamber. The hour spent with their families had flown by. Now they waited for Nocao, Ramin and Horum to arrive for a meeting with Neberun. Sean had travelled in royal transports before, but those vessels were nothing compared to the opulence on display here. Everything was gold-plated. A circle of wide, cushioned seats encircled a large throne. The chamber walls were windows into viewing tanks, showing exotic species in their natural environment.

Sean moved closer to the first window and peered through the glass. Obscure aquatic creatures swam through the crystal clear water. A flat pancake-looking fish flipped over and flashed a bright light at them.

Sean shielded his eyes. 'Whoa!'

Bella laughed. 'It's a camera fish!'

The next enclosure supported a zero-gravity environment, with luminescent amoebae swimming between the floating rocks.

'What are those things?' Bella said, moving closer to the glass. 'They look like jellyfish.'

'I don't know. Makes you realise, there's so much of the universe we haven't seen.'

'Sure is.'

Bella moved to the next window. Colourful birds zipped between the branches of a spindly tree. 'They're pretty birds.'

Sean recognised their bright yellow-red plumage straight away. He stopped short. An icy finger shot down his spine. 'And deadly.'

'Really? They're so cute. Are you sure?'

'I'm sure. They're slitherquills. They have a poisonous spike hidden beneath their tail feathers.'

'Urgh!' Bella moved on. 'Nocao's taking a long time to join us. Do you think there's something wrong with Horum?'

'I hope not. Maybe they're just having regular baby problems.'

'I doubt they're changing nappies. If that's what you mean.'

Sean chuckled. 'Horum's definitely not a baby.'

'Si, he was nearly as big as us.'

'Maybe they're teaching him to walk and talk before he comes in here.'

'That's quick for a newborn.'

'We don't really know anything about Isharkute offspring. They could be like newborn foals. They stand and run within the first ninety minutes of being born.'

Bella nodded. 'I hadn't thought of it that way.'

The chamber door slid open. Nocao, Ramin and Horum entered.

Ramin held Horum's hand, guiding him inside the chamber. Horum took everything in with wide, inquisitive eyes, looking like a child on his first day at school. He was half the height of Nocao, who was now half the height of Ramin – a picture-perfect Isharkute family!

'Horum, say hello to Sean and Bella,' Ramin said.

Horum spoke in a youthful, high-pitched tone. 'Hello.'

Sean and Bella replied in unison. 'Hello!'

'Horum, remember the human greeting custom we practiced,' Ramin said.

Horum nodded and offered his hand. Sean shook Horum's hand with a warm smile. Horum smiled back. His striking blue eyes harboured no prejudice, just a willingness to learn and connect with those around him. He was like a sponge, soaking up the world for the first time.

'Bella is a human female,' Horum said as he shook her hand.

Bella nodded. 'You've grown up so quick!'

'Have I?' Horum said in an inquisitive voice, looking to Ramin and Nocao for confirmation.

'Compared to a human baby, yes, you have,' Ramin said.

'The first few days after birth are crucial for bonding and intellectual growth,' Nocao explained. 'That's why Ramin and Horum remained secluded during our return to Earth.'

'The role of parenting has almost skipped an entire generation of Isharkute,' Ramin said. 'Thankfully, Hemket was there to guide my transition, with Nocao observing. His generation will be the ones who pass this knowledge on to the next.'

Sean made the Isharkute sign of the cosmos. 'Horum, humans have also learnt an important gesture, taught to us by your people, the Isharkute.'

Horum joined his thumbs and fingers together, as if he'd made the sign a hundred times before.

Emperor Neberun finally entered the chamber, flanked by four royal guards. After almost two years spent in Earth's orbit, little had changed for Neberun. From what Sean heard, the Emperor spent most of his time in stasis because of his age. He appeared older and even more frail than Sean remembered him – if that was even possible.

'You have my deepest gratitude,' Neberun said, acknowledging each of them. 'You rid the Empire of its greatest scourge and ensured the future of our species.'

Neberun ambled into the centre of the room and stood before Horum. His old, dark-blue eyes lightened a little. With the aid of his guards, Neberun knelt on one knee.

Sean glanced at Nocao in shock. He never thought he would see the Isharkute Emperor kneel before anyone.

'Horum,' Neberun said, taking Horum's young hand in his, 'you are a symbol of hope, of life, and of peace. Future generations will remember this moment, when our race was saved in the darkest hour, not by force or violence, but by compassion, friendship, and family.'

Horum nodded, understanding every word.

Neberun eyed the guards, and they assisted him to his feet. The simple effort made him puff. His grasp on life seemed driven by a desire to witness the continuation of his species. He caught his breath and continued. 'Ramin, have you chosen who will father your son Horum and guide him into adulthood?'

'I have,' Ramin replied, turning to Nocao.

Nocao did a double-take between Ramin and Neberun with a surprised look of *Who, me?*

'Nocao is not much older than a child himself,' Neberun said.

'True, but he has experienced more than those twice his age. I could not imagine an Isharkute more suited to the honour.'

Neberun nodded thoughtfully and fixated on Nocao. 'Nocao, son of Horumbut, member of the Guild of Sciences, do you accept this responsibility?'

Nocao's mouth hung open. For a long time, he said nothing. Horum peered up to him with large, expectant eyes. Nocao straightened his shoulders and composed himself. A proud smile came over his face. 'I would be honoured.'

Horum beamed, almost jumping on the spot.

Neberun nodded. 'Good, it's settled then. Now, return to Earth – show the world what you have achieved.'

*   *   *

Thirty minutes later, Sean found himself standing on the Giza Plateau, overlooking the rebuilt city of Cairo. A healthy mirage of lights sparkled under the orange-pink sunset. The metropolis had risen from the ashes. With the help of the Isharkute, even the Great Pyramid and Sphinx had been meticulously reconstructed from the decimated blocks. Returning to the plateau gave Sean a sense of closure. This was where it all began, exploring the opening beneath the Sphinx with his dad, William, Carla, and the excavation team, all those months before.

Hundreds of television reporters, journalists and photographers packed the area before them. Cameras flashed incessantly. Voices screamed for their attention. Isharkute vision drones hovered overhead. Vessels hung in the sky for a bird's-eye view. Behind the on-ground wall of media, a crowd of human and Isharkute onlookers stretched all the way back to the outskirts of Cairo. The sea of heads and waving arms had no end.

Nocao and Ramin stood by Horum, explaining what all the fuss was about.

'It's like the entire world has come out to see us,' Bella remarked.

Sean nodded, realising he didn't feel a hint of nervousness. He smiled to himself, remembering when he first arrived in Egypt – how intimidated he was by meeting his dad's team of thirty people. Now he faced billions.

General Hazim El-Amin took to the podium and addressed the worldwide audience with the confident voice of a born leader. He introduced them one by one to rapturous applause, summarising their extraordinary adventures.

Hazim finished his address. 'The universe is ours to share. Together, we're standing on the precipice of unparalleled knowledge and technological advancement. The future has never looked so bright; a future now assured by the actions of the heroes standing before you. Without them, we could not welcome Ramin, and the first Isharkute born in decades, his son Horum.'

The million-strong crowd erupted into rapturous applause. The force shook the ground and rattled the stage. Sean glimpsed the Great Pyramid, half-expecting the blocks to vibrate free and tumble down the side.

Ramin led Horum to the front of the stage. The applause rose to an almost unbearable level. Hazim directed them off the rear of the stage to shake hands with innumerable officials, generals, leaders, and high-ranking Isharkute.

Sean found a familiar face amidst the chaos, Admiral Powell. They met each other with open arms and embraced.

'Sorry I didn't get out there to help you, kid, but I was caught up here on Earth.'

'That's all right. What happens now?'

'Go home, spend some time with your aunt and uncle. We've got plenty to discuss, but it can wait a few days.'

Sean was intrigued. 'What do you mean, like a debriefing?'

'Sure, we'll do that, but there's something else I want to propose.'

'What is it?'

'A job.'

'What job?' Sean asked, butterflies racing through his stomach.

Powell winked. His blue eyes glinted with excitement and the promise of things to come. Sean was happy to let it go, confident his future would follow in the footsteps of his father, full of exploration and adventure.

*   *   *

Sean pushed his bedroom door open to find his room the way he'd left it two years before. His black custom-built PC dominated the desk, surrounded by hard drives, cables, a VR headset, headphones, and speakers. Two of his mum's Africa-themed watercolours were pinned to the board over his desk, surrounded by pictures of *Juliette*

IV, robot schematics, and blueprints of the Great Pyramid. Star charts and astronomy posters were stuck to the ceiling.

It all seemed so familiar, as if he'd never left.

He walked past his desk, amused at the clutter of gadgets. The technology seemed so old and archaic now. He could never go back to his old life, not after everything he'd seen. It had been two days since the media frenzy in Cairo, but he couldn't stop thinking about his brief conversation with General Powell.

What would his new life entail?

There was no way he could live here now, not with a media circus hounding his every move.

Sean sat on his bed and peered through a crack in the blinds. The flashing lights from the news vans and police cars illuminated the bushes outside his window. Was Bella experiencing the same attention back in Italy? He couldn't wait to see her again. Nocao and Horum were returning to Akanae with Ramin, where she would live from now on. Nocao had his hands full, busy coming to grips with being a new dad.

Sean felt a little lonely. It was hard being away from his friends.

Janine poked her head around his door. 'Everything okay?'

'Yeah, thanks for looking after my room.'

Janine smiled. 'We don't have much food in the house. Steve and I haven't been here for a couple of weeks. We've ordered pizza. Is that okay?'

'Sounds good. I haven't had pizza in ages.'

'It'll be here soon...that's if the delivery person can get through the commotion.'

'I'm sorry about that.'

'It's not your fault, Sean,' Steve said, leaning into his room. 'We're just glad to have you home, even if it's only for a few days.'

'I'm glad to be home.'

'We'll let you know when it's here,' Janine said, closing the door.

Sean sat on his bed and looked up at the *Earthrise* poster. One corner had peeled off, obscuring half the image. He stood up and pressed it back into position, then picked up his LED torch from the bedside table and laid back. He flicked the torch on and off, spotlighting Earth the way he used to before going to sleep.

The drowsiness crept up on him. He really wanted pizza but couldn't hold back his heavy eyelids. He let himself drift into a deep, well-earned sleep.

A Special Journey

Six months later, Sean found himself millions of light-years from Earth, standing in the hall of the Ancients. He was leading the first contingent of human scientists, mathematicians, astrophysicists, biologists, botanists, geologists, theologians, priests, and rabbis through the portal. Members from all the Isharkute guilds were represented as well, making a team of sixty-five galactic pioneers. Everyone looked up to him, eager to embark across the vast network of portals connecting the universe.

Their expressions of awe and wonder reminded Sean of his younger, naïve self, standing beside his dad as they opened the doors to the Hall of Records.

At the beginning of his journey, he was the student.

Now, he was the teacher.

Sean had been working on his speech for the past two months; starting the day he was appointed the position as team leader. His words deliberately echoed the speech his dad gave that fateful night in Egypt.

He took a deep breath and began.

'We're not here for personal gain, but to further our knowledge of the universe. Our future relies on more than just understanding the past, it requires our deepest respect and humility. The Ancients left their world to show us the universe is far greater than what we can see, hear, or touch. The journey of discovery starts within each of us. Beginning with every cell. Every atom. We're made up from the same matter as stars and planets, as they are from us. When ready, we can follow in the Ancients' footsteps into a new plane of existence outside our universe. But we have more than a lifetime of discoveries and understandings to make before then. It may not be our generation, or even the next, but one day, those who take the first steps will look back and remember that without our sacrifices, it never would have been possible.'

The crowd applauded.

Sean peered through the wall of faces. Admiral Powell and General Hazim stood at the back of the group, nodding in approval. Beside them, Nocao, Horum and Bella watched on, applauding, and smiling with pride. Bella and Nocao had also taken on leadership roles in this new mission. Horum was destined to follow his father Nocao into the Guild of Sciences, experiencing firsthand the breadth and beauty of the universe. Together, the four of them would venture into the unknown, bound forever as friends and family.

Sean bristled with excitement, knowing the greatest journey of all was about to begin.

A Note From Andrew D. Connell

Thank you for reading *The Spearhead of Creation*. Working as a self-published author, the success of my writing relies on you, the reader. Your reviews are the most effective way to introduce new readers to my books. If you enjoyed this book please consider leaving a review on Amazon or your place of purchase. A simple sentence, or solitary one-word review is often enough, but if you're willing to write more I'd love to hear your thoughts.

Subscribe to my monthly newsletter at *andrewdconnell.com* for the latest news and upcoming releases.

— Andrew D. Connell

About The Author

Andrew Connell was born in Melbourne, Australia, in 1972. He studied film and television at the Victorian College of the Arts and has since worked as a writer, editor, and director of both short films and television programs. He has also written several award winning screenplays. Andrew lives in Melbourne with his wife and three children.

Acknowledgements

As always, special thanks to my family for their love and support.

Proofreading by Susan Uttendorfsky.
adirondackediting.com

Cover artwork by Wayne Nichols.
wnichols.com

The Sean Livingstone Series

Crown of the Pharaohs
A Sean Livingstone Adventure (Book One)

Ark of the Gods
A Sean Livingstone Adventure (Book Two)

The Spearhead of Creation
A Sean Livingstone Adventure (Book Three)

Also available:

Crown of the Pharaohs (Special Edition)
Includes the prequel novella:
Monsters, Myths, and Microchips
A Sean Livingstone Adventure (Book Zero)

andrewdconnell.com

Made in the USA
Las Vegas, NV
21 July 2021